DEAD HARVEST

OTHER BOOKS BY ANTHONY GIANGREGORIO

THE DEAD WATER SERIES

DEADWATER
DEADWATER: Expanded Edition
DEADRAIN
DEADCITY
DEADWAVE
DEAD HARVEST
DEAD UNION

ALSO BY THE AUTHOR

DEAD RECKONING: DAWNING OF THE DEAD
THE MONSTER UNDER THE BED
DEADEND: A ZOMBIE NOVEL
DEAD TALES: SHORT STORIES TO DIE FOR
DEAD MOURNING: A ZOMBIE HORROR STORY
ROAD KILL: A ZOMBIE TALE
DEADFREEZE
DEADFALL
DEADRAGE
SOUL-EATER
THE DARK
RISE OF THE DEAD
DARK PLACES

DEAD HARVEST

Anthony Giangregorio

DEAD HARVEST

ISBN Softcover ISBN 13: 978-1-935458-00-5
ISBN 10: 1-935458-00-0

This book was printed in the United States of America.

For more info on obtaining additional copies of this book, contact:
www.livingdeadpress.com

Acknowledgments

Thank you to my wife, Jody, for all her love and support, and to my two sons Domenic and Joseph.

And a big thanks to all my friends for listening to me when I'm on a rant about my next story idea and for sharing their own ideas with me.

Though there is no greater joy than in reading a work of literature, I can honestly say there is but one more even grander, and that is to create the work myself and then have the opportunity to share it with others.

AUTHOR'S NOTE

This book was self-edited, and though I tried my absolute best to correct all grammar mistakes; there may be a few here and there.

Please accept my sincerest apology for any errors you may find.

This is the second edition of this book.

Visit my web site at undeadpress.com

What Has Come Before

One year ago, a deadly bacterial outbreak escaped a lab to infect the lower atmosphere across America, unleashing an undead plague on the world.

With rain clouds now filled with a killer virus, to venture outside in the rain was tantamount to suicide.

To get caught in the rain and exposed to the bacteria would be an instant death. But that wasn't the end. Once dead, the host body would rise again, becoming an undead ghoul, wanting nothing more than to feed on the flesh of the living.

The United States was torn asunder, civilization collapsing like a house of cards in weeks.

But mankind survived, eking out a dreary existence, always keeping one eye on the sky for the next rainstorm.

Only one year after the zombie apocalypse, the world has become a very different place from what it once was. Gone are cell phones, the internet, restaurants and shopping malls; now all lost relics of a culture slowly fading into history.

In this new world, the dead walk and a man follows the rules of the gun, where the strong are always right and the weak are usually dead. Major cities are nothing but blackened husks, nothing but giant tombs filled with walking corpses. Across America, though, smaller towns have become small municipalities with makeshift walls protecting them from both live and dead attackers. Strangers are not welcome and are either shot on sight or made to move on, that is, if they are not exploited by the rulers of the towns.

Through the destruction of what once was walks a man, crushing death beneath his steel-tipped boots. Before he was an ordinary man, living a quiet life with a wife and a career, but the rules have changed and so to, has he adapted, becoming a warrior of death who wields a gun with an iron hand, but shows mercy and wisdom when it is needed.

His name is Henry Watson, and with his fellow companions, Mary, Jimmy and Cindy, by his side, he travels across a blighted landscape searching for someplace where the undead haven't corrupted everything they touch, and where he can lay his head down in safety.

Though life is fleeting, each breath means the possibility of life, and a better future for all.

Chapter 1

Henry Watson stood at the bow of the cruise liner, watching the waves drift by beneath him. The Pacific Ocean was empty, no other vessels in sight.

He glanced up at the dark storm clouds overhead, watching them drift lazily by. A storm was coming, not always a good thing when you were at the mercy of the ocean's currents.

His right hand reached down to check his sidearm, the Glock 9mm resting comfortably in its holster, and his panga, a long sixteen-inch blade that rode his right hip. The motion was unconscious, the gesture the same as a person double-checking that their wallet was still where it should be. A pump action shotgun hung across his back, but every time the wind caused it to move, it reminded him it was still there.

He thought back to almost a year ago, when clouds like the ones above him would have signified death. Back then, the clouds had become contaminated with a deadly bacterium. Rainfall was a death sentence to any foolish or unlucky enough to be caught in it.

But death wasn't the end.

The bacteria would reanimate the body after death, causing the host body to live again in a state of undeath, what was once called a zombie or ghoul in the old horror movies.

Now the unimaginable had become reality, and in less than three months, all of America had been consumed by the walking dead. Civilization, fragile at the best of times, crumbled like a deck of cards. Police and fire services were the first to go, followed by telephones and the internet. Sure, the satellites were still orbiting the earth, receiving and sending communications, but without human hands to coordinate the signals, and power to retransmit, the satellites became nothing more than space junk floating in the darkness of space.

Henry had been a regular guy back then, with a wife and a job. He chuckled to himself, thinking back to when it had all started to fall apart. If someone had asked him where he thought he might be in a year, the answer sure wouldn't have been adrift on a cruise liner in the middle of the Pacific Ocean with the undead ruling the land.

Thunder clouds rumbled overhead and he looked up automatically. Luckily, the rain was harmless now.

Whatever bacteria had inhabited the clouds had slowly burned off, whether from the freezing temperatures of winter or the scalding heat of summer. Or perhaps it had just run its course, infecting the world and then dissolving into mist, its job complete.

Like the infamous flood from the bible, humanity had been washed from the earth in a tidal wave of death, only leaving small enclaves to try and pick up the pieces.

Across the United States, cities had become deathtraps, where thousands upon thousands of the walking dead now remained, as if somewhere in their rotting brains, they knew the cities were theirs. Major metropolitan cities had been nicknamed the deadlands due to the high population of ghouls, and only someone stupid or foolish enough to enter would ever risk entering the massive tombs.

But there was still hope. Smaller towns and villages had barricaded themselves inside their walls; using whatever was at hand to make the makeshift barricades and protect themselves from the undead menace. Some towns piled automobiles four and five high, using cranes; while others used wire fencing or barbed wire. Others used cinderblocks and concrete.

Armed guards would then guard the perimeters, always watchful for the undead.

Though numerous, the zombies weren't very intelligent and only their numbers were a threat to the survival of the remaining population of the earth.

Strangers were rarely welcomed in these places, the citizens always wary. With the fall of civilization, the world had slid back to the times of the Old West, where the law of the gun was final. Each town was independent of the others, the leaders dictating what the rules would be. In one town, stealing bread would get you a few lashes with a whip, while in another, the same crime would have you hanged...or worse.

The Boss' of these towns were all hard men and women, some fair, some evil, only becoming ruler by taking what wasn't theirs; usually by force. Opportunistic men had seized the chance to grasp power and now held onto it with an iron grip.

Henry had come upon a few of these men and so far he had buried them all. Whether it was luck, or some divine intervention that was beyond his control, he and his companions had made it out of scrape after scrape, always on their own two feet.

Footsteps pulled him from his reverie and he turned to see a beautiful woman in her early twenties walking over to him. Her brown hair blew about her face, caught in the wind, and her porcelain skin seemed to almost glow in the falling darkness of the storm clouds. On her hip was a .38 Police Special and she carried it like it was a part of her. In a small leather sheath on the left side of her hip, she wore a small Bowie knife, more for casual use than as a defensive weapon.

Mary Roberts wrapped her light coat around her tighter and smiled when Henry turned to look at her. "Hey. I was wondering where you got off to," she said in a soft voice.

Henry turned fully around, both his arms leaning on the railing that lined the deck.

"I just wanted to get out of there; it was a little too noisy for me."

Mary nodded, knowing exactly what he meant. "Yeah, you've got to admit, Sparrow likes his wine and women."

Henry nodded at that. Sparrow was the name of the man who now technically owned the cruise ship. The Sea Princess was a massive cruise ship that could berth almost two-thousand people. At the moment, though, there were less than two hundred men, women and children on board, all the refuges Sparrow could find.

He was an avuncular, almost grandfatherly figure with a white shock of hair on his scalp and a thick pair of coke bottle glasses. His voice was hoarse from too many cigarettes and the man had only stopped smoking because he had run out of his supplies of the precious tobacco; coffee being the second thing the man adored.

He was the defunct captain of the ship, one of the few men on board who knew how to operate it. A few crew members from the original staff of the liner still worked on board and it was these people that had kept the ship afloat and moving all these months since the dead first began to walk. Since then, Sparrow had sailed from place to place, searching for survivors and supplies.

Sometimes he would come upon derelict ships, some civilian, some military. On these ships he would usually find valuable supplies and fuel, usually enough to get him and his people to the next derelict ship.

But he would also find the undead, hiding inside bulkheads and storage compartments, eager to feed on the scavengers. Since Henry and his friends had joined up with Sparrow and his crew, they too, had helped in the scavenging operations. There were many yachts, and military vessels floating on the deserted waters now, all filled with either a bounty of supplies or a hold full of the undead. On the last ship found, a pleasure yacht worth more than a million dollars; Henry, Jimmy, Sparrow and the others involved in the search had discovered a ship full of ghouls, all hungry for the flesh of the boarding party. It had been a tough fight in the confines of the ship to eradicate all the ghouls, but in the end they had succeeded and had found a ship full of food and fuel. The original owners of the ship had tried to outrun the plague, but had only succeeded in dying out on the water instead of on dry land.

The dingy had been missing and Henry wondered if survivors had used it to try and escape the ship of the dead and if they were even now floating somewhere out on the water.

Thinking of the missing dingy reminded Henry of how he and his fellow companions had found their way into Sparrow's crew.

That was how Sparrow had found Henry and his friends. They had been adrift in a small dingy off the coast of South Carolina after having to make a hasty getaway from an irate Boss. The Boss of the town had wanted Mary and Cindy to stay with him and be part of his personal harem, one he had already grown to more than ten women. Of course, the women had declined, and before any of the companions knew it, they were in the midst of a firestorm of bullets and had quickly taken their leave, battling all the way to the coast and only then were they lucky enough to find a dingy moored to the pier. They had kept up a running cover fire and Jimmy had managed to get the small outboard motor running. Henry had then managed to detonate a gas tank of one of their vehicles, and in the ensuing explosion, the four companions had taken their leave by escaping out into the ocean. They had traveled for days until the gas in the engine, and the spare tank, had run out of fuel. Then, with almost all hope gone, Sparrow had sounded his fog horn and had appeared over the horizon to save them.

They had been out of food and only had one canteen of water between them. If Sparrow hadn't come along, Henry loathed thinking what might have happened to them. He snapped out of his reverie when Mary nudged him slightly, wanting him to pay attention to her.

He turned to look at her, her face as beautiful as ever.

"Where's Jimmy and Cindy? They okay?" He asked her.

She nodded, smiling. "Oh, yeah, they're fine, Jimmy's telling Sparrow jokes and the old man is laughing it up, plus, I think he's taken a shine to Cindy."

Henry grunted at that. "I was afraid that might happen. Seems the man chases after anything in a skirt. Think it'll be a problem?"

Mary shook her head, fighting to keep the hair out of her eyes. "No, she's a big girl and I think Sparrow's attraction is harmless. She can handle herself if he gets too grabby. Why, you think there could be trouble?"

Henry let out a sigh, and turned back out to the water. "Trouble? Shit, Mary, in a world where the dead walk, trouble has lost a lot of its original meaning, don't you think?"

Before she could answer, he continued talking, his question rhetorical. "Come on, let's get back inside and keep an eye on them, we don't want Jimmy getting jealous and getting us all in hot water." Then he pushed off the railing and started for the doorway that would lead back to the dining hall deep inside the ship.

Mary glanced out onto the ocean herself, admiring the dark clouds, flashes of lightning and the rolling waves. Then, she too, turned and followed Henry back inside.

Their other two companions were down belowdecks alone, and if Mary knew Jimmy, he was bound to get into trouble.

Chapter 2

"So then the guy says; that's not my wife, that's my dog!" Jimmy Cooper said with a mischievous grin that had Sparrow laughing so hard he almost fell off his chair.

Sparrow continued laughing and Jimmy turned and looked at Cindy Jensen, his girlfriend for more than six months. She had long blonde hair and deep blue eyes and a figure that had most men drooling. She was a sharp contrast to Jimmy's skinny frame and brown hair. They were almost the same age, only a few months separating them and had clicked from the moment Jimmy had spotted her in a small town on the outskirts of Virginia. Since then, the two had become inseparable.

She had stayed with him when trouble had brewed in her town, making their threesome a quartet, and now the four of them traveled across what was left of the United States, hoping to find somewhere safe from the undead threat.

Cindy repositioned herself on her chair, her rifle hanging on its sling on her shoulder uncomfortably. But she refused to take it off. Better to be uncomfortable with the weapon than to need it at a time it was out of reach. Jimmy also carried his weapons on his person. A .38 Smith and Wesson rode his hip and a pump action shotgun--identical to one Henry owned--was slung across his back along with a six inch hunting knife that hung from his belt. Both Jimmy and Cindy looked ready for war instead of just relaxing with Sparrow. But both friends had learned to keep their weapons handy or pay the consequences in blood.

With tears in his eyes Sparrow sat up, still laughing. "Jimmy my boy, you are one funny guy! You must keep your friends in stitches all the time!" He laughed.

Cindy leaned in close and nudged Jimmy with her elbow. “Oh yeah, he’s a regular laugh riot,” she jeered.

“Hey, I resemble that remark,” Jimmy said, grinning at Cindy, which had Sparrow laughing even harder.

Cindy leaned in close so only Jimmy could hear. “My God, he’s your biggest fan; just what does he think is so funny about you?”

Jimmy frowned at her. “Hey, at least someone can see me for what I am, an entertainer. Maybe if the world hadn’t gone to shit I could have been famous, like Steve Martin or Jay Leno. So lay off, it’s nice to be appreciated.”

She sighed. “Are you serious? The only reason he’s laughing is because he’s so full of booze. He could run the engines on this ship by just breathing into the fuel tanks.”

“You’re just jealous,” he told her.

She leaned back in her chair and sulked. “Hardly,” she added and looked to her left just in time to see Mary and Henry entering the room from one of the many entrances. If Henry had been worried about trouble between Jimmy and Sparrow, it was quickly washed away like one of the waves outside the ship’s hull. Sparrow was having a great time, enjoying Jimmy’s jokes like he was the son the older man had never had.

Henry, with Mary by his side, strode across the room, his head looking all around him. He was admiring the architecture for the hundredth time. He had always wanted to take a cruise with his late wife, Emily, but had never gotten around to it. Now of course, it was far too late.

Emily was somewhere back in the Midwest, probably nothing but a dried husk. Henry tried not to think of her like that, but instead tried to focus on his wife when she had been alive, full of life and hope.

Henry took in the room like a general would a battlefield, his eyes roaming over each face and body, searching for any hidden threats.

There were more than fifty people in the room, seeming like a drop of water in a large pool. The room was massive, able to hold and feed more than five hundred people in one sitting. The room was set up in a large circle with ornate stairways--plush carpeting and hardwood where appropriate--leading up to circular balconies that hovered over the main room. From these balconies, a patron could dine while looking down on the massive room, complete with crystal chandeliers and a large water fountain sculpture in the middle of the room. Due to the shortage of water on the ship, though, the fountain was obviously off, but it had once made a grand sight.

The fifty people now dining and sitting with Sparrow were of all shapes and sizes. There were fat, skinny, young and old, plus a few hardened souls that were Sparrows bodyguards.

Henry's eyes lingered on these men for a second longer, watching their hands to see if anyone was going to reach for a weapon. Though he knew he should be safe here, he and the others welcomed into Sparrow's little group with open arms, old habits died hard. Multiple men had said one thing to Henry and done the exact opposite and he would be damned if he'd be caught with his pants down again.

When Henry had caught Sparrow's eye, the old man sat upright in his chair, setting his drink down.

"Henry, my boy, where'd you go? And the lovely Mary, always good to have you back with us," Sparrow slurred the last words, the man more than borderline drunk.

"Just needed a little air, I don't like to be inside," Henry said as he stopped by the man's chair.

Sparrow looked up into Henry's face, not the least bit uncomfortable. "Fine, that's fine, how about a drink? We still have plenty left from that barge we found a couple of days ago."

Henry shook his head and instead reached for a glass of water, then sat down next to Sparrow. One of Sparrow's guards had to move out of the way, but the man knew not to argue with Henry. Sparrow had already told his men that Henry and the other companions were to be treated with respect.

The reason for this was simple.

A few days ago the cruise ship had come upon a floating barge. At first it had seemed empty and Sparrow's security force had boarded the barge and had searched it. Once they had found nothing threatening, Sparrow had boarded the small vessel, always liking to investigate for himself what was onboard. At the time, Henry and the others had only been with Sparrow for a few days and were still considered outsiders, but when Sparrow had entered a small room at the rear of the barge and had been attacked by a lone ghoul, it had been Henry who had acted fast and had caved in the rotting figure's head with the butt of his shotgun, Sparrow's guards only staring in shock.

After saving Sparrow's life, the man had welcomed Henry and the others with open arms, Henry and Jimmy now becoming his favorites. Unfortunately, this didn't go over too well with Spencer, Sparrow's second-in-command and head of the small security force on the ship. Spencer felt Henry was pushing him aside and was worried about his position with Sparrow.

Spencer sat at the table, as well, watching and listening to everything being spoken with a devious frown on his lips.

"What's wrong, Spence', you look pissed off," another crewman asked Spencer.

Spencer turned to look at his friend. Mickey was one of the security guards on the ship and followed Spencer around like a puppy dog. On top of that, he was Spencer's lover, though as far as Spencer knew, no one else on board knew he was gay. The two men had been an item for months and it had been almost dumb luck that Spencer had found him in the first place. With the world the way it was, he would have thought the old prejudices would have been forgotten; the need for survival winning out. But instead it had only gotten worse, and now, without political correctness, Sparrow didn't have to put up with a gay second-in-command if he didn't want to. Instead, he could leave his ass on some derelict boat and be done with him. And Spencer knew that's just what would happen to him and Mickey. Sparrow was an old man and was set in his ways and many times had shared his feelings about Blacks, Jews and queers, as he called them. No, Sparrow was as racist as they came and Spencer knew to keep his personal life discreet and hope for the best. If he was found out, well, he would deal with that when it happened.

Spencer shook himself from his stupor and smiled at Mickey, careful not to show too much emotion and make the other men around them suspicious.

"I'm fine, Mickey, I'll talk to you later, when we're alone."

Mickey grinned a little at that. "Same place? The boiler room at eleven?" He asked.

Spencer nodded, subtly. "Yeah, and make sure no one sees you. We've come too far to screw it up, now. So do me a favor and go check topside; make sure everything's okay. I don't trust Williams up in the command center. That guys a moron."

"Sure, Spence', no problem," Mickey said and finished off his drink. Then he set his glass down on the table and left. Spencer wanted to watch him leave, he always liked to see Mickey from the rear--he had a nice apple-shaped ass--but controlled himself. It wouldn't look good for the security chief to be checking out his men. Instead, he turned back and glared at Henry over his own drink. Henry never looked his way, as he continued insinuating himself next to Sparrow.

But the truth was that Henry could have cared less about Sparrow or Spencer. Spencer had nothing to worry about, Henry only wanted to make landfall where he and the other companions could make their departure.

Spencer sat at the opposite end of the table, watching Henry cozy up to his captain. Under the table, his hands squeezed tightly into fists, the knuckles turning white. Henry was a problem for Spencer and he knew one way or another, the man needed to disappear. But he knew if he openly challenged Henry, Sparrow would disapprove. So he had already decided Henry needed to have an accident. What that accident would be exactly, he hadn't worked out just yet, but he knew it would come to him in time.

Across the table¬--a table large enough to sit twenty people easily--Henry laughed and smiled while Jimmy continued telling jokes, enjoying himself with his friends and Sparrow.

For Henry, it was nice to let his guard down, even if it was just a small amount, and enjoy life once again; even if it was only temporary.

Out on the ocean, the dead couldn't reach him or the ship and it was good to just pretend that life was normal and that things were the way they used to be

Chapter 3

Sparrow slowed his laughing and slowly regained control of himself.

"Ah, Jimmy, you're wonderful, I haven't laughed so hard for quite some time."

Jimmy shrugged. "Hey, what can I say, it's a gift."

"Or a curse for the rest of us," Cindy jibed next to him.

Jimmy frowned at her. "Lighten up, Cindy, it's about time someone realized my comedic talents."

Cindy was about to answer him with yet another jab when a crewman walked into the room, distracting her. She watched the man walk toward the table, which took him a few seconds to cross the wide open space separating the entrance from the dining table, but eventually the man reached them and leaned down next to Sparrow.

Sparrow stopped laughing and his face went serious, all business now. He nodded a few times, listening and then waved the man away.

He sat up straighter in his chair, showing a sobering visage to the world, almost all signs of his drinking now gone, and made eye contact with each of the personnel at the table.

"I've just been told there's a ship coming up off our starboard bow. Looks military, Navy probably. He turned and glared at Henry.

"You up for another adventure, my friend?"

Before answering, Henry first snuck a glance at each of his friends, all nodding their approval, then he looked back to Sparrow.

"Yeah, Captain, we're ready if you need us," Henry told him. Sparrow slapped the table and looked to his second-in-command.

"Spencer, get the men ready. I want to be on that ship and taking its treasures five minutes after we've pulled alongside her."

"Aye, sir, I'll get it done." Then Spencer jumped to his feet and headed out of the giant hall, with barely a backward glance at Henry and the others.

Sparrow stood, as well, tossing his napkin onto his plate. The food had been nothing special, just scavenged supplies from a dozen ships. They had a choice of a buffet, everything from canned carrots to pasta in a can. Despite this, the companions hadn't eaten as well as they had on the ship in quite a while.

"Henry, join me in the control room and we'll talk some more. I want to supervise Williams, make sure the man is capable of steering my ship."

Henry nodded and then looked to Jimmy. "Go on, Henry, we'll finish up here and meet you on deck." Jimmy told him, gesturing to both Cindy and Mary.

With a scraping of chairs on marble tile, everyone stood up and each went their own way. All the crew and passengers of the ship that had been at the dinner table all moved away, all having respective duties to attend to when a new ship was sighted. In seconds, everyone was gone, leaving Jimmy, Mary and Cindy alone.

"Well, ladies, it appears it's just the three of us now, what do you think we should do to keep ourselves occupied?" Jimmy said with his eyebrows waggling up and down on his forehead.

Mary leaned back in her chair and folded her arms across her chest. "Not in your wildest dreams, Jimmy."

"Yeah, not to mention you can barely handle me," Cindy jibed, nudging her boyfriend in the ribs.

Jimmy sighed. "Perhaps, but a man can dream, can't he?"

Both Mary and Cindy looked at one another and then at Jimmy, saying the same words at the exact same time.

"No, he can't," they both said together, flatly.

Jimmy frowned and then stood up, going to the small table with the food spread across it. He was still hungry and had been so busy telling Sparrow jokes that he'd barely eaten anything.

"Well," he mumbled to himself, heaping canned vegetables and canned meat on his plate, "we can fix that."

Henry followed Sparrow through the corridors of the ship and up ladders, until finally coming to an elevator.

"After you, Henry. This will take us up to the tower, as you already know."

Henry nodded and stepped inside the elevator, Sparrow right behind him.

The doors closed and the elevator shot upwards, canned music issuing out of the speakers.

Sparrow started snapping his hand in tune with the music. Henry looked at the man and Sparrow grinned.

"I love this song," he said, now humming along with it.

Henry only grunted. Inside the elevator, with its polished steel doors and strained music floating out of the speakers, it was almost as if the world was fine and the past year was nothing but a bad dream.

Then the elevator jolted to a stop and the doors opened and Henry was brought back to the real world. Where once the control tower of the ship would have had dozens of men and women operating it with crisp white uniforms and possibly matching hats, as well, now there were a ragtag group of people, all in old clothes and unkempt hair.

The second Sparrow stepped out of the elevator; the man at the wheel turned and called out: "Captain on the bridge!"

Sparrow raised and lowered his hands, wanting everyone to get back to work. "That's okay, people, as you were." Sparrow then walked over to the front window of the control room and picked up a pair of binoculars.

Looking out onto the water, Sparrow peeked out the side of them to check that Henry was next to him.

"Did I ever tell you how I wound up running this ship and all the people on it?" He asked Henry casually.

Henry shrugged slightly. "Not really. You've hinted at a few things and I sort of figured out the rest. You obviously worked on the ship before all the shit went down, right?"

Sparrow nodded, the binoculars bobbing with him as he scanned the water in front of the cruise ship.

"Yup, that's it exactly. I was a purser, if you'd believe it, but I liked to hang out on the bridge on my time off. Some of the guys would show me how stuff works, the rest I figured out on my own," he gestured to a small metal closet to the rear of the bridge. "There's a manual for everything in there."

Sparrow pulled the binoculars from his face and handed them to Henry to take a look. Henry placed them to his eyes and scanned the horizon while Sparrow continued talking.

"The rest is probably obvious. When everything started happening last year, the ship was in dock. Then they canceled the last cruise. It was me and a few others living on the ship at the time and when a couple of hundred of those dead things showed up on the pier, well, me and a few others decided to just cast off and get the hell out of there. We floated without power for a while until one of the guys was able to get one of the engines running. We were only going about three knots to conserve fuel, but then what's the rush, right?"

Henry lowered the binoculars and looked to Sparrow. "How much fuel you got left?"

Sparrow shook his head. "Not much. We've kept going by finding fuel in the derelict ships and boats that are out here. If that ever dries up, I guess we'll just float with the currents. Sometimes I do that anyway when there's nothing around to salvage. As long as we have food and water we can live out here forever. Hell, we could start families and to hell with dry land. Let the dead have it and the living will take the water. At least we're safe out here."

"So you've been on this ship ever since the shit hit the fan? You never went back on land?"

Sparrow nodded; his face grim. "Yup, ever since the bad rains first fell and started all this shit. Way I see it, there's nothing left on land for me anyway. Nothing but death and despair from what you and a few others have told me. Figure I'll spend the rest of my days on the ocean."

Henry grunted and raised the binoculars back to his face and continued searching the horizon. "Nice idea, but it will never work. Sooner or later you'll run out of either food or water and you'll have to go scavenging on land. There's no way around it, there's just not enough ships out here. Now maybe if you just sailed off for some deserted island somewhere...”

Sparrow shook his head. “No, not enough fuel to make it even halfway. Then where would we be? No, I’m afraid this is where we’ll be for the foreseeable future, for better or worse. Sailing around the coasts of what was once America.”

Henry was about to answer back when his eyes caught the flash of metal on the horizon. With the storm clouds overhead, the sky was growing ever darker, and with no lights on the ocean it became an inky blackness that consumed all in its wake.

The derelict vessel was dark; no lights could be discerned through the binoculars. That bode well that the ship was deserted. The only question was why. Why did the crew abandon the ship and let her float on the currents like a piece of driftwood?

Lightning flashed, reflecting off the spires of the ship and Henry lowered the binoculars and handed them back to Sparrow.

“Over there, just to the right of center,” he said. “Wait for the lightning and you’ll see it.”

Sparrow did as directed, and when the next lightning flashed, his mouth curved up into a wide grin. “Ah-ha, got you, you bastard. It’s a Navy vessel if I’m right, it’s hard to tell from so far away. We should be there in another hour or so. Until then, how ‘bout a drink to pass the time?”

Henry shrugged once again, the gesture ingrained in his makeup. “Sure, why not.”

Sparrow slapped him on the back and the two men walked to the rear of the bridge where maps and charts were spread out. Sparrow opened a small cabinet and pulled out a bottle of Jack Daniels. The bottle was more than half empty and the liquid swished inside the bottle like the sea outside the tower’s windows. His eyes opened wider when he held it up for Henry to see.

Henry only nodded. He had never really been much of a drinker, but as the cruise ship slowly chugged closer to what could only be called a ghost ship, he figured a shot of liquid courage could only help.

Chapter 4

The boarding party patiently waited for the men to finish securing the lines to the derelict ship. Next to Henry stood Jimmy, the man fidgeting with excitement, like he was going on an adventure instead of into the unknown.

Other crewmen nearby shifted uncomfortably in nervousness and anticipation of the coming events. No one knew what would be onboard the dark ship. It could be full of food and supplies, much needed by the men and women of the cruise ship, or it could be full of the undead, all just waiting for the unknowing men to enter their trap.

Behind Henry, Spencer stood waiting for his captain, his SMG in his hands. All the men carried some form of automatic rifle, whether it was an Uzi, an M-16 or an AK-47. One man carried a Steyr SSG-70 RIFLE, though the weapon was more suited for sniping than a close quarter battle, but if the enemy was close enough it wouldn't really matter and would still prove useful.

Sparrow pushed his way to the front of the line. Henry and the rest were standing at the opening to a cargo hold, the large opening like a square hole in the side of the ship. This would be the perfect height to lay the massive planks of wood from the cruise ship to the derelict ship, the planks landing on the latter's handrails.

A flash of lightning lit up the sky and Henry caught the chipped words on the side of the ship.

The **U.S.S. Miller**, it read.

So it was a naval vessel. If Henry was right, then he was looking at the side of a frigate. A frigate was about half the size of a naval destroyer and was used for mostly search and rescue operations, although it had many more duties, such as searching for enemy submarines during war time. It had a set of gun cannons at the forward and aft decks, and amidships had a space designated for helicopters to land.

Henry looked up at the darkened bridge windows, a chill crawling up his spine.

For just the briefest of moments, he could have sworn he saw a face looking back at him, but it had come and gone so fast that he just assumed it was a stray shadow, or perhaps a trick of the light.

"Something wrong?" Sparrow asked him while they all waited for a few men to get the planks across.

Henry shook his head slightly. "No, just thought I saw something up there in the windows."

Sparrow nodded himself, agreeing with him. "Don't worry about it. These deserted ships give me the willies too. You never know what you'll find. Every one of them is like a floating haunted house."

With a loud thud of wood on metal, the planks were dropped onto the handrail of the Miller. Sparrow was the first over, walking the planks and dropping down to the deck of the frigate like a tight-rope walker.

"Come on, men, let's see what we've got here," he told the rest of the boarding crew.

One at a time, each man crossed the ten feet to the frigate, eight in all counting Henry and Jimmy. Henry watched as the boards sagged in the middle and he was surprised to see them hold.

Mickey moved up next to Henry and climbed up onto the edge of the plank. "Don't worry, they'll hold. They just bend in the middle a little. That's why we have those brackets on the ends."

Henry noticed for the first time that there was corroding, heavy metal brackets screwed into the edges of the planks, thereby preventing them from slipping.

Mickey waved at him with a smile, and then with his right hand out for balance, and his left hand holding his weapon, he slid his feet across the planks.

Jimmy climbed up onto the edge. It was his turn, now, and he glanced down to Henry. "I guess this probably isn't the best time to tell you that I'm scared of heights."

Henry frowned. "Just get going, will ya?"

But Jimmy wasn't ready yet. "Okay, how 'bout I can't swim?"

"Will you please go, you're holding up the line." Henry snapped at him.

"How about vertigo? Would you believe that?"

"Either go or get off the damn plank, or so help me, I'll shoot you myself!" Henry yelled at him. "This isn't the time or the place!"

Jimmy held his hands out in surrender. "Fine, sheesh, what a bully. Look, I'm going." Then Jimmy turned and quickly moved across the plank like an acrobat at the circus.

The only men that were left to go across were Spencer and Henry. Spencer held out his hand to Henry. "After you," Spencer said politely.

Henry smiled back. "Thanks, Spencer," he said and then climbed up onto the plank.

Spencer waited patiently. With no one around but one of his men, who was to stay behind and guard the planks, all he had to do is wait for Henry to walk out to the middle of the planks and then he would lift them up and topple him into the inky black depths of the Pacific. The other guard would say nothing about it, as he was loyal to Spencer

Henry started across, oblivious to his coming doom. The frigate was covered in mist and shadows, the others already onboard the derelict ship now waiting for Henry, their forms lost in the shrouds of darkness; the light fog that had been slowly covering the two ships seeping into every open doorway and opening.

Spencer already had his hands on the planks, prepared to lift with his back when a voice called from behind him.

"Hey, how's it going?"

Spencer stepped away from the planks and turned to see both Cindy and Mary walking up to him.

He smiled politely and nodded. "Ladies, it's going fine. Everyone's over, just me left and we'll be ready. What are you doing here?"

Mary shrugged, since she had met Henry she found herself mimicking him with the gesture. "No reason, seems we couldn't join you guys, us women folk thought we'd come for moral support."

"Uh-huh, well that's great, but I need to be going. The others are waiting for me." Then he climbed up and quickly slid across the divide, making sure to not look down or back at the two women. He had missed his chance to take Henry out, but that was all right. There were a lot of dark corridors and hallways in the frigate and a stray bullet could come from anywhere.

Mary stood there watching the retreating Spencer and then she turned and looked at Cindy.

"What was that about?" She asked her friend.

Cindy shook her head. "No idea." She walked over to the planks and looked down into the canyon that separated the two ships. "Damn, that's a good drop and I'm not that good of a swimmer. Maybe it's better if we just wait here. Can't say I'd want to fall down there."

Mary chuckled at her statement. "Honey, if you fell down there, you'd have more important things to worry about then trying to swim. Namely the frigid water and the two ships crushing you like paste. Or better yet, getting sucked under and chopped up in the propellers."

Cindy frowned. "Thanks, I feel a lot better now," she said sarcastically.

Mary smiled back. "Anytime, glad to help."

With a smile to the guard near the planks, the two women plopped down on the deck and got comfortable. They would keep an eye on the planks themselves and make sure nothing came over that wasn't supposed to.

It wasn't that they didn't trust the crew of the Princess to do their job; it was just that neither of them trusted the crew of the Princess to do their job. They had come too far and seen too much to put their fate in anyone's hands but their own.

So with the guard staring at them, Mary and Cindy got comfortable and stared back, while the planks creaked softly from the motion of the waves, constantly shifting subtly as the two ships moved back and forth in the constantly moving currents, straining at the mooring lines to be free.

* * *

Henry looked around at the nervous faces of the men surrounding him, Jimmy already by his side. Spencer had just dropped down off the planks and all were ready to start searching the frigate.

Sparrow pushed his way through some of the men until he was standing next to Henry and Spencer.

"Henry, you're with me. I like the idea that you've got my back," Sparrow told him.

"But, sir, usually I go with you on these searches," Spencer told him.

Sparrow nodded. "Yes, that's true, Spencer, but this time I want Henry with me. You take the men and search the forward section and I'll go aft with Henry, Jimmy and Mickey. We'll meet at the galley in the middle of the ship in fifteen minutes."

Spencer seemed like he was going to protest, his mouth open. But then he closed his mouth and nodded. "Yes, sir, you're the boss."

"That's right, I am," Sparrow grunted.

Sparrow moved off down the deck, the railing a thin black line on his right. Henry looked over the railing and marveled at the small flickering of light. Sparrow noticed him looking and pointed down to them.

"Cool, huh? It's some king of fluorescent algae or something. The hull moving through the water disturbs them and they seem to flicker."

"Yeah, I've never seen that before, but then again, I lived in the Midwest. Not too many oceans around."

Sparrow only nodded and then continued forward. He slowed as he approached a bulkhead door. The door had steel pins that could be turned to secure the door in place; three on the top, three on the bottom and two in the middle on both sides of the frame. The proper term or slang was to dog the door. Each door had a gasket around the inside and if the door was closed and all the pins were turned, the door would be watertight, thereby protecting the ship from flooding in case of it sinking. The entire ship was like this, compartmentalized, as flooding and fire were the two most dangerous things to a naval vessel.

Sparrow undogged the door and opened it wide, the door squeaking loudly in the night, the echoes bouncing off the bulkheads to be lost in the darkness.

Sparrow turned to Henry and grinned. “This is the fun part. Walking into the unknown, having no idea what’s waiting around the corner.”

“If you say so,” Henry said, gripping his shotgun just a little tighter. He wasn’t happy about entering the bowels of the ship, but understood it as a necessary evil. Before they could ransack it, they needed to make sure it was uninhabited, by either living humans or the undead.

Sparrow pulled out a flashlight and turned it on, the thin beam slicing through the darkness. Slowly, with his SMG in his right hand and the flashlight in his left, he started down the corridor.

Henry refrained from using his own flashlight, not wanting to waste a hand holding it. As he followed Sparrow, though, he had wished he had considered taping it to the end of his shotgun like Jimmy had done. Jimmy held his weapon in front of him, the beam illuminating Sparrow’s back. Shadows from the flashlights played out across the bulkheads, giving everything a haunted house feel.

With the engines of the frigate off, the ship was preternaturally quiet, only the sounds of their footsteps breaking the silence. Numerous doors, all closed, lined the corridor and Sparrow slowed at each one, cocking his head to listen if anything stirred within. Inside the compartment, these doors were all standard wood construction, complete with doorknobs. The ship smelled of mold, and something else, a staleness that said no one had walked these corridors in quite some time.

The corridor doglegged to the right and Sparrow followed it, his flashlight beam leading the way. The deeper they moved into the bowels of the ship, the more signs of once human habitation became obvious. Miscellaneous items started to appear on the deck at their feet as they walked. Jimmy used his flashlight to illuminate some of them and Henry saw everything from a baseball cap with the ships logo on it to photographs of friends and family; the photos now scratched and wrinkled from countless boot soles.

“Where do you think everyone went?” Jimmy asked Henry as they skulked down the corridor. Sparrow was in the lead and Mickey brought up the rear.

Henry shrugged; the gesture invisible in the darkness. "Don't know. Maybe we'll find the evacuation boats gone or whatever the hell they call them. Maybe everybody just abandoned ship."

"Yeah, but even if they did, where would they go? I mean, I would think the safest place to be would be on a ship if you're lucky enough to have one."

"Jimmy, I wish I had an answer for you, but I don't," Henry said, in a low voice. The ship felt like a giant tomb, even if there were no bodies on board, it just didn't feel right to talk loud.

Sparrow came upon a ladder and he flashed the beam of light down the steep staircase. In naval terms staircases were called ladders. Henry's father had been in the Navy and a lot of the terms came back to him as he remembered some of the stories his father had told him. The only exception was that his father had been on a submarine. He had been stationed out of San Diego, but his mother had stayed in the Midwest near her own mother and father.

He had seen his father very little when he was young and even less when he was older; both he and his father had little in common, with the exception of being father and son. Now the man was probably dead or worse, walking around somewhere as a walking corpse. Deciding those kinds of thoughts did nothing positive for him; he pushed them away, concentrating on the situation at hand

Still, just being in a naval vessel brought back nostalgic memories for Henry.

He was pulled from his daydreaming when Sparrow stopped by something hanging on the wall at the top of the ladder. Henry moved closer and examined the schematic of the ship bolted to the bulkhead. The map was behind a sheet of plexiglass and the bright light of the flashlight made it hard to read, but then Sparrow cupped the light with his hand and the reflection dimmed.

Henry spotted the red circle and then used his finger to trace the lines that showed the other places of value inside the ship.

"If we're here," he said, pointing to the red circle, "and if we stay on this corridor, then we'll be able to reach the galley, but if we go down that opening," he pointed to the ladder, "and follow that corridor below us, it will take us to the engine room."

Sparrow nodded, listening to Henry. “Good, let’s check out the engine room first and then we’ll backtrack to the galley and meet up with the others.” He smiled back to the others. “So far it looks good around here. You could say it’s a free lunch, especially if their food locker is still full.”

Sparrow turned and moved down the ladder, only pausing to play the flashlight back and forth. Quickly, the others followed and then with Sparrow once more in the lead, they moved down the corridor to the engine room.

While they walked, more signs of life were evident, though not as positive as they would have preferred. The bulkheads, though once painted a dull gray, were now splashed with maroon, the dried blood dripping down the walls like some kind of abstract art by a mad painter. Dried pools collected near the edges of the deck, where the bulkheads met and though long dried, everyone made sure to step over each pool. There were also uniforms, ripped to shreds and covered in blood. As for the owners of these uniforms, there was no sign.

Finally, Sparrow reached a larger hatch, dogged closed with a white sign with the words **ENGINE ROOM** glued to the middle of the heavy, gray-metal opening, just below a small circular window. The small window was two-inch thick glass and was made to withstand the pressures of being deep underwater if the compartment flooded.

Sparrow flashed his beam at the window, trying to see inside the room.

“I can’t see shit through this little window. We’ll have to open her up and go inside.”

“Okay, how do you want to do this? We can’t just go walking inside like we’re on a picnic. We need a plan. Who goes where and where to shoot at whatever’s in there if the need arises,” Henry told Sparrow.

Sparrow slapped the bulkhead, his grin wide. “You see? That’s why I wanted you with me. You think of things I don’t. Okay, you take point and tell us what to do.” He looked at Mickey in the back. “You listen to Henry now, he know his shit.”

Mickey nodded. “Yes, sir, not a problem, Captain.”

Henry looked through the small window, seeing what lay on the other side of the hatch, then he stepped back and gestured to Jimmy.

"Jimmy, take a look inside," Henry said, pulling Jimmy to the door and having the younger man take a quick peek through the porthole so he could get the layout of the room, then Jimmy pulled back and nodded.

"Okay, Henry, what's the plan?" Jimmy asked.

Henry quickly went through instructions on how they would enter the engine room. Henry would go first and take the right, while Jimmy would go left. Mickey would follow third and stay in the middle. Henry explained to Mickey about how to only shoot in front of him, keeping his fire contained, counting on both Henry and Jimmy to take the sides.

"What about me? Where do I go?" Sparrow asked from the side of the corridor.

"You follow us in. You're the Captain and so you need to take the less risk."

Sparrow was about to argue, but Henry put his hand up to stop the old man.

"No arguments, that's just the way it has to be. If something happens to you, then where will your crew be? From what I saw, the only person who might take over for you running the ship is Spencer." Henry shook his head, negatively. "No, you need to hang back and we'll call you in when the coast is clear."

Sparrow's shoulders slumped just a little and the man nodded. Though he wasn't pleased with Henry's decision, he understood the rationality.

"Fine, Henry, you're in charge of this little recce. That's why I had you come along. Me and my crew have spent to much time on our ship to really know how to fight these dead things. Every now and then we find a few hiding in these ships, but they're always easy to kill."

"All right, then, let's see what's inside," Henry said, undogging the hatch and pushing it open. The hatch creaked on rusty hinges and slammed against the doorstop mounted to the bulkhead, bouncing slightly and stopping.

With a deep breath, and a small prayer, Henry leaned his head down, not wanting to whack it on the low doorframe, and stepped over the small ledge of the frame near his feet and entered the engine room.

Jimmy had just started to enter behind him and Henry was about to tell him to move to the side when a dark shadow lunged out from the darkness, knocking Henry to the deck.

Death and decay filled his nostrils and he desperately tried to get his hands out from between himself and the heavy weight on top of him.

In the wan light of Jimmy's flashlight, now bobbing around the room like it was a bouncing ball, Henry stared up into the face of death.

And then jaws and teeth descended, blocking out the light.

Chapter 5

Henry's world was nothing but his own tortured breathing and the guttural growls of the snarling creature struggling to reach him, as it squirmed and twisted on top of him. A flash of something he'd once heard shot through his mind, how when you were about to die you saw your life in bits and pieces in your mind. But as he struggled with the ghoul on top of him, all he saw was rage. The zombie was nothing more than death incarnate and he'd be damned if he'd let the son-of-a-bitch win today. With a surge of adrenalin, he shifted his weight, managing to pull his hands out from between himself and the corpse's body. Freeing his shotgun, he knocked the ghoul's arms to its sides, giving himself a precious second to gain the upper hand.

Just as the head darted down to try and bite his face, he jammed both hands under its chin, keeping it away from him.

His stomach rolled inside him when both his hands sunk into the gelatinous ooze that was once the creature's skin. Henry could feel the distinct impression of the zombie's jaw, and then his thumbs slid around to actually lock around its spinal column.

Bits of gore dripped off its head to drop onto the deck around his face.

One particularly nasty gobbet fell onto his forehead, the jello-like substance oozing down his face to drip off his cheek and strike the deck below him.

The ghoul was like a wild animal, gnashing its teeth as it anticipated chomping on Henry's exposed flesh. Then the weight was lifted off him and he was able to breathe again.

Out of the corner of his eye, with only the dull gloom from Jimmy and Sparrow's flashlights to see by--both lights pointed in different directions--Henry watched Jimmy throw the zombie to the deck and crack its skull like a ripe melon with the butt of his shotgun.

The corpse dropped to the deck with a massive head wound that had pieces of its skull falling to the floor. The head bounced twice, red liquid and brains oozing out to spill onto the deck.

Henry blinked for a moment, and when he opened his eyes, Mickey appeared hovering over him as if by magic, his hand out to help him up. Henry took the man's hand and with a heave, was brought back to a standing position.

Leaning over, trying to catch his breath, Jimmy moved next to Henry, his eyes constantly watching the shadows.

"You okay?" Jimmy asked with eyes filled with concern.

Henry nodded curtly. "Yeah, I'll live, just give me a second. Jesus Christ that bastard came out of nowhere." He looked up into Jimmy's face. "Thanks, buddy, that deader almost had me."

"Anytime, Henry, feel free to pay me back if I get into a jam."

"Done," Henry said, wiping his face with his sleeve.

"What's a deader?" Mickey asked from beside the two men, his eyes also watching the shadows nervously.

"It's just a nickname for the dead fucks, that's all," Jimmy told him.

Mickey opened his mouth and nodded, not really understanding. "Oh, okay, right."

Henry walked over to the dead ghoul, examining the now still form. It had once been a man, but other than that there were no tell tale pieces of identifying characteristics. The body was clothed in dirty, blue coveralls, the name **OLSEN** handwritten in black marker on the breast pocket of its shirt.

"Who do you think he was?" Jimmy asked, studying the body next to Henry; nudging it with his foot to make sure it was dead.

"Don't know," Henry said, "probably one of the crew who somehow got infected and then came down here to die, maybe." he shrugged. "There's really no way to know for sure what happened to him, other than he's dead, now and forever. He's finally at peace."

"Yeah, and you almost joined him," Jimmy added with a slight grin

"I'm comin' in, I'm sick of waiting out here like an old woman," Sparrow called from the hatch.

Henry waved him inside. "Come on in, it's safe, now. If there were more still in here, then believe me, we'd know about it. They're not too smart. If they know there are humans around, they go to 'em like a bee to honey."

"Uhm, actually, Henry, bees make honey, not go to it," Jimmy said wryly.

Henry gave him an evil look. "Whatever, you know what I mean, so if the school lesson is over, what do you say we search this place and get the hell out of here? I for one have already had my fill of ghost ships."

Jimmy and the others nodded, all agreeing with him.

"Sounds good, Henry, sounds real good. We just need to check the level on the fuel tanks and then we can go," Sparrow said, while moving into the darkness, his flashlight in front of him.

With Henry and Jimmy, followed by Mickey, they all moved deeper into the engine room. In a few scant minutes, Sparrow found the tanks, and after a quick inspection, looked up with a smile.

"We're in luck; they're not full, but there not empty. There's a good week's worth of juice in these tanks. Now all we have to do is get some people over here and start siphoning it out."

"That's great, Sparrow, glad to hear it." Henry said as he checked the battered watch on his wrist, the small glowing hands illuminated in the gloom of the room. "It's about time we go meet the others in the galley."

"And hopefully get some food," Jimmy added.

Everyone moved back through the engine room, stepping over the prone corpse.

Henry chuckled while he stepped back through the hatch and into the corridor. "That's my Jimmy, always thinkin' with his stomach."

Jimmy smiled from ear to ear. "Hell yes, can't get far without a full stomach, no matter how tough a guy thinks he might be."

"Amen, son; that is so true. You know, Henry, you just might have a philosopher on your hands here," Sparrow said while they moved slowly up the dark corridor.

Henry let out a bark of laughter that echoed off the walls and immediately regretted it. Though he hated to admit it, he was still a little shaken by his encounter with the dead sailor.

"Oh, really, well maybe I'll just start calling you, Professor, how 'bout that?" Henry asked Jimmy.

Jimmy rubbed his chin with his free hand and nodded. "I like the ring of that. Professor Cooper, it just might work."

"Forget it, Jimmy, not now and not ever," Henry told him with a wide smile.

Jimmy glared at him, but a moment later his visage cracked and he smiled back. With the tension broken for the moment, the four men moved deeper into the ship, until they were only a few minutes from the galley.

Jimmy was talking quietly with Mickey, while Sparrow and Henry led the way. Sparrow continually swept the flashlight back and forth across the small corridor, trying to illuminate each door they passed. If there were stirrings behind the doors, none heard it and so after making sure they were secure, they would move on. There was nothing inside those rooms that the cruise ship required. The only things needed were fuel and food, the order interchangeable.

Henry slowed at a corner junction, and his finger trailed across yet another plexiglass covered map of the ship.

"Looks like the galley and mess hall is just past this door," he told the others, pulling his finger back and wrapping his hand around his shotgun. Whatever was in the galley, he'd be damned if he'd be caught off guard again.

"Well, come on then, dammit, times a wastin'. Spencer and the others should already be waiting for us," Sparrow said and pushed past Henry to get at the hatch that was as big as a standard door.

"No wait, we need to make sure it's safe!" Henry called out to him, just as Sparrow wrapped his hand around a small protuberance in the middle of the metal hatch and pushed it open.

The instant the door opened all the men in the corridor felt the urge to gag. The sweet smell of decay and decomposition filled their lungs and threatened to choke them like they were all drowning in a lake of molten lead. Eyes watered and the air became filled with flies, everyone now batting at them with their hands, trying to keep them from landing on their exposed flesh.

Henry was about to yell at Sparrow, tell the man to close the damn door, when the multiple retorts of firearms could be heard coming from inside the galley.

A man yelled over the roar of gunfire and Sparrow turned to Henry, his eyes wide. "That's Spencer, he's in there. We've got to help him!" Sparrow screamed.

"Shit, I know we do," Henry growled, already ripping a piece of cloth off his shirt and wrapping it around his face to protect himself from both the smell of death and the buzzing flies. Next to him, Jimmy was doing the same, and with a nudge to Mickey, the younger man copied Jimmy, ripping his t-shirt in half and wrapping it around his face like a bandito about to rob a train.

More gunshots could be heard and screams filled the corridor.

"All right, Jimmy, you take the right and I've got the left. If it moves, kill it. That's it, let's get going." Henry ordered, prepared to step into the galley.

"What about me and Mickey?" Sparrow asked quickly, his eyes wide with worry for his men inside the galley.

"You and Mickey take the middle, just watch your fire; don't stray into Jimmy's or my fire path, that way we maximize the kill zone!"

Sparrow nodded and slapped Mickey on the arm. The younger man looked scared, real scared, and Henry could only hope the kid could keep it together long enough to do what had to be done.

Without a clue as to what was waiting for him inside the galley and mess hall, Henry raised his shotgun and charged inside, the others right behind him.

Chapter 6

If Henry had thought the odor was bad out in the corridor, he was almost knocked unconscious when he stepped inside the mess hall.

The charnel house smell was so bad only his iron will kept him from vomiting the contents of his stomach across the bloody and chipped decking under his feet.

With the exception of a few flashlight beams moving about erratically, the mess hall was in complete darkness. The room was large enough to sit and feed more than fifty men at a time. Tables and chairs, similar to picnic tables, but made of plastic and metal, were bolted to the deck and spread out in neat rows around the room, with an isle in the middle for pedestrians to move through easily. A broken and shattered television, once mounted to the corner bulkhead, now lay hanging by its electrical cord like an overripe apple ready to drop from its tree branch and dozens of DVDs were scattered across the floor beneath it like dead leaves fallen from the same tree.

Across the room, Spencer and his men were shooting indiscriminately into the shadows that made up the far bulkhead. Jimmy came up behind Henry and flashed his light to where the men were shooting and Henry let out a silent gasp.

More than twenty zombies were gathered against the bulkhead and on the nearby tables. All were covered in gore from head to toe, large chunks of rotting meat in their hands, other chunks appearing to look fresher, the bright red gristle glistening in the dull light of the flashlights.

Jimmy moved the light downward and the tight beam illuminated the partial remains of what was once a human body. The body had been ripped to shreds and now resembled nothing but a large hunk of meat that had been torn apart by ravenous dogs. The eyes from the severed head of the body gazed up at nothing, reflecting the beam of light as Jimmy played the light over it.

Even with more than half the body missing or destroyed, Henry recognized the corpse as one of Spencer's men.

At first the zombie's did nothing, merely accepting being shot by Spencer's men, one at a time, as they continued feeding on their prey, but then one more perceptive than the others realized there was more meat in the room, and after standing up and approaching Spencer, others slowly followed.

Spencer shot the closest one, the body jumping and twitching as round after round struck its torso. Blood and gobbets of red and black exploded out its back to cover the ghouls behind it, but with the exception of slowing it momentarily from the force of the shots, it continued onward.

"Shoot them in the head, goddammit, the head!" Henry yelled across the mess hall.

If any of the men heard him, none gave an inclination. He looked to the opposite side of the room to see the opening that would lead into the kitchen. Ominous shapes moved about, flirting in-between large stainless-steel kettles and ovens.

Turning back to the charging ghouls, he realized they were in serious trouble.

Soon more than half of the zombies were up and on the move, arms held out, jaws already glistening with blood, snapping open and shut in anticipation of the food in front of them.

Henry ran across the room, shooting the closest ghoul next to Spencer in the head in a spray of red mist and bone fragments. Pumping the shotgun, the expended cartridge falling out to be lost amongst the feet of the men and darkness, Henry lined up another shot and sent a barrage of death into a dead crewman of the U.S.S. Miller.

The body flew backward to knock over two more behind it, and Henry pushed in close against Spencer, glancing to his right to see Jimmy firing round after round at the oncoming crowd of undead crewmen.

"Spencer, you've got to shoot them in the head or all you'll do is piss them off!" Henry yelled at the man from no more than a foot away.

Spencer turned to stare at Henry, his face wide with either anger or panic. In the dim light it was hard to tell.

"Don't you think I know that?" He screamed over the gunshots around him, smoke now filling the air from all the gunfire.

"Well then fucking do it!" Henry screamed back, kicking an approaching zombie crawling on the floor in the head and then shooting it in the face. It was thrown back by the blow, the face disintegrating into a red mist, the body falling to the deck with a thump.

Spencer's men poured bullets into the zombie horde like they grew on trees, almost all their shots striking the ghouls in the chest or lower torso. Bodies fell to the deck, writhing and wiggling as ligaments and muscles were ripped apart by bullets, but still they came onward; crawling if they had to, but not giving up.

Sparrow was to Henry's right now, their formation at entering the mess hall totally gone to shit. It was pure pandemonium, as men panicked and shot at any shadow they saw, instead of concentrating their firepower on the undead threat.

Instead of blowing the corpses to hell in seconds, the ghouls had managed to get in tight with the men, hand to hand and hand to teeth now becoming the battle of the day.

Henry and Jimmy moved back to the door, Spencer near him and Sparrow by his side.

"Fall back, dammit; this is all going to hell, fall back!" Henry yelled.

Spencer shot him a look of hatred, but even he had to agree that was the most prudent course of action.

Spencer followed Henry, Jimmy and Sparrow to the hatch leading back to the corridor they had entered by, the other men now cut off. Screams of the rest of the boarding party filled the mess hall and every now and then a gun would fire. Spencer stopped and looked around worriedly, his eyes trying to peer into the gloom,

"Mickey, where's Mickey?" He screamed.

Henry didn't know what was so important about this one man, but he too, started to try and find the younger man in the smoke and gloom.

"There he is!" Jimmy yelled, pointing to the middle of the room. Mickey had been cut off from the others, and as he fired at two approaching ghouls, he didn't see one was sneaking up on him in his blind spot. "Mickey, behind you!" Spencer screamed to the man, but Mickey was oblivious; the gunshots and screams of his dying friends filling the mess hall like a crescendo.

Spencer was about to charge into the fray, heedless of his own welfare, when Henry grabbed the man's arm and held fast.

"Let me go, goddammit, I need to help him!" Spencer roared.

"It's too late, there's nothing you can do for him...look!" Henry yelled, pointing.

Spencer turned back to see Mickey falling under the ghoul that had attacked him from behind, the man uttering one frightened cry before he was overwhelmed completely by the snarling corpse. No sooner had he gone down then the other two ghouls, neither fatally wounded by Mickey's marksmanship, swarmed over his flailing body and began to rip him apart piece by bloody piece.

"No!" Spencer screamed, "Mickey!"

Jimmy helped Henry pull Spencer through the door just as a half-dozen ghouls came at them, distracted by Spencer's calls.

"What the fuck is his problem?" Jimmy screamed at Henry, struggling to pull Spencer through the doorway.

"I don't know, just keep pulling or he's dead...and us too!"

With the growling, struggling Spencer between them, Henry and Jimmy pushed and pulled the man through the hatchway. Sparrow was ready and just as Henry's foot crossed the frame; Sparrow slammed the hatch closed, a ghoul bouncing off it with a loud and meaty thwack.

Spencer ripped himself away from the hands of Henry and Jimmy and immediately pushed past them to reach the small porthole on the hatch.

"Mickey...no!" He screamed, pounding on the metal fruitlessly.

Henry and Jimmy stared at Spencer's back, not quite understanding what was happening. Was Mickey family to Spencer? Perhaps a cousin or even a brother? Why was the man so torn up about this one man in particular when all the other men on the boarding party had been killed like lambs to the wolves?

For a few scant seconds all that could be heard in the corridor, other then Spencer's protests, was the sound of heavy breathing while the men tried to regain control of themselves.

Sparrow moved next to Spencer, who was still peering through the porthole, frantically trying to see Mickey.

"I'm so sorry, son, but he's gone, you know that," Sparrow told him quietly.

Spencer spun around and stuck his hand out, directly at Henry, his index finger aimed at Henry accusingly.

"You, you did this! You stopped me when I could have saved him! He died for nothing!" Spencer spat, drool sliding out of the corners of his mouth in his anger and frustration.

"What the fuck are you talking about?" Jimmy yelled at the man. "If it wasn't for Henry, you'd be zombie chow right about now. He saved your worthless life!"

Henry placed a hand on Jimmy's shoulder. "That's okay, Jimmy, he's just upset. He's obviously lost someone close to him."

"Don't see why, Mickey worked under Spencer as a deckhand, and gopher. I mean, it's terrible we lost him today, but not any more so than losing the other men. They were all good men and will be missed." Sparrow stated to Henry and Jimmy with Spencer staring at the floor, shoulders heaving with internal struggles as he tried to wrap his mind around the fact that his lover was dead.

"You don't know what the fuck you're talking about, Sparrow. Mickey was more than just a deckhand to me!" He yelled at Sparrow, though even in his grief he was careful not to cross the line and be absolutely disrespectful. Sparrow had saved his life back when the zombie outbreak first started and he would never forget it, no matter how upset he might be at the moment.

"Oh, really? Well then, why don't you enlighten me and the others here on what the hell you're talking about?" Sparrow asked Spencer.

Spencer turned back to stare at the three men, hands clasped tightly into fists. He debated finally telling Sparrow about him and Mickey, but even as he was about to speak, a small voice in his head told him not to, that it didn't matter now that Mickey was gone.

"Forget it, Sparrow, just leave it alone." Spencer then turned his wide eyes on Henry. "Look, big man, I don't care what you've done for Sparrow or that your friend here thinks you saved me. In my heart I know you cost Mickey his life and I'll tell you this, in front of my Captain. You and me are gonna settle this account real soon."

Then, wiping tears from his eyes, he pushed past the three men and stomped down the corridor, his hand out to the right bulkhead to feel his destination, the corridor pitch black, and his flashlight now missing, lost in the mess hall. His footsteps slowly faded away until they were gone.

"Would someone please tell me what the fuck just happened here?" Jimmy asked Henry and Sparrow.

Henry shrugged. "I have no idea. I thought we were doing a good thing by saving his ass, not ending up getting into a feud with him."

Sparrow patted Henry's shoulder. "Don't worry about Spencer, Henry; I'll have a talk with him. For now, let's get back to the ship. I'll need to send more men down here with enough firepower to take out that...what would you call it...a nest?...of zombies and then we can see what food is left in the storerooms. I just hope it's not all for nothing. Bullets don't come cheap, you know. Not to mention the human loss today."

Henry turned and started back up the corridor, the same way Spencer had gone just moments ago, Jimmy and Sparrow behind him.

"You're really gonna go in there and take on all those deaders? Do you really think it's worth it?" Henry asked quietly. The sounds of the zombies in the mess hall quickly faded away, thanks to the heavy metal hatch being closed and dogged.

Sparrow nodded. "Uh-huh. If there's fuel in the tanks then there should be food in the kitchen. We need that food, Henry, even more than we need bullets."

Sparrow said the last sentence with conviction, then said: "Are you two boys gonna help out with the clean-up or what?"

"If it's all the same to you, Sparrow, old buddy, I'd like to sit the next dance out." Jimmy told him as they walked slowly down the corridor. Both Henry and Jimmy were more relaxed, now, having already checked this part of the ship, but even under their calm exterior there was a tension, both men ready to shoot anything that appeared out of the dark.

"I'd like to agree with Jimmy, if it's all right with you, Sparrow," Henry said.

Sparrow sighed and nodded; his face hard to see behind the beam of the flashlight. "I suppose so, I've got enough men to do the job, but I could still use your help."

Henry weighed the man's words, thinking. "Well then, how 'bout this, let me think about it for a little while, huh? I mean, it's not like you have to go right back in there. Let the plan keep for a couple of hours."

"Fair enough. That I can do." Sparrow smiled and then pushed past the two men to take the lead once more.

Jimmy looked to Henry in the darkness, wanting to discuss things more, his face only a dim outline, and Henry shook his head. "We'll talk later," was all he said to Jimmy.

Jimmy nodded, understanding. The two men had traveled so long together sometimes it was like they knew each others thoughts.

With their footsteps echoing off the bulkheads, the only three survivors, plus Spencer, worked their way back through the ship, looking forward to reaching topside once more.

Sparrow's mood began to grow sullen. He wasn't looking forward to telling the boarding party's families that their husbands, fathers and sons hadn't made it out alive.

Both Henry and Jimmy picked up on this and the rest of the journey back to the upper deck was one in silence, only the creaking of the ship, as the waves struck the hull, to keep the men company.

Chapter 7

More than an hour had passed since Henry, Jimmy and the others had returned to the cruise ship. Sparrow had bid them goodbye and had gone off to the bridge to find some men for the clean-up of the naval ship's mess hall and galley.

After meeting up with Cindy and Mary, the two weary men had filled the ladies in on what had occurred and what might come next.

They had talked over multiple ideas and had then split up once again, the women heading off to see what they could find out from the rest of the crew and passengers.

Similar to a small town, everyone on the ship always knew what everyone else was doing and it was only a matter of time before someone let a particularly juicy nugget of information spill by accident.

As for Henry and Jimmy, both men went to find a place to unwind.

Henry had decided to return to a small gym on the aft end of the ship. The front of the room was filled with all types of weights and cardiovascular machines, but the rear part of the room was large and empty. Large rubber mats lined the floor and at the front of the room, the walls were covered in mirrors that reached to the ceiling. Also in front, was an eight-inch high stage; preferably where the aerobics instructor would have positioned himself while he stretched and bent muscles to burn fat off of overweight passengers.

Henry had found the gym quite by accident and had soon found that it was virtually always empty. The ship had an identical gym near the front of the ship and most, if any, of the passengers used that one.

Henry was far to wired to rest or sleep, so had decided to go workout for a while. Now that he had a physique to maintain, he enjoyed working out, feeling the adrenalin pumping and his own heartbeat thumping in his head, as he strived to push himself harder to curl that one more pound or one more leg press.

Jimmy had sat in a corner watching him at first, making cracks and jokes whenever possible.

Finally, Henry had stopped bench pressing weights and had stood up and then dragged Jimmy over to the mats.

"All right, tough guy, you've been busting my balls for long enough. If you're so damn tough, then let's see what you got." Henry told him this with a wide smile, enjoying the comradeship.

Jimmy had started stretching and bending, looking like he was about to go run a marathon. "Are you sure you want to do this, old man? I mean, I wouldn't want to hurt you, or have you break a hip."

Henry placed a hand on each hip and frowned. "Just you wait, Mr. Big Shot, we'll see who's laughing in a minute.

Jimmy continued to stretch, and then, without warning, he took off directly at Henry like a sprinter. Henry hadn't expected the younger man to attack without warning, but inwardly he was impressed. Rules of contact for fighting in the new world they both lived in were irrelevant. The only goal was to destroy your opponent as fast as possible, and nothing more.

Jimmy charged at Henry, head first, for all purposes resembling a bull, but Henry reacted just a little faster than Jimmy expected. Henry sidestepped Jimmy, and when Jimmy charged past him, he dropped his hand over the back of Jimmy's neck like a karate chop, but at the last instant pulled the blow.

Still, Jimmy went tumbling head first to the mats, but rolled over his head and came up in a crouch; if facing the wrong way. Jimmy hopped into the air and came down facing Henry.

"That hurt, you old bastard," Jimmy said, rubbing the back of his neck.

"Could have hurt a lot more if I'd wanted it to. Lesson one, never take your eyes off your opponent," Henry told him flatly.

Jimmy sneered slightly and this time moved in slower, trying to find Henry's weak spot. Not wanting to scare him away, Henry dropped his guard slightly, giving Jimmy the advantage he thought he'd found. Jimmy stepped into his punch with his right fist heading for Henry's jaw, but Henry reached out and blocked the blow, then grabbed Jimmy's arm and then pulled him toward him. Jimmy went flying off his feet, and Henry threw him over his hip.

Jimmy landed in a heap of arms and legs, and this time he looked mad.

Jimmy pulled his knife then, waving it in front of himself like he was in a brawl in the back of an alley in some seedy city.

"That was low, Henry, you pretended so you could let me in, didn't you."

Henry nodded and pulled his panga in one fluid motion.

"Now, Jimmy, it's all in fun, put the knife away and we'll call it quits."

Jimmy shook his head. "Nothin' doin'. This ends when I prove to you I can handle myself. I'll make a bet with you, Henry. The first person to draw blood has to clean the others weapons for a week."

Henry frowned slightly. "Now Jimmy, the last time we made a bet like that you lost, you don't want to lose again, do you?"

"Don't you worry, I won't lose this time. I've gotten better, while you're gettin' older. You'll see. Besides, out there in the real world they don't play. It's either the real thing or nothin'."

Henry realized maybe he'd hurt his friends ego just a little and now Jimmy needed to save face with him.

With a loud sigh that filled the room, Henry nodded. "Fine, first blood, but be careful, there's no hospitals around here, last I checked."

Jimmy chuckled at that, now moving closer like a wild animal. "Don't worry, Henry, I'm just gonna nick ya, like you accidentally cut yourself shaving."

"Hmmm, we'll see about that, junior," he cupped his left hand to Jimmy. "Bring it on."

Jimmy started to move in, making playful swipes at Henry. He still had to be careful not to really hurt his friend. Despite his bravado, he'd regretted pulling the knife on Henry the second he'd done it, but his ego wouldn't let him back down.

Now, if Henry happened to nick him fair and square at least he could hold his head high.

So far Henry was only on the defensive, his larger blade an advantage. But Jimmy was wiry and quicker and continually slipped under Henry's guard.

Then Jimmy took a chance, slashing at Henry's thigh. Henry blocked the blow with his blade and then tried to nick Jimmy's arm, but Jimmy managed to jump out of the way at the last second.

"That was close, old man. But still to slow. What's the matter, the arthritis acting up again?" Jimmy quipped, smiling as he bobbed and weaved around his friend.

"Very funny, you are so damn funny; I can't believe you don't take your act on the road?" He joked back, knocking a blow aside and trying to come in under Jimmy's guard.

Jimmy tried to hop back, but Henry dropped to the mats and swept his leg out and knocked Jimmy to the floor like a toppling bowling pin. Jimmy rolled up and just as he was on his knees, Henry had the panga at his throat.

"Uh-oh, looks like someone just lost a bet?" Henry said with a smile, breathing heavily from the exertion.

Jimmy didn't move a muscle, knowing the razor sharp panga was a hair's breathe away from his Adam's apple.

"Uh, sorry to disappoint, old man, but before you start gloating, maybe you should look down."

Henry did as he was told and looked down to his groin to see Jimmy's knife, poking his thigh, just below his testicles. The point of the knife had ever so tenderly poked his skin, eliciting the smallest bubble of blood to seep onto his pants.

Henry lowered the panga and stepped away from Jimmy, the younger man doing the same.

"Son-of-a-bitch, you sneaky bastard," Henry said, wiping sweat from his brow. "That was nice, very smooth. I never saw it coming."

Jimmy leaned back and stretched, trying to breathe in oxygen faster and slow his beating heart. "I thought that's the idea. I learned that trick from you. Remember when we were at the mall?"

Henry did actually. They had spent the winter at a New England shopping mall and when the snow had been high outside the walls of the mall, the snow plows now gone forever, Jimmy and he had spent many hours at the sporting goods store, wrestling and boxing. Henry had boxed in college and had been surprised how easily it all came back to him when he started to work out regularly.

Now his once flabby arms and beer belly were replaced by hard muscle.

He was twice the man he had been physically before the world had crumbled. Health wise, he was in the best shape of his life, if only it hadn't taken the fall of civilization to transform him. Jimmy, too, was a more muscular specimen of the human male. When Henry had first met him he had been a skinny kid who could barely point a gun straight, but now the man was all muscle, though still skinny, his size belaying his strength.

The two men had formed a friendship in fire and were closer than most brothers now. Henry was proud to be bested by Jimmy, like a father would be that his son had become the victor. It was the normal stage of life that sooner or later the son would win over the father.

Not that he would ever tell Jimmy that. The young man had a big enough head as it was; Henry wasn't going to add to it.

With both men relaxing, their breathing coming under control, Henry sheathed his panga, Jimmy doing the same with his knife.

"That's enough of a workout for now, what do you say we find the girls and see what's up? Sparrow should probably be ready for whatever he's gonna do by about now," Henry said.

"Are we going back to the other ship? You know, help him out?"

Henry rubbed his jaw. "I've been thinking about that. He wants us to come and we need to stay on his good side. What do you say if we just go as backup; in case his men run into trouble. That way we shouldn't need to do anything but stand around and look important."

Jimmy shrugged. "Fine with me, whatever you say is okay with me, let's just do something. It's the waiting around that drives me crazy, you know that."

Henry grinned at that statement. Jimmy was notorious for wanting to charge into a situation without thinking, favoring action over contemplating. Henry knew it was just youth, and if he was lucky enough to survive long enough, Jimmy would eventually grow out of it.

"Fine, let's go, I'm thirsty as hell and I need a shower, even if it's with salt water."

Jimmy nodded and the two men grabbed what gear they had and left the gym.

With the door closing, the gym grew quiet, but then a side door opened behind a set of barbells and Spencer stepped out. He had been at the door the entire time the two men had fought and talked, listening intently.

Rage burned inside Spencer while he had watched Henry spar with his friend, wanting nothing more than to put a bullet in him. But he wasn't sure he'd get a kill shot, and even if he did manage one, Jimmy would have surely attacked.

No, he needed to make sure the odds were entirely on his side. He's have to if he was to succeed. He thought of Mickey then, remembering his lover's face as he was pulled down to be ripped apart on the deck of the mess hall under a wave of bodies. He'd take Mickey's screams with him to bed every night for the rest of his life, he knew this without having slept even one night after his loss.

But he knew one way to help squelch those screams. By smothering them with the screams of Henry and his friends. They had stopped him from going in and saving Mickey. He knew he could have reached him in time, at least that was what he told himself over and over so many times he was just about convinced it was true.

Now all he had was revenge, a burning that started in the pit of his stomach and worked its way up to his throat. An acidic flavor so strong he could taste it.

Henry needed to die; he had to die, if Spencer was ever to find peace again.

Stepping back into the back room, the door clicked shut again, leaving the room in solitude once more.

Chapter 8

Just as the two men stepped out of the gym and into the hallway, a young boy no more than thirteen ran up to them. The boy's face was covered in acne and his voice cracked when he talked.

Henry smiled at the sight. Watching as the boy ran up to them, a look of concern on his face. Henry had met the boy before and he thought his name was Tom or Ron, or something along those lines.

"I finally found you guys," the boy's voice squeaked as he slowed to a halt in front of Henry and Jimmy. "I've been looking everywhere for you."

"Well then, you weren't looking in the right place, because we've been here for a while now," Jimmy quipped back.

The boy nodded, not interested in debating the subject one way or the other.

"Sparrow sent me to fetch you. He's on the bridge. He wants to talk with you guys before he sends the clean-up team over to the other ship."

Henry looked to Jimmy and then back to the boy. "That's fine, son, we were just about to do that very thing. We just want to find our friends first."

"You mean the pretty blonde girl and the one with dark hair?" He asked.

Henry nodded. "That's them; you don't know where they are, do you?"

The boy grinned, proud of himself. "Sure do, they're in the main dining room getting some grub. I can take you there if you want. I know a few shortcuts to get you there quickly."

"Sure, kid, lead on," Jimmy said, starting to move after the boy.

Henry chuckled at Jimmy's vernacular for the boy. It seemed like Jimmy was the one being called kid not so long ago.

Henry took up the rear, the boy weaving in and out of corridors. He knew his way around the ship, that was for sure. But then why wouldn't he? For almost a year the cruise ship had been his home. To him the corridors and hallways were like the alleyways and main streets of a city.

In this new world the boy found himself in, there would be no proms or school dances, only the constant struggle to eek out an existence. At least on the cruise ship there was a relative amount of safety. Compared to being on land, the ship was a virtual fortress. Even if the dead could swim there would still be no way for them to enter the ship from the water.

Eight minutes later, the boy turned a corner and Henry recognized the wide, grand opening that led into the main dining room.

As both he and Jimmy stepped into the room, Cindy and Mary waved to them, both sitting at a table near the side of the massive room.

Like walking into a mausoleum, their footsteps bounced off the high ceiling and far walls until they had reached the two women. Both men sat down, Jimmy reaching out for a pitcher of water and pouring himself a glass. Across the room, spaced apart at other tables, were a few other late night diners, all of them minding their own business.

"Okay, you found us, son. Tell Sparrow we'll be there in a few minutes." Henry told the boy.

"But he told me to get you right away, and not to goof off."

Henry's face grew hard, but only slightly. "That's okay, son, tell Sparrow we'll be there in a few minutes," he repeated. "Trust me, it'll be fine."

With trepidation, the boy looked to Henry and then Jimmy and then the others; then nodded curtly. Without another word he was off, his legs carrying him across the room like a sprinter in a fifty yard dash.

"What was that all about?" Mary asked, askance of Henry.

Henry shrugged. "Sparrow wants to see us on the bridge. He wants us to go back over to the other ship and help clear out the nest of deaders, that's all.

"And are you?" Cindy asked from across the table. She was just finishing a bowl of canned pears, relishing the syrup in the bottom of the bowl. She couldn't even remember the last time she'd ate canned pears. Maybe when she was back in college, perhaps?

Henry shot a quick glance to Jimmy, who was munching on a bowl of pretzels.

"It's up to you, man, whatever you want to do is fine with me, I told you that already," Jimmy said, spitting small pieces of pretzel onto the table while he talked.

Cindy reached over and slapped his arm, pointing to the crumbs. Jimmy looked embarrassed and took another drink of water to wash his mouth out.

"Well, let's wait and see what he has to tell us when we get to the bridge," Henry said, standing up and making sure all his weapons were in place. It was an unconscious thing, one he did constantly now.

Jimmy finished his glass of water and wiped his mouth on a stray napkin. "So much for a shower," he said ruefully.

"Maybe it's better this way. We'll see what the old man wants and then, hopefully, we can shower. It's late; he can't want to go over there now. Better to wait for sunrise, the more light, the better." Henry said, starting to walk across the dining room, but not before nodding to Cindy and Mary. "We'll see you girls later. Just watch yourselves. I know it seems safe here, but you never know anymore," Henry told them. "You get what I'm sayin'."

Mary smiled, leaning back in her chair. "Don't you worry about us women folk, Henry, we'll be just fine. You go see what the big, strong men want on the bridge and we'll be waiting for you to return with a warm bed and a hot meal." The words were dripping with sarcasm and Henry smiled wanly. Neither Mary nor Cindy were fragile waifs that needed protecting. Both women had proved they were warriors in their own rights.

Henry waved to them one last time. "Whatever you say, Mary, but remember what I said." He called to her. Then both Jimmy and Henry had reached the grand opening again that exited into the main corridor.

With one final look at both women, both of them disappeared from sight.

The bridge was a few minutes away, up many stairs and corridors until they reached an elevator that went to the uppermost part of the ship.

Elevator music played softly as the car shot upwards and Jimmy snapped his fingers, humming with the tune.

Henry turned slightly to watch his friend and Jimmy stopped when he noticed he was being watched.

"What, I haven't heard any music in a while. Even this shit sounds good right now."

Henry only grunted and then looked forward once again, his reflection glaring back at him from the polished elevator doors.

His eyes roamed up and down his body, barely recognizing himself. Where there was once the flowering of a second chin and a beer belly, now the body of a man ten years younger looked back at him. Though Henry would feel a few aches and pains when he woke in the morning, overall he was in the best shape he had ever been in. Not bad considering most of the United States, and for all he knew, the rest of the world, was nothing but a shambles.

The car slowed to a halt with a slight jolt and the doors separated. The first thing Henry noticed was the grand view out the wide windows that surrounded the bridge. It was raining out, something that had gone unnoticed in the interior of the cruise ship.

Sparrow turned at the sight of the two men and moved over to them, a smile on his face. Though smiling, his eyes were filled with worry and exhaustion. It was a hard job the man had inherited, more than two hundred people relying on him to keep them safe.

"Ah, you're here. Good, come in, come in, I want you to see something," Sparrow said quickly, ushering the two men onto the bridge. Henry and Jimmy tried to take all the activity in one glance but it was next to impossible. There were at least five other people on the bridge, all moving about at specified tasks. One man stood at the front of the bridge, a large wheel in front of him, used for steering the ship, like in the days of old.

Others were checking instruments and yelling into two-way radios.

Henry moved up to one of the closest windows and looked out and down on the massive ship. To the sides, and in the distance, only shadows playing across the ocean. The waves rolled and churned, the cruise ship acting like a rubber duck in a child's bathtub.

"Wow, look at those waves. You'd hardly know it inside the ship," Jimmy said watching with wide eyes.

Sparrow nodded, proud of his ship. "That's right. The ship has stabilizers that help control the rolling. Sometimes it'll be rough as hell up here, but inside the ship you could put a pencil on a table and it wouldn't roll off."

"Uh-huh, so why did you want to see us, Sparrow? It's been a long day and both of us could use some rest," Henry told the man.

Sparrow nodded and pulled Henry over to a small table used for navigation. On it was a piece of notebook paper with a rough sketch of the mess hall and the surrounding corridors. "I did this from memory," he said with his hand pointing to the drawing. "I've already decided to go in at first light. I'm taking five men with me, all armed to the teeth. We're gonna step in there and blow anything that moves to hell. What I want to know is, are you with me or not?"

Henry ground his teeth while he stared at the paper. It showed the two entrances from the front and rear of the mess hall. Sparrow had sketched arrows with small stick figures for his men.

"Yeah, about that," Henry said, glancing to Jimmy, who nodded to go ahead and tell Sparrow. "Jimmy and me talked about it and we decided to just go in as back-up for your men. We'll hang back in the corridor and if things get dicey we'll be there to help, but otherwise we're staying out of it."

"But why? You both are two of the best fighters I've seen in a while. Why won't you lead the charge, or at least help coordinate it?"

"Because we think this is futile. Whatever's in that galley isn't worth any more lives then you've already lost. Leave the ship alone and let's go after the next one. From what I've seen, they're everywhere out here."

Sparrow chewed his lip, thinking. Then he shook his head from side to side with a finality that Henry knew well. "No, Henry, thank you for your opinion, but we need what's on that ship. First light we go."

Jimmy glanced out the windows and then back to Sparrow. "Yeah, but what about the weather? It's lookin' pretty bad out there. Could it be a problem with the two ships tied together?"

Sparrow turned and looked out the windows as well. Only the bow of the frigate could be seen, bouncing up and down on the water. So far neither ship had collided with the other, but as the waters grew worse, anything was possible.

"Don't see as we have a choice in the matter. If I cut her loose, we'll loose her in the storm. Shit, we'd never find her again." He walked away from the table and looked out onto the waves, the current pulling them along at a steady pace.

The engines are off right now, only emergency power for the lights and walk-ins in the kitchen. My men said they'd be finished with sucking the tanks dry in a couple more hours. Then everyone's gonna rest up and we'll start fresh at dawn."

Henry sighed, knowing there was no use talking the man out of his fool's errand.

"Okay, Sparrow, it's your show, we're just visitors, just make sure your men are wearing protective gear, that way if they get attacked, maybe they can escape without a bite."

Sparrow turned and walked back to Henry, his hand out for the man to take. Henry shook it twice and then Jimmy did the same.

"I already owe you my life, Henry, and that's why I'm not forcing you to be in the main assault, but it's good to know you'll be there, even if it's as back-up. See you in the morning. I'll have Tom fetch you a little before it's time to go."

Tom, that's what the kid's name was, Henry thought. "Okay, Sparrow, we'll be ready. And I hope I'm wrong about this and everything goes smoothly."

Sparrow stood a little taller and pushed out his chest, looking like a sea captain of old. "I hope you're wrong too, Henry, because if you're not and we loose the rest of the fighting men on this ship tomorrow, then there will be no one left to scavenge but the women and children."

Henry understood. Though women could be as hard as men, it was still grueling work crawling about the deserted ships they came across, looking for supplies and dealing with whatever horrors might still be left behind. Most women just didn't have the stomach for it. Plus, if they had children to look after, they would be less inclined to want to risk their lives.

Henry and Jimmy walked back to the elevator and Jimmy pressed the call button. The elevator opened immediately, and the two warriors stepped inside.

As the doors closed with a soft hiss and the car began to drop away from the bridge, Jimmy turned to look at his friend and mentor.

"You really think things are gonna go bad tomorrow?"

"Yeah, Jimmy, I'm afraid I do. Don't ask me why, 'cause I wouldn't be able to put my finger on it, but we've been through too damn much for me not to at least get a sense when things are off." He looked at Jimmy's face in the reflection of the elevator doors. "Why, you don't have that feeling? Not even a little bit?"

Jimmy shook his head. "No, sorry, I guess I'm not a psychic as you."

Henry said nothing; both men finished speaking for the moment. With the canned music of the elevator piping in through the speakers, both men stood like statues.

All Henry could think about was that he prayed his hunch was wrong and that tomorrow would just be another raid and clean-up.

Meanwhile, the storm grew closer and the waves grew higher, the mooring lines growing taught, holding the two ships fast together on a desolate sea; like two lost souls in the night.

Chapter 9

Though dawn was fast approaching, the sky overhead was dark as night. The storm was almost in full bloom, tossing the two ships around like a child's plaything.

Henry, Jimmy, Cindy and Mary all stood around the wooden planks that spanned the opening between the two ships. To their right was Sparrow with Spencer and seven of his best men, all armed to the teeth. The men looked like they were going to war, instead of going into the bowels of the dead frigate to clean out the nest of zombies.

It was early in the morning and Henry had not enjoyed the best night's sleep. He had dreams of his late wife again. Lately she had visited him constantly in the deepest caverns of his mind and he wondered if he still felt guilt for her death. Through no fault of his own, he had been instrumental in her death, but when she had turned into a zombie and had attacked him, what choice did he have? He had acted on instinct, grabbing a heavy skillet and caving in her skull. Logical reasoning would tell him he did what he had to do to survive, but his emotions, the real him, still hadn't come to terms with her death, even almost a year later. That was the last time he had ever seen her. Not the best picture to take with you for the rest of your life. He wiped his face clear of water, the rain a constant annoyance. But at least it wasn't deadly to touch or drink anymore, which was always a Godsend.

As Henry watched Spencer checking his men, he thought to himself perhaps that it wasn't far from the truth. Though dead, the undead could be just as ferocious as any live enemy; more deadly in fact. The ghouls felt no pain, nor exhaustion. They worked as a team with only one goal in mind, to consume human flesh.

Mary wrapped her arms around herself, trying to fight off the morning chill. Rain fell into the cargo hold through the massive opening, washing the deck clean.

"I don't like this, Henry. Especially after you told me how Spencer flipped out. The man practically called you out right there on the ship. Just make sure you don't turn your back on him."

Henry fixed the strap to his shotgun, positioning it better on his shoulder. "Don't worry, Mary. That's exactly what I intend to do. Sparrow's boys are doing the heavy lifting. Me and Jimmy are just there for extra support if need be. You just stay here with Cindy until we get back. With this storm brewing, I want us all to be in the same place in case there's trouble."

"Don't worry, Henry, we'll be here," Cindy said as she hugged Jimmy. The two of them had spent the night making love, enjoying every night they'd had on the ship. The privacy was something they didn't get a lot of anymore and they took full advantage of it.

"You two just come back in one piece," she finished, stepping away from Jimmy.

Sparrow walked up to them and nodded to Henry, Jimmy and the women. "Hello, all; hope you slept well," he said politely.

"As well as can be expected with all the bouncing around," Henry said. "I thought you said this ship had stabilizers. It was pretty rough last night."

Sparrow nodded, knowing what Henry meant. The storm had grown in strength overnight to the point that even the massive cruise ship was a slave to the currents.

"Sorry, Henry, but even Mother Nature can be too much for this old rowboat. So are you two ready to go?"

Henry and Jimmy nodded. "As ready as we can be given the circumstances. Is it too late to talk you out of this?" Henry asked him one more time.

"'Fraid so, Henry, so let's get this party started," he said in a loud voice so all could hear.

Spencer began organizing his men, pushing them onward and over the planks that crossed the rift between the two rocking ships. Whatever emotions he had displayed yesterday were now gone, only a grim resolve to do what was needed. Besides, he had his own agenda this morning. The dead bastards who had killed his Mickey were on that ship and he was looking forward to blasting them all to hell.

"All right, you pieces of shit, lets get moving, one at a time over the planks, move out!" He yelled, his men obeying.

Henry watched them line up and proceed over the planks. Some of them looked like they were scared shitless, while others wore a mask of determination.

One at a time, they moved across the boards, the wood bending in the middle. Five of the seven men had made it across easily when trouble struck when the sixth man was crossing. He was a middle-aged man with a balding hairline and large ears. He was about halfway across when a particularly large wave crashed against the two ships, causing the planks to buck and shift like they were alive. The man was thrown off balance, and before he could so much as utter a surprised yell, he was over the side and falling between the two hulls. Henry ran over to the opening and looked down, but the man was already lost. The rain pelted his face and he tried to see through the spray, but it was hopeless. One man lost before the foray had even begun.

The seventh man swallowed hard and stepped up onto the planks, now realizing his destiny was in the hands of the ocean. Moving as fast as he could, the man tight roped across the divide and jumped down onto the railing of the frigate.

Spencer went over next, sneering as he walked by Henry. "Watch your step, pal, wouldn't want you to fall or anything." He quipped sarcastically, climbing up onto the planks and walking across like he was going for a stroll in the park.

Sparrow was next, not hearing the exchange between Spencer and Henry, and with a nod to the two men, he climbed onto the edge of the planks and then scurried across, much smoother than Henry would have given him credit for, the man being in the shape he was in.

"Well, old man, it looks like it's just us left," Jimmy said to Henry. "Who's first?"

Henry held his arm out in a gesture that said, you first and said: "After you, Jimmy, and be careful."

With a quick look over his shoulder at Cindy, the woman blowing him a kiss, he climbed up and then quickly scurried across, hopping down to his relief.

Last up was Henry and before he climbed onto the planks, Mary walked over and placed her mouth near his ear so she could talk over the growing tempest. "Be careful, I don't want to lose you today," she said into his ear.

He turned and patted her shoulder and said: "Wish me luck!" Then hopped up onto the planks just as a large wave crashed against the massive cruise ship. The planks buckled and Henry grabbed the side, glad he wasn't out in the middle where there would have been nothing to hold onto. Then, when he felt the ship had settled down as much as it was going to, he sucked in a breath and started across. He was more than halfway across when another large wave crashed against the frigate, causing it to jump as it fought to break free of its moorings to the cruise ship.

Henry barreled forward; knowing to stop would be his death. He wobbled back and forth, the planks jumping like a snake beneath his feet, and just as he would have fallen into the churning water below, he jumped for the railing of the frigate, landing hard on his side, expelling all the air in his lungs. Jimmy was there the second he impacted the deck and helped him to his feet.

"You okay? Shit, that was close," Jimmy said over the rain and waves.

Spencer pushed by Henry, having seen the whole thing. "I told you to watch your step," was all he said, and then led his men down the decking until they could reach the hatch that would lead them into the bowels of the ship.

Cursing under his breath, Henry stood up, leaning against the railing for support.

"See, I told you things were going to be bad, didn't I?" He told Jimmy.

Jimmy smiled, his hair plastered over his head like a school boy from the rain and spray. "Well, I don't know, Henry, look at the bright side?"

Henry blinked his eyes clear of moisture. "The bright side? What the hell could be good about all of this?"

Jimmy's smile grew ever wider. "Well, you could have followed that poor bastard into the drink, instead of making it over here in one piece."

Henry gave that some thought as the two men started after the others. "Jesus, Jimmy, you know what? If that's the bright side, then things are only gonna get worse before they get better."

Jimmy only grunted in reply. They moved down the side of the ship and when the two men reached the hatch that Spencer, Sparrow and the six men had entered, they also entered the darkness, like they were explorers entering a cave or massive tomb.

As the hatch slammed shut behind him and he flicked on his flashlight, Henry could only hope that the massive tomb wouldn't claim himself or Jimmy, as well.

Chapter 10

Walking down the dank, dark corridor was treacherous, the deck constantly shifting under their feet as the frigate was tossed about on the waves of the tempest. It reminded Henry of a carnival ride he had been on as a boy, nothing but a few planks of wood with rollers and hydraulics under them to make the floor unstable.

That ride had been fun and he had gone on it two more times that day. If only he had the option of getting off the ride he was on now.

In front of Henry and Jimmy was the last man in the line, the boarding party quickly moving through the maze like a mouse to the cheese. Spencer and Sparrow's voice could be overheard over the footsteps of the men as they made their way to the mess hall and galley. Henry noticed the same musty odor permeating the corridor, but he noticed a new one, as well.

The stink of fear.

The men all knew what had happened to their predecessors and all were nervous, though all tried to keep it from showing.

In the gloom of the corridor, only the beams of the flashlights to see by, the men moved closer to the mouth of the dragon.

Seven minutes later, the small party slowed and then stopped. Sparrow called for Henry to come to the front of the line and the man pushed and shoved his way through the guards until he was once again staring at the large hatch that led into the mess hall.

"Well, we're here," Sparrow said simply.

"Yes, we are. I wish you'd change your mind about this. Let them stay there and rot for all eternity. Let's just leave this damn ship and move on to the next one. At least we got fuel here," Henry pleaded to the captain one last time.

Sparrow shook his head, his jaw set in his resolve. The ship jumped on a wave and all the men were tossed to the side of the starboard bulkhead, one crying out in pain.

"Well, then at least wait for this damn storm to pass. It'll be hard enough in there without the damn deck jumping underneath us," Henry said, still not wanting to give up on changing the man's mind.

"Look, Henry, I respect your opinion, but this is my ship now and these are my men, so if you're not with us, then stand aside."

Henry sighed, but did as he was asked. Spencer moved past him and shot him a sneer that summed up how he felt about Henry in one look. Henry ignored him. If the man had hard feelings about him that was fine; as long as he kept his weapon holstered then the two of them would have no problem.

Sparrow moved across the few feet separating him from the hatch, prepared to open it, while Henry slowly slipped to the back of the line next to Jimmy.

"He won't listen, huh?" Jimmy asked in a subdued voice.

"Afraid not, he's got his head wrapped around a treasure-trove of food and supplies just waiting for him in there."

"You don't think there's food in there?"

Henry shook his head slowly. "All that's in there is death. Stay sharp and be ready for anything," he told Jimmy.

Jimmy answered by pumping his shotgun, sliding a shell into the chamber.

Sparrow had undogged the hatch, and with a loud squeak of hinges, the portal opened wide. The charnel house stench, mixed with the fragrance of an open sewer, wafted out of the hatch to permeate the corridor.

All the men gasped at the redolence, but Sparrow shouted them down.

"All right, men, shoot first and let God sort them out," he called as he stepped into the mess hall.

Spencer was on his heels and the six men all followed, stepping inside and lining up in a row, similar to a firing squad. The deck pitched once more and like dominoes the men all bumped against each other.

Henry and Jimmy moved to the hatch and looked in, only bystanders on this particular foray.

Once again the zombies had moved to the opposite end of the room, once more eating the undisguised human meat. Now there were new body parts to add to the old, the remnants of the first boarding party. At the moment, none of the ghouls acknowledged the presence of the new men in their midst, until a more observant one on the edge of the others perked its head up and let out a gurgling moan. The others, like it was a call to arms, also looked up from their feeding and as one, all stood up and started to crawl towards the firing line.

"Okay, boys, let the dead fucks have it!" Sparrow screamed, letting rip with the mini-Uzi held in his hands.

The other men did the same, each firing indiscriminately into the pile of dead human flesh as it slowly came at them. The deck rolled under their feet, causing some of the men to lean into the one next to them, knocking the aim of the others off target.

Bodies danced and wiggled, their flesh becoming riddled with bullets, the staccato sound of the gunfire filling the room like a thousand small drums. Then a massive wave struck the frigate, so hard it was slammed against the hull of the cruise ship, feeling like a battering ram.

Men went flying across the room, trying to grab something to hold onto, but there was nothing. They became nothing more than playthings that were tossed into the horde of zombies like they were being served up for dinner. Screams and shrieks of pain overrode the moaning ghouls as they fell on top of the boarding party.

Sparrow went down in-between two undead sailors, their duty uniforms now covered in gore and blood. In each of their chests in black stencil, their names could be seen if the light hit their shirts just right, not that Sparrow needed to know the names of his killers.

Spencer was tossed to the floor with the others and he quickly rolled away from grasping hands, firing his rifle as he rolled. He was about to climb to his feet, when he stopped in shock, looking up at the shadow of a face he recognized.

Mickey's slack-jawed eyes gazed down at him, large portions of the dead man's flesh missing.

Spencer was dumbfounded, so happy to see his lover alive his sense of reason hadn't kicked in to tell him the man was dead.

"Mickey? Oh my God, you're alive!" Spencer yelled over the din around him. A flashlight rolled across the deck, knocked around like a child's ball and when it flashed on Mickey's stomach. Spencer's eyes went wide.

Mickey's stomach had been ripped open and his intestines hung out like live eels, swinging back and forth as the corpse moved about. Spencer's mouth went wide when he realized the truth; that his lover was long dead.

Lying on the floor, he brought up his rifle, knowing he had to shoot Mickey if he wanted to live. Mickey leaned down, mouth gaping wide, teeth dripping scarlet as he prepared to attack Spencer. Spencer was about to squeeze the trigger, and at the last second stopped...his grief overwhelming him.

Instead of firing, he let Mickey fall onto him, his lover's dead teeth covering his lips like an embrace. Spencer closed his eyes and imagined everything was fine, until Mickey's teeth slammed closed and ripped Spencer's lips from his mouth like pulling taffy from a stick.

Lipless, Spencer screamed his pain, realizing what he was doing was madness, his sense of survival overriding his loss for his lover. But it was too late, as Mickey dove down again, after swallowing his lips whole, he ripped Spencer's throat out, the man's shrieks turning into gurgles of loss as he slowly lost consciousness.

Jimmy watched all this from the hatch, holding onto the frame for support while the ship tossed and turned. "We've got to go help them!" He screamed. Prepared to charge in there and try to save Sparrow or some of his men. Henry held him fast with an iron grip to his arm. "No, it's too late. I told the old fool not to go in. I'm not risking you or me on a fool's errand!"

"But we can't just let them die!" Jimmy tried to reason with him, his eyes constantly moving from the carnage in the mess hall back to Henry.

Henry grabbed Jimmy and slammed him against the bulkhead. "Dammit, Jimmy, they were dead the second they stepped foot in there, I tried to tell Sparrow, but he wouldn't listen!"

Just then a shadow appeared at the hatch and Henry swiveled his waist and shot the zombie in the chest, blowing it away from the hatch with the force of the shot.

The zombie, its chest a shattered mess, rolled onto its side and began regaining its footing. Henry knew he needed to dog that hatch and retreat before both he and Jimmy joined the others in death.

Henry moved toward the hatch, prepared to swing it closed, when yet another wave threw the ship around on the surface of the ocean, causing Henry to slam against the bulkhead so hard he saw stars. Jimmy was thrown, as well, both men falling to the deck in a daze. Only a second passed before Henry shook off his fugue and climbed to his feet, but as soon as he did, he saw the hatch was blocked by a swell of dead humanity.

"Shit, they're coming out; it's too late to close the hatch, now! Come on, we need to get the hell out of here or we're next!" He yelled to Jimmy, reaching down and pulling the younger man to his feet.

Jimmy shook his head to clear it, having received a hard bump to his forehead when he had fallen. With eyes blurry, he turned to see the ghouls trying to exit the mess hall. Bringing his shotgun up, he fired two quick shots, so close they sounded as one, and the first ghoul in line shuddered from the blasts. But his shots were rushed and only struck it in the shoulder and chest, slowing it down for a heartbeat as the ones behind it pushed forward, keeping the wounded corpse upright.

"Forget, it, retreat, it's over!" Henry yelled, already starting to move down the corridor, his flashlight bobbing and waving while he ran.

Jimmy muffled a curse and shot one more time, taking off half the face of another creature as it forced itself through the hatch, the others around it slowing it down. It looked like a parody of the Three Stooges, as they all tried to get through the hatch at the same time.

Jimmy spit onto the deck and then turned to run, Henry already around the next corner.

"Come on, Jimmy!" Henry yelled stopping to make sure his friend was coming.

"Go, I'm right behind you!" He called back, jogging as he fought to maintain his balance on the constantly shifting deck.

The moans of the dead followed behind him, as they flooded out of the mess hall, free at last.

Chapter 11

Henry and Jimmy struggled their way through the bouncing corridors. It was like the men had been placed inside a giant blender, the deck constantly jumping up and down below their feet.

Outside the walls of the ship, the storm was in full bloom, rain and wind blasting at the two ships with a vengeance. The frigate was still moored to the cruise ship and just as Henry and Jimmy reached the rail that led to the planks, they both stopped short.

The planks were gone, now having fallen into the churning water between the two ships.

Henry held onto the railing for dear life as the smaller ship crashed against the hull of the cruise ship. The sound was unbelievable, like a hundred automobiles crashing together at the same time. Looking across the divide at the opening into the cruise ship, Mary and Cindy leaned out, calling to them.

"Henry, the planks fell into the water, how the hell are you gonna get back!" Mary called to him, her face covered in concern.

Henry looked at her and then at the water below, both he and Jimmy holding on when the frigate crashed yet again into the cruise ship's hull. After striking the hull, the frigate would bounce off and only the mooring lines would stop it from floating away, but similar to an elastic, they would immediately pull the ship back to the hull again and again. The bow of the frigate was already a mangled mess of metal, jagged pieces hanging off it like a crushed child's toy after a particularly nasty temper tantrum.

Henry held on as the frigate crashed again and he was beginning to realize there was a rhythm to the motions of the ship. It would crash and then rebound, only to crash yet again. He noticed as the frigate struck the cruise ship that there was only a few feet separating the two hulls.

Wiping water from his face as the rain sluiced over his head, he yelled to Jimmy, next to him. Such was the fury of the tempest that he had to yell or risk his voice being lost in the storm.

"Jimmy we've got to make a jump for it when the frigate crashes into the ship!" He called to his friend, his mouth only a few inches from his ear.

Jimmy's hair was matted to his face and he looked like a wet dog coming in out of the rain.

"What, are you serious? That's fucking crazy!"

"Maybe, but it's our only chance of getting back before the lines snap and we float away!"

Jimmy pursed his lips, looking at the divide just as the two ships crashed together yet again. Shaking his head, he tried to look at Henry through the water in his eyes, his pupils wide with what would come next.

"It's crazy, but you're right; it's the only chance we've got!"

Henry nodded and then turned back to Mary. "We're gonna make a jump for it, we need you to catch us when we do!" He called to Mary.

Cindy looked at both men, understanding what he had just said and her jaw went slack. "Are you crazy? That's suicide!" She screamed.

Just as she finished her exclamation, one of the mooring ropes snapped, sounding like the crack of a pistol. All eyes went to the dangling rope and everyone knew Henry was right. They had only seconds before the remaining two lines snapped and the frigate floated away on the waves of the storm.

Henry looked to Jimmy and nodded. "All right, on the next one. When the ship gets close, jump for it and pray to God we make it!" He yelled, only some of what he was saying getting through to Jimmy.

Jimmy shook his head clear of rain and an instant later was coated once more. The rain would drip into his eyes, reducing his vision, and he had to keep his teeth closed and breathe through them like a filter or else risk the freezing cold water filling his mouth and choking him.

He nodded his affirmative and both men prepared to jump.

The first zombie, who had left the mess hall and had followed them through the darkened corridors of the frigate, chose this exact moment to make its presence known, stumbling onto the deck and striking the railing hard. Others were right behind it, all shambling out into the rain. One or two lost their balance on the bucking deck and tumbled over the side to be lost in the waves.

Henry spotted the first one when it was no more than three feet away, the darkness, plus the water spray blocking almost all sight.

Without warning Jimmy of the incoming threat, he pulled his Glock from its holster and shot the zombie point blank in the forehead, the ghoul falling backwards and landing in the arms of the one following it. The corpse dropped to the deck and the others crawled over it, one slipping and falling over the railing to join its brothers before it.

Jimmy turned and ducked at the sound of the Glock and his eyes went wide. He screamed a curse that was lost on the wind and pulled his .38 from its holster, quickly firing again and again at the shambling creatures. With the deck rolling beneath him, his aim was off and only two more dropped to the deck, but there were more behind it, and as he watched the faces, he saw a few new ones to boot, including Sparrow and Spencer, now part of the new crew of the living dead.

Henry fired again and patted Jimmy on the shoulder, just as another mooring line snapped. The frigate pulled away farther from the cruise ship, only coming back when the longer line finally went taut. Henry knew the weight on the line must be immense and they were lucky that it had held for as long as it had. But he knew the odds were the next time the line would snap, casting the frigate away to be lost forever in the deadly current.

"We have to go, Jimmy, it's now or never!" Henry screamed as the frigate slowly bounced back toward the cruise ship.

Jimmy could barely hear him, and as the frigate struck the cruise ship yet again, Henry grabbed Jimmy by the shirt collar and pointed the man toward the opening in the cruise ship's cargo hold.

Both men leaped just as the frigate had rebounded and for a moment all they could see was the black depths of the channel between the two ships. Though they had jumped at the almost perfect time, they were still off and when they finished their leap, they came up short.

Outstretched arms and hands wrapped around the ledge to the cargo hold and both men struggled to hold on, feet kicking below them like dangling bait on a hook. Both Mary and Cindy tried to lift the men inside, but the weight of their water drenched bodies was too much for them.

Suddenly another wave struck the opposite side of the cruise ship and sent the ship leaning at a dangerous angle. Miscellaneous items slid out of the cargo hatch and fell into the water below, some of the pieces barely missing the flailing bodies of Henry and Jimmy.

"Pull us up, for the love of God, pull us up!" Henry screamed, Jimmy adding his own choice words.

"What the hell do you think we're trying to do?" Mary screamed back, pulling with all of her slight frame. Henry had to have fifty pounds on her, at least, and Cindy was in the same predicament with Jimmy's hanging body.

The lone mooring line grew taut and then the frigate began its return trip towards the cruise ship. Henry glanced over his shoulder to see the huge hull begin floating back at them like a giant piston, only this time both Jimmy and Henry were on the hull and would be crushed to death when the two ships collided yet again.

With Mary and Cindy struggling to pull them up, Henry realized they wouldn't be in time. Before he could tell Jimmy what he knew was their only chance for survival, he reached out and wrapped his arms around the man's smaller frame.

"Henry, what the fuck are you doing? Let me go or we'll fall!" Jimmy screamed as his fingers started to slip and Cindy let out a yell of hopelessness as she desperately tried to pull her boyfriend back up into the cargo hold.

Henry shot another look over his shoulder and realized he had only seconds to live; the massive hull coming at them like a giant battering ram.

"Jimmy, there's no time to explain, just trust me when I tell you, if you want to live, then let go!"

"What! Are you mad? We'll drown!" He yelled, though despite his arguing his hands were still slipping with the added weight of Henry.

"Just do it, I've never steered you wrong before!"

Whether Jimmy would have let go on choice was taken from him when his hands, finally becoming so numb he couldn't feel them, started to lose purchase, and both he and Henry started to slide off the edge of the cargo hold.

"Henry, no, you're falling!" Mary yelled, too shocked to even know what to say.

Jimmy started to slide downward, and his eyes locked with Cindy's for only a heartbeat as he fell into the inky depths of the churning waves. In that brief heartbeat, he sent all his love and sorrow that they wouldn't be together again, and that his life was over so quickly.

Then both Henry and Jimmy landed in the cold water and sank below the waves, just as the two hulls crashed together, gouging a massive hole into the side of the cruise ship where they had been hanging seconds ago. When the frigate bounced away, the last mooring line snapped and the frigate continued across the waves, in seconds lost in the wind and rain of the storm.

Mary and Cindy leaned out, trying to spot the two men.

"Henry!!" Mary called out. "Jimmy!! Where are you?" She screamed to no avail.

Cindy looked down into the black water and the tears falling down her face were lost amidst the rainwater constantly pounding her head and shoulders.

"Oh my God, they're gone!" She screamed in shock while looking out into the water.

Then another wave struck the side of the cruise ship and the ship tipped almost horizontal. Both Mary and Cindy were thrown out of the cargo opening, their arms and legs wind-milling as they dropped through the air and into the icy-cold water.

Sinking under the waves, Mary tried to hold her breath, quickly losing sight of Cindy. She reached out and locked onto something, and pulled it toward her. She looked up at it just as the current tossed her above water and she sucked in a desperate breath of air, trying not to take in the frigid sea water.

Then something bumped her and Mary looked into Henry's unconscious face and her heart jumped in her breast. She had found him. Pulling the man to her, she desperately struggled to hold them afloat.

Another wave crashed over them and Mary made sure to hold his arm with an iron grip while they were tossed around the water like they were the most insignificant items in the world. For a few desperate heartbeats she didn't know which end was up, and took a chance, praying she was going in the right direction and not swimming downward where she would run out of oxygen and drown.

When her lungs screamed for air and she thought she would have no choice but to breath, her head broke the surface and she sucked in precious gasps of air mixed with water. This time, though, she ignored the water that went into her lungs, causing her to choke and gasp when she tried to expel it.

She was breathing and that was all that mattered.

Next to her, Henry's head lolled from side to side and she struggled to keep his head above the water. She had no way of knowing that when he had fallen into the waves, to avoid being crushed by the colliding hulls, his head had struck the side of the frigate, causing him to black out.

Mary struggled to stay afloat, but realized it wouldn't be long before her strength would be gone, sucked out of her limbs from the cold water and churning waves.

Then something bumped her and she reached out desperately, pulling whatever had struck her towards her and Henry.

It was a small chest, with ropes around the sides, used for storage in the cargo hold. The chest was the lifeline she needed, and Mary wrapped her arms around the rope, holding both her and Henry fast to it, with wave after wave pounding into them mercilessly.

All she could do was hold on and do her best to keep Henry's head above water, while the two of them were slowly pulled out deeper into the storm and lost from sight of the cruise ship.

Mary sent out a silent prayer that Jimmy and Cindy were alive somewhere close, and then added one more for her and Henry, as well.

After that, she closed her eyes and concentrated on surviving another second, another minute, until all time was lost between the waves.

Chapter 12

Though the average human being doesn't give it a second thought, in many ways the body is a completely separate entity from the thinking and reasoning mind.

The body itself has many separate procedures that run independently, not needing to receive any thoughts or concern from the mind. There are lungs to be filled with oxygen, blood to be pumped and food to be digested and broken down for its nutrients; none of which require actual thought from the person. Only when one of these procedures actually breaks down does the mind become cognizant of the complexities of the human body it inhabits and sometimes controls.

Which is why Henry was floating in a deep abyss that seemed to have no ending, nor beginning. Images of past friends and family danced past his mind's eye, seeming to beckon him to come to them. They're bodies seemed to morph into odd shapes and then flutter away to be lost in the mist that surrounded everything; the air defying transparency and instead becoming almost opaque.

It took a while for him to realize they were all dead and now wanted him to join them in their self-exiled oblivion. He watched in horror as their faces melted like wax statues and flesh turned to soup to puddle at their feet.

As the visions began to turn violent and the faces began to distort into horrible images of death and decay, rotting hands reached out for him, desperately trying to pull him to them and he fought and screamed to break free. Hands like tiny claws swiped at him, one appendage wrapping around his left arm and yanking him off his feet.

If he was truly standing.

In his vision, up was down and down was to the left, all completely distorted. He felt himself being pulled into a hideous rictus of a mouth; one that grew in size as every second passed. He screamed, but his throat was raw and he ended up letting out nothing but a pathetic wheeze. The roar of the cavernous maw grew ever larger until it started to transform and distort.

A soft sound, as of cascading waves floated to him, piercing the nightmare visions and sounds.

At first he thought there was a light in front of him, the fabled light he had heard about all his life in church and Sunday school. But soon he realized the light was external, not internal, and that even with his eyes closed the light pierced his eyelids, causing the darkness to take on a yellowish aura.

Something bumped his feet and caused him to grunt in pain.

Rolling over, he slowly opened his eyes, the white light now stronger. Quickly, he closed his eyes again and allowed them to adjust. When he thought it was time, he tried again, this time opening them more slowly.

At first there was nothing but yellow circles around his vision, and then slowly, ever so slowly, his vision cleared and he looked up at a clear blue sky; a few seagulls floating on the gentle air currents high above him, calling one another as they searched for food.

Something struck his feet again and he tried to look around himself, but his neck protested drastically and he stopped.

Closing his eyes again, he tried to do a mental inventory of his body, flexing each arm and leg and then each finger, one at a time, until he was satisfied, that though bruised and battered, his body seemed intact with no broken bones.

He lay there, not moving, sucking in each breath, staring up at the birds as they swooped and called out to one another again and again. The birds battled constantly with each other. One would find a juicy fish or flotsam in the water and no sooner would it try to fly away with its prize, then the others would swoop down and attack, trying to dislodge the food from its beak.

Something struck his feet yet again and he let out a soft yelp of pain. Deciding it was now or never, he grimaced from the pain and slowly raised himself to a sitting position. His vision grew foggy yet again, but after a few moments it began to clear and he saw he was on a beach, the pure white sand going off on both sides of him. Looking down to his feet, he saw a cargo chest, the rope connected to it intertwined around his right leg. Every time the waves came into the shore, the chest would strike him.

His head continued to spin and he felt the lightheadedness of wanting to faint again, but with his will alone, he fought it off, though for how long was unknown.

Wincing in pain, he leaned forward, and with protesting and numb fingers, managed to extricate his leg from the rope, the waterlogged chest now being sucked out into the water, only to be pushed back once more, but this time missing his prone body.

Spitting sand, he looked out across the beach, wondering just where in all the deadlands he could be. His combat instincts, honed after a year of battling the dead and living hard in the harsh new world, made him immediately look around him, making sure there were no present threats. He grunted softly when he saw the beach was deserted.

He was alone, that was true, no other people, alive or dead, in sight; except for one other person.

A low groan sounded from behind him and he turned to see the unconscious form of Mary. She was about three feet behind him, partially buried in the sand, and so he hadn't spotted her when he had first revived.

Turning over, he crawled like a dog on all fours until he had reached her. Brushing her hair from her face, he saw she had a large bruise over her right eye, a small bump there, as well.

She moaned again, and he picked her up, cradling her body in his lap as his own muscles protested. Whatever had happened to him and her, they had gone through the ringer and were then spit out whole.

Another seagull cawed and screeched above him and he looked up and watched as it dove into the surf, coming back with a small fish in its mouth. He looked away when he became dizzy and then back down at Mary's face, doing his best to wipe the sand from her cheeks and lips. He was exhausted, and could barely sit up, but knew he had no choice. A small flicker of hope had begun to grow in his chest. If Mary was alive that was something, it meant he wasn't alone. Mary Roberts had become the daughter he had never had, but had wanted so much. The two had formed a bond of trust and love that could never be broken. Now he knew he had to do something and quick. Both of them were exposed to the harsh sun and were utterly exhausted with no way of knowing where they were or how dangerous the area was.

He looked around again, this time behind him. There was no sign of Cindy and Jimmy and he wondered if they were all right. The last thing he remembered was falling into the water as the frigate came crashing back to the cruise ship. He had felt the impact of his body striking the water when both he and Jimmy had entered the ocean and then...nothing.

On unsteady legs, he rose to his feet, a wave of nausea overcoming him the moment he stood upright. At the top of the beach were a few bungalows, looking like their owners had left for the off season and would be returning in a few months.

He felt his stomach spasm inside him and he leaned over and vomited what felt like a gallon of sea water. Wiping the salty taste from his mouth with his soggy shirtsleeve, he shook his head to clear it.

The moment he was thinking more clearly, he reached for his weapons, though his arms moved far to slow for his taste. His shotgun was gone, probably lost in the ocean somewhere, but his Glock was still in its holster, the strap securing it in place still snapped closed. Reaching further down his hip, he sighed when he felt the comforting feeling of the panga's sheath, the handle still poking upward. Pulling it out, the sun glinted on the wet blade, causing him to wince and close his eyes once more. He would have to clean it and soon or risk the salt ruining the honed blade.

Deciding the blade would be fine for the moment; he sheathed it once again and pulled his sidearm. Water spilled out of the barrel and Henry knew the weapon would be useless until he could give it a good cleaning. The saltwater would be devastating to the delicate weapon, but he knew the first item on the menu was to get Mary mobile and then to find shelter for the two of them. After that, they would head off to search for Jimmy and Cindy.

Before he could do anything else, though, the rumble of an engine floated to his ears. Turning around, he was mildly surprised to see a four-by-four red jeep speeding toward him, the tires of the vehicle shooting sand behind it as it made its way along the shore.

Henry looked at his Glock in his hand, muttering a few choice imprecations about the situation he now found himself in. Mary was unconscious behind him and he could barely stand on his feet, the feeling of fainting coming back with a vengeance as he pushed his body harder than it could take in its present condition.

The jeep moved closer and his hand instinctively reached down and tried to pull the panga from its sheath, but the sky seemed to spin again and he felt a sharp pain in his head. The concussion he'd received when his head struck the hull of the ship when he had gone under now showed itself, causing his vision to lose focus and the beach to start spinning.

He tried to fight it, standing erect, though weaving, as the jeep came closer. He had no way of knowing if they were friendly or not, but he knew better than to believe in the faith of humanity. Too many times he had seen that under the face of humankind was an ugly underbelly that cared only for itself, and would destroy any unfortunate enough to stray into its malevolent path.

Standing defiant, he was just able to catch a glimpse of the three men riding in the jeep. All wore white and were armed with heavy assault weapons, the sun glinting off the metal, telling Henry the weapons were well maintained. Then darkness fell once more and Henry collapsed to the sand, the panga falling from his hand to be killed, or worse, by whoever was approaching, but he was far to stick upright next to him; his body falling heavily next to Mary.

He tried to stay awake, knowing he was probably about too weak to remain standing, let alone conscious.

And then, though he fought it with all his being, oblivion claimed him once more as the rumbling engine of the jeep grew ever closer.

Chapter 13

For the second time that day, Henry battled his way from the abyss of unconsciousness to the world of wakefulness. His eyes opened slowly, but instead of being blasted by the bright light of the sun, there was only a dull glow from a small lamp in the far corner of the room.

Wait...a room? But how? The last thing he remembered was collapsing on the beach as either adversaries or friends had approached him.

Raising his arm and rubbing his face with his hand, he was pleased to see he wasn't tied or secured to the bed in any shape or form. That bode well for him. If he was unrestrained, then perhaps the people in the jeep had been friendly.

Looking to the right he was very happy to see Mary slumped down in a small wooden chair, her head rolling on her shoulder as she slept. She had her hair pulled back in a bun and a small bandage over the wound on her forehead. She was now dressed in white, her clothes similar to pajamas or a karate outfit.

With the exception of the small table which held the candle, the bed and Mary's chair, the room was bare.

Sitting up, Henry waited for the familiar feeling of nausea to overwhelm him and was surprised when he felt fine. Flexing his arms, he grunted with approval that nothing was broken, as he had surmised before on the beach. There was a small window near the only wooden door in the room and he saw it was now dark outside. He looked down at his wrist to see his watch was missing, and as his mind snapped into combat mode, he realized his Glock and panga were missing, as well.

Feeling naked without a weapon, he threw off the wool blanket he was under and set his feet onto the cold wooden floor. A sharp twinge from his ribs came to him, his face contorting in discomfort. Readjusting his position, the pain went away. Evidently he had bruised some ribs in his past ordeal. Guess he didn't come away as unscathed as he'd thought

Standing up on shaky legs, he walked over to the window and looked outside, his eyes taking in as much information as they could in the first glance.

What he saw was a small town, complete with clean streets and picture perfect buildings. He noticed all the buildings were no higher than three-stories tall and the few people that walked by the window on the street were also wearing white clothing, the same as Mary's.

He also noticed a man standing on the stairs of the building he was in. The wooden door would open directly onto the guard. While the man seemed to be very relaxed, it wasn't hard to notice the large shotgun the man had slung over his back and the holster that carried a sidearm. The make of the weapon was unknown from Henry's position, but he saw the belt the man wore carried spare clips and a six-inch hunting knife. Whatever was going on, there was a guard watching his building. Henry's gaze lingered on the guard for a few more seconds and then he looked back out onto the gloomy street.

As more people moved passed the window, his eyes searched their bodies for weapons and he was surprised to see no one was armed. The lights in the street were one of the more surprising things to behold. Instead of torches or some other type of burning material, the streetlights were on, casting the street in front of the window in a yellowish glow in the falling dusk.

A car drove by slowly, not wanting to hit the few pedestrians that moved out of the way for it to pass. Henry's mouth hung open, shocked at what he was seeing. The street looked like a normal street in any city across the United States before the dead had begun to walk.

A faint stirring came from behind him. He turned around to see Mary opening her eyes, and with a wide smile, she stood up, stretching while she moved over to him.

"Hey, there, it's good to see you awake. I was beginning to get worried."

"How long was I asleep for?" Henry asked her, hugging her at the same time he talked.

Mary squeezed him hard, burying her face in his shoulder. Then she let go and stepped back a foot.

"All day. Ever since you we were found on the beach, I was told. The doctor said you had a mild concussion. They just let me back in here to see you a little while ago."

Henry rubbed his face and chin, contemplating. "Doctor huh? So where the hell are we? Where's our weapons. Have you seen Jimmy or Cindy yet? Who's in charge around here? Are they assholes like the others or are they normal for a change?"

Mary held her hands in front of her for Henry to slow down.

"Wait, will ya? I can't remember all that." She held up her hand, the fingers wide and started counting. "As for the doctor, yeah, they have a doctor here. His names Doc Rivers and he know his stuff. As for where we are, we're in California, on the coast. As for our weapons, they're being cleaned by the guy in their armory. Said we'd get them back when he's done with 'em. Uhm, what's next...oh, the guy that's in charge is about as good as you can get. He's a Reverend and he gathered all the people in this town when the dead started walking; as for Jimmy and Cindy..." She shook her head to add to her words. "I'm afraid no one's seen them. They probably didn't make it. Hell, Henry, you and me were damn lucky. If I hadn't found that chest and hung on for dear life, we both would have drowned."

Henry had listened to her patiently, though all he wanted to do was run outside and go into action. Not that he knew what that action would be, but anything was better than just standing there listening. But he knew there was a time for action and a time for planning and this was definitely the time for the latter.

"Okay then, so when we get our weapons back? What's the plan? You've been awake longer than me. Do we try to escape from here or what?"

Mary shook her head as if Henry had said the most foolish thing in the world.

"On the contrary, Henry. I think we should stay. This place is great. This might just be the place we've been looking for all this time. I mean, they have power here, running water, and they seem to have a decent moral compass, too." She walked to the window and gazed out into the street. "No, Henry, I think this just might be what we've hoped to find all these months."

Henry grunted, folding his arms. It was like Mary was under some kind of spell.

"Okay, Mary, we'll see what this place has to offer, but once I'm feeling better I still want to see about searching for Jimmy and Cindy. I'm not just going to forget about them."

Mary turned away from the window and walked back to him, hugging him again. "That's okay, Henry, once you see how great this place is, you'll agree with me. Now what do you say we get you back to bed and I'll have someone get the doctor."

Henry did as she requested and was glad for it. The second his head hit the pillow, he felt like he could sleep for a week. Mary went to the wooden door and knocked on it. A moment later the door opened a crack and the security guard Henry had seen outside on the stairs looked inside.

Mary filled him in about Henry being awake and the man nodded, his head disappearing and the door closing once more.

Henry lay prone in the bed while Mary told him what had happened during the storm and how she had managed to find a floating chest that had become their life preserver.

Ten minutes passed and then there was a knock at the door. Before Mary could go to it, the door opened and a small man in his late sixties stepped inside. He, too, was wearing an all white outfit and he looked over his glasses at Henry.

"Well, well, look who's finally come around. I have to tell you, I was beginning to become worried." The little man said while he slid into the room, his feet barely rising enough to propel him forward.

Doctor Rivers was a white man with a receding hairline and a sunburned scalp from not wearing protection out in the sun. He had a small mustache that looked almost comical on his face and his eyes were a dark blue, which seemed to catch everything. He set down the small black bag he had in his right hand on the foot of Henry's bed and then proceeded to open it, digging around for a few items, such as a thermometer and a blood pressure gauge.

Without preamble, he stuck the thermometer into Henry's mouth and then began to wrap the blood pressure gauge around his left arm, squeezing the small balloon on its end. Henry winced as the wrap constricted his arm and then let out a sigh when the doctor released it, the air wheezing out of it like an old man who had smoked far too many cigarettes in his lifetime.

"You're doing fine, Henry. You should be up to snuff by morning, with the exception of a few pains around your chest. You bruised a few ribs on top of your mild concussion."

Henry was about to ask how the man could know his name, but then he realized Mary must have filled the doctor in.

Henry said nothing, merely watching the doctor work. After Doc Rivers finished up a few more tests, such as flashing a penlight into Henry's eyes, the man nodded happily and then stood up from the bed, packing his medical supplies back into the bag and then heading for the door.

"I'll have someone send you some food, both of you, and tomorrow you'll meet the Reverend.

The Doc turned then, his head leaning forward so he could look over his glasses. "He knows about all the weapons you were found with and that you were on the beach. No one goes on the beach anymore, not since..." he trailed off then, knowing he had said too much.

"Well, anyway, the Reverend will tell you what he wants you to know, goodnight all, and the food will be here shortly."

He banged on the door twice, and the guard outside unlocked it, letting the doctor out of the room. The guard poked his head in for just an instant, nodding when he saw Henry and Mary by the bed. Then he pulled his head back and the door closed and was locked with a silent click.

Henry immediately turned to Mary, curiosity in his eyes, as if she would know what the hell that conversation had been about.

She shrugged, moving over to him and sitting on the edge of the bed. "I have no idea what that was about. I came to a little after we got here and they put me in here with you after the doctor had checked me over." She touched her bruise on her forehead. "He said this isn't so bad, just a slight bump that should be fine in a few days."

Henry crossed his arms and frowned. "Well then, I guess whatever happens next is out of our hands. Guess we should just make the best of it until things look like they're going the wrong way."

Mary leaned against him and Henry hugged her. "Do you think Jimmy and Cindy are dead?" She asked in a soft voice.

He sighed, those same thoughts flying around his mind, but until Mary had said something, he hadn't wanted to bring those thoughts into reality by speaking them. And frankly, at the moment he was just too tired to care. Until he was back up to peak strength there was really nothing he could do for Jimmy or Cindy.

"I just don't know, honey, I just don't know," he said quietly.

The two friends sat together, holding each other, as the night enveloped the building. Henry looked out the window once again, from the bed, and could see a small amount of sky over the neighboring buildings and he wondered if Jimmy and Cindy were alive under that same sky or were they still in the cold depths of the ocean's currents.

Chapter 14

Jimmy came to with a start, the van he was riding in bumping and jumping one to many times, the last jump enough to wake him from his fugue state. He quickly realized he was lying on the floor in the rear of a van, the area open, only the remnants of mismatched paint from where the shelves had been removed from the sides, resembling a mad artist's sculpture.

With nothing but a rough blanket for padding, the van's jouncing about was mighty painful to his already bruised and battered body.

Next to him, sleeping fitfully, Cindy was slowly coming back to reality and he reached out and touched her, glad she was real and not just a figment of his imagination.

Memories of the storm-tossed night flooded his mind, as he recalled the harrowing adventure in the watery depths of hell.

After falling over the side of the cruise ship with Henry on his back, Jimmy had landed in the water and had quickly become disoriented. He had concentrated on just staying afloat between the waves until he had been shocked to see Cindy next to him, Mary swimming next to her, as well. Mary had spotted Henry and with a yell, had swum off, leaving Cindy and Jimmy alone. Cindy had found a piece of floating debris and had helped Jimmy wrap his already numb hands around it.

He had remembered losing sight of Henry and Mary and then, when another large wave had crashed over them, he had lost sight of his friends for good.

After that it had been one wave after another, struggling to hold his breath long enough for the debris to return to the surface. Cindy had wrapped her arm in his and the two had held on for their life, sometimes falling asleep as the hours wore on.

How he had wound up inside a van was a mystery, one he was sure would be solved soon enough as the driver and passenger both turned their heads in unison at the sound of his groan, and smiled.

"Hey, Pete, it looks like our two water-logged friends are awake," the passenger said to the driver.

The driver, Pete, nodded and then turned back to the road. "Well don't just sit there like an asshole, Ben. See if they need help," Pete scolded him.

Ben nodded briskly and then climbed out of his chair and slid into the rear of the van with Jimmy.

Cindy had come around now and was blinking frantically, trying to chase the cobwebs from her mind. Jimmy reached out and grabbed her arm, shaking her. For a moment, the young woman didn't seem to recognize him, but then her eyes focused and she smiled in surprise and relief.

"Jimmy? Is that you? Oh, thank God, I thought we were going to die," she said with relief flooding her voice.

Jimmy nodded, grinning slightly. "Yeah, babe, it's me, in the flesh, though a bit pruny at the moment." He looked up as Ben moved next to him, the man holding his left hand out to steady himself against the van's walls.

"Hey, dude, you want some water?"

Jimmy nodded and took the water, drinking half before handing the rest to Cindy, who disposed of the remaining liquid in seconds. The liquid was cool and hit the spot, clearing her dry throat and filling her empty stomach.

Scratching his head, Jimmy reached down to find his .38 was missing as well as his shotgun which was nowhere in sight. Looking across at Cindy, he didn't see her rifle anywhere.

"Are we prisoners? Did you guys capture us or something?" Jimmy asked cautiously. If they were prisoners, the two men were awfully cavalier about it, offering them water where Jimmy could easily attack Ben and take the weapon strapped to his hip.

Ben shook his head back and forth. "Hell, no, you're not prisoners. We found you guys on the beach while we were scouting and now we're taking you back to our town. Unless you don't want to, I mean, but I wouldn't recommend walking around here without a vehicle or serious firepower. The dead ones are everywhere, man, and they'll eat you for breakfast and make you one of them by lunch."

"And where exactly are we?" Cindy asked, wiping her mouth with the side of her sleeve.

"You mean you don't know?" Pete called back from the driver's seat. The van bounced and the definite sound of an impact reverberated through the metal and Pete slapped the steering wheel. "Hah, got you, you dead fuck! That's two points for me, Ben. Make sure you mark it down!" He called excitedly.

Jimmy and Cindy looked with questions written on their faces and Ben only shrugged.

"It's a little game we play; how many dead ones we can take out on our supply runs. Shit, you two were lucky we found you when we did. It was almost dark and the dead fucks really come out in force at night," Ben told them

"So, where are we exactly? I mean, what state are we in?" Jimmy reiterated, hoping to get a more direct answer this time.

"You're in beautiful, sunny California, on the coast actually; about ten miles from San Diego. We managed to barricade ourselves inside our town when the rains came and totally wiped everyone out. Now there's about a thousand of us, spread out across the town. The old timers hang out on the outskirts, but the rest of us have set up Main St. like party central. It's like Mardi Gras every night," Pete called back from the driver's seat.

"It's a good thing it was us who found you instead of those bible thumpers," Ben told Cindy and Jimmy.

Jimmy looked to Cindy as if she would know what Ben meant, but Ben was already elaborating.

"There's another town a few miles down the coast from us. There's a Reverend there who set up his own little township. Only thing is, the guy's crazy as a shithouse mouse. He thinks all the shit that's happened is because God's not happy with us mere mortals or some such crap. He thinks this is the Rapture or something and if we don't all stop our sinful ways, then we're all going to Hell or something." Ben leaned back and slid to the floor at a particularly nasty bump of the van. "I ask you, if this isn't Hell we're living in now, then I don't want to know what the real Hell looks like."

"Amen, brother, amen," Pete joked from the front.

"So where are our weapons? Did we lose them on the beach or what?" Jimmy asked carefully. So far these two men were more than friendly and he didn't want to do anything to rile them. But if he was worried, he didn't need to be.

"Relax, man. We found your weapons. A shotgun and a .22 rifle, right?" Ben asked.

Both Jimmy and Cindy nodded.

"There on the floor near the front seat. But they're pretty fucked up from the water and sand. We need to get them to our armory. We got a man there that'll fix 'em right up for you."

"What about my .38? Did you find that, too?" Jimmy asked hopefully.

Pete nodded, and held the weapon up with his right hand, his left on the steering wheel. "Sure did, man, but it's all wet, plus we didn't know if you guys were cool or not, you know, if you was one of them bible jerks, so we took it and your knife for safekeeping. Once we're back at the town, you'll get them back. But first you need to meet out leader and shit. Once that's over, we'll get you a place to crash." He looked over his shoulder for a second, the van swerving slightly. "Hey, if Merle likes you guys and let's you stay, why don't you come out and party with us later tonight?"

Jimmy looked at the man dumbfounded, shocked that he would even ask. Both Jimmy and Cindy were alone in a strange place with their friends missing and these two chuckleheads wanted to go out and party.

"Uhm, we'll see, guys, we're a little tired, after floating around in the ocean all night and lying unconscious on the beach all day," Cindy said sweetly, batting her eyes slightly at Ben; only Jimmy picking up on her subtle bit of sarcasm.

It worked extremely well and Ben blushed. "Oh, that's cool, we was just askin'. You don't have to if you don't wanna."

Jimmy nodded, slightly, feeling the sweat dripping down the inside of his shirt to pool in his lower back. For the first time he realized how warm it was in the van. Only the windows on the doors were open and they were only cracked a small bit. Jimmy moved around so he was facing forward and crawled up to the driver's seat, his head ducking low to look out the windshield.

Sitting on the floor of the van, he couldn't see everything he might have wanted too, but he was still able to see the tops of the palm trees as the van shot down the road.

"Holy shit, we really are in California," he said mostly to himself.

Pete, thinking he was talking to him, nodded happily. "Sure am. Welcome to heaven, my friend," he smiled. But then his smile faltered a little. "Well, except for the dead ones that is."

Ben nodded. "Yeah, and don't forget those bible freaks, they're not much better."

Cindy moved up closer to Jimmy. "You mentioned them before. Who are they exactly? Are they dangerous?"

Ben had crawled back to his seat and he shrugged slightly. "Sort of. Mostly they keep to themselves, but whenever our two towns meet on foraging expeditions, there's always trouble. They don't compromise for nothin'. If they get to a nearby town that's deserted and we're already there, they want us to pack up and leave all the goodies to them. They say it's what God would want." He turned then and looked both Jimmy and Cindy in the face. "Believe that? It's what God would want. They mean that they should flourish and we should die or if not that, then get on our knees and beg for them to let us join them."

"Bunch of crazies, if you ask me," Pete said from the driver's seat, just as he had to swerve around six or seven zombies in the road. Jimmy peeked over the dashboard and was able to see a few bloated faces as the van weaved in and out of the small group of walking corpses. What he saw made his stomach turn ever so slightly. He was used to the sight of death by now, having seen it more than he would care to, but sometimes, the sight of a rotting zombie was still a little much to take.

That didn't bother him though. He figured every zombie was once a human being; with feelings, hopes and dreams. And the second he forgot that and became totally inured to the sight of them, well, then he thought that would be the day he lost just one more ounce of his own humanity.

The van shot through the corpses, clipping at least one with the bumper. The ghoul was hit on the hip and sent flying across the shoulder of the road. What happened after that was a mystery, the van continuing onward.

For the next hour or so, Jimmy watched the palm trees and the wrecked homes that lined some of the road, Cindy doing the same with dusk slowly falling. The homes were set back, ornate gates protecting the homes from intruders. But now almost every gate was open wide, some moving back and forth in the wind, their rusted hinges squeaking, in desperate need of lubrication.

Ben saw Jimmy looking and he pointed to a few of the homes. "We cleared all these houses out months ago," he said looking out the window of the van. "We got a lot of good shit, I tell ya. But now we need to go further inland to find more supplies. We've been growing our own food, though. We've got a few green thumbs in our town that do a great job."

"Not me, man, I've got what they call a black thumb," Pete said. "I kill whatever I touch." He sighed slightly. "It's too bad, really. Farm duty ain't that bad. Beats the hell out of coming out here and risk getting bit every damn day."

Ben patted Pete's shoulder. "That's okay, man. I'm in the same boat. Some of us lead and some of us follow, ain't that what Merle says?"

"This Merle sounds like a smart man," Jimmy said from the floor.

Both Ben and Pete's eyes lit up, a clear case of hero worship.

"Oh, yeah," Pete said first, beating Ben to the punch. "Merle's great. Shit, we probably all would have died if it wasn't for him. He was the Mayor before and it was his idea to quarantine the town last year and not let anyone in. Then when he knew shit had really hit the fan, he started us building our wall around the town."

"We've seen that before in other places," Cindy told the two men.

"No shit? Well how 'bout that," Pete said happily. "Guess great minds think alike, I guess."

Both Cindy and Jimmy had to hold back a laugh at Pete's words. Though Pete and Ben were nice enough, both were dumb as posts. Cindy was reminded of the typical surfer boys she'd seen on television back when there was television.

Cindy smiled back politely and the van slowed a little, Pete sitting up straighter in his seat.

"We're here," he said with a smile.

"Finally," Ben added.

Both Jimmy and Cindy sat straight up, craning their necks to see over the dashboard. When Jimmy was able to see where the van was going, his jaw dropped open and he uttered a soft: "Wow, would you look at that."

In front of the van, more than two stories high, was a massive stone and steel wall. Birds sat perched on top of it, cawing at the new arrivals. The wall was massive, with armed guards walking along the outside.

Zombies crawled along the bottom of the walls, desperately trying to climb up the stone slabs and reach the meat inside the town. Huge spotlights crisscrossed the road, illuminating the undead as they moved and shambled about constantly. Every now and then a rifle would crack as a guard decided to take a zombie out.

As the van drew closer, the road became lined with the scorched bodies of corpses. Dozens of them were piled high like cordwood, most only dim shapes in the falling darkness. There were also Jersey barriers spread out on the road leading up to the main gate. They were positioned so that any vehicles approaching had to weave around them, and by that the vehicles couldn't gain much speed and try to ram the front gate.

The place was something out of medieval times, a fortress with everything but dragons flying in the distant sky.

Whatever this town was, it was one of the most prepared towns Jimmy had ever seen in his travels across the deadlands.

Ben looked at Jimmy and his face beamed pride. Though he was used to the sight, he still was impressed every time they arrived at the entrance to his town.

With the van slowing and preparing to enter the maze that led to the main gate, Ben looked on proudly.

"Welcome to Stardust Cove, guys," Ben chirped happily.

Jimmy only looked back at Cindy and she nodded, her jaw set tight. She was thinking the same thing that had flashed across Jimmy's mind. If the town was that impregnable from the outside, then it would be just as difficult to leave if they decided they didn't want to stay.

But for now, they were both weaponless and tired, exhausted from their ordeal, all they could do was relax and hope the town was better than the last one they had been in back in South Carolina.

Jimmy held out his hand for her to take and she did, squeezing it tightly.

Whatever would happen, they would face it together and to hell with what came next.

Chapter 15

It was just a little past nine o' clock at night when there was a soft knock on the door and the head of one of the security guards poked his head inside the room.

"If you two are ready, the Reverend would like to talk with you now," the guard said in a civil tone.

Henry nodded and stood up from the bed, trying to stretch away some of the aches and pains he still felt. He had managed to doze off easily, with Mary curled up in his arms, and had slept soundly until being woken by the guards.

Shaking Mary awake, she opened her eyes, for a moment not knowing where she was. Then reality crashed back and she was instantly alert, coming to her feet next to Henry.

He held his hands up, placing them on her shoulders to calm her down. "Whoa, girl, relax, it's all right. The guard said the Reverend wants to see us now."

She blinked twice and nodded. "Oh, of course. I was having the strangest dream..." She petered off then, as the dream already began dissolving like the mist on a sunny morning.

"Save it for later, Mary, right now let's see what the leader of this town wants from us."

Together, they walked out into the clear night air, Henry immediately admiring the palm trees that lined the streets and front lawns of some of the buildings.

The darkness was pushed away by the streetlamps, but Henry noticed the light seeping through some of the windows of neighboring buildings. He also detected the faint odor of engine smoke in the air, assuming it had to be from one of the generators that were powering the town's facilities.

With the guard in the lead, his weapon slung casually over his shoulder, Henry and Mary followed the man up and down the winding streets of the town. As they passed by a side street, Henry slowed just a little, looking to the end of the street where a large warehouse was situated. He noticed an alarming amount of activity there, the portable lights surrounding the building all on high and a multitude of guards walking around the perimeter. There were also numerous trucks, all in many shapes and sizes, but having one thing in common, namely that they were all cargo trucks, capable of carrying large loads enclosed inside their walls. Off to the side were even two eighteen wheelers, their chrome bumpers glistening in the glare of the spotlights.

"Hey, buddy," Henry called to the guard. "What's going on down there? Sure seems like a lot of activity."

The guard stopped walking and covered the few paces separating him from Henry and Mary. Looking down the street, the man shrugged slightly.

"It's nothing you need to worry about, stranger; it's just a project the Reverend is working on." He gestured slightly with his hand for Henry to keep moving. "Now, if you'll continue walking, the Reverend is waiting."

Mary pulled his arm slightly. "Come on, Henry, there's time to sight-see later, right now let's go meet the boss man of this place, I don't want to be rude and keep him waiting."

Giving in to the pressure, Henry grunted, and with one last look at the warehouse, he continued walking, the guard now next to him.

As they walked, Henry leaned closer to Mary. "What the hell has gotten into you?" He asked her softly. "Ever since I woke up, you've been acting like you're in some kind of trance."

Mary smiled sweetly. "I have no idea what you're talking about, Henry. It's just that this could be the place we've been looking for all this time. They've got the undead situation in check and this is a peaceful place to live. We could be happy here, don't you think?"

Henry stared at her for a few seconds, trying to understand what she was saying. Somehow this place...this town had brainwashed her into thinking she was in some kind of utopian Paradise.

They walked in and out of streets for another fifteen minutes and it was only when they reached what was obviously the main street of the town that they walked in a straight line, staying on the same sidewalk for more than ten minutes.

When they reached the City Hall of the town, the guard gestured for them to go up the stone walkway without him.

Henry believed they had taken a circuitous route to the Reverend's office, though why was anyone's guess.

"Just go through those doors at the top and take a right," the guard said. "The Reverend's office is right there, you can't miss it."

Henry nodded and, with Mary at his side, moved up the steps. His eye roamed over the front of the building, noticing a few places where there were what looked to be scorch marks, as if from a fire. Whatever had happened in the buildings past, it hadn't been pleasant and peaceful like Mary's opinion of the town.

Stepping inside the large hallway, Mary by his side, Henry admired the décor. There were statues of famous leaders at intervals along the hallway and a large painting of the town hung on the wall, directly across from the main doors. A small desk sat below the painting, where a concierge would have sat a year before. The floor consisted of white marble tiles, polished to the point it looked like ice. Henry walked over to the painting and looked down at the small plaque below the painting.

"Painted in 1972 by Arthur Feldman; the town of Sunset Bay," he read out loud, his voice echoing in the empty hallway.

"That painting is our pride and joy," a deep voice said from behind Henry and Mary.

Henry spun on the balls of his feet to see a man in his late fifties staring back at him. The man was at least six-feet tall and wore the classic vestments of a Protestant Reverend. He had a small set of rimmed glasses perched on his nose and he had a full set of dark brown hair.

A vintage M11-A1 pistol rode his hip in a leather holster.

The man smiled at Henry and Mary and his polished white teeth seemed to almost glow in the faded light of the hallway.

He started walking to Henry and Mary, his right hand held out in a greeting. "Welcome to Sunset Bay, it's so good to finally meet you both," he said in a cheerful tone.

Without even thinking about it, but instead responding to the familiar gesture, Henry reached out and shook the Reverend's hand. The handshake was firm, but not to pretentious. Letting go, Henry stepped back a pace as the Reverend then shook Mary's hand.

"My name is Reverend Carlson and I hope you're feeling better," the Reverend said, looking to Henry as he still clasped Mary's hand.

Henry nodded. "Yeah, thanks, I'll be back to normal in a few days, thanks for asking. My name is Henry Watson and this is..."

"Mary Roberts, ah yes, we've already met, though you weren't quite yourself then. It's good to see you up and about, as well, my dear."

"How do you know my name?" Mary inquired. For the life of her she didn't remember telling anyone her name.

The Reverend smiled, charmingly. "That's easy, my dear, when you were brought in you were mumbling incoherently, and when one of my men asked you your name, you told him, though I highly doubt you even knew what you were saying."

Mary only stared back, her mouth bent at an upward angle as she tried to remember any of what the man had told her. None came to mind.

"So, Reverend, this is a pretty nice set-up you've got here. Electricity and fuel and safety. The big threes that mean a healthy life nowadays." Henry told the man.

Reverend Carlson gestured that they follow him into his office and Henry and Mary did so, Henry flashing Mary an inquisitive look when the Reverend's back was to them, the brief flash of his eyes asking how the Reverend knew her name, not buying the man's story.

Mary only shrugged and followed the two men into the office.

Reverend Carlson gestured for his guests to take a seat in the large leather chairs that sat in front of his desk like soldiers on watch.

"Please, have a seat, we have so much to discuss."

"Oh, and what about? If I can be so forward as to ask," Henry said with as pleasant a tone as he could muster. He could feel it coming, like it did every time he and his friends found themselves at the mercy of a Boss of whatever town they found themselves in. The leader would always want them to do something, or perform some task that was usually far too dangerous for his own men, thereby using the disposable labor that was Henry and his companions.

Only they were down by two personnel now, neither the whereabouts of Jimmy or Cindy known.

"Not at all, Henry, not at all." The Reverend leaned forward in his chair, his hands cupped on the desk in front of him. Henry thought the man was preparing to give him a speech or sermon.

"Are you a religious man, Henry?" The Reverend asked.

Henry shrugged and leaned back in his chair. He had a feeling this conversation might take a while.

"Not particularly, no. Especially after all the crap that's rained down on the world. Why do you ask?"

Reverend Carlson pursed his lips as if he was contemplating how to start. Finally, the man did, inhaling deeply so he would be able to get out the most words in the smallest amount of time.

"The walking dead plague that has befallen the world is not an accident, Henry. In fact, I believe it's God's will. You see, man has wandered so far from the path of righteousness that if it wasn't the undead that had brought us to our knees, well then, sooner or later it would have been something else. A virus, perhaps, or a meteorite that would be so huge as to bring about the next ice age. Man has become nothing more than a decadent beast that wallows in the mud like the most inferior form of life. Only through the Lord will man ever attain his rightful place by his side once again." His eyes had slowly grown wider as he continued his speech and Henry could see the man was slightly off-balance, though until this moment the Reverend had hid it well.

"There's something in the city that I need you to get for me." Reverend Carlson said flatly.

"Uh-huh, and why may I ask does it have to be me that goes and gets this item? Surely you have plenty of men to do your bidding," Henry stated plainly.

The Reverend nodded slightly, agreeing with him. "You are correct in that assumption, with the exception of one fact. Three weeks ago I had a dream. In that dream the Lord spoke to me and told me that I would have a man and woman, like Adam and Eve, come to me. They would be far from home and would need my help. In gratitude for my help, they would be eager to do as I ask."

His eyes flared with intensity and Henry could almost see the fire burning within them.

"I believe both you and Mary are those people, Henry, and I need your help desperately." He pressed a button on the underside of his desk and a moment later, three guards strode in, weapons in their hands. Henry couldn't help but wonder where they had been stationed if they had arrived so fast. All three men wore hard faces and carried their weapons as if they were prepared to use them at a moments notice.

Mary shifted uncomfortably in her seat, staring at the three guards.

The Reverend was making a statement, without ever uttering another word.

"So, what do you say, Henry? Will you help me? I'd prefer you to acquiesce voluntarily."

Henry looked into Mary's eyes and she nodded. The look she gave him seemed to say she would have helped even if the guards hadn't entered the room.

Which seemed odd. Mary usually wasn't one to capitulate so quickly. Just one more mystery to be added to the half dozen he already had.

Sighing, he leaned forward in his chair. Though inside himself he was rolling with tension, he pasted an air of calm over his visage.

"Sign me up, Reverend, always happy to do the Lord's work."

"Wonderful," the Reverend said; his face filled with pleasure. He looked up at the first guard and waved the man toward him.

"Ralph, get us a bottle of wine, I want to celebrate this occasion," he told the man excitedly.

Ralph was a heavy set man with chubby cheeks and a red face. He grunted softly and then slipped out of the room. He was back in a moment with a canter of wine and three glasses. Placing them on the desk, he stepped back, waiting for further orders.

"You can go now," the Reverend told Ralph. "I believe if there was going to be any trouble here tonight, then the time has passed, hmmm?" He glanced at Henry as he said the last words.

Henry only smiled back innocently, acting as if he was unaware of what the Reverend was inferring to. After pouring the wine into the glasses, all three picked one up and the Reverend beamed pleasure.

"To the Lord and his good works," he said loudly.

"Uhm, yeah, sure, the Lord," Henry said, just trying to stay in the man's good graces.

"To God," Mary said sweetly.

Reverend Carlson drank deeply and polished off half his glass in one sip. Both Mary and Henry watched the man, their mouths slightly agape. Then they each took a sip and placed their glasses back down on the desk.

Wiping his mouth on his sleeve, the Reverend slammed his glass on the desk and smiled.

"Well, then, I believe our business is concluded. Go with God, my friends. Ralph will see to your needs and in a day or so, when Doctor Rivers says you're fit; you can set off on your quest, like the warriors of old once did."

Ralph stepped inside again and Henry could only assume the man had been signaled once again. Then with Henry and Mary on their feet, they were ushered out of the office and back into the hall.

Ralph pointed with the barrel of his weapon at the main doors and Henry started walking, Mary at his side.

"Henry, what about..."

He cut her off with a wave of his hand. "Later," he said simply, not wanting to talk in front of the guard.

She nodded and the two of them walked back down the street, weaving their way back to their room. There were less people out now, though as Henry passed the warehouse he had seen earlier, he still noticed a beehive of activity around it. Trucks were rolling in and out and men in white bio-hazard suits were moving about. Henry filed the scene away for dissection later; for the moment he had enough on his plate.

It took less time to return to their room this time, Ralph taking them on a more direct route and soon they were on the street that their building was located on.

When they had reached the door of their room once more, they were ushered inside and the door was closed, Ralph giving them a polite nod as he exited. Henry walked over to the door and tried the knob, not surprised to see it was locked.

"Guess I'm bunking with you tonight," Mary said as she looked around the room, now the two of them alone once more.

Henry grunted. "Yeah, guess so, just do me a favor though, huh?"

"What's that?"

"Just try not to snore like a locomotive. It's been a rough day and I need my beauty sleep," he joked.

She slapped him lightly on the shoulder, but he winced in pain, it was one of the spots still sore from the battering he'd received in the ocean.

"Oh, Henry, I'm so sorry, still sore?"

He chuckled at her question. If there was a part of his body that didn't ache, he had yet to find it, but stoically he only shrugged, even that causing him a twang of pain.

"Yeah, a little, but I'm sure I'll be better tomorrow." he sat down on the bed and kicked off his boots, the footwear still soggy from his dunk in the ocean. "Look, Mary, about earlier..." he said, talking about when he had shut her up.

She held out her hand to stop him and walked over and sat down next to him on the bed.

"No, it's okay; I know what you meant, and you're right. We've got more important things to worry about right now. Like where Jimmy and Cindy are...or even if they're still alive."

Henry put his arm around her, consoling her. "Don't worry, Mar', we'll find them. Like Jimmy always says, until I see a body, they're still alive, right?"

She nodded slightly, her hair falling in front of her eyes. "Yeah, I guess so. That sounds like Jimmy." Then she yawned, which in turn caused Henry to follow suit.

"Dammit, woman, don't do that. You know it's contagious."

"Sorry," she chuckled and then stood up and kicked off her own boots, also still soggy. Next she peeled her moist socks from her feet and draped them over a small chair. "Here, lay down and I'll get yours for you," she told him.

Henry stretched out on the bed and she peeled his socks off. His feet looked like shriveled prunes and he wiggled his toes at her.

"They look like a man of eighty years old," he said, still wiggling his toes.

She giggled and turned to hang them next to her own socks.

"You know, Henry, maybe what the Reverend wants us to do won't be so bad," she said, trying to be positive. When Henry didn't answer, she turned to look at him and found he was fast asleep, his chest rising and falling slowly. He was still exhausted from his ordeal and she had to admit, she was pretty wasted, as well.

Walking over to him, she covered him with the blanket at the foot of the bed and then lay down next to him. She felt safe near him, like a daughter with her father and as she closed her eyes, she found herself drifting into that realm where sleep was just over the crest, wakefulness still refusing to let her go.

Just as she felt herself slipping into the waiting arms of slumber, she thought of Cindy and Jimmy and prayed they were still alive and were, hopefully, looking for her and Henry, too.

Chapter 16

The van pulled through the gate and slowed to a stop. Ben leaned over his seat and gestured for Jimmy and Cindy to get out while Pete walked around the back of the van and opened the rear doors.

"Well, guys, I guess this is the end," Ben said solemnly.

For a brief instant, Jimmy thought the man was telling him that Jimmy and Cindy were about to die.

"Excuse me?" Jimmy said softly with a lump in his throat. His mind was already trying to figure out how he could stop the man from hurting Cindy and himself and had placed a hand on Cindy's shoulder, so he would know where she was when he went into action.

"It's the end of us being together. From here on someone else will take you into the town. Me and Pete have to be somewhere else." Ben's eyes creased as he studied Jimmy's face and posture.

"Oh, wait...you didn't think." He started to laugh then, loud and long. "Hey, Pete, they thought we was gonna kill them!"

Pete stood at the rear of the van, his body outlined by one of the spotlights inside the gate. "No shit? Now why the hell would we go and do that. If we was gonna kill them we could have done that on the beach when they were lying dead to the world, helpless as a newborn kitten."

Jimmy started to laugh with the two men, forced at first, but when he realized he and Cindy were truly safe, the laughter slowly came more easily.

"Sorry, guys, but if you've seen some of the shit I've seen you wouldn't be laughing so hard."

Pete slowed his laughter. "Well, buddy boy; you don't have to worry none. As long as you can take care of yourself, you'll be fine around here. It's a rough place, that's for sure, but if you're careful, you'll be fine. Now come on out of there so me and Ben can get going."

Pete turned and called to someone that neither Jimmy nor Cindy could see from inside the van. A moment later footsteps could be heard and a large man with rolling mounds of muscle stepped into view. An M-16 rifle was slung across his shoulder and a large machete was strapped to his hip.

Seeing the machete made Jimmy think of Henry and his panga and a pang of loss crept inside him. Pushing the emotion back down, he focused on the task at hand. There would be time to think about Henry and Mary later, when they were safe somewhere. The only question was where that might be.

"Hey, Bert, these people were found on the beach a few miles from Sunset Bay. They looked like a couple of drowned rats."

"No shit?" Bert said in a deep bass voice. "Lucky you found them before the crazies did."

"Yeah, no shit, we already told them a little about them people, but feel free to tell them more," Ben called from the driver's seat.

Jimmy and Cindy climbed out of the van and stood together, Jimmy still trying to be prepared for anything while the men talked.

"Nah, I'll let Merle tell them about us and them. He doesn't like it when we steal his thunder, you should know that by now," Bert warned.

Jimmy listened and read between the lines. Without meaning too, the two men's conversation had already given something away of the town's leader.

Pete shrugged next to Jimmy. "Hey, man, give us a break. It was a long ride, we had to talk about something and the tape deck was broken."

"Not my problem, Pete, now you better get going. Ned needs you at the garden. He needs to load up a bunch of shit in the van, so git or I'll blow your lazy ass off." Bert threatened, actually slinging his rifle around casually.

Pete held up his hands to stop the man and started back to the passenger side of the van. "All right, man, don't get crazy, we're goin'," he said and climbed into the van. But before the van surged away, Pete tossed Jimmy a look. “Hey, Jimmy, maybe I'll see you at one of the bars later. If I do, I'll show you the ropes and we'll get good and wasted, too.”

Jimmy could only stare at the man. The last thing on his mind at the moment was going to a bar.

With Ben back in the driver's seat, the van skidded away on a plume of dust and smoke, Pete waving like a hick just out of the bayou, hanging out the passenger window.

Jimmy and Cindy were left alone with Bert, while behind them other men walked the tall wall. Bert gave each of them a once over and then gestured with his chin, not feeling threatened in the least by the two strangers.

“Okay, you two. Follow me and I'll bring you some place to sleep for the night and in the morning, I'll bring you to see Merle, our leader. He was the mayor when everything went to hell last year. As for me, I'm the head of security, so if I tell you to jump you best try to figure out how fucking high I want you to. You understand?”

Both Cindy and Jimmy nodded. “Sure, man, it's cool. We appreciate you taking us in,” Jimmy said gratefully.

Bert nodded curtly, happy with Jimmy's answer.

Bert waved to one of the men on the wall that he was leaving and clicked the two-way radio on his belt twice. A second later, two clicks came back to him on the speaker and he started walking away from the wall, gesturing for Jimmy and Cindy to follow.

Bert walked across the wide open area around the gate until he stopped at a small lot filled with cars. He climbed into a massive four wheel drive truck complete with chrome wheels and custom exhaust.

Climbing up into the driver's seat, he gestured for Jimmy and Cindy to do the same from the passenger side. Both did as told and a half minute later, the truck roared to life, and with a belch of smoke, Bert pulled out onto the main road that would bring them to the town's main street.

“I know what you're thinking,” Bert said while he straightened the large vehicle on the pavement and surged forward.

“Oh?” Jimmy said simply.

"Yeah, you're thinking what this truck must be doing to the ozone layer, what with it belching smog like an oil refinery, but I figure the last thing me and the rest of the people who are still alive on this mud pit of a planet need to worry about is the fuckin' ozone layer. Am I right or am I right?"

Cindy giggled at Bert's joke and Jimmy flashed her an angry stare. "Actually, I was wondering where you got the gas for this truck and the others I saw."

Bert reached in his pocket and pulled out a bent cigarette, the package wrinkled and crushed. Lighting it from the cigarette lighter on the dash, he blew the smoke out the window and leaned back in his seat, the engine roaring beneath the chassis.

"We got lucky. There's a large tank yard about ten miles from here. All the gas we'll ever need. The trick is getting it, though. The damn walkers have the place surrounded and every time we go in, we have to shoot a shitload of them. The more we kill, the more that take their place. It's a goddamn nightmare, is what it is."

Jimmy nodded, understanding. "There's no way to close the place off? Maybe enclose it so the deaders stay out?" He suggested while watching the few buildings and structures fly by the window.

"Deaders?" Bert asked, and then realized Jimmy was referring to the undead. He shook his head heavily. "No, man, the fences are all knocked down and there are large holes in other areas. Plus, there was a big fire there back when everything went to shit and that entire area is unstable. No, we just get in and hook up to one of the tanks that are still intact and fill an old tanker trunk we got parked just near the gate. Maybe you saw it when you came in.

Cindy and Jimmy both said no. Truth was, in the darkness, and with all the activity going on, the last thing either of them would have noticed was a truck sitting in the lot, even if it was as big as an eighteen wheeler.

"So, what about you two? Where'd you guys come from? Can't say there's much worth being here for unless you like sunshine and dead fucks."

"Uhm, we were in a boat and it capsized. We got washed ashore. That's about it really," Jimmy said, not wanting to give anything away that could jeopardize his standing with Bert or this Merle character. Next to him, Cindy nodded, agreeing with his story.

Bert pulled the truck into a parking spot and turned off the engine. They had parked at the beginning of the town, the answer to the unspoken question of why apparent for both Jimmy and Cindy to see as they looked out the windows of the truck at the tableaux spread out in front of them.

The two lane blacktop that cut down the street was filled with at least two hundred people. Various carts, such as what would be found at a flea market or a swap meet, were scattered about the area as the vendors attempted to hawk their wares.

Climbing out of the truck and slamming the door, Jimmy and Cindy did likewise.

"We walk from here on in. There's no vehicles allowed on Main Street. This is where most of the townsfolk hang out. Merle believes in having fun, so as long as no one gets hurt, anything goes."

The three of them started walking toward the melee, and within two minutes, were at the first buildings that defined Main Street.

Cindy looked down at a man and a woman rutting on the sidewalk, oblivious in their passion as other people walked around them, while a few spectators stood around cheering them on. Others paid them no mind, but continued on with whatever errands they were about.

"I can see that," Cindy stated, her eyes wide as she watched the man slam his enormous member into the writhing woman. Askance of her, Jimmy was also watching with wide eyes, the tip of his tongue poking out of the corner of his mouth. She elbowed him in the side to get his attention.

"What? What I do? I'm just watching," he exclaimed, his eyes darting between the exhibitionists and Cindy's face.

"Exactly, cut it out. And don't get any ideas." Then she walked away from him, following Bert who had started moving into the crowd of people.

Jimmy took one last look at the couple, and with a sigh, started forward, as well, still doing his best to keep the couple in sight until they were lost behind the other people moving about the street.

The noise was deafening. Vendors argued for the best price for their goods and townspeople talked with each other and called out prices they were willing to spend; all under the lights of the streetlamps. Doorways were open on both sides of the street, light spilling out onto the sidewalks, and where once hardware stores and bakeries were the norm, now there were scantily clad women in low cut tops and skirts, all trying to entice the men, and sometimes women, to come into the buildings with them for a dalliance. Others contained men and women who were obviously selling drugs, small packets of chemicals in their hands as they tried to get the pedestrians to sample their wares.

Though Jimmy wasn't very religious, it all reminded him of some kind of Sodom and Gomorrah from the bible, where it seemed the pleasures of the flesh was the theme of the day. Everywhere he looked there was another form of decadence, whether it was S&M with two men or a three way with three women of all ages, shapes and sizes. Some openings even had children in them as the adults that should be protecting them were instead feeding on their naiveté and fear.

Though sickening to watch, it was at the same time fascinating. These people were delving into their basest desires as there were now no laws to fear but the ones the Boss of the town decided to enforce.

A loud commotion was coming from one of the open doorways and Jimmy grabbed Cindy's arm and steered her toward it, curious. "Let's see what all the noise is about," he told her.

Bert saw where he was going and nodded. "Oh, you'll like what's in there. It's one of my favorite spots," he said with a wide smile. "Come on, we got time before you have to see Merle."

Jimmy continued on, glad for the approval of Bert and stepped inside the doorway. A large brute of a man with an aluminum bat stopped his progress, but Bert slipped in next to him and slapped the larger man on the arm.

"It's okay, Matt, they're with me."

The man lowered the bat and grunted, the only time he came close to speaking. Jimmy looked at the man hesitantly, and then with Cindy at his side, slid by the monster of muscle.

Bert followed, chuckling at Jimmy. "Ah, don't be scared of Matt, his bark's worse than his bite."

"Uh-huh, it's not his bark I'm worried about," Jimmy commented and moved down the small hallway that was about twenty feet long. At the end of hall it opened up onto a large room filled with people.

The cacophonous noise filled the room so a person could barely hear themselves think. Copious amounts of alcohol and marijuana were being shared by the clientele and the atmosphere was of a wild party, though more intense than the scenes Jimmy had seen outside in the street.

It had once been a bowling alley, but had since gone through some major construction. There was now a balcony that surrounded the entire room (stairs leading up at the end of the corridor) so the spectators could look down onto the open area below. Six foot high fences had been built from one end to another of the room, so that the bowling lanes were now individual corridors.

It reminded Jimmy of something he had seen back in high school when a few of his friends had thought it amusing to race mice. Only in this construction there wasn't cheese at the end of the maze nor were there mice as the contestants.

What Jimmy looked down on were three zombies, each in its own corral, chained by the necks, while at the opposite end were live human beings, each tied up with their hands over their heads, the heavy bindings bolted to the wall above them. The prisoners thrashed about wildly, trying their best to escape, but it was obvious even to Jimmy from high up in the balcony that their struggles were futile.

The prisoners consisted of two men and a woman, all in the middle of their lives. The oldest had to be at least twenty-five, though with all the blood and bruises, plus swollen faces, it was difficult to tell.

Cindy was the first to voice her shock and surprise.

"What the hell is going on down there?" She gasped, watching the zombies as they pulled at their chains.

"It's the races, what else?" Bert stated, as if it was the most normal thing in the world.

"Races? You mean you race those creatures? Why the fuck for?" Jimmy asked, his eyes still studying the grotesque scene below him. "And why are those people shackled down there?" The moment she asked the last question, she figured she already knew the answer, but still the inquiry came from her mouth

"What for? Why, for the hell of it. Got to do something with 'em, right? Instead of just shootin' them in the head, that is. This way we get rid of some of the rabble and have some fun at the same time."

"Rabble?" Cindy said simply, as she watched the crowd below. She could see numerous men moving through the crowd, taking what looked like bets on the coming race.

"Yeah, those poor fucks down there did something to piss Merle off. This is how he deals with them. Figures it gets rid of them and teaches the rest of the townspeople a lesson."

"Oh, and what lesson is that?" Jimmy asked, though he was fairly certain he already knew the answer.

"Simple. Don't fuck with Merle or you'll wind up gettin' your ass bitten off." Then Bert leaned in closer to Jimmy, almost like a close friend would do to pass on some sage advice. "Best you pay attention here, stranger. Or you might wind up in the races next."

"I'll do that," Jimmy said coldly, not liking where the threat was going, but helpless to do anything about it without any of his weapons. Shit, they had even taken his hunting knife. But as he looked around the room below him, he wondered if it would have even made a difference if he'd had his weapons. If he or Cindy tried anything, they wouldn't last long with so many guards around. Jimmy scanned the room and it was easy to see the other guardsmen scattered about the room. These men, and one woman, all had hard faces and appeared disinterested in the coming games. Jimmy made sure to mark their positions, just in case.

He thought of Henry then and what he would have made of the present situation. He could almost imagine hearing his voice, telling him to stay sharp and watch everything, for even the smallest tidbit of information could spell the difference between life and death.

At the front of the bowling alley, a man wearing a shiny black suit stood up and waved his hands. He reached up to a rope hanging over his head and Jimmy could see it was connected to a pulley system that connected to the corrals that held the zombies. With a loud yell from the man, and a louder cheer from the crowd, he pulled on the rope and the gates holding the zombies came up.

For a moment, the three zombies stood where they were, not realizing their small prison had become larger, but after being poked and prodded through the fencing by what could only be called animal trainers, they were shoved out into the alleys. One at a time each ghoul spotted the prisoners at the opposite end of the alley and almost at the same time, they began moving forward, growling and drooling, hands out in front of them like some bad actors in a Frankenstein movie.

The crowd went wild, some of the closer spectators climbing onto the fence so they could get a better look at what was coming.

Cindy turned and looked at Jimmy, her eyes filled with emotion. “Jimmy, we’ve got to stop this, those things are gonna kill those people!”

“I know, babe, but there’s nothing we can do. Even if we wanted to, we’re outnumbered and unarmed. Best to let this shit sort itself out.” He shook his head. “I’m sorry, but there’s nothing we can do for them. Pray they die quickly is the best we can do for them.”

Cindy’s eyes creased with pain and frustration at her helplessness and she turned away from him to watch the progress of the three undead corpses as they shambled down the alleys. All three were disgusting specimens with blue and blackened skin and flesh that was so tight on their faces and arms that it looked like it was painted on.

One corpse, number 2, according to the sign strapped to its back like a marathon runner, had a large gaping wound in the middle of its chest. Jimmy could see the blackened clothing around the wound and figured it must have been from a gunshot. That was also when he noticed the other two ghouls had signs of their own, each with the number 1 or 3 on them.

At the moment, Number 2 was making good progress, though Number 1 was close behind, albeit in another stall. The prisoners started wailing now, knowing what was coming next; one of the prisoners high-pitched keening rendered the air like a police siren, overriding the screams of the spectators.

Then it happened as the entire room knew it would. True to form, Number 2 reached his prey first, immediately sinking its blackened teeth into the prisoner’s neck. Blood shot from the wound around the ghoul’s mouth to bathe the alley in scarlet as the prisoner's shrieks slowed, his blood filling his throat and drowning him. The woman prisoner was next; Number 1 reaching her only moments after Number 2 had started feeding. He dove into her body head first. Its teeth sinking into the first thing they came in contact with, namely the woman's right breast. Her tattered shirt was ripped from her body, along with a long vermilion ribbon of flesh.

As she screamed to God to save her, the zombie spit out the material from her shirt and chomped happily on her flesh, one pink nipple sticking out of its mouth like a pacifier. Then finishing off the piece, it dove in for more, the woman screaming louder and the spectators roaring with excitement like they were at the Coliseum watching Gladiators do battle.

Finally, Number 3 reached his prisoner and started consuming the face of the hapless man, the man's arms jerking and bucking under the onslaught, but with his arms tied over his head, all he could do was add his own screams of agony to the cacophony of the others.

All three prisoners were ripped apart, slowly at first, but as the zombies grew more voracious, their ministrations grew wilder until limbs were being torn from bodies and blood began to sluice across the alleys to pool in the gutters of the alleys, where bowling balls would once end up after unskilled players took their chance with the game.

Cindy had seen enough and she turned away to look at Jimmy. Her pallor resembled a clean white sheet and she gasped and swallowed before she spoke. "Jimmy, I really want to go now, can we please?"

Jimmy nodded, agreeing with her wholeheartedly. "Sure, babe; I know what you mean." Turning to Bert, he saw the man was totally wrapped up in the visceral scene below him. Jimmy reached out and grabbed the man's arm.

"Hey, Bert, we want to go, we've seen enough," he told him in a tone that said he would not be denied.

"What, now? But it's just getting' good," he screamed, his eyes wide while he watched the carnage below.

"Sorry, man, but we really want to go. With or without you, it's fine with us," Jimmy said in a flat tone that said he wasn't going to argue about it.

Bert turned away from the scene below and then looked at Jimmy, then back down below. Sighing he nodded. "Fine, it's pretty much over, anyway. At least I saw who the winner was. Later, when the guys are talking about it at the barracks, at least I'll know what happened." He smiled then, and slapped Jimmy on the back. "Thanks for coming in here, Jimmy. If you hadn't, then I would have missed all this."

"Sure, glad to help," Jimmy answered snidely.

Bert slapped Jimmy on the back again, this time more hardily. "Come on, then, and I'll get you two fixed up for the night. We've got a small hotel inside the perimeter where we keep guests. That is the few times we have new people here." He started working his way through the crowd. "I bet you're tired after all you've been through today."

Jimmy only nodded. Truth was he could barely keep his eyes open, he was so exhausted, and Cindy's countenance was no better. They both needed time to recover from their ordeal from the storm and also to get a minute alone to discuss their situation.

As the three of them started to weed their way through the crowd and out into the darkened street, the noise and activity still going strong, Jimmy turned to Cindy and made sure only she could hear him.

"This place isn't what I thought it was. As soon as possible, we need to get the fuck out of here," he said into her ear.

She nodded and moved along so as not to fall behind him. "Jimmy, I'm way ahead of you, the moment we saw those poor bastards in there, I knew it was time to go."

Jimmy grinned slightly at her then, he should have known, of course. If there was one thing about Cindy that he loved and trusted, it was her grasp of the obvious. With revelers jostling them as they made their way through the busy street, both Jimmy and Cindy followed Bert's back as the large man cleared a path through the throng of people, knowing even if they wanted to slip away, they would still have the hard task of escaping the town's high walls.

No, better to meet this Merle character and see what he had to say and hopefully get their weapons back, then, at the first opportunity that came their way once they were outside the walls, they would take a chance and sneak away into the surrounding countryside.

Once they had escaped there was still the almost impossible task of searching for Henry and Mary along the coast. And hoping the two had been fortunate enough to survive the wild ride of the ocean waves.

The trick was; just how were they going to get outside those walls again?

Chapter 17

Henry was pulled from sleep by a sharp knocking on the door of his room, or prison, depending on how he wanted to look at it. Without waiting to be given permission to enter, Ralph stepped in, holding a tray of food, the smell of coffee preceding him into the room.

Henry blinked twice and sat up; Mary still snuggled up on the bed next to him.

"The Reverend is having an assembly in one hour in the town square. He wants you two to be there," Ralph said brusquely, while tossing two sets of white jumpsuits for Mary and Henry to wear onto the end of the bed.

"Oh, yeah, and what's going to happen there that's so important that we need to be there, too?" Henry asked the man as he stood up from the bed and walked over to the table with the tray of food. The moment his nose sensed the coffee aroma, his stomach began to growl, like a hungry beast woken from its slumber.

"You'll see when you get there. Let's just say one of the Reverend's commandments has been broken, so he wants to remind everyone who's in charge around here. He does it every now and then. Guess you got here at the right time, huh?" Then he stepped out of the room, leaving any further questions unasked.

Mary was awake now, hearing the voices in the room, and she sat up, stretching. Looking to Henry, she cocked her head like a lovelorn puppy.

"Now, that was weird. What he said. Rather cryptic, don't you think?" She asked.

Pouring himself a cup of coffee, and then one for Mary, he walked back to the bed, handing her the cup. She inhaled the soothing fragrance and took a sip, careful not to burn her tongue.

"Guess we'll just have to wait and see. Until then, you hungry?" Henry asked while walking back to the table and sitting down at one of the two chairs in the room.

There was an assortment of fresh fruits and a loaf of bread, accompanied by a jar of grape jelly. Without waiting, Henry dove in, devouring two oranges and three slices of bread before Mary had finished dressing and sat down across from him.

Feeling better after a good night's sleep, his body was craving sustenance and he was happy to appease it.

When she was comfortable next to Henry, Mary reached for an orange and sighed. Her socks were now on her feet once again, dry and warm over her cold skin. She reached down where her .38 would have been and frowned when she realized it was still missing. She thought it funny that only a year ago she would never have wanted to ever touch a firearm, but now it was as much a part of her as her shirt or shoes.

"What's wrong?" He asked around a mouthful of bread.

"Nothing really, it's just...I can't believe Jimmy and Cindy are gone. And now we have to go do something for the Reverend. It just won't be the same with just the two of us."

"I know, Mary, but what do you think they would want us to do? I'll tell you what," he answered for her, not really expecting an answer. "They would want us to keep on going; that's what."

"Yeah, I know, it's just..." She tapered off, Henry knowing what she was thinking.

"Listen, once we've done what this guy wants, we'll see about slipping away and looking for Jimmy and Cindy. Until now, lets eat, I'm starving," he said, reaching for another slice of bread and lathering it with jelly.

She nodded as she peeled an orange. He was right, she knew that, but deep down inside her she had a gnawing feeling that something was wrong.

She just couldn't put her finger on it.

* * *

When they had finished eating and were thoroughly dressed in the fresh new clothes, a knock came at the door. Before either one of them could say anything, the door was thrust open and Ralph was there again, a hard look on his face.

"It's time to go and we need to move fast or we'll be late," he said quickly, his head disappearing before Henry or Mary could answer.

Henry looked to Mary and gestured for her to go first.

"After you, my lady," he joked.

She curtsied politely and started forward. "Why thank you, good sir."

Henry followed her out, and a second later, they were both standing on the sidewalk, the sun overhead shining down on everything, almost cleansing them with its brilliance. The smell of salt floated on the morning breeze, making Henry cringe slightly. He'd had enough of the ocean for the time being and had no inclination to go near it anytime in the future.

"It's this way," Ralph told them as he started down the sidewalk.

"Hey, what about our clothes? White really isn't my color," Henry said with a little crassness to his voice.

"They'll be cleaned and returned to you later today. Happy?" Ralph asked him over his shoulder.

"Yeah, actually, thanks."

Henry and Mary followed Ralph down the streets, both admiring the town better now that it was daytime. The buildings were all quaint and clean, looking like they had been maintained even after the town had secluded itself behind its chain and wooden fences. Pedestrians moved back and forth along the street, and children played ball, running and laughing as they kicked it back and forth.

Mary smiled, watching the children. It was nice to see people who seemed to actually be happy and thriving despite all the loss in the past year.

Rounding a bend in the street, Ralph directed them up a small alleyway. The sun was slightly blocked here and shadows fell on old garbage cans and a faded green dumpster.

Cutting through the shortcut, the three of them came out on the fringes of a small crowd. With only the backs of the people facing them, neither Henry nor Mary knew what was happening, but as soon as Ralph reached the first person at the rear of the line, he tapped him on the shoulder and the gawker quickly stepped aside once he saw who wanted passage by him. Almost the entire crowd wore white or pieces of the white uniform that seemed predominant in the town.

Soon, others moved out of the way, the crowd parting like the fabled Red Sea, but instead of Moses at the lead, it was just plain Ralph.

Henry watched some of the faces as he passed through the crowd. Some leered at him warily, others with what seemed to be fear. Mary smiled and said hello to some others in the crowd, but when none returned her greetings, she decided to stop.

Eventually the front of the line became clear and Henry and Mary stepped out onto a wide open field with a long stage with a podium in the middle. The crowd surrounded the stage on all sides, and when Henry looked up, he received his first glimpse of the Reverend Carlson that morning.

Next to the man on the large stage was a giant cage, about seven feet high. Chicken wire surrounded the entire metal frame, doing a nice job of keeping the two prisoners inside. The cage was split up into two parts, the right side holding a desiccated zombie with one missing eye and only one arm.

Its clothes were in tatters and the reek of death carried across the heads of the crowd to assail Henry's olfactory senses. Next to him, Mary gagged and covered her nose with her arm.

Henry looked back up after he had adjusted to the smell of the dead thing in the cage. If the other spectators were bothered by the redolence, they did an excellent job of hiding it.

Seeing the dead ghoul in the cage was bizarre enough, but it was what was in the second part of the cage that was even more of a mystery. A very frightened man stood in the next cage, only a thin piece of chicken wire protecting him from the snarling creature of death. Henry could see the man was on the verge of a total collapse. His pants were wet from where he had released his bladder and there was a dark stain on the rear of his pants—probably from when he had shit his pants in terror.

The Reverend was standing very still, a bible lying on the waist-high podium in front of him, his head bowed low. His black vestments were ironed to the point of crispness and the creases on his pants looked like they could slice flesh if given the chance. On his hip was his handgun, a sharp contrast to the vestments of God, not to mention the dark color of his clothing compared to the almost white cloth almost all of the townspeople wore on their persons.

The Reverend reminded Henry of every televangelist he had ever seen on TV, right down to the large poster of the man's head plastered on the wall of the stage behind him.

"What are they going to do to that man?" Mary asked Ralph, her curiosity getting the better of her. Though from other places she'd been, she had a crawling feeling in her gut that told her she already knew.

"You'll see; it won't be long now. The Reverend needs to give his sermon and then he'll take care of the heathen." Ralph's eyes seemed to light up as he spoke, the first time Henry had seen any inflection on the man's face since he had first met him.

Up on the stage, the Reverend raised his head and smiled slightly. A hush grew over the crowd and all eyes locked onto the man in black.

"My children, you may believe that you have to die to be judged by the Lord, but I am here today to tell you that just ain't true. In the new world the Lord has thrust us in, we can be judged by him at anytime, day or night. Some of you may think the fires of Hell are far away from you and that there is nothing to worry about, but the fires aren't just around the corners, waiting. No my children, the fires are with you, with us, right now. It is here, now and forever and will be as long as we are mortal. For you see, man is a sinful beast. As we fornicate, drink and gamble our lives away from this world to the next, I stand before you today to say enough! Those of you who have sought shelter in my bosom have learned the ways of the Lord, but what of those across the way? What of those heathens in Stardust Cove who still continue to sin despite all our warnings? The clock of eternal damnation is still ticking my friends and I'm here to tell you it has already struck midnight and we are done!"

The Reverend began waving his arms out in front of him as if he was possessed. Though the morning was cool, his forehead broke out in perspiration and his face turned red from his activity.

The crowd seemed to almost mimic him, each one growing in their own fervor.

"We are done, my children, so stick a fork in the ass of mankind and flip us over on Satan's spit, because we are not going to Hell people. No, we are not, because we are already there, now! So sayeth the Lord, Amen!"

"Amen," screamed the crowd, some of them clapping. The Reverend held his hands up to silence them.

"This brings me to the festivities of the day. This man was found on the beach four days ago and when he was asked politely, he informed us he was from Stardust Bay, that foul pit of depravity."

Henry studied the prisoner a little more closely and he could now see the bruises covering the man's face and what looked like cigarette burns on his arms. He could only assume when the Reverend said the man was asked what he really meant was tortured.

"We have a special punishment for this prisoner, my friends, one you should all know well. Since this man wants to sink to the level of the demon spawn that claw at our gates, then so shall he become one of them." The Reverend nodded and two guards moved closer to the prisoner. One held a .45 pistol in his hand, the other a short sword no more than two feet long, but more than adequate to reach into the cage and puncture the hapless man.

"Go on, you know what you have to do. Do it or we'll put a bullet in your head now and end it." The guard with the gun spoke to the prisoner, his tone one of edged steel.

The prisoner turned away from him, shaking his head frantically. As if a switch had been pulled, the man spoke at last. "No fucking way am I doing that. Screw you; put a bullet in my head, then. You'd be doing me a favor. You're all nuts, especially that asshole who thinks he's a priest!" His eyes flared angrily. "Fuck you, you prick!"

The guard with the sword stabbed the man in the buttocks then, sinking the tip three inches into the man's flesh. The prisoner wailed with the pain and tried to pull away, but the only way to even try to escape the sword was against the chicken wire that separated him from the zombie. The dead creature banged against the wire, enraged at the smell of live meat so close and yet so far.

"If you want, we could just open the cage and let it have at you. Just do what you were told earlier and get it over with. It won't be so bad," the guard with the handgun said.

To punctuate his words, the other guard jabbed the sword into the man's side, slicing into the meaty part of his stomach. Screaming with tears rolling down his cheeks, the crowd roaring obscenities at him, the prisoner realized that defying his captors would get him nothing but more pain and with his will broken, he sighed and nodded, weeping the entire time.

"This is when it gets good," Ralph said, his breathing heavy. Mary scooted to the side of him, moving closer to Henry.

"I don't like where this is going, Henry," Mary said while she watched the prisoner getting stabbed on the stage.

"I know, Mary, but there's nothing we can do, so for the love of God, just stay there and watch. If you don't like it, then close your eyes. Remember, we have no weapons and are helpless here for the time being. Just play along...please. Don't do like you did in that other town a few months ago. Just stay calm."

She nodded, knowing he was right. In a past town they had visited only a few months ago, Mary had let her conscious get the better of her and she had put a similar prisoner out of his suffering and had ended up bringing the entire town on top of her and the rest of the companions. It had only been luck, and a little skill, that had allowed them to escape in one piece.

"I'll be fine, Henry, don't worry about me. I know there's nothing I can do for that man and though it makes me sick..." She trailed off as another wail of pain came from the prisoner. He was bleeding in multiple places now, his already filthy clothes now even worse.

Henry noticed for the first time there was a small opening in the chicken wire around chest level of the prisoner. With the sword waving in front of him and the handgun there, as well, the prisoner did what Henry thought no man in his right mind would ever do, whether under torture or not. He stuck his hand into the hole so that the zombie could bite him.

The zombie looked down at the limb sticking out of the hole in front of it and seemed to stop for a moment, not believing its good luck. Then it dove in, biting a three inch piece of flesh from the man's arm and shooting blood out of the cage like rain to splatter the front of the crowd. The prisoner roared in pain and terror and pulled back his arm, but the damage was done. Trying to wrap the arm with a piece of filthy shirt, the prisoner hugged the arm to his chest while scarlet slowly spread across his already sodden shirt and began to drip onto the floorboards of his cage. The zombie had ripped a major vein with its teeth and without a tourniquet; the man didn't have long left on this earth.

The zombie chewed merrily, happy to be eating, its mouth covered in vermilion. The guard with the handgun made a disgusted face and then walked up to the cage and shoved the barrel of the weapon through the wire. In one quick shot, the guard shot the zombie, part of its head exploding as the creature fell to the cage floor, bits of flesh still sticking out of its mouth.

Next to the zombie, the prisoner wept tears of fright and sat down on the floor. He was breathing heavily and Henry realized that the man was doomed. He could see the blood still seeping out of the bandage and dripping over the man's boots and pants. The man's complexion was pale, more so than before and Henry could see the man was dying. Around him, the crowd was throwing epitaphs and imprecations, howling and yelling while the man's life slowly faded away.

But Henry knew that wouldn't be the end to the man's ordeal. The sun moved across the sky and the crowd continued to watch. Checking his watch, Henry realized they had been there for almost two hours. A few vendors had begun walking through the crowd, selling water and food. It was one big party, the townsfolk talking amongst one another and throwing their discarded food stuffs onto the stage at the cage.

As for the prisoner, he slowly slid into death until his eyes closed and his chest stopped moving. When this happened a hush grew over the crowd as they all watched, eyes transfixed on the prone corpse lying still on the floor of the cage. Then, as a few more minutes went by, one of the crowd let out a yell. "A finger moved. I saw a finger move!"

The Reverend stood up from his chair, where he had taken refuge after his sermon. There was a large umbrella over it and he had sat quietly all this time, until the spectator had called out. Now he stood and walked over to the cage.

"Hush, children, it's almost time," he said quietly.

"Oh my Lord, they're actually doing it," Mary said next to Henry.

He silenced her, not wanting to draw undue attention to them and watched with the rest of the crowd. He had to admit in all the ghouls he'd killed, there hadn't been many times when he had actually witnessed one being born, though the metaphor sickened him.

Then it happened, just like the sun rising in the morning and setting at the end of the day. The prisoner's eyes snapped open and the vacant gaze looked out on the crowd.

"He has risen, so sayeth the Lord!" the Reverend screamed, raising his arms in front of him.

"So sayeth the Lord," the crowd returned, all of them jumping and clapping; some of the older folk fainting.

"The mass is ended, go with God and follow his teachings, and may death avoid you for another day," the Reverend preached and dismissed his flock.

"It's done, come on, the Reverend told me to bring you to the rear of the stage after the ceremony," Ralph told Henry while the crowd clapped and started to disperse.

"What's going to happen to that man now that he's turned? Are you going to kill him?" Mary asked as they moved through the crowd.

Ralph shook his head. "Naw, that guy'll take the place of the other critter until another prisoner is brought in. Then the cycle will start again and that guy will be put down." He smiled then. "It's all the Reverend's idea. He likes to remind the good folks of this town that there are worse things than death nowadays."

"Ain't that the truth," Henry said quietly.

With the sun rising in the sky, Henry and Mary were escorted to the waiting Reverend who was now sitting at a small table surrounded by four chairs. The man was sitting under another umbrella, this one having its pole in the middle of the table like the man was about to have a picnic. On the table was a pitcher of lemonade and two more glasses plus his already full one.

Seeing Henry and Mary round the stage, he sat taller and smiled. “Ah, at last. Come sit down and we’ll talk about the little excursion I need you to perform for me,” he said with a glint in his eyes.

Looking at one another, Mary and Henry sat down while the Reverend poured each of them a glass of lemonade.

We have so much to discuss,” he said and leaned back in his chair, smiling. “Please, drink up, it’s fresh squeezed, you know. After all, this is California.”

Knowing he was trapped for the moment, Henry grinned slightly, and with a casual gesture, picked up his glass of lemonade and took a sip, Mary doing likewise.

The liquid was cool and wet and it slid down his throat to fill his stomach. But no sooner had he swallowed the liquid then his head began to feel groggy and his vision started to blur.

The Reverend’s face became blurry, and though he tried to focus, nothing would cooperate, his hands becoming weak and his head feeling too heavy to hold up.

He heard laughter coming from behind him and recognized the voice as Ralph’s. Then the Reverend began to snicker, too.

Turning to Mary, he saw she was already unconscious, her eyelids were closed, and her head was lying on the table; her glass having fallen from her lifeless hand to bounce in the dirt at her feet.

Trying to stand and confront Reverend Carlson, only his force of will still keeping him conscious, he stood up on unsteady legs.

“What did you...” was all he uttered, then the blackness swarmed in and he once again found himself tumbling into a black abyss with no bottom, while the grating laughter of the Reverend floated across the void to follow him into the darkness.

Chapter 18

Jimmy rolled over in bed, sat up and stretched; his aching muscles protesting. He stopped moving for a moment and just gazed down at Cindy as she lay sleeping next to him. Her blonde hair was spread out around her head like a halo and she sighed softly in her sleep. Jimmy smiled slightly while he continued watching her, admiring the strong features that made up the contours of her face and the slim, curvaceous form under the clean white sheets they had both shared last night.

Bert had brought them to a two-story bed and breakfast on the opposite edge of town and had assigned them a room for the night. If there were any other occupants in the other rooms, neither Jimmy nor Cindy had heard a peep out of them. Both of them had been elated to find the shower and toilet worked and had each enjoyed a shower alone and then had finished off with a shower together, enjoying the precious time they had alone.

Jimmy had brought the subject up of them being alone and had ended up throwing their moods into one of melancholy and moroseness. If they were alone, then it was because neither Mary nor Henry was with them, and wondering where their friends were was worse than knowing they were actually dead. Cindy had wanted to broach the subject with Bert, but Jimmy had stopped her before she had said anything. Bert didn't need to know there were two more of them out on the beach somewhere.

If he did, he might be tempted to go out and search for them, and though Jimmy would like to see Henry and Mary safe, he also didn't want them trapped inside this town of depravity with him and Cindy.

Jimmy's smile grew wider as he continued looking down at Cindy's sleeping form, remembering the previous night. After the shower, they had both retired to the bed and he had to admit they had ended up delving into a little depravity of their own. Remembering how soft her skin had been and the feeling of her warm breath against his own flesh as they had made love made him slowly become aroused.

Lying back down, he slid in close to her, his now hard member brushing against her leg. She opened her left eye slightly, her right one buried in the folds of the bedding. She grinned at him and stretched slightly, trying not to move too much and ruin her position.

"You've got to be kidding," she said coyly. "Again?"

"Hey, I'm young and in my prime, give a guy a break," Jimmy quipped back as his hand caressed her left breast.

Sighing, she rolled over and sat up, totally ignoring his ministrations.

"I have to go to the bathroom, I'll be right back," she said brusquely and stood up, naked to the world, and walked to the bathroom. Jimmy watched her go, admiring her buttocks as they swayed with her walk. God he was horny, it was like last night had never happened.

A minute later he heard the toilet flush and the sink running, then Cindy reappeared, standing against the frame of the bathroom in a sexy pose.

"There, now I'm ready, if you think you're up to it," she stated flatly, her eyes creased in seduction.

Jimmy tossed the sheets from him, the cool air of the room giving him goosebumps and grinned, looking down at his aroused organ.

"Does this look like I'm up to it?"

She ran across the room and jumped onto the bed, falling into his arms. Lying on top of him, her body warm and inviting, she nodded. "Why, Jimmy, I do believe you're happy to see me."

Jimmy grabbed her butt cheeks; one in each hand and squeezed so hard she giggled and squealed with delight.

"You better believe it, babe, and now I'm gonna show you," he said and began kissing her passionately on whatever part of her was closest to his lips

With the revelers from the previous night already rousing to start a new day of depravity, Jimmy and Cindy made love in the light of the morning sun, and for the moment, the rest of the world was irrelevant.

* * *

One hour later, both Jimmy and Cindy were dressed and waiting for someone to come for them. It happened five minutes after the passing of the hour and neither Jimmy nor Cindy was surprised to see it was Bert again.

With a quick rapping on the door, Bert stepped into the room, not waiting for either of them to answer the door.

“Knock, knock, you all decent in here?” He asked, his face falling when he saw they were. Obviously, he was hoping to catch them in a compromising position as was evident by the way he leered at Cindy while she lay stretched out on the bed.

Jimmy cleared his throat and stood up from the chair he had taken up as his resting place across the room.

“Hey, Bert, ‘bout time you got here. We’ve been ready for more than an hour.”

Bert shrugged slightly. “There’s no rush, Merle always sleeps in. He wants you to come now, though. There’ll be food there so you can eat, too.”

Jimmy walked across the room and took Cindy’s hand. “Shall we?”

She smiled at him, her face still flushed from their activities under the sheets a little while ago. “Yeah, I’m ready, let’s go.”

Bert led them out into the sunlit morning and Jimmy and Cindy had their first look at the town of Stardust Cove in the daylight.

Other than a few less shadows, the street looked much the same as the night before. A few townspeople walked around with a trash barrel and a broom, picking up all the trash that had accrued in the street from the previous night. As they walked by them, none looked up, but concentrated on their work. Jimmy caught a brief glance at one of the men and he saw a beaten down look of exhaustion and pity.

"Ignore them," Bert said. "They're the scum of the town, no better than street sweepers. They're lucky we let them stay at all."

Cindy wanted to say something, but Jimmy flashed her a look that told her to be silent. Now was not the time to debate the town's politics. Especially without so much as a knife to defend themselves.

Bert started walking and Jimmy and Cindy followed.

"So when do we get our weapons back?" Jimmy asked while he walked next to the large security chief.

"Soon, probably. Merle decides stuff like that and I don't want to cross him by going over his head."

"Sounds fair," Jimmy replied, struggling to keep up with the larger man's wide steps. "So what kind of guy is this Merle? Is he cool or what?" He asked, trying to glean any information out of the large man.

But Bert wouldn't bite and just shook his head back and forth. "You'll see soon enough, we're almost there." Just when he had finished his words, they rounded a street corner and slowed when they came upon a small crowd of men and women in the street. Bert waved one of the security guards that were in the crowd over to him and asked him what was happening.

"Another OD, that's all. We're getting him out of here now. The poor bastard should have known better than to fuck with that shit," the guard told Bert.

"That's fine, Mathews, get it done quickly and restore order; the sooner the better," Bert told the man. Then he started walking again, pushing his way through the crowd. Then he stopped and waved the guard back to him. "Did the stiff have any family?"

The guard shook his head no. "Not as far as we can tell, sir."

"Okay, fine. Dispose of the body over the wall like the others. The piece of shit doesn't deserve a real burial."

"Yes, sir," the guard said and disappeared into the crowd.

As they walked on, Jimmy asked Bert what that was all about.

"Sometimes we just chuck the corpses over the wall and let the zombies eat 'em. There's not enough room in town to bury everybody. So if there's no family, then over the wall they go."

"That's horrible," Cindy blurted out, not realizing she had said it so loud.

Bert turned to her and shrugged. “Don’t see how that is, Miss. They’re dead, right? It’s not like they can complain.”

“He’s got a point there, babe,” Jimmy said with a wan smile.

She pursed her lips and frowned. “You would agree with him, despite how barbaric it is.”

“I don’t know, Cindy, sounds pretty reasonable to me. Beats digging a hole.”

Huffing in frustration at Jimmy and men in general, she pushed past him and walked a little faster, making sure to keep one eye over her shoulder to see where Bert was going. Ten minutes later, Bert called to her and stopped in front of a large three-story house on the outskirts of the main drag of the town. From where they stood, the wall of the town could be seen easily, the large barricade cutting through some of the backyards of the adjacent homes on the street. Jimmy marveled once again at the large wall, and wondered how the town had managed to build it while keeping the dead at bay.

Bert waved for them to move up the walkway. “This is it; this is where Merle lives and runs the town. He doesn’t like City Hall anymore. Says the old ways are dead and there’s no reason to adhere to them anymore.”

Jimmy took a step or two with Cindy at his side and stopped when he realized Bert wasn’t behind him.

“Aren’t you coming in?” Jimmy asked.

Bert shook his head. “Nah, I’ve got rounds to do and a shift change to check on. Make sure everyone showed up who was supposed to and shit like that. I guess that’s why I get paid the big bucks. Sometimes some of my men party too hard and I have to kick them in the ass to keep them in line. You’ll see once you get into the rotation with the others.”

Jimmy’s eyebrow went up a little at the statement, but he controlled the surprise on his face. So he was going to be a guard once everything was said and done.

“What’s Cindy going to be doing?” Jimmy asked. She stood next to him, waiting for an answer, curious as well.

Bert picked his teeth with a finger and spit out a piece of gristle--the morsel from breakfast--onto the path. “Dunno, probably go to work in one of the bars. They always need strippers and bartenders. We'll see what she's good at." As he turned to walk away, he called over his shoulder to the couple. "There's always a place in the brothel. Those bitches get worn out pretty quick and we can always use some new blood."

Cindy was about to yell at the security chief and tell him there was no fucking way she was going to be a prostitute, but Jimmy held her arm and squeezed tightly, stopping her. He shook his head and his stern expression told her not to say anything.

Her eyes flared anger and she almost snapped at him, but then reason kicked in and she stopped herself.

"Well, see you guys later. Merle's waiting inside. Oh, and if you think you can sneak away or something, then take a look up in that second floor window. There's a man with a sniper's rifle aimed at your heads, so I suggest you get inside and don't delay."

Jimmy and Cindy turned, looking where Bert had gestured, and sure enough, in the middle window, the curtain pulled back and tied with a piece of string, was a man with a rifle; the barrel aimed at the two of them. Jimmy acted casual and waved to the man, grinning widely, knowing the man could see his visage as clear as if he was standing next to him; the magnification of the rifle's scope more than powerful enough.

The sniper never shifted position, looking for all purposes like a statue. Turning to Cindy, who was filled with anger and frustration at the past few minutes of conversation, he gestured for her to follow him.

"Well, come on, babe, we might as well go meet the man behind the curtain."

Frowning, she nodded and the two of them walked up the path and entered the doorway that led into the house of the man who ran Stardust Cove. What waited for them inside was unknown, but then it wouldn't be the first time they had entered the unknown and come out free and clear.

They could only hope this time would be no different.

In the window above the doorway, the sniper disappeared from view, the curtain falling back to cover the opening, a gentle ocean breeze blowing inward, filling the house with the smells of morning.

Chapter 19

Mary was floating in a dark abyss from which there was no escape. She flailed her arms and tried to pierce the darkness with her eyes, but there was nothing. A hissing, similar to white noise covered all sound and she felt like she was inside a television screen that was turned to a non-channel.

For only a moment, she wondered if she was still in the ocean, having just fallen into the water from the cruise ship and even now she was breathing in water, the cold liquid suffusing her lungs as her body began to spasm in its death-throes under the cruel waves of the ocean.

Then a voice sliced through the obsidian blackness of her world and she felt herself being pulled toward a light. It was far away, like a pinpoint at the end of a mile long tunnel, but slowly she felt herself floating toward it. She didn't know what lay at the end of that light, but it had to be better than the barren world she now found herself in.

The Reverend Carlson's voice penetrated the white noise and darkness surrounding her and she began to hear his words more clearly. He spoke softly, telling her she was fine and that he had a set of tasks for her that she needed to perform.

Lost in the hypnotic spell the Reverend had her under; all she could do was nod, the subliminal orders becoming imbedded in her subconscious. Time was irrelevant and when the Reverend finished with her, he told her she would wake feeling a little groggy thanks to the sedative he had administered to both her and Henry in their drinks. He said she would have no memory of their conversation and that she would only do as he bid her when the time was right. Until then, she would go on about her life as if nothing had changed.

Henry stirred next to her and slowly began to wake up, grumbling in his sleep.

Sitting in the seat next to the Reverend in the back seat of the motor home they were presently riding in, Ralph shifted uncomfortably.

"Watson's coming to, sir. Are you gonna wake her up soon?" Ralph asked a little uncomfortably. He hated watching the Reverend work his hocus-pocus and always wondered if the Reverend had ever done it to him. He knew the man had done it to some of the guards when he had needed information about the town and had managed to make a few moles in the barracks. In fact, even the man who was doing the snitching didn't actually know who the culprit was. The perfect spy, one who didn't even know he was guilty.

"Just give me a moment longer, Ralph. This is the second time I've had her under since we found her and her associate, and I want to make sure she is fully committed to what I've told her needs to be done when the time's right. When I saw her last night, she seemed to be wavering slightly," the Reverend told Ralph.

"Wavering, sir? What do you mean?" Ralph asked.

The Reverend leaned back and sighed. "I mean that not all my subjects are susceptible to my machinations. Watson here happens to be one of them. You saw when I tried to give him suggestions earlier. Nothing happened. Some men and women just have wills that are simply too powerful to break with the power of suggestion." He gestured to Mary as he spoke. "But no worries, she will suffice."

"We're almost at the rendezvous site, Reverend," the driver of the motor home called from the driver's seat.

"Good," the Reverend nodded, "tell the other car to pull up alongside us and post guards, but not to shoot any dead ones unless they have no choice. I don't want my two guests spooked."

"Yes, Reverend, the driver said and then picked up a two-way radio off the dashboard, speaking into it softly.

The Reverend quickly wrapped up talking to Mary, then he snapped his fingers and Mary began to stir, while Henry did likewise in the adjacent seat.

The Reverend leaned back and waited for his two guests to come back from the depths of unconsciousness while outside the motor home, the other car was disgorging men, all moving about with purpose as they set up a small perimeter around the two vehicles. When Henry finally opened his droopy eyelids, he was greeted by the grinning face of Reverend Carlson.

"Ah, Henry, so good to see you're awake again. Welcome back to the land of the living. Or should I say, the living dead. I'm terribly sorry about what happened, but I'm afraid you were drugged," the Reverend said politely.

Scratching his head and sitting up, his stomach rolling slightly from the movement, Henry frowned. He noticed he was wearing his old clothes again, now clean and dry, as was Mary. He was glad; white had never really been his color.

"Yeah, I kinda figured that one out on my own. The question is; why the hell did you do it? I already said I'd do your little mission for you."

The Reverend nodded, cocking his head to the side. "True, but I figured this would solve the problem of you changing your mind. You see, while you've been sleeping, I've taken the liberty of loading both you and Mary into my mobile home and driving down the coast to where I'll be leaving you."

Mary groaned next to Henry and he looked over to see her waking up. She didn't look to good and he sympathized, knowing just how she felt.

Smacking his lips, they were so dry; Henry looked out one of the windows of the rolling camper. It was bright outside, the sun high in the sky. Other than a few buildings in the distance, the area was vacant.

"Where are we?" Henry asked hoarsely, smacking his dry lips. "And how about some water, I'm thirsty as hell."

The Reverend slid a pitcher of water and an empty glass across a small table to Henry, acting like the perfect host.

"Here, this should take the edge off," the Reverend said. Henry poured himself a glass of the warm liquid, not caring if he spilled some of it on the table. He was done being polite to this asshole who considered himself a man of God. He had met plenty of people that thought just because they wore a certain type of clothes that made them more than they were.

Mary sat up, rubbing her face with her hands and looking around curiously while her eyes focused on her surroundings. Henry polished off his glass of water and then poured another, handing it to Mary. “Here, Mary, drink this, it’ll make you feel better.”

She took it and downed half before she had taken another breath, then after finishing the rest, she looked around again. “Where the hell are we?”

“That’s what I just asked him and he’s about to tell me, so listen up,” Henry told her.

“Yes, please do. I’d prefer to only have to brief you once,” the Reverend said, haughtily, standing up and walking over to the door that would lead out of the motor home. “Come with me, both of you.”

Opening the door, Ralph behind him, Reverend Carlson stepped outside into the sun.

Henry stood up, woozy for a moment as the rest of the drugs worked their way through his system. Helping Mary to her feet, he led her out of the motor home and into the sun.

The light was blinding, and they blinked a few times, trying to adjust to the harshness of the day. The black two-lane asphalt seemed to absorb the heat of the sun like a sponge and heat waves could be seen a little ways in the distance. As his eyes adjusted to the daylight, Henry noticed a few shambling figures on the horizon, moving towards them slowly. They were slow moving and would take quite a while to reach them, so at the moment there was nothing to fear. Plus, the four guards surrounding the motor home were well armed and alert.

The Reverend turned to Mary and Henry, pointing down the empty road with the index finger of his right hand. “This is the main road that leads to the San Diego Naval base,” he said almost casually, as if he was giving directions to a lost family on vacation. “I want you to enter the base and find the Lincoln Research Facility. If what I’ve been told is correct, then there is a cure for the zombie plague in there.”

"You're joking right? There's a cure in the base, and after all this time no one's used it." Henry shook his head in disbelief. "It doesn't make sense."

"Perhaps, but it's all I've got and I'm willing to risk the lives of you, Mary and a few of my men to see if it's true."

"So what do you need us for? Surely you could just send your men inside and find what you want."

Shaking his head in exasperation, the Reverend started walking around the side of the motor home, circling like a homing pigeon. Henry didn't know if the man was still talking to him or was just on a rant, but he listened quietly.

"No, Henry, you don't understand. When I had this dream…this vision… it told me that you would come and that it had to be you that searched for the Holy Grail, the cure. No one else can go unless you lead the charge. I hope you understand."

"Even if I don't, does it really matter?" Henry asked.

"No, I'm afraid it doesn't," Reverend Carlson said brusquely.

Mary spoke up then. "What about weapons? Surely you don't expect us to go in there unarmed. If there are deaders in there, and there's no reason to think there aren't, we'd be slaughtered before we were halfway inside."

"Ah yes, your weapons. Ralph, get them will you?" The Reverend asked of his security chief. Ralph ran across the lot to the other vehicle and reached inside and popped the trunk. Walking around quickly, he leaned inside and pulled out a large cotton bag--similar to a gym bag. Carrying the bag back to Henry and the rest he dropped it in the dirt.

"Careful you idiot, those weapons are valuable!" The Reverend snapped at him.

"Sorry, Reverend, I wasn't thinking," Ralph said, humiliated.

"Exactly, and that's why you're not going to the base. I can't trust you to get the job done. Plus, I need you to help with that other task I need to finish."

Both Henry and Mary waited for the man to elaborate further, but when he didn't, Henry spoke up.

"So, are our weapons in the bag?"

Leaning down and unzipping it, Reverend Carlson reached in and started pulling out weapons, Henry's eyes lighting up when he saw his Glock in the man's hand.

"Here you go, Henry, all cleaned and ready to go. You'll find it has a full clip as well as a few more extras in the bag."

Henry barely heard him, but was already popping out the clip and checking the slide to make sure it was in full operating order after its dip in the ocean. The smell of gun oil came to his nose and he grunted with satisfaction, slapping the clip back in and cycling a round into the chamber. For one brief moment he stared at Reverend Carlson, wondering if he should attempt to put a bullet in the man's head right here and now and end this charade, but no sooner had the thought popped into his head, then he heard the sounds of rifles cocking, and safety's being taken off.

Turning, he saw the other guards all moving slightly closer, and Ralph now had his weapon leveled at Mary.

"Now, you weren't thinking of reneging on your promise, were you Henry?" Reverend Carlson asked in a hard voice.

Henry smiled widely and slid the Glock into the empty holster on his hip. The odds were against him at the moment and he knew when to lay his cards down.

"Of course not, Reverend, Just checking to see all's in order."

"And is it?"

Sullenly, Henry nodded. "Yeah, I guess it is."

"Excellent, then let's finish giving you the rest of your armaments and then we'll see you on your way." The Reverend dug around in the bag and pulled out Henry's shotgun and Mary's .38. She took her handgun with a slight smile, carefully going through it to make sure it was in good working order. As for Henry's shotgun, the weapon was empty, the Reverend handing him a box of shells.

"You can load that when you're on your way and not before. He handed Henry a two-way radio. "This is for when you're finished. Two of my men are going with you and their orders are to kill you if you so much as blink the wrong way, so I suggest you do what is required of you and return with the cure. Do you understand everything that's been told to you?"

Nodding brusquely, Henry frowned, knowing he and Mary were trapped for the moment. He would just have to wait until later and see if there might be a better opportunity for him and Mary to slip away once they were inside the base. The first thing would be to dispose of the two guards and then try to find a way out of the naval base in one piece. Until then, he was just glad to have his weapons back and felt a pull at his heart when he saw his trusty panga come out of the bag, Ralph taking over for the Reverend and handing it to him by the hilt.

Whatever would happen next, at least they were armed, now. And in any fight, that was half the battle.

Chapter 20

The front hallway of the house was dark and musty and Jimmy curled his nose slightly at the redolence within. The smell of stale beer and something else...the odor of old sex, permeated the air.

Next to him, Cindy also covered her nose, her eyes creasing as she inhaled the aroma. Without knowing where to go, both of them began walking, following the hallway deeper into the house. A large stairway led to the second floor, the carpet now dirty with bits of lint scattered here and there. The house had once been magnificent, the crown molding and ornate designs on the doorframes evident, but there was also a feeling of despair, like a once healthy man now wallowing in the last stages of cancer, his body fat wasted away, his skin hanging on his bones.

Cindy looked to Jimmy, her eyes asking what he was thinking. “Where do we go?”

Then a few noises came from a room off the far end of the hallway and Jimmy slowly started to move toward the sound, Cindy at his back. The hairs on the back of his neck stood up, a tingling feeling crawling up his spine. He was unarmed and the feeling of helplessness was overwhelming after more than a year of always being armed.

As they grew closer, the noise began to clarify itself, a gargling slurping noise that reminded Jimmy of pigs eating slop. Reaching the closed, but not latched door, he pushed it open, the hinges squeaking in the gloom.

As the door opened, Jimmy’s eyes immediately took in the room for possible threats. There were three wide windows at the back of the room, and bookcases filled both sides, the books looking aged and worn by both time and use.

A dull red carpet lined the middle of the room, the edges not quite reaching the walls. A large oak desk filled the center of the room, dominating it to the point there was nothing else a person's eyes would look to once entering the space, plus two empty chairs to the side.

But it was the man seated a few feet behind the desk that was the most imposing, if imposing could be used to describe the fat sack of flesh that was at the moment leaning back with his pants down to his ankles and a naked woman of indiscernible age on her knees in front of him giving him felatio.

Her head was bobbing up and down at a rapid rate and one of the man's hands was firmly holding her head down so even if the girl had wanted to stop, she would have been unable to. The man's face was scrunched up in either pain or ecstasy and as both Jimmy and Cindy stood there watching, the man let out a grown and bucked his hips, the girl literally gagging on his member.

A second later, the man relaxed and pushed the girl away from him as if he was discarding a piece of wrapping from a candy bar. She fell to the floor, her right hand wiping her mouth, and reached across the few feet separating her from her clothes.

"That's all for now, leave me," the man said in a deep baritone voice, dismissing the woman. With his pants still down and his flaccid penis now hanging between his legs, the man looked up to see Jimmy and Cindy watching him. If the man was embarrassed at being caught in a sex act, he gave no show of it, but instead slid his lower body under the desk, the chair's wheels gliding across the floor.

"And who the fuck are you two?" He asked brusquely.

"I'm Jimmy Cooper, and this is my girlfriend, Cindy Jansen," Jimmy stated. "You sent for us?"

"Ah, yes, the two who were found on the beach, right?"

Jimmy nodded. "Yeah, that's us," Jimmy answered.

"So what do you think of my town?" Merle asked.

"Don't really know yet. I guess the best word to describe it is different."

"Oh, really? How?"

Cindy chose that moment to speak up. "Well, for one thing, people seem to have sex anywhere they want and the way you had those people killed at the bowling alley last night. That was pretty harsh."

Merle leaned forward in his chair, the leather creaking slightly. Both Jimmy and Cindy were more than a little uncomfortable, knowing the man was nude behind the desk.

"Listen up, you two; though I don't owe you a goddamn explanation, I'm going to give you one anyway. Call it your indoctrination into my town. As for the sex my people like to have, well, there ain't much else to do anymore and with the world in the state it's in, I figure fuck and have fun for as long as you're still alive. And as for those three prisoners you saw in the bowling alley, they were malcontents and one was a spy for Sunset Bay." He leaned forward even more. "You have heard about them, right?"

"Not really, no one would really tell us anything, just bits here and there," Cindy said.

Merle beckoned for them to sit down in the two chairs near his desk. Once Jimmy and Cindy were seated, Merle leaned back in his chair again, a cigar appearing in his hand miraculously. Jimmy was just glad the desk blocked his view of the large man's lower half. He had already seen all he wanted to of the bovine mayor.

Lighting the cigar, he blew a cloud of smoke into the air and squinted his eyes slightly. Though he was a large man, his face was slightly leaner, a sharp contrast to the rest of him.

"Sunset Bay was always a place of religion, even before the world went to shit. There's a Reverend there, Carlson's his name. Well, he decided this zombie thing is the end of the world and that we are just as bad as the damn dead fucks walking around outside the walls I've had built. You see, the man was always unstable and now with everything that's happened, he's finally cracked. He wants to have us all killed here in Stardust Cove and he's gone to great lengths in the past to try."

"Oh, like what?" Jimmy asked, waving smoke from his face.

Merle didn't seem to care if the smoke was bothering his guests, and continued his tale.

"Well, let's see, there's been so damn many. Ah, I have it. A few months ago he somehow got his hands on some dynamite. If I had my guess, I think he got it from the San Diego Naval base a few miles from here. Well, he had someone try to sneak in and do one of them suicide bombing deals, but we caught the guy before he had a chance to set off the explosives." He sat taller in his seat and grinned widely at his two guests. "You know what I did with the guy?"

"What?" Cindy asked, curious despite herself.

"I cut off his head and sent it back in a box. Then I had one of my men drop it off outside their gate in the middle of the night. To this day, I don't know if that crazy bastard got my message, but I do know after that thing's became quiet for a while. You know, you'd think things would be bad enough with the dead walking around like a bunch of senior citizens doing their exercises at the mall, but I've got to worry about some psychotic priest as well."

"Okay, so you got troubles. So how do me and Cindy fit into it?" Jimmy asked frankly.

Merle chuckled at that. "Fit in? I hate to break it to you son, but you don't. You two don't mean a goddamn thing to me except two more mouths to feed. Now we got a good thing going here and as long as newcomers pull their weight, I got no problem with strangers coming in from the outside. But for all I know you two are the next plan of that crazy fuck to bring my town down around me, so until I know I can trust you, you'll be watched."

"Make's sense," Cindy said. "So, what do we do around here until you know we aren't spies?"

Merle's eyes moved up and down Cindy's lithe frame, undressing her with his eyes. "Well, honey, I think I already know where you should go."

"No way, Merle, I already know what you're gonna say and it ain't gonna happen without a fight," Jimmy said, his body language showing the tension in his limbs.

"Whoa there, partner, at ease. I was just suggestin' it. It's okay. Some of the ladies around here like it."

"Well, not me, thank you. Bert said something about a bar. I worked in my Uncle's bar about a year ago. Can I do that?"

Merle sighed. "I suppose so, though it's a damn waste, I tell ya." He looked to Jimmy. "How 'bout you, where do you think you're gonna go?"

Jimmy's visage was hard and he spoke in a low tone. "You tell me, you're the Boss, right?"

Merle laughed then; smoke billowing out of his mouth like a chimney stack.

"That's right, I am! And you're one of the smarter ones around here to realize that right off the bat. Some men just don't get it. Actually, Bert already called dibs on you, so I was thinkin' there's a place in my security staff, if you want it. It's the best place to work. A clean bed and good food. If the people that protect me aren't fit and healthy, then what chance do the rest of us have, right? How are you with a weapon, I hear you were found with some water damaged firepower."

"I can handle myself in a fight," Jimmy stated flatly.

"How about those dead fucks, can you keep your head in a pinch?"

Jimmy decided not to share his past history of traveling on the road with his friends and how he had probably brought down more zombies than Merle's entire security force combined.

"Yeah, I can handle myself. Those dead things don't intimidate me."

"Good, then it's settled. You get to Bert and you," he pointed to Cindy, "go to the Dollar Bar at the end of Crescent Street. I happen to know they need a bartender and waitress there."

"Oh? And what happened to the person I'm replacing?" Cindy asked.

Merle leaned forward, placing his arms on the desk. "Honey, that is a story you can hear from Betsy if she wants to share it with you, now the both of you get the fuck out of here, I need to take a shit and I want to be left alone."

Jimmy stood up, as did Cindy, and the two left the Mayor alone.

"Hey, close that door behind you!" Merle yelled to Jimmy.

Jimmy did as he was told, the door clicking softly. Walking back down the hallway, Cindy looked at Jimmy, the concern clear on her face. "Well, what do you think?"

"I think Merle's one classy guy, for one thing," he said sarcastically, "and second, I don't want to get on the wrong side of that guy if I have a choice, how 'bout you?"

"I think I don't want to know what happened to the bartender I'm replacing."

Walking out the front door and into the light of day, they were greeted by Bert. He had been waiting for them, chain-smoking to pass the time, a lit cigarette hanging out of his mouth while he leaned against a light post. Three more butts lay on the sidewalk near his feet, like fallen soldiers after a losing battle.

"So how was your meeting with my Boss?"

"It went fine," Jimmy said. "He said I'm with you."

Spitting onto the sidewalk, Bert stood up. "Figured as much, especially after everything I told him about you." He looked at Cindy. "How 'bout you, love, where you goin'?"

"Bartender, at the Dollar Bar," she told him.

Bert seemed disheartened, and Jimmy had to guess he was disappointed she wasn't going to one of the brothels.

"Oh, I guess that's good, too. All right then, come along and we'll get the both of you situated." He started walking then, the others following.

"Once we get you armed and stocked up there's a little mission I'm going on with a few of the men. Figure it'll be a good a place as any to see how you do in a pinch," Bert told Jimmy as he strolled down the sidewalk.

"Ready when you are, bro. Just say the word," Jimmy said, walking behind the larger man. All he knew was that it would be good to have his weapons back and if not the ones he came in with, then any weapons would do.

Walking back onto Main Street, the revelers already in full swing, Jimmy and Cindy prepared to become one of the townspeople of Stardust Cove.

Chapter 21

The small four-cylinder Honda sputtered down the lonely road, weaving in and out of the few derelict cars in the way. Most of the burned and broken vehicles had been pushed out of the way months ago, leaving a maze large enough for the small car to wind its way through. Henry watched some of the vehicles as they drove past. Some still had bodies propped up in the seats, desiccated corpses still wearing their gold watches and pearl necklaces. Now, all those possessions were nothing but trash. Even scavengers weren't interested in the once prized bling. Now food, water and weapons were the price of the land, life and death hanging by a string, the mystical Fates waiting in the wings, ready to cut any particular string at a moments notice.

In the driver's seat was a man named Wilson, a hard man with a perpetual scowl and a long scar that ran down the right side of his face. In the passenger seat was another man. His name was Lewis and he was the almost exact opposite of Wilson. Where Wilson was hard and strong, Lewis looked like he was about to break down and cry at any second. Lewis' complexion was a pale white that had Henry wondering if the man had ever ventured outdoors before this mission. Whenever Wilson would talk to him, Lewis would flinch slightly. Henry couldn't help but wonder how, out of all the guards to go with them, why Lewis had been picked.

Lewis carried a weapon in his lap, as did the rest of them; an old weather-beaten Thompson .45 machine gun. Watching the man, Henry wondered if he knew how to handle it or would just end up shooting himself or one of the others by mistake.

In the back seat, Henry watched the heads of the two security guards he'd been saddled with. Internally, Henry had already made up nicknames for the two men. Wilson was Laurel and Lewis was

Hardy. As the two men conversed with each other, the names made more and more sense. Wilson was by far the dominant man and Lewis bowed to Wilson's every whim.

Sitting with Henry in the back seat of the small car was Mary. She had her .38 sitting on her lap and she now carried an extra weapon, a lever-action, .32 caliber Winchester rifle. When she had received the weapon, she had surprised everyone by quickly working the lever to make sure the load was clear and then easily sliding in six cartridges. She ejected the first shell and then slid it in once again, making it now the last in line, now satisfied the rifle was in good working order. Mary had picked up a lot of skill with firearms over the months of wandering the deadlands and sometimes Henry forgot she wasn't the fragile woman he had first met on a lonely highway in the Midwest.

The rifle had a few scratches on its butt stock, but otherwise seemed to be almost new. She laid the rifle in-between her legs as the Honda drove over a rough patch in the road, barely noticing the jouncing. Her brown hair blew in the wind from her open window, the warm California air keeping her from sweating to profusely.

"Are we there yet?" Henry asked, sounding like a five-year-old pestering his father.

"Yeah, buddy, another minute or so. The gate for the base is around the next corner," Wilson snapped at him. "So shut the fuck up until we get there!"

"Gees, Wilson, I'm starting to get the feeling you don't like me," Henry jibed back.

Wilson only growled something unintelligible. He didn't like having two strangers with him on this mission, but he did what he was told and the Reverend told him to bring them.

Mary smiled at Henry's crack. "You know, Henry, you sounded a lot like Jimmy there for a minute."

He turned to look at her and his eyes were filled with loss for his missing friend. "Oh, yeah? Maybe I'm channeling him from somewhere. After all, we need a wiseass in the group and Jimmy's not here to bug Wilson, so I guess it falls to me to do it."

"I guess so," Mary answered, thinking of Jimmy fondly.

Henry gazed out the window again onto the road, the Honda cruising down the highway at a steady gait. Every now and then a blur would fly by, some unknown roamer staggering about. Henry had come up with names for the zombies almost a year ago. He had gotten tired of calling them zombies as it sounded like he was living in a bad Italian horror movie, so he had dubbed the zombies that liked to move about all the time, roaming around the countryside looking for fresh meat, roamers, and the ones who were idle, usually found in one's, two's and three's inside towns and cities, deaders.

It made him feel he had some small control of his life, and Mary and Jimmy, and later Cindy when she had joined their group, had also started to call the undead by their nicknames.

Another ghoulish face flew by the window and Henry leaned forward to look out the front windshield. There were more of the undead now, the Honda weaving in and out of the bodies like a new driver taking his test for his license, the zombies nothing but orange cones instead of rotting piles of pus.

As the Honda rounded a bend in the road, the front gate to the naval station came into view and Henry had his first sight of what had happened to the once great base.

The Honda continued on, dodging the few corpses still walking or lying unmoving, decomposing in the sun. The American flag that had once flown proudly at the main gate was now hanging by a thread, the material destroyed by the elements. As the Honda drove through the open gate, Henry thought the flag was a good metaphor for how the world was now; old and worn out.

The guard shack was nothing but rubble, the abandoned car that had run through it parked just a few feet away. Looking into the base, Henry could see the distinctive markings of fire. Blackened and burnt structures soaked up the sunlight like tunnels for the opening to Hell. Though disturbing, the sight was nothing new to Henry. He had seen so much destruction and carnage in the past year it came as second nature to him. Prone bodies littered the pavement, some nothing but dried tendons and bone. Before the base had fallen, the base personnel had put up a fight. Now all that remained of the battle were rotting skeletons bleached white in the sun.

Just inside the gate, Wilson slowed the Honda and then stopped it, slamming the transmission into park and opening the door like he was going into a market to grab some smokes and would return in a moment.

"Come on, let's get a move on. We're walking from here on in," the head guard said as he climbed out of his seat.

"What's wrong with driving around in the car? It's small, but it's still better than walking around exposed," Mary said as she watched Wilson stretching his arms and legs from the cramped confines of the car.

Lewis was climbing out of the car now, leaving his door open wide for Mary to get out, the Honda only being a two-door.

"Nothin' doin' doll. Just after that building over there, the roads are clogged with cars and shit. We need to walk from here. Sorry if it'll bother your dainty feet, though."

Mary ignored the comment and climbed out of the car, making sure her rifle was in front of her as she did. Henry said nothing, but did the same, Wilson watching him as he left the Honda. Henry saw him looking at him and spoke up.

"What's wrong, do I have a booger on my face?"

"Not funny, Watson. No, I was just thinking about how fucked up all this is. Why the hell do you have to come with me, anyway? I don't need you here and I don't want you here." Wilson spit.

"Look, pal, I don't want to be here either, but it's not like I have a choice, so what do you say we just try to make the best of it. You watch my back and I'll watch yours. Now which way to the research lab?"

Wilson gestured with his M-16. "It's this way, I think. Truth is; no one's been here from the town for over six months. Back then the base was crawling with dead ones so we stayed the hell out."

"So what's changed now?" Mary asked, scanning her surroundings. "There were a few deaders in the area and they were slowly walking towards the car, but the group had at least five minutes before the flesh eaters became a danger.

Wilson shrugged. "Not much actually, but about a month ago we sent a few scouts over here, and when they came back, they said the base was almost deserted. Guess most of the dead ones moved on when the food ran out."

Henry rubbed his chin, feeling the beginnings of a beard coming in. "Yeah, that's possible, but there's sure to be some still lingering around in the shadows and in some of the buildings. Best to stay sharp."

"I'll give the goddamn orders around here, Watson, I'm in charge!" Wilson snapped at him.

Holding his hands up in surrender, Henry pacified the man. "Fine, whatever, you're in charge."

"And don't you forget it," he grunted at Henry.

"Hey, Wilson, when your scouts came in here, did they actually go into the buildings or did they just walk around out on the streets?" Henry asked.

Wilson looked aggravated by the question, but he answered Henry. "Far as I know, they didn't go into the buildings. They said there wasn't enough time, but they did search most of the streets and there were almost no dead ones around. Does that answer your question?"

Henry shrugged. "Yeah, I guess so, but I've got to tell you, your Intel sucks. Those idiots didn't do anything but walk around where it was safe."

Wilson glared at Henry, already getting tired of his opinions, but Henry only smiled back, wearing the same wiseass grin Jimmy had always been so fond of using.

Wilson looked away and then glanced around at Lewis and Mary while he repositioned his two-way radio on his hip and waved them on. "All right, let's move out. From what we know, we think the research building is in the middle of the base. From here it's about a half mile walk or so."

"Oh, boy, a hike, just what I wanted to do today," Henry quipped, but he began walking. Wilson flashed him a dirty look, and then instead of commenting, he raised his rifle and shot a walking corpse that was getting a little to close for his liking. The body fell back like it had been slapped in the head, but from the distance separating it from them, Henry wasn't able to see how accurate Wilson's shot had been. In the long run, dead was dead, so it didn't really matter too much. The sun was high in the sky and in another hour or so would begin its descent, the full moon already peeking out from behind a few fluffy clouds.

Forming a line, with Mary and Henry at the rear, the four explorers moved out, while the wandering dead slowly followed.

Chapter 22

Outside in the streets of Stardust Cove, dusk was falling once again, while inside the Dollar Bar, Cindy moved out of the way of the thousandth grasping hand that was seeking her behind. She silently swore to herself that the next man to goose her would get her fist in his face.

The Dollar Bar was a seedy dive that would have been low on the list of well-to-do of California even before the collapse of civilization. The layout of the bar was set up in a triangle with the counter at the rear of the room and a jukebox off on the left side. In the recent past, the owner had built a small platform with a pole, and even now, two girls danced and gyrated to the music and the catcalls of the men and women in the room. Beer flowed freely, with other spirits among them, all more than enough to get the average customer drunk. Hard alcohol was in short supply and would cost any man a pretty penny if he cared to imbibe. The more popular was a homemade moonshine that would peel the paint off an automobile, but would get you a good buzz...if it didn't kill you.

Cindy checked the clock on the wall, sighing when she saw it was just going on eight in the evening. She had been there since early afternoon and her feet were killing her. Working in the bar reminded her too much of her past, when she had worked for her lecherous uncle in Pittsfield, Virginia. If it hadn't been for Jimmy and his friends, she would probably still be there, or worse, locked up after finally killing the dirty old man who was supposed to be her uncle, wanting to protect her, but instead wanted to be her boyfriend.

But then she recalled that the town of Pittsfield had been wiped from the map when the undead had breached the walls. So if she had actually still been there, she would have probably ended up as lunch for the hundreds of undead that had swarmed into the town, killing all who had lived there.

Still, she couldn't help but think of her lecherous uncle. Just thinking about the way he would look at her made her skin crawl and it was only her force of will that made her push the distasteful thoughts away and focus on the present.

Jimmy should be arriving soon, after finishing whatever mission he had gone on with Bert and some of the other guards. Dodging a pair of grasping hands, she moved through the crowd and slipped behind the bar. Finally able to take a breather, she leaned on the counter and sighed.

"Hang in there, Cindy, only four more hours and you can get off for the night," a heavy set woman in her late forties told her. The woman's name was Betsy and she was the owner of the Dollar Bar. Her husband had run the bar before her, but he hadn't been so lucky months before and had been attacked by a group of the undead when an unfortunate outbreak had happened in the town's limits. With nothing else to do and a little to old for the brothels, Betsy took over the bar and ran it with an iron hand. Though a hard woman, she was a fair woman, as well, and Cindy had taken an instant liking to the woman. In some ways Betsy reminded her of her dead mother.

"Thanks, Betsy. I've got to tell you, I can't believe this place. If one more guy grabs my ass, so help me..."

Betsy chuckled at that, trying to speak over the loud music and general din of the bar. "I know it's rough, honey, but if they think you're gonna sleep with them, then they usually give you a good tip. You just have to learn to humor them a little more."

Cindy nodded, knowing she was getting good advice, but praying she wouldn't be in the town long enough to need it. Inside the town's walls, money was still valued, Merle controlling the town's treasury. Though the money was basically worthless, it still made most people feel at least a little like things were still normal, and the use of money was far easier than a barter system.

Since leaving Merle's house earlier that day, Jimmy and Cindy had been separated and she had yet to see him again. With them away from one another, trying to plan an escape was impossible, so for the time being, Cindy had to accept her fate and work at the Dollar Bar.

A table at the side of the room called for more beers, and sighing, Cindy poured more drafts and started the ordeal of trying to reach the table without being either goosed or bumped. She was halfway there when a hairy arm reached out and wrapped itself around her, pulling her out of the aisle, the tray in her hand toppling off balance, and the contents falling to the floor with a crash that was lost in the cacophony of the room.

"Whoa, there sugar, I've been waitin' all night to get my hands around that sweet body o' yours," a burly man with a goatee brayed into her face. His breath smelled of old cigars and stale beer and she tried not to vomit into his face.

"Get your goddamn hands off of me!" Cindy snapped, trying to extricate herself from the massive arms.

"Whoa, there, Stew', I think you got a fighter there!" One of the other men sitting at the table yelled out, to great balls of laughter from the other three men who were with them.

Struggling uselessly in the man's arms, Cindy did her best to try to escape his clutches, but the man's arms were like steel tendons and would not give even an inch. His other hand crawled up her waist until he was cupping her right breast. Squeezing it roughly, she cried out in pain, knowing things just went from bad to worse. She tried to look over the heads of the other men and women in the bar, desperately hoping Betsy would see her predicament and help her, but she was hidden from view. She was on her own, as frightening as that seemed, but she had faced hordes of zombies with Henry, Mary and Jimmy at her side, and she'd be dammed if she was going to surrender to one stupid hick who thought he was God's gift to women.

"Come on, doll, there's a room in back where you, me, and my friends can get more comfortable," Stewie told her as he picked her up and started to carry her through the other patrons. Cindy kicked and tried to elbow the man in his side, but her blows were ineffective. She was just beginning to get a creeping feeling in her gut that she might not be able to get out of this one when Stew grunted and fell to his knees, dropping Cindy to the floor. She fell hard, but rolled with the motion, coming up in a crouch a moment later. Her face beamed with a smile when she saw what had saved her from being raped by Stewie and his friends.

Jimmy stood behind Stewie, his shotgun in his hand. He had used it like a bat and had clubbed Stewie on the back of the skull, knocking the man to his knees from the blow. But Stewie was large, almost twice the size of Jimmy, and with a roar of anger, he spun around to see what had hit him.

"Did you just hit me, little man?" Stewie screamed, and his face scrunched up in anger, spittle flying from his mouth. On top of everything, Stewie was more than a little drunk.

All at once the music stopped in the bar and the entire crowd turned as one to see what the commotion was about. A circle appeared around Jimmy and Stewie, all faces looking forward to a good fight.

Jimmy swallowed hard, his gulp almost a tangible thing as he looked up at the monster in front of him. Stewie had more than a foot in height and was almost twice as wide as Jimmy. While he stared upwards, his neck bent like he was looking at a high-wire act in the circus, Jimmy felt like David preparing to fight Goliath, only he was all out of slingshots.

"Uh, yeah, that was me. That's my girl you were about to take in the back and rape and I didn't want you to do that to her." Jimmy whispered, his heart beating so loud in his chest he thought it would explode. He was scared shit and not because he was a coward, but because only a man with no common sense wouldn't be. As he stared up at the behemoth in front of him, he desperately wracked his mind for what he was going to do to not get ripped to pieces by this brute.

"Would it help if I said: please don't?" Jimmy asked with a slight smile.

"No, it wouldn't and hitting me was the biggest mistake of your very short life, because I'm going to rip your head off and shit down your neck. Then I'm going to take your woman into the back and fuck her until she bleeds. What do you say about that?"

Jimmy took one step backward and looked up at the man with a smile. "Are you sure there's no way we can talk about this like two civilized men? Do we have to resort to violence to settle this? Come on, let me buy you a beer and we'll work this out."

Stewie started laughing, his bellow floating across the room. All eyes were watching him, like they were hypnotized in preparation of the slaughter to come. They'd seen this brute in action and knew there would be blood spilt in a matter of moments. A few were betting on the battle, but most wouldn't take the odds offered. Jimmy was done for, the man just didn't know it yet, was the general consensus.

Stewie raised his fists in the air, preparing to bring them down on Jimmy and pound the smaller man to the floor. But for just a moment, he paused and looked down at Jimmy. For some reason he couldn't figure out, Jimmy wasn't moving, he just stood there and stared up at him, his shotgun leveled in his hands. That's when Stewie realized he had made a tactical mistake in assuming Jimmy was just like the rest of the townsfolk and would battle him bare knuckles.

Instead of thinking he was going to be battling the smaller man with only fists and legs, Jimmy had decided he would stand no chance of surviving the encounter and had instead slowly brought the shotgun he had used for a club around until it was staring up into Stewie's chest.

Stewie blinked twice, not believing what he was seeing and Jimmy nodded that it was true, yes, it was going to happen. Then before Stewie could so much as yell, Jimmy squeezed the trigger, sending both barrels of death into Stewie's chest. The large man was thrown back like a mighty wind had blown into the bar and had attacked only him. A table was behind him, and Stewie landed on it hard, the legs snapping as his body crushed the wood into splinters. Blood sprayed the spectators standing behind him, splattering them with ribbons of red.

As for Stewie, he was dead before the table had settled under his body, his eyes staring up at the ceiling in disbelief at what had occurred. The bar was absolutely silent, no one believing what had just occurred. Then Jimmy looked around at the other faces and screamed at the top of his lungs, pumping the shotgun and sending fresh rounds into the weapon for emphasis.

"You people listen up. That big ape would have killed me and none of you were going to a damn thing to stop it. The moral of this story is, don't bring your fists to a gunfight. I'm with security now, so if you don't like it, then tough shit. Now get this piece of shit out of here and clean this place up!" The last words were directed at Stewie's friends who, with a heave and a groan, dragged the still form of their friend out the back door of the bar.

"This ain't right, Bert's gonna hear about this," one of the men said as he dragged Stewie away.

"We'll see, buddy, but until then do what the fuck I say or you'll be joining him," Jimmy snapped, gesturing to Stewie's bleeding corpse.

The man said nothing, lowering his head and concentrating on the grim job of removing his dead friend. Jimmy knew this wouldn't be the end of this. Surely, sooner or later one of the gorilla's friends would be looking for payback. That was okay, when they tried, he'd be ready.

Jimmy saw a blur out of the corner of his left eye and was preparing for an attack from an unknown assailant when Cindy jumped into his arms and gave him a big kiss.

"Talk about good timing, thanks, lover," she said, kissing him all over. "I missed you today."

"Evidently not that much if you were about to go into the back with the Incredible Hulk."

She pushed him jokingly. "Very funny, I know you saw what happened and that's why you came to my rescue. Thanks for that, I was really starting to get worried."

Around them the music had started up again and the beer and moonshine was starting to flow once again. In another five minutes the entire episode would be forgotten.

"Happy to help, I'm just glad I got here when I did," Jimmy told her.

Cindy took his hand and walked him to the bar where Betsy was watching, still holding an old shotgun in her hands. She had been about to jump over the bar and see what the gunshot had been about when she had heard Jimmy's voice and had then seen what had happened. After that, she had stayed behind the bar, prepared for whatever came next.

Cindy gestured to Betsy. "Jimmy, this is my boss, Betsy. She's good people."

Jimmy nodded and took the beer Betsy slid across the counter at him. Picking up the glass, he took a hardy sip, always keeping one eye on the glass mirror lining the wall behind the counter, just in case someone wanted revenge for Stewie's killing now instead of later.

"That was something else, son. Nobody's ever taken down Stewie before, not like that anyway," Betsy told Jimmy.

Jimmy shrugged. "That's me, always thinking outside the box."

Betsy grinned, and then moved away to help another patron refill his mug, then she returned back to Jimmy and Cindy.

"Nice place you have here, Betsy, is it always like this?" Jimmy asked after setting down his glass.

"Nah, this is a slow night," Betsy said with such a casual tone that Jimmy almost laughed out loud. That was when Bert walked into the bar, a large frown creasing his face. Jimmy turned to his new security boss and gave the man a brief nod of acknowledgement.

Bert gave Betsy a wink and picked up the glass of beer she had already placed in front of him, ready to drink deeply.

"That's why I love ya, Betsy, you always know what I'm thinkin'" Bert smiled as he took a drink. After finishing off half the glass in one swig, he slammed it onto the counter and looked at Jimmy. His frown was back and he didn't look happy.

"One of my men just told me there was a shooting in here and that you might have been involved. Is that true, Jimmy?"

Jimmy looked to Cindy and then Betsy, prepared to tell Bert what had happened and suffer the consequences if there were any to come, when Betsy spoke up first.

"Yeah, there was a shooting, Bert. It was with Stewie. The stupid asshole that he is, he tried his luck with the wrong person tonight and wound up eating dirt for his trouble. It was self-defense. I saw it all."

"Uh-huh, and who, pray tell, was the shooter?" Bert asked this question despite the fact he obviously knew who it was.

"It was me, Bert, I shot him. He was about to take Cindy into the back of the bar and rape her and I wasn't about to let that happen. When he called me out, I took him down."

Bert stared at Jimmy, Jimmy doing the same back. Neither man blinked until Bert finally grinned. "All right, Jimmy, fair enough. Plus, if what Betsy here says ain't true, I'll find out soon enough. Just 'cause you're with my team doesn't give you the right to go around shooting people, no matter how much they might deserve it. But if you had to shoot someone, I can't imagine a better asshole to do it to. Stewie was a real jerk, that was for sure."

"Amen," a few patrons who had overheard the conversation said.

"It's the truth, all you have to do is ask," Cindy said defiantly. "He saved me." She gave Jimmy a big kiss on the cheek again and Jimmy blushed.

Putting the weapon back under the counter, Betsy slapped her hands together to get Cindy's attention over the din of the room. "All right, sugar, playtimes over. Back to work. You've still got a few more hours to go and there's money to be made."

Cindy did as she was told, flashing Jimmy one more smile and then nodding to Bert. Then she moved off into the middle of the room to take some orders and see that everything was getting back to normal. As she walked by the broken table Stewie had landed on, she slowed and watched the seventeen year old girl that was washing the floor of blood and tossing sawdust on any of the heavier spots. The girl reminded Cindy of herself and she placed her hand on her shoulder. The girl looked up and smiled slightly, then got back to work. Cindy let her do her job and focused on hers.

Jimmy finished his beer and patted Bert on the arm to get his attention.

"Listen, thanks for understanding. If there had been any other way..."

"Yeah, I know, sometimes a man has to do things he doesn't like. At least if he wants to stay alive," Bert said with an almost poetic rhythm.

"Look, if you're done with me for the day, I want to go take a shower and rest up until I have to come back here and get Cindy."

"Sure, you did a good job today, Jimmy. You should work out fine here." Bert told him as he took another beer from Betsy. He was done for the night and was planning on getting good and drunk.

"Thanks, that's good to know," Jimmy answered back, pushed off from the counter, and then worked his way through the crowd of revelers, heading out of the bar and into the warm night.

The smell of wood smoke was hanging on the wind still from some wildfires that had been burning less than a week ago in Lawson valley and the surrounding areas of Jumal and Rancho Bernado. One of the other guards had filled him in, telling him all about how with the Santa Ana winds blowing in full force and no fire firefighters around anymore to try and slow the flames, the conflagration had burned across thousands of acres until finally dying out on their own. Almost all of Malibu was now nothing but ash. Burnt and blasted buildings littered the landscape like a picture from a bombed London back in World War 2.

Jimmy was just glad the town he had ended up in was on the coast and fire was a less dangerous foe than the undead milling about the stone walls.

That had been his mission today.

He, Bert and three other men had driven out of the town and into the blackened landscape, looking for anything useful. Charred corpses had been everywhere and the charnel house smell had been overwhelming at times. In the end, there hadn't been much to salvage, the blighted terrain all but ash and wreckage.

But as Bert had said on the way back to the town: "At least now we know that there's nothing left here we can use and we can just write all of this area off as useless."

Jimmy had agreed with the larger man. A solemn mood had hung over them all as they had driven back empty handed. Bert and the others had hoped that there might have been at least some survivors. Human survivors. In the past few months it had been harder and harder to find other live humans, the fire now sealing off a large part of California from the town. They were slowly becoming an oasis surrounded by a sea of the undead with the water at their backs; the town of Sunset Bay the only other survivors.

Bert had started to share a few things unknown to the rest of the town with Jimmy, how in a few more months, supplies would become harder to find as they slowly stripped the surrounding area clean. One of the few places they had not gone, though they knew there were supplies there, was the naval base a few miles away to the west.

Jimmy had asked him why they hadn't gone there and Bert's visage had grown hard while he stared out the window of the transport.

"Because there's nothing there but death. Every building is filled with the dead ones. To go there would be utter suicide. That's why we steer clear of the place."

While Jimmy walked through the warm night air to his room to shower and then rest for a few hours, he thought of that base and the army of the undead hidden within its blasted walls, and said a silent prayer that Bert or Merle wouldn't be foolhardy enough in their desperation to want to go there.

He had known places like that before on his travels with Henry and the others and knew to go into a place like that would be almost certain death.

Reaching his building, he put thoughts of the base out of his mind and focused on the shower he would be enjoying in a few minutes. While overhead, high in the night sky, the full moon looked down on him and the town as the revelers partied long into the night.

Chapter 23

The same full moon that was looking down on Jimmy was also watching over Henry and Mary. It had taken another two hours to make their way through the shattered remains of the naval base, not all of it pleasant.

Before they had made it a thousand feet into the base, more than twenty ghouls had come out of hiding and had sought to attack the foursome. Wilson, never one to shy away from a fight, or his orders, ordered the four of them to lay down a line of fire, and within one minute, all the zombies were horizontal, some of them still twitching or trying to crawl over their fallen brethren despite their shattered kneecaps or just plain missing legs.

Wilson had picked up a heavy sign post, once used to identify the street they were on, and had used it to systematically bash in the heads of any of the undead survivors. Ten minutes later, breathing heavily, he dropped the post and walked back to the others.

"See? What did I tell you, piece of cake," he gasped from his exertions. His boots were covered in gore, despite the fact he had taken care not to get covered in too much blood and bits of brain matter.

"Piece of cake?" Henry said. "Of course it was. There were only twenty of them and four of us, all having serious firepower at our disposal. But what if there's more inside some of these buildings? If they get to close, then using our weapons won't be an option. Maybe we should just pack this mission in and head back," he finished, trying to reason with Wilson.

Wilson's visage grew dark as he stared at Henry and Mary. Lewis seemed to take a step back, not wanting to receive any of his leader's wrath. Wilson was a man who could bring great misery down on his underlings if he saw fit and though he wanted to tell Henry to be quiet and just do as he was told, he was too scared to say anything with Wilson within earshot.

"Go back? You coward. I don't know why the fuck I had to bring you with me, but I'll tell you this. I always succeed on my missions. We'll find that cure and we'll bring it back or we'll die trying." He turned then, with his back to Henry and started forward, kicking a decapitated head out of his way. "Now, come on, it's getting dark and I want to be out of here before it's full night."

Henry turned to Mary and frowned. "Die trying, he says. That's what I'm afraid of. Look, Mary, stay sharp, I'm starting to get a real bad feeling about this place and I don't want this to be our tomb, okay?"

"I hear you, Henry. I've got the same feeling myself. It's like there's something itching at you just below the surface, but I can't put my finger on it."

"Exactly, so stay triple sharp, because I think things are gonna get worse before they get better."

"Will you two idiots hurry the hell up!" Wilson yelled from fifteen feet away. He wasn't used to working with civilians and he was even more surly than usual.

Henry sighed and picked up his pace, Mary next to him. Lewis was off to the right of Wilson, walking wide to make sure nothing came at the group from one of the open doorways of the nearby buildings.

Walking through the abandoned base gave Henry a feeling of being in a ghost town. Papers and debris blew everywhere, catching in wire fences and under tires of derelict vehicles. Dried and desiccated corpses littered the streets and sidewalks, some of them with bullet holes in different parts of their bodies.

"There was a fight here once upon a time," Henry said, leaning over and checking a corpse. It had been a woman once, the tattered dress and moldy purse near the body the only identifiable traits to tell him it was once female.

The corpse had a large gunshot wound to the chest, an even wider one on her back. She had died hard was the only thing Henry could discern from the tableaux below him and he muttered a silent pray for the woman and the thousands of others before her.

The barracks came next on their journey and the signs of a struggle were even more predominant here than in the other streets they had passed through. Nearly every window was shattered, bodies hanging out windows and scattered around the buildings. One poor soul had died and had caught his leg in a wire or rope. His corpse now swung back and forth from the roof, like a haunted trapeze show in a circus of the damned. A large pile of bodies, looking like a macabre pyramid was set up off to the side of the road. The bodies had been set on fire a long time ago, the charred remains nothing but blackened ash with bits of scaled bone peeking through.

A head of one of the bodies had survived the incineration and hung over the rest of the pile, balancing precariously on a few chipped bones, looking for all purposes like a discarded child's doll. As the foursome walked by the pile, a brisk wind caused the bodies to shift and the head fell off its perch to roll across the road and stop at Henry's boot.

Picking up the skull, Henry felt like Hamlet, but decided this wasn't the time for scholarly pursuits and tossed the skull back toward the pile. The head rolled and bounced like a warped soccer ball until it disappeared into the ash.

No one spoke, the scene weighing heavily over all of them. The world was nothing but death nowadays, and though they weren't dead yet, inevitably they were all headed in the same direction. If a zombie didn't kill them, then eventually time would do the deed for the undead ghouls.

Proceeding through the streets, more zombies began popping out of their hiding places. As they moved through the abandoned cars, they were constantly on the lookout for any hidden menaces. Henry had one eye on his surroundings and his other one on Lewis. The man was growing increasingly erratic, despite Wilson trying to beat some courage into the man. It was almost to the point that Henry was going to talk to Wilson about it, but that discussion was taken out of his hand when a large group of undead came around the corner and charged at the foursome. Lewis had been closest to the horde, and though he raised the Thompson and began firing, his aim wasn't focused properly, and almost none of his shots were head shots. His bullets went through leathery skin, causing a few ghouls to step back from the blows, but soon they were moving forward again like the incident had never occurred.

The others began strafing the dead, but with Lewis in the middle, they had to pull their shots or risk killing one of their own.

"Dammit, Lewis, get the fuck out of the way or so help me I'll shoot through you!" Wilson yelled at the man, but Lewis was hearing none of it. His cries of fright carried across the din of weapon's fire while the man desperately tried to keep the undead at bay.

Mary fired her rifle repeatedly, the Winchester growing hot from continuous fire. Spent casings littered the ground below her feet, and like a seasoned hunter, she quickly ejected the last round and started to reload while Henry covered her.

Henry fired again and again, but he already knew what was coming. He had seen it too many times before and every time only sickened him a little more.

A zombie was struck in the shoulder just in front of Lewis and it fell to the pavement, writhing for a minute. Lewis didn't see the dead creature roll onto its stomach and start to crawl on its hands and knees toward him. Lewis' attention was focused above the waist as he cycled the Thompson dry and then quickly tried to reload before becoming overwhelmed.

That was when the crawling zombie reached him, and in one fluid motion, reached up and sank its rotten teeth into his calf. Lewis screamed in surprise and pain and fell to the ground, his weapon clattering away to land near another zombie. By coincidence this corpse was dressed in the dried, bloodied rags of a soldier and for just a heartbeat, the pale white face looked down at the weapon as if it recognized what it was.

Henry stared amazed as the ghoul picked up the weapon and held it in his hands. But whatever remembrance from a past life ended there. The dead soldier merely swung the Thompson like a club, not understanding the mechanics of it.

Henry didn't wait for the creature to get another chance to remember something from its past life and sent a spray of death at its face that knocked it over, sending the newly acquired weapon spinning from its hands to become lost under a dozen shuffling feet.

Lewis flailed on the ground, trying to escape the teeth and clasping hands on his leg, but other ghouls soon caught him and held him in place as teeth and nails dug into his soft flesh.

Screaming with pain, Lewis called out for help, but the others were occupied keeping the line of undead at bay.

Slowly, they gained the upper ground, their weapons proving to be the master of the battle.

Before Henry or Mary realized it, the battle was over, twitching corpses lying on the ground, some still active, but unable to cause any real threat.

Wilson walked over to Lewis and shot the zombies on top of him, eradicating them like vermin, then he looked down on the bloodied man. He was still alive, though he had multiple bites and tears across his body. His bright red blood pooled under him, causing Wilson to take a step back, not wanting to get his boots covered with any more gore than they already were.

"Help me, please," Lewis begged, spitting blood in a bubbly froth from his mouth.

Wilson shook his head. "Sorry, Lewis, but you're beyond help. There's only one thing I can do for you," the man said flatly, aiming his M-16 at Lewis' head.

"No, don't do it, I'll be all right, I'll..." Lewis screamed; his hands going up to block his head like that alone would stop a bullet to the brain.

Wilson never hesitated, sending two rounds through Lewis' hands and into the top of the man's head. Lewis jerked from the impacts, one of the rounds exiting down and out of his chin. Blood spurted everywhere and Wilson danced backward with amazing grace to avoid becoming saturated by the geyser.

As quick as it had started, the blood flow ceased, only a small amount of spittle still seeping out of the wounds.

"Damn, man, those fucking head wounds," Wilson said while walking back to Henry and Mary. He shot a few zombies on his way, making sure they were down.

Henry studied the man's face, wondering if there was any remorse there at all for having to kill one of his own men. If Wilson knew what he was thinking, he didn't say, but then he stopped walking in front of Henry and Mary and ejected his clip, slamming in a new one from a small munitions bag he carried over one shoulder.

"If you're expecting me to say something, then you can forget it. We all know what would have happened if we let him live. If I hadn't killed him, then there would just be one more of them to deal with later."

"I know that. But it's just...the way you did it. Christ, Wilson, you didn't even give the man a chance to say his last words," Henry said softly. While Henry was a hard man, never having a problem with doing what had to be done, whether that was killing someone or not, he still had compassion and mercy, something that was slowly dwindling away to nothing in the heart of the deadlands. If it had been up to him, he would have given Lewis a few more seconds, maybe a minute or two to say his peace, perhaps give a message to pass on to loved ones. It would have risked nothing and been the humane thing to do.

"So what if I didn't? Shit, Watson, this isn't day camp out here, you know. He was bit. And when you're bit, you're dead."

"But what about this cure we're supposed to find? Couldn't that have saved him?" Mary asked hopefully.

"A cure? Christ, if you believe that then you're more naïve than your friend here," he said to Mary, gesturing to Henry with the barrel of his M-16

"Then you don't believe there's a cure for the plague in one of these buildings? Then why the hell are we out here?" Henry asked suspiciously.

"We're out here because I was ordered to, that's why. It doesn't matter what I believe. If I'm told to do something, then I do it. That's what makes an army strong. If every friggin' soldier wanted to debate an order he was given than where the hell would any of us be? No, I was told to come here and we're here. So let's move out before any more of these dead bastards show up."

Henry wanted to debate the subject more, but Wilson started moving again. Mary looked to Henry for advice and he shrugged, realizing that for the moment the only thing they could do was continue on.

While Henry walked behind Wilson, he debated if he should shoot the man in the back and then make his way out of the base with Mary. He actually raised the weapon and his hand hovered over the trigger, but at the last moment he stopped. Two reasons floated to the forefront of his mind. One was he was a lot of things in the new world he had been thrown into, but a cold blooded killer wasn't one of them, and two, what if there really was a cure somewhere in a research building on this base? Just waiting for someone to find it and dispense it to the survivors. Though slim, the chance was worth the risk, if not for him, then for the rest of humankind that would come behind him after he was gone. It could be his legacy to the world if he was one of the men to find the valuable prize.

Lowering his weapon, he stepped over a fallen body and moved further into the streets of the base. Mary followed, her eyes constantly searching for attackers. With the initial horde taken down, there were only sporadic threats quickly taken down without incident.

As the three survivors moved through the base, passing the large mess hall and into the complex of buildings set aside for education and research, their spirits were high.

They had made it this far with only losing one of their number, and though tragic, was still a feat on its own.

Twenty minutes later, Wilson slowed to a stop in front of a large brick building with blackened red bricks on its façade and shattered windows.

"I think this is it," he stated cautiously, picking his way through the wreckage blocking the door.

"What makes you think that?" Henry asked, his eyes scanning the building for anything that would indicate its use before the destruction of the base.

Wilson leaned over and picked up a battered metal sign. There was a lighter spot on the bricks from where the sign had fallen above his head, a few of the bricks actually having fallen from the wall, thanks to gunshots that had weakened the mortar holding them in place.

"This is why," Wilson said and tossed the sign at Henry's feet. The sign skittered across the pavement and Henry used his boot to stop its momentum. There were faded words in black on a white backing that read: Research and Development, Bldg. 72.

“Fair enough,” Henry grunted, Wilson actually flashing a wan smile at Henry, pleased at being right.

Wilson stepped into the shadows of the main lobby inside the building, pulling a large military flashlight he’d carried connected to his waistband off its clip to illuminate the darkened corners of the room for any signs of trouble. An ornate oak and granite counter-like desk stood in the middle of the room, piles of debris and dust covering its surface.

With Mary right behind him, Henry stepped into the lobby, as well, whistling softly at the sight that greeted him. At one time there had been quite a battle for survival in the large lobby. Desiccated body parts and skeletonized corpses littered the floor, not to mention dozens of black spots; where dried blood had turned to a fine powder to cover large expanses of tile, seeping into the grout lines that connected each tile to the other.

Bullet holes pockmarked the ceiling tiles and continued down the walls. Whoever had tried to make a last stand here had not given their lives up easily.

Wilson cleared his throat at the far end of the lobby, impatient to continue exploring. Henry only nodded at the sound, understanding and both he and Mary crossed the open area until they were with Wilson once again.

Wilson had spent his time inspecting the large board that had listed all the names of the research companies that had once been housed in the building. His finger moved from name to name, some of the letters of words now collecting on the floor like sawdust, and he nodded energetically as he saw the ones that looked the most promising.

Looking over his shoulder, Henry did the same. Though he wasn’t happy to be in the base, if he wanted to leave soon, then the best chance would be to find what they were looking for so they could all go.

Satisfied where he wanted to go, Wilson stepped back from the board. “All right, you two, we need to go to the third and fourth floors. From what the board says, that should be where the cure is located.”

“Yeah, if it’s really here and not a figment of your Reverend’s imagination,” Henry told him unhappily.

Wilson ground his teeth angrily and was about to retort back, when he heard a sound coming from the front of the lobby. All three warriors turned as one to see more of the undead filing through the shattered glass doors.

"Shit, more of them," Wilson spit, bringing his M-16 to bear so he could begin firing, but Henry held the man's arm and pulled him toward the stairway that led to the upper floors.

"No, wait, don't waste the ammo. Let's just go and we'll find another way out of here when we leave."

Wilson seemed to hesitate, like he wanted to just kill as many of the undead as he could find, but reason won out and the man assented, lowering his rifle and double-timing after Henry and Mary.

Once through the stairwell door, Mary stopped long enough to pick up a stray piece of wood lying on the stairs. Shoving it through the handle, the wood made a half-ass lock that should be more than enough to stop the walking corpses from entering the stairwell after them.

"There, that should hold them for a while," she said proudly in the beam of Henry's flashlight. The stairwell was almost pitch black and without the beams from the flashlights, they would have been helpless if there had been a threat hiding in the stairwell.

"Good job, Mary, now just pray we don't have to come this way again," Henry told her, and then started to move up the stairs.

Mary frowned a little, her great idea speared through the heart by Henry's statement. "Well, one thing at a time, why don't we," she told him, following the two men upward around the spiraling stairs.

Wilson stopped at the first floor door and placed his ear to the metal. "Watson, come here and listen, will ya?" He asked, with a wave of his hand. Henry did as requested, and when he placed his own ear against the cool metal of the door, he heard the distinctive sounds of groaning mixed with more guttural, animal sounds.

Removing his ear carefully, he locked his jaw. "I don't think we want to see what's behind door number one, Bob," he told Wilson, his Let's Make A Deal joke going right over the man's head.

"Very funny, looks like they're in the building, too, maybe they've been in here all along," Wilson said.

"Maybe, if they are, do you want to call this off?" Henry asked hopefully.

"No way, Watson, I told you before, I do what I'm told and we'll get the cure or die trying, now come on, it's already late." Then he turned his back on Henry and started up to the next floor.

"I wish he'd stop saying that, it's like he's on some kind of friggin' holy war." Henry said and looked to Mary for support, but she only shrugged, not really having an opinion on the subject.

"Well, let's go, I wouldn't want to keep the man waiting," Henry told her. She nodded slightly and patted his arm, then with a smile of support, headed up the stairs after Wilson. Henry hovered at the door for another moment, listening to the moans coming from the other side, and then something slammed against the door, making a dull thump. Though hardened to violence, in the quiet solitude of the stairwell the noise still made him jump slightly.

Feeling slightly embarrassed, like a person does when they accidentally fall up the stairs, but relieved that no one was around to witness it, he headed upwards after the others, leaving the moaning behind.

Chapter 24

Wilson stopped climbing the stairs when he reached the third floor landing. The fire door leading into the main floor was slightly askew, at least allowing for easy access onto the floor.

Henry and Mary stood behind the soldier, with their breathing shallow in their chests for fear of disturbing something either dead or alive on the darkened floor.

"All right, on three," Wilson said while he prepared to open the door and charge onto the floor. Henry nodded, and with a quick look to Mary to make sure she was prepared, Wilson counted down to one and pulled the door open, running inside at full speed.

Though his flashlight was in front of him and some sparse lines of moonlight seeped in through shattered skylights that lined the hallway, Wilson missed the prone corpse lying on the floor at his feet. Like stepping on a banana, the man went head first onto the dust covered carpeting, a hundred balls of dust filling the air like a whirlwind.

Coughing and sputtering, spitting dust from his mouth, and desperately trying to see through the haze, he didn't see the torso of the zombie crawling toward him. The creature had no legs, only its arms dragging it forward. Half its neck and face had been eaten away and a hundred flies and maggots infested its carcass as it dragged itself inevitably along the faded red carpeting.

Unaware of the danger he was in, Wilson struggled to wipe his face clean, while Henry jogged up behind him. Just as the torso zombie was about to sink its rotting teeth into Wilson's outstretched arm, Henry stepped over the prone soldier and brought his panga down in a gut-chopping blow that severed the head from the ghoul's shoulders and caused the head to roll away like a child's kickball that has rolled away from its owner on the playground.

Finally clearing his vision, Wilson looked down the open neck wound of the headless corpse and jumped back with a frightened yelp.

Henry chuckled softly, not wanting to antagonize the man, but still finding amusement in the scene.

"Nice one, Rambo, maybe next time you'll watch where you're going," he told Wilson and reached down to help the man back to a standing position.

"Holy shit, that fucker would have bit me for sure. If you hadn't done what you just did, well, I don't even want to think about it." His countenance softened slightly. "Thanks, Henry, I mean it. Maybe I was wrong about you."

Henry didn't let it slip that the man had just called him by his first name for a change instead of his last. Perhaps he was being authentic.

Henry nodded slightly, as well, acknowledging the round-a bout complement. "Yeah, maybe you were. So come on, let's get moving." He glanced at Mary. "Mary, we okay back there? Any problems?"

She shook her head no. She was still in the doorway of the fire door, her ear cocked to hear anything amiss in the stairwell. "No, we're good; the wood seems to be holding the door in place down there, no unwanted guests."

"Yet," he grunted in reply.

"Yet," she answered back and stepped into the wide hallway to catch up to the two men. When she arrived aside them, she stopped moving and cocked her head as if she was listening to something. Henry was about to ask her what was wrong when she held up her finger to quiet him.

"Shhh, I hear something, it sounds like...music."

"Music, up here? Shit, this place is as dead as it gets, don't see how you could hear anything but echoes," Wilson said disapprovingly.

"Well, shut up and listen for a second and you'll hear it, too," she snapped at him. Wilson was about to answer back when for that brief instance of silence he picked up the faint sound of music. All three stood perfectly still, listening. It was an old song, from the sixties. It sounded like some kind of waltz or serenade.

"Come on, I think it's coming from down here," Henry said, taking the lead. Wilson came in second and Mary took up the rear. All three moved slowly across the darkened hallway, their flashlight beams bouncing off the walls and ceiling.

Eventually, they reached the last door on the floor. The entire floor had a large hallway that went up the middle with doors on both sides, the layout much like a ladder. It was the last door on the left that seemed to call to them, like the sirens of the ocean pulling sailors to their doom on the rocks of the shore.

Mary stopped at the door and listened once again. After a full minute, with the two men behind her growing impatient, she gestured to the door.

"This is it. This is where the music is coming from."

Henry and Wilson listened carefully for another moment and the distinct melody could be heard more easily now that they were closer. It sounded hollow and far away, but there nonetheless.

"I'm going in, I want to see what's in there," Mary said while reaching for the handle to the door.

"Dammit, wait a second, Mary," Henry told her. "We have no idea if there's a dozen men with guns waiting to shoot the first person to open that door or if there's a shitload of deaders waiting to rip out our throats. Wait a second so we can make a solid plan that won't get us all killed."

"Fine, what's the plan, chief?" Mary asked, imitating Jimmy.

He frowned slightly at the jibe, but then wiped his face clean of emotion. Now was not the time for petty squabbles. Though Henry had always been the defacto leader of the companions, Jimmy, Mary and Cindy, deferring to him, they still almost always made decisions by way of a democracy and only fell back to listening to Henry without question when debate wasn't an option.

Evidently, Mary felt this was one of the latter times and though she hesitated, it was clear she wanted to just go inside and see what the grand mystery was.

"All right, Wilson, when I kick open the door, you go right and I'll take the left. Mary, you take the middle. If there's anything in there, we'll blow it to hell before it knows what hit it," Henry told them both.

Wilson answered him by bringing up the M-16 and aiming it at the door;

Mary doing the same with her Winchester. Sucking in a deep breath, Henry brought up his shotgun and then kicked the door in with his left foot so hard, the interior handle lodged in the wall inside the room.

All three rushed in, one after the other, the door limiting their attack, but instead of finding a horde of zombies, cannibals or violent humans, there was nothing but an empty waiting room, complete with a dead secretary leaning over her desk.

All three let out the breaths they hadn't been aware they were holding and studied the room. The music was still playing, and Mary realized it was filtering through the thin wooden door at the back of the waiting room.

With the other two behind her, she made her way to the door and cautiously opened it, after a brief nod from Henry telling her to go ahead, of course.

The door creaked on hinges that could use a good lubricant, but other than that, all was silent. Wilson was admiring the corpse of the secretary, the body nothing more than dried skin wrapped around a skeleton. He reached over the body and picked up a framed photograph that had fallen off the desk and onto the floor. The picture was of a black haired woman with another man, perhaps a husband or boyfriend. They were standing on a street corner and the Hollywood sign could be seen in the distance behind them. Wilson stared at the picture, lost in thought, then he came back to reality and gently placed the picture back on the desk, as if he wanted the corpse to be able to see it for all eternity as she lay rotting in the waiting room.

"Wilson, come in here, you might want to see this," Henry called from the other room, having entered the room behind Mary.

Wilson stood up and cleared his face of any emotion, looked away from the corpse, and then stepped through the doorway.

Mary was standing by the only window in the small office, this particular pane of glass still in one piece. The wan light from the moon cast its luminance down onto her face, making her look even more beautiful than usual. When he caught Henry looking at him oddly, he quickly looked down at his feet and cleared his throat. "Um, you called? Find something?"

Mary picked up the cassette radio in her hand, the cassette still playing. At first, Wilson didn't understand why the radio could still be playing. There were no radio stations broadcasting and the batteries should have gone dead long ago. Then Mary turned the radio over and showed Wilson the top of it. There were two black panels with lines going through them.

"This is a solar collector. This radio must get charged everyday when the sun comes up and then it must play until it dies again," she said. And to back up her assumption, the cassette was already beginning to run down, the music becoming garbled. Mary flicked the off switch, turning the radio off once and for all. Then she set it back down on the windowsill.

"Wow, that's a little creepy, to think its been playing every night for at least a year," Henry said while staring at the small radio.

"Well, that's all great and everything, but if that's all you found in here then let's move out and finish checking this floor. We still have the fourth floor to recce if there's nothing around here," Wilson said. Then he turned and walked back out into the waiting room, this time not even noticing the dead secretary.

Henry looked at Mary with a thoughtful expression on his face and she smiled slightly at him.

"You know, it's funny," she said.

"Oh, how so?" Henry asked.

"Well, it's funny to think that no matter what, even if every human is wiped out one day, all this shit will still be here, just waiting for someone else to come and pick up where we left off." She looked down, checking for any stains on her boots. "That is, if you believe in aliens and stuff."

He chuckled. "Aliens? Honey, we live in a world where the dead come back to life and want to eat us. Aliens don't seem that far a stretch. Come on; let's get going, the sooner we're done here the better."

She nodded and the two walked out of the room, the radio silent forever. As an afterthought, Mary closed the door again, feeling like she was closing the door of a crypt. Then with Wilson at the main door, they all stepped back out into the hallway to continue the search for the laboratory that, hopefully, actually existed and could be found with a cure for the plague.

* * *

The next two hours passed slowly with the three warriors finishing their search of the third floor and then moving up to the fourth. The fourth floor was in about the same condition as the others, stained carpeting and a few mummified bodies lying about.

There was one thing different about this floor, however, compared to the ones before it. This floor had a large desk in the main hall and a secured metal door with a vacuum seal around its frame. The door would have been a formidable opponent, probably only explosives managing them access past its confines, but for the fact that the door was open wide, the darkness beyond beckoning like a cave with a dragon waiting for the knight to slay it. All three stood in front of the door, each knowing what the next move would be.

To enter into the black abyss and see what they could find.

Wilson was in the lead once again, Henry and Mary behind him. This time the man showed more caution, waving his flashlight back and forth like a blind man with his cane. He wasn't about to trip over a hidden object twice in one day.

The atmosphere was one of desolation, the lack of light an oppressive, tangible thing. There were no skylights overhead on this floor which was odd. All the other floors had a complex design of mirrored steel tubes inside the ceiling that reflected light from the openings on the outside of the building, thereby illuminating the room with natural light despite the fact the floors were not on the utmost top of the building, plus the odd design of the building's architecture.

The building itself was made up so that from the outside, the roof resembled a stairway, thereby allowing the floor below the one above it to receive natural light from the skylights.

Now they were on the top floor and it was even odder that the builders of the building had not taken into account the natural light that would easily be accessed by skylights. Unless the original architects had known something the three searchers did not.

That the top floor was exclusively dedicated to research of biological agents, viruses, and bacteria and therefore would need to be sealed off entirely from the outside world. What an irony if there had been a release of a dangerous contagion and it had managed to escape the lab because of a broken skylight.

But none of the three warriors knew any of this, though Henry had seen enough movies to know what a lab and containment zone was.

Walking softly, their boots making no noise on the dusty tile, they moved deeper into the lab complex. This floor was made up into only a few rooms, each with its own sealed door.

"All the doors are open," Mary said as she looked down the open frames until her light petered out in the murky depths.

"Yeah, it's like everyone just got up and left, but didn't care about closing up behind them," Wilson said, his voice echoing in the darkness.

"You think there are any viruses or stuff that could kill us in here?" Mary asked, her eyes scanning the darkness.

"Doubt it," Henry said. "Whatever would have been in here should be long dead. Still, best not to touch anything if you don't have to."

Both Wilson and Mary agreed; the advice sound.

"Well, let's see what we can find. The cure's got to be around here somewhere," Wilson said and started moving forward.

The three moved slowly, expecting something to jump out of the dark at any moment. Still, all was quiet.

By the time they reached one of the inner labs, they all stopped and looked around. This lab was slightly different than the others. For one thing, this lab contained dozens of test tubes in holders on three large steel tables. Bunsen burners stood unlit and cold underneath many of the vials and papers were scattered everywhere. But it was what was found at the far end of the room that told the three of them they were in the right place. There were large rectangular tanks the size of coffins and inside each one was a zombie. Ten tanks in all lined the wall, stacked five high and dozens of tubes went in and out of the multiple holes that lined the side of the tanks. Rubber gaskets kept the tubes from leaking out any of the precious fluid that was still inside the tanks.

"Oh my God, I don't believe it," Mary gasped as she stared at the tanks.

It was what was in the tanks that made her so shocked. In each tank was a zombie, still active, though severely deteriorated. The creatures barely had the power to move, let alone somehow attack Henry and the others from inside their glass prisons. They had not fed in almost a year, trapped in the tanks like fish in a dentist's waiting room.

Henry walked over to one of the tanks and stared at the grotesque mockery of a human being. Its face was all but melted off, its eyes long gone. Its white teeth shone in the glare of the flashlight and its nails could be seen on its skeletal hands, long and dirty, the ultimate customer in need of a good manicure.

"Jesus Christ, they must have been using these guys for experiments, trying to see if they could find a way to reverse the plague or something," Henry said while he studied the ghoul.

Wilson's face perked up with hope. "This must be the place, then, we found it! This is where the cure is! All we have to do is find it," he uttered excitedly, running over to one of the tables and starting to root through the piles of paperwork.

Henry heard him, but paid him no mind, concentrating on staring at the macabre face floating in the tank. He moved from that one to another above it, this one containing a smaller form, a child or perhaps an older person at one time before the plague had infected them. This one still miraculously had eyes and they followed Henry's movements as he moved around the room.

"It's so horrible, how could they do that to people?" Mary asked, moving closer to Henry. Though the scene was utterly horrible, she still found it hard to look away from the grotesque shapes.

He shrugged. "They were probably already dead and had returned again before they did this to them, Mary."

"Yes, but do you think they feel pain? To be trapped in there for so much time with no one and nothing but the darkness. It's horrible."

While the two were talking, Wilson was hard at work searching for something, anything, which could be considered a cure. So far he had been out of luck. All the test tubes were empty; whatever chemical contained inside them long dried up and evaporated. As for the papers, he had no way of ever deducing what they could mean. There were complex formulas and diagrams, some with drawings of the anatomy of male and females, arrows pointing to sections of the brain and organs. As he continued ransacking the place, his nervousness began to grow. To come this far only to find nothing.

And what about the Reverend? Though he was a man of God, he was far from forgiving. He would not be pleased with Wilson when he returned empty handed.

And Wilson knew damn well, he didn't want to end up inside the wire cage on the podium with a ghoul ready to eat his face off for his failure.

As he tore the place apart, tossing paper into the air and knocking items to the floor in his frustration, Henry and Mary ignored him. The two companions seemed almost mystified by the tanks with the decomposing bodies in them. Wilson had no idea why, and frankly, he didn't care.

Wilson had reached a side door at the far end of the lab and opened it, not even considering there could be something on the opposite side that might want to attack him.

The door swung wide and before Wilson could react, a rotting, jelly-like corpse lunged out of the darkness to wrap itself around his neck.

He screamed from surprise, gagging on the decayed smell of death. The meat on this particular corpse had dried up long ago, internal organs all but dust. What exactly was keeping it moving was a mystery, a puzzle one the scientists had struggled with until he and the others were all wiped out.

The rotting corpse still wore its lab coat; the material now stained maroon with bits of black and gobbets of dried meat from when its skin had slid from its face and neck like melting ice cream.

There was a name tag over the right breast, it read Dr. William Fredericks. Fredericks had been a biochemist, called onto the base when the military put together the co-op of scientists and doctors to try and battle the zombie plague. He had been one of the last to become infected when a strain had splattered from a broken test tube and had sprayed the nearby researchers. Fearing what would come next, Fredericks had barricaded himself in the far room, hoping to wait out the terror until help arrived. Unfortunately, he had been exposed, as well. When he died and had then returned, he had been trapped inside the room for almost a year, the dim intelligence still left in his brain far from accomplishing the task of opening the door.

Wilson screamed, Fredericks lunging at the surprised man, the dead scientist finally enjoying the taste of freedom and a meal long overdue.

When Fredericks sank his teeth into Wilson's shoulder, Wilson had panicked, his trigger finger squeezing the trigger of the M-16. Bullets sprayed everywhere, tracking across the ceiling and then back down toward the vats against the far wall.

"Mary, get down!" Henry yelled, pulling her to the floor and kicking over one of the steel desks to protect them from the hail of bullets.

Huddling behind the table, the rounds ricocheted like steel rain, denting the table, but saving both of them from serious injury. One dent appeared exactly next to Henry's head, and if the table had been made of wood, he would most definitely be dead right now. Behind them, the vats shattered, spilling their contents out onto the floor, the odor of death and decay causing Henry and Mary to gag on their own vomit.

The moment the bullets stopped, Henry jumped up and ran toward Wilson to try and help the man. Wilson had managed to get his rifle in-between the rotting face and his own body and he was desperately trying to toss the body away from him, but the stringy arms were like iron and wouldn't budge. Henry ran as fast as he could across the room, and just when he reached the two men, one dead and one alive, he brought back his foot like a place-kicker and let his heavy boot fly directly at Fredericks' head. The steel toe connected just below the jaw and the brittle spine snapped like a twig, the head separating from its body to bounce off the wall. A small trash barrel was below it, and by total coincidence, the head dropped into the barrel, like an office worker shooting crushed paper while passing the time to go home.

Ignoring the coincidence, Henry helped Wilson to stand. Wilson was already sweating. He had a large wound over his right shoulder, but otherwise was fine.

Wilson's eyes bore into Henry's, knowing his fate. He was about to tell Henry about it when Mary screamed from across the lab.

The vats having been shattered, the zombies within had finally been released from their clear prisons. Like the worst nightmares that Henry and Mary's minds could ever imagine, the creatures crawled and struggled to regain their feet. Mary was directly across from them and those with eyes turned to gaze at her, yellow teeth flashing in the beam of her flashlight.

"Uh, Henry, I could use some help over here!" She called as she slowly tried to back away from the ten grotesque life forms. She was managing to stay calm, but something inside her wanted to just run away like a scared little girl.

"Wilson, your wound is bad, but you're not dead yet. I need your help to deal with these things and get us out of here alive. Are you with me?" Henry asked.

With a sheen of perspiration covering his face and neck, his face pale in the beam of the flashlight in Henry's hand, he nodded. "Yeah, Henry, if I'm gonna die, then I want to take as many of those dead fucks with me as I can. Let's save your friend."

Mary fired the Winchester at the closest zombie, her aim askew, only its arm blowing off from the force of the blast to skitter across the floor and be lost in the darkness like a dead eel. The creature never slowed, only continued forward, wanting nothing more than to feast on Mary's soft flesh.

Wilson and Henry ran across the lab, careful not to trip on discarded furniture, and upon reaching Mary, Henry reached down and grabbed her arm.

She screamed when he grabbed her, trying to pull away, thinking a ghoul had circled around and was attacking her, but she quickly realized it was Henry and stopped fighting him.

"Come on, Mary, it's time to go," he said briefly, helping her to stand.

Wilson had started firing nearby, spraying an entire clip at the ten shambling figures. Their treacle-like movements were confusing, the shadows of the flashlight making it hard to pinpoint one target, so Wilson just sprayed bullets where he could. He was rewarded with two head shots, the other bullets only thru-and-thrus. Henry leveled his shotgun and shot the closest ghouls, one receiving the barrage of death in its jelly-like torso. The creature was severed at the waist, the top half falling over to splash in the murky water from the shattered tanks. The legs fell over and remained motionless, but the top half began crawling forward. Henry waited for it to be only a foot away and brought his boot up and slammed it onto the head, twisting his foot as his weight crushed the soft skull. Blood and brains oozed around his foot, a squishy sound coming from the sole of his boot as he pulled it away.

Pulling his boot back, he slammed it onto the floor and started to back away from the eight ghouls straight out of his nightmares. They seemed to move as one, as if only one mind controlled them. Was it possible? Could they somehow be telepathically linked?

Anything was possible in the chamber of horrors the three hapless humans now found themselves in. The flashlight beams seemed to almost glisten off the corpses bodies, as if they were coated with Vaseline or vegetable oil.

Wilson grunted, feeling dizzy from his wound and Mary helped him to stand, wrapping her arm around his chest. He grunted a thank you and then slowly they started retreating out of the room.

Henry fired shot after shot, the spent casings falling to the floor like metal rain until he was out. Swinging the shotgun over his shoulder, he pulled his Glock and sent three rounds at the nearest face of horrors, the grizzly countenance exploding in a spray of blood and brown brain matter.

"Go, out the door, I'm right behind you!" Henry yelled to Mary, as he shot three more rounds at shadows. Whether he hit something was never known, as he was already turning around and running for the door. He felt the faintest breeze brush by his face, a claw-like hand reaching out to caress his cheek, and he would never know how close he had come to being dinner for one of the terrors in the dark.

Then he was past the doorframe and he slammed the door shut behind him. After turning the lock, he ran for a chair near an overturned desk and quickly jammed it under the handle.

"Do you think that's necessary?" Mary asked from across the room. She was leaning against a far wall with Wilson. The man's bleeding wound had begun to slow, the blood only seeping now. If it wasn't for the fact that he had become infected, the wound wouldn't have been fatal. Still, at the moment, there was far too much going on to worry about that right now.

Henry left the chair at the door, satisfied it would hold for at least a little while and ran across the room and out into the corridor. Upon reaching the stairwell door, he opened it and was greeted by the sound of crashing and then the sound of dozens of feet as they began moving up the stairs. The distinctive howl of the undead floated up the stairwell, a song of death he had heard far too often in the past two days.

Running back to Mary, he stopped her when she began moving toward him, Wilson leaning heavily on her.

"No, can't go that way, the door at the bottom gave in and they're coming up the stairs," he gasped, out of breath from all the exertion and tension of the past few minutes.

"So what, let's just blow 'em to hell and get out of here," Wilson said confidently, though he looked far weaker than he was trying to act.

Henry shook his head. "Can't, there's too many of them. We need to find another way out. There's more than one stairwell, we just need to get to another, that's all."

With a sudden unexpectedly, the door leading to the lab shook on its hinges; the chair sliding an inch from the pressure being placed on the door. All three faces turned as one and Henry swore under his breath. The door rocked again, and by the sound of it, there was more than one body banging on the opposite side of the door.

"Jesus Christ, I don't believe it, but they're working together. There's no way that door would be shaking like that if it was just one or two of them. We need to go now, before it's too late; come on," Henry said and began leading the way deeper into the main corridor, now moving to the opposite side and hopefully, freedom.

They passed many doors, but Henry ignored them all. They were all dead ends. They needed another stairwell, which was the only way to escape the trap they now found themselves in.

Upon reaching the far end of the corridor, Henry let out the breath he hadn't known he'd been holding when he saw the sign on the door that read: north stairwell.

Pushing down on the horizontal bar, he opened the floor into more darkness. Flashing the beam of his light down the stairs and then upwards, as well, he saw nothing but dust. Listening carefully, he waited for the sounds of movement, but none came to his ears.

"Okay, this is as good as it gets, let's go and keep an eye on our rear. Don't want anything sneaking up on us."

With Henry in the lead, they made their way down the darkened stairs. Wilson was moving better, the initial shock of his wound passing. The man was strong and had balls, Henry had to admit and was fighting off the infection with everything he had. It was a shame in the end it wouldn't matter. In a different time and place Henry could have called the surly guard a friend, the past few hours causing the two men to grow closer as only a battle for survival will do. But for now he was merely an uneasy ally. Henry still needed to find a chance to escape, and by the way things were going, it shouldn't be too hard. Wilson knew once they were clear of the base he either had to go his own way or die. He couldn't be allowed back into the town, not with the infection inside him. Henry had already decided that he would leave it up to Wilson what he wanted to do.

As he walked down the steps, Henry quickly reloaded his shotgun, pulling shell after shell from his pockets. They reached the bottom floor without incident and Henry smiled wildly when he realized this stairwell led directly to the outside. Cautiously, he pushed the outer door open, the warm night air filling the stairwell, washing the scent of fear and sweat from their bodies.

All was quiet. If there were other ghouls in the area, they weren't in the immediate vicinity.

"Coast is clear, let's go...and stay sharp," Henry said and stepped out into the moonlit night. Mary and Wilson followed and soon they were away from the building and making their way out of the base. A few zombies were scattered around here and there, but with the exception of one ghoul that got to close and Henry disposed of with his panga, they avoided the rest, not wanting to call attention to themselves by firing their weapons needlessly.

Upon reaching the car, Wilson slumped against the bumper, glad to finally rest. He was sweating profusely and it was clear the infection was taking hold.

"Well, Wilson, I guess this is where we part ways," Henry said flatly, holding his shotgun level with the man's chest. Mary saw what he was doing and did the same; both weapons trained on Wilson. If he so much as moved a muscle, he would be dead before his body hit the road. Henry wasn't pleased that the man was dying, but then again it did make a difficult problem simpler. With Wilson dead, there was no one to stop him and Mary from leaving the base and heading out on their own, hopefully to find Jimmy and Cindy.

"What do you mean by that?" Wilson asked innocently.

Henry blinked twice. Surely the man couldn't be so daft as not to understand what was going on here.

"I mean, this is where we say goodbye. Mary and I are getting out of here and we're not going back to the town. I told you this was a damn fool mission, but no one would listen to me and now Lewis is dead and you're gonna be following him real soon. So drop the rifle or you're gonna see if there's a God even quicker than you thought."

Wilson cocked his head to the side in contemplation. "Yeah, you'd think that, wouldn't you, but I'm afraid things won't be working out quite the way you planned. You see, I was ordered to kill you whether we found the cure or not; that you were disposable. The Reverend only kept you alive when we found you so he could send you on this mission. Now that it's over, you're not needed anymore."

Henry chuckled slightly, admiring the man's confidence.

"Maybe you don't realize who's in charge here, now. It's me and Mary who have the upper hand, now drop your weapon and step away from the car or I'll kill you right here and end this."

Wilson stood up, a wide smile crossing his lips.

"You know, you're right, of course. You would have the upper hand with the exception of one thing."

"Oh, and what's that?" Henry asked, curious despite himself.

"You didn't know that the Reverend sent me with an Ace up my sleeve. A secret weapon so to speak, in case everything went to shit, like it has now." He turned casually to Mary and spoke one word to her. "Righteousness," he said as cool and clear as he could say it.

Henry was about to ask him just what the hell he thought he was doing, when Mary's face seemed to go blank, her face losing all emotion, and she slowly turned her body toward Henry, raising the Winchester so that it was aimed directly at his face. From the corner of his eye, Henry saw Wilson doing the same with his M-16, his smile so wide it should have split his face in two.

"Mary, what the hell do you think you're...?" Henry began to say, and then she squeezed the trigger, the blast of the weapon rolling across the deserted road.

Chapter 25

"Is everything going as planned?" Reverend Carlson asked from where he stood on the loading dock of the brightly illuminated warehouse, overlooking everything like a general preparing for war. He was wearing one of his black suits and an off white shirt, but it was the bleached white collar predominant on his neck that called the most attention to itself. The outfit was impeccably clean, one of the few vices he let himself indulge in. After all, cleanliness is next to Godliness isn't it?

The man he was talking to nodded. "Yes, Reverend, we're almost finished loading the first truck and the second one is waiting. As soon as the first one pulls out we'll start loading the second."

"Excellent, this is God's work you're doing here, son. Don't ever forget that," he said, patting the man on the shoulder, "Now go, and get to it, and make sure the others know I'm pleased with their efforts, but make them work faster. I want to be heading out by first light."

The man nodded, glad the Reverend was happy for the moment, because if the Reverend wasn't pleased then he and the other men would be in for a world of hurt. The man left the Reverend then, running away down a side ramp to find the foreman for the loading dock. They had only a few more hours until first light and there were still more than half of the warehouse left to load into the two trucks.

The Reverend watched the man leave, pleased at his momentum. The Reverend enjoyed being obeyed. His eyes glanced across the dock at the line of zombies ten feet away waiting for their turn to be loaded into the semis, while his men were herding chained zombies out of the warehouse at the opposite end at the same time. These men wore white bio-hazard suits that prevented them from accidentally becoming contaminated by the ghouls. The suits were made of a heavy material that could withstand a bite from one of the creatures. So far only one man had been attacked and his suit had saved him from being bitten and then having to be killed after becoming infected.

Reverend Carlson watched as body after body of decomposing, walking corpses were ushered into the back of the large trailers.

He had planned this for months, having his men collect as many zombies as they could per day. He had more than a thousand now and all were about to do God's work. He winced slightly as the wind shifted, the stench being unbearable. But he would persevere. The zombies were God's creatures after all, no better or worse than himself.

Well maybe not entirely equal.

He had a plan for his sister city of Stardust Cove. He planned on bringing the semis in under the guise of food supplies and a goodwill gesture from himself to Merle, the mayor or Stardust Cove. He was confident the pompous fool would believe he was being generous and perhaps wanted to make amends for past indiscretions. Once the trucks were inside the town's massive stone walls, he would throw open the doors of the trailers and like the Trojan Horse of Greek mythology, the zombies would swarm out and wipe out the decadent town once and for all.

If any of the townspeople managed to survive and make it to his town's city limits, then he would consider them one by one on whether they deserved to be saved. After all, he could always use slave labor and with their town destroyed, the refugees would be willing to submit to anything compared to the alternative.

Yes, the Rapture was coming to Stardust Cove, but it was Reverend Carlson who was the architect, not God.

No, wait, perhaps that wasn't true. If God worked through him, then in the end, wasn't it God who was actually the architect of the town's downfall?

Perhaps, but he preferred not to get too philosophical in times like these. For now, he was just enjoying watching all his plans finally coming to fruition.

By the next morning the trucks would be ready and he would send them out to do his work. He would be there, as well, of course, following in his own vehicle. He would wait a good distance from the town and when he knew it was utterly destroyed; he would send his men in to burn everything to the ground. He was fortunate enough to have a dozen flamethrowers with full tanks, complements of the naval base, plus a special package of C-4 that he planned to use. One of the few things his search parties had been fortunate enough to find before the undead had become too unruly inside the base.

That made him wonder how Wilson and the others were doing. The girl had been hypnotized easily and Wilson had orders to use her when the mission was over. She was to kill Henry, and then once the man was dead, she was to turn her weapon on herself and commit suicide.

Suicide may be a sin, but The Reverend was willing to make an exception this once. He knew the moment he met them they would be trouble if he kept them around, so he had decided to use them instead of just killing them. Using all the weapons at your disposal was the mark of a good leader and the Reverend believed himself to be an excellent one.

He had adapted to the new world he found himself in adequately by throwing out any of the old rules he didn't care for and only keeping the ones he liked. Others, he simply adapted to suit his needs. He was a reverend in name only now, but he kept up the appearance so that the townspeople would follow him. It seems people will follow a man of God much more easily if they believe that the man actually believes himself to be following a higher power.

The Reverend smiled in the moonlight, admiring the shuffling bodies as they were moved into the trucks. The men had long poles with ropes on the end, connected to a pulley system. It was identical to what dog catchers used when capturing wild dogs. Some of the walking corpses were unruly, trying to escape or attack their captors, but the poles did their job nicely, keeping snapping teeth from tender flesh. If only they knew of the smorgasbord that awaited them, he wondered if the undead would be more cooperative, knowing to wait would allow them all the meat they could ever desire. But, no, though they might be God's creatures, the zombies were nothing but brain dead fools, acting only on instinct.

But that was all right. Things were going as well as could be expected and soon, by the end of the next day, he would be the leader of two towns, with the excess townspeople killed off, like the fat of a steak cut away and thrown to the dogs by a diligent butcher.

In the end, when the smoke had cleared, he would be the ruling power on the Californian coast, and when he had gathered all who wished to follow him, he would then begin his real campaign; which was to wash across the rest of California, collecting souls. And when they had been consolidated into his growing army, then the rest of America would fall, all becoming absorbed one town at a time, enclave after enclave, until he was the master of it all.

And any who did not want to join his grand design will be crushed under his shoe like an errant bug.

Oh yes, a new age would be dawning for mankind and it would all begin in the morning with the destruction of Stardust Cove.

There was about to be a harvest of souls on the coast of California, a dead harvest.

Chapter 26

Mary stood quietly, guarding Wilson, while Henry traded words with the man. Unexpectedly, Wilson turned to her and smiled. Then he uttered something to her that seemed to penetrate into her unconscious mind.

Like she was sleepwalking, she turned her weapon away from Wilson, and in one fluid motion, squeezed the trigger with the barrel of the rifle aimed directly at Henry's shocked face.

Mary remembered almost nothing of what happened after Wilson spoke that one word to her: righteousness. It was like her mind was a television that someone had decided to turn off when they were tired and ready to go to bed one night. One moment she was looking at Wilson, her Winchester aimed at the man while Henry talked to him, the next she was sprawled on the ground looking up at the moon and clouds in the night sky.

Her mind was fuzzy, and then she saw stars that weren't in the sky, as someone slapped her face so hard her teeth hurt.

That was when her memory flooded back to her and the last five minutes came slamming into focus. It was then that she realized what she had done and a hole in her heart opened up when she realized she had shot her rifle directly at Henry.

Then the world spun and she collapsed to the pavement, unconscious.

* * *

Five minutes ago.

"Mary, what the hell do you think you're...?" Henry yelled as Mary squeezed the trigger of the Winchester directly at his face.

If he ever thought about that moment in time again on some lonely night in the future, he would always wonder why he didn't see his life flashing before his eyes.

He had always heard that upon a person's death, their life would play like an old movie across their mind, showing all the trials and tribulations they had suffered until their final moments on earth.

Henry saw none of that. What Henry saw was Mary's face go blank and her eyes seemed to gaze at nothing and he knew whatever was happening to her was not in her control.

Just as she fired, he dropped to the ground like a sack of potatoes, his body going limp, letting gravity take over. Though his reactions were quick, he was still not quick enough to escape the entire blast of the rifle. As his head fell low, the blast flew over his head, singing the top right corner of his hair.

In that brief instance, he noticed the odor of his charred hair and his testicles went up inside his abdomen, thinking he'd been shot and just hadn't felt the pain yet.

Then he remembered almost nothing, his instincts kicking in.

Wilson was leveling his M-16 at him, as well, his finger tightening on the trigger. When Henry dropped to the ground, he immediately started to roll, the rounds from the M-16 digging up the pavement, missing his torso by inches, though pieces of gravel bounced up to sting his cheek.

Rolling to his knees, Henry was already firing the shotgun, the blast hitting Wilson in the chest.

The man flew over the hood of the Honda, crashing to the ground heavily, but Henry was already focusing on his next target.

Mary.

He didn't want to kill her and he knew it would break his heart if it came to that, but if it came down to either him or her than there would be no argument.

Mary's blank stare gave her the illusion of one of the zombies she had battled so valiantly in the past and the only reason Henry was able to hold his fire was that he immediately could see she was only moving at half capacity. It was like she was a puppet controlled by someone else's strings or she was fighting her own internal battle inside herself as she tried to stop herself from shooting her closest friend.

Either way, Henry racked his mind for a safe way to disable her without killing her.

Mary fired again; the shot going wide just as Henry lunged out of the way, rolling across the shoulder of the road. His leg kicked something metallic and he saw a dusty hubcap reflecting in the moonlight. Reaching down, he grabbed it and then as quick as he could, stood up and threw it like a frisbee directly at Mary. The hubcap flew across the ten feet separating the two combatants, wobbling slightly in the air. Mary was already preparing to fire another shot and Henry realized he had left himself exposed out in the open. If the hubcap missed her, then Mary would have an easy target of Henry, killing him with the next shot to the chest.

But the hubcap flew true, striking her just above the eyes. There was a dull clank when it struck the bone of her forehead and she was knocked off her feet, the shotgun falling to the ground by her feet.

Not waiting a second longer, Henry ran across the distance separating them and kicked the Winchester away from her grasping hands. Mary's eyes were unfocused as she struggled to pull herself up.

"Sorry, Mary, but this is for your own good," Henry said and he slapped her across the face so hard he thought he might have knocked one of her teeth out. Mary's head rocked to the side and her eyes became unfocused again. She moved her head slightly, and then almost like she was going to sleep, her eyes closed and her head dropped back to the pavement.

Henry reached out and quickly felt for her pulse, grunting happily when he felt it strong and sure. She was only unconscious. She would live another day, the only question was when she woke up would she be herself or something else?

Deciding he didn't want to take any chances, he quickly ripped the sleeves from her shirt and used them to bind her arms.

Once she was secured, he picked her up, her Winchester on her chest, and carried her the few short feet to the Honda, laying her on the hood. Looking over the car to check on Wilson, he saw the man was dead, lying face up, his open eyes seeing nothing. His chest was a bloody mess, and just as Henry let go of Mary, Henry saw Wilson's finger's begin to twitch.

The man was coming back, the previous bite flooding his system with the virus.

With Mary secured, Henry reached down and pulled his panga from its sheath. Then with a slight sigh, like he was about to do some boring yard work, he strode around the car towards Wilson. With three hard thwacks of the panga, Wilson's head was severed from the shoulders and Henry held it up to look into the face. Wilson's eyes were open now and he stared at Henry, the mouth trying to speak and bite at him.

With a disgusted yelp, Henry tossed the severed head across the street to let it roll onto the shoulder. In the shadows of the night, he couldn't see it anymore and didn't care where it had landed.

Deciding it was time to go, he was preparing to pick Mary up and put her in the Honda when he realized two things at the same time. The first was that the front left tire was flat, collateral damage from the gunfight that had just occurred. The second was that the radiator was leaking water all over the street, the liquid looking like blood in the flickering shadows of the night.

Muttering imprecations under his breath, he then realized he was about to have company. The shadows that had stayed at bay surrounding him had suddenly come to life and the distinctive sound of shuffling footsteps could be heard coming closer.

Deciding the car should get him at least a few miles before it overheated, and not caring about the flat, he picked Mary up, tossed her into the front passenger seat and quickly dug in Wilson's pants for the keys to the car, ignoring the wet material that had absorbed the man's blood.

For just a moment, he started to worry, his heart fluttering when he found nothing, but then he realized the keys were farther down the front pocket than he first thought, and instead of trying to squeeze his hand inside, he used his panga to cut the pocket, slicing into the flesh of Wilson's leg a good inch. That was fine, though, Wilson didn't seem to mind.

With the keys in his hand, he ran around to the driver's door, kicking the first zombie to reach him away. Jumping into the car, he slammed the locks for the doors home and started the engine. It sputtered for a second and then started, sputtering just a little more, and Henry honestly thought it was going to stall. But then the motor evened out, and with another sigh, and silent prayer for his good luck, he slammed the transmission into drive.

After driving in a tight circle, knocking shadowy forms away like bowling pins, he pointed the Honda the way they had come hours before, and with the one tire flap, flap, flapping, he drove away from the base, leaving the pursuing zombies in the distance.

Mary groaned next to him, and he glanced at her face, her visage only a dim outline in the moonlight. She had a lot of explaining to do once she woke up and he was eager to listen, but for now he concentrated on driving, fighting the steering wheel as the tire slowly shredded from the rim, leaving bits of rubber behind him like a trail of breadcrumbs for any who sought to follow.

* * *

Mary stirred in her seat uncomfortably and slowly returned to consciousness.

"Oh, my head is killing me. What happened?" She asked, looking around her as she attempted to get her bearings and focus her vision.

When she turned her head to the left, she was greeted by Henry's dour expression. He was sitting quietly in the darkness of the car, with his shotgun in his lap and the barrel touching the floor. He was playing with a cigarette lighter he'd found in the ashtray, flicking the small lighter on and off; his face glowing in the flicker of light for a moment each time it flared to life. He was patiently passing the time it took for Mary to revive.

She pulled her hands away from her face to see there was still a bit of torn shirt hanging from her wrist from when she had been tied up, by who, she could only guess; not that she could blame him.

"That's what I'd like to know. You nearly blew my head off back there at the base and, if you don't mind, I'd like to know why."

Mary shook her head, clearing some of the cobwebs from her mind, and tried to remember what had happened. It all came back in a misty haze, jumpy like a picture from a projector. She remembered Wilson saying something to her and then it was like she was on autopilot.

"I tried to shoot you, didn't I?" She formed the sentence into a question, not quite knowing what was real and what she may have imagined.

Henry only scowled more, his eyes seeming to almost glow in the wan light of the cigarette lighter. It was well past midnight and they were a little more than two miles from the naval station. That was when the little Honda's engine had finally overheated and stopped running. As for the flat tire, the last of the rubber had fallen off more than a mile ago and Henry had driven on the steel rim, the rim gouging a jagged line in the street that followed behind them into the distance.

"Yeah, you did, and I need to know why. Especially if you're gonna try and do it again. I need to know I can count on you not to shoot me in the back every time I look away from you," he said flatly.

She nodded, the gesture making her head hurt. "I know, Henry and I think I can explain. I don't know if it's all true or just in my imagination, but this is what I remember..." Then she started to tell him about the Reverend and the meetings she'd had with him, and how at the end of those meetings, she wouldn't remember what they had talked about. It was only when she tried to kill Henry, something that went so far against her personality that she was almost able to overcome the hypnotic suggestion, that she recalled exactly what had happened to her.

Henry sat quietly, listening to her talk, not so much as nodding to what he was hearing. When she was finished with her story and was beginning to get worried that he wouldn't understand, he slapped the steering wheel in anger, making her jump.

"That son-of-a-bitch. You know, it's pretty goddamn clever when you think of it. He made my own friend my worst enemy." He looked at her with a wide grin. "And it would've worked if you had been a better shot."

She frowned at that, almost insulted. "I'll have you know, I'm pretty sure I hesitated, which gave you enough time to avoid getting a new haircut. You're welcome."

He gazed at her, the statement sinking in, then he stared more intently at her, his eyes growing hard, and said the word: "Righteousness."

Mary simply blinked back, looking at him like he was crazy.

"Righteousness what?" She asked curiously, expecting him to keep talking when he stopped.

"Righteousness. That's the word Wilson said that had you going all Terminator on me. I guess it doesn't work anymore."

"Does that mean you can trust me again?"

He shrugged. "Guess so, it's not like I have a choice." Before she could answer him, he was opening his door and stepping out into the warm night air. She pulled the torn bit of shirt from her wrist and tossed it to the floor of the car and then opened her own door, standing up slowly. A slight wave of dizziness came over her, but it quickly passed within a half minute. She let out a silent breath and looked around her surroundings for the first time. They were parked in front of what looked like a small mini-mall. There were six storefronts lined one next to the other, a small cement sidewalk connecting them like a cheesy boardwalk.

One was a Chinese restaurant, the other a copy store. The one next to that was unknown, the sign having long disappeared. It was the one closest to the end that caught her eyes, though. It was a clothing store and as she looked down at her own filthy clothes, the torn shirt especially, and wondered if there might be anything left or if the place was cleaned out.

"So, what are we doing here?" She asked, walking around to the front of the Honda. The hood was still warm, telling her the car had only recently stopped.

"Doing here? Not much, unfortunately. The cars crap, it's not going any further. We need to get back to the beach and then start looking for Jimmy and Cindy. If they're still alive, then they're probably at one of the closest towns around here. Hopefully they're looking for us, too."

"Uh-huh, look, before we get going again, can we see if there's some clothing in that store? I could really use a change of outfits," she said, holding her arms out to show how filthy she was. Henry looked over at her and nodded, then looked down at his own attire, seeing much the same as on her. They were both filthy, and if a bath or shower was out of the question, then a set of clean clothes would do wonders for their morale.

"Okay, why not, I could use some new duds. But stay sharp, we don't know what's in there and I don't want to lose one of us over a new shirt."

"Amen to that," she answered, retrieving her Winchester from the car, and began walking excitedly toward the store with Henry right behind her. If she noticed he had his shotgun leveled toward her she gave no sign, as it could just be the night shadows playing tricks on her eyesight. But even if it was true; she knew that after what she'd done, betraying him like that, she would have to earn his trust again, like a child learning to walk for the first time. One step at a time, she thought, while she moved past the shattered windows of the storefronts. The Chinese restaurant looked like it had seen a fire in its past, the odor of burned material still noticeable. Inside the open pictured frame of its shattered front, Mary could see the blackened tables and partially burned menus littering the floor. There was another smell, as well. That Chinese food smell that permeated every Chinese restaurant she'd ever gone into. Even the fire couldn't totally destroy the redolence of a thousand pupu platters.

"You in the mood for Chinese?" She asked playfully.

"No, I'm good, my stomach can't take all the msg's they put into it, not to mention the cholesterol. Emily wouldn't even let me near the stuff, said it was either the food or her. And I chose her." He became slightly melancholy then, thinking back to his wife and how happy they'd been together, at least until he'd had to kill her. That had put a damper on their marriage that was for sure. But with the passage of time slowly moving on, he was beginning to accept her death and the millions of others that had perished along with her; now nothing more than dust and memories.

"We're here," she said when she had reached the door to the clothing store. There was a sign painted on the glass of the door that read: Debbie's Fashions.

Though the window was cracked, it wasn't shattered and for the hell of it, Mary tried the door. She was mildly surprised when it opened inward when she pushed on it.

Henry was at her back and he grunted. "You know, that's a fire hazard."

"What is?"

"The door opening inward. All doors are supposed to open outward, that way if there was a fire, then all you had to do is push and you were out. Opening inward like that, a crowd would prevent the door from opening by the pushing people against the door and then everyone dies. It happened in the Coconut Grove fire. Since then all doors have to open out."

"No kidding?" She asked.

He smiled. "No kidding, just one more bit of useless information nowadays, I guess. Come on; let's get us some new duds."

She nodded slightly; pleased he was talking to her again, and then stepped inside, her Winchester tracking back and forth. For just a moment, as she entered the store, the floor seemed to undulate like a live thing, but then Henry flashed his light into the room, illuminating it, and whatever shadows she thought she saw were gone.

Henry noticed the perplexed look on her face and asked: "What's up? You see somethin'"

"Uhm, no, I guess not, probably just my eyes playing tricks on me, let's go."

It was dark in the store, despite the moon being high in the sky; the glow not enough to penetrate the dirty front windows. She almost jumped when Henry stepped on a high-heel shoe, cracking it, his weight too much for the cheap footwear to bear. The echo from the crunch reverberating off the walls like it was a massive cave. His flashlight moved back and forth, the dull beam playing over the store. She almost fired her weapon when the beam illuminated a mannequin in the corner, but held off at the last moment.

Henry chuckled at that. "Don't worry, I think she's harmless," he joked, referring to the inanimate body.

"Says you. You never heard of killer mannequins?"

"Only in the movies, Mary, now pay attention. Let's scope this place out, get what we need, and then get going. I want to get back to the beach by sun-up."

She turned and moved deeper into the store. It wasn't that large, the rear of the store and its dressing rooms dimly seen in the illumination of the flashlight.

Mary slowed as she passed a rack of clothing, she thought she heard purring, like from a cat and was racking it up to her imagination again when she heard the distinctive sound of a cat crying, its mewling floating to her ears. Using the barrel of the Winchester like a probing stick, she pushed a few dusty dresses to the side of the metal rack and let out a soft gasp at what she found.

"Hey, Henry, come here and look at this," she said as she leaned down and stared at the mother cat and her five kittens. The mother hissed once, but when Mary stopped moving, the mother relaxed slightly. Mary's eyes roamed over the mother cat's body. It was nothing but skin and bones; the kittens too, were ridiculously tiny. She idly wondered how much milk the mother could even be offering the tiny babies.

Henry came up next to her and looked over her shoulder. "Huh, cats. Well that should at least mean the place is devoid of any deaders. I doubt the cats would have made up a home here if there was." He leaned away from her and started rummaging through a few racks set up in the men's section. Though a few of the racks were empty, there was still a bounty of clothing available.

Mary pushed the clothing back to the position she'd found it, leaving the felines in peace. It made her happy to see such a small piece of nature, still struggling to survive, despite the harshness of the times.

A scratching sound came from off to her right and she turned her head quickly, trying to see what had made the sound, but all she was greeted to was the wind blowing the few faded clothes nearest the window.

Deciding it must have been the metal hangers clicking against the bars that held them, she decided to find what she would need so they could move on.

Henry was already trying on a new pair of pants, looking comical in his boxer shorts. She smiled widely, while watching Henry try to get into the jeans he'd found. They were a size too small and he was squirming like an exotic dancer to get his legs into them.

"What, you think this is funny? This is all I could find, dammit."

She held back her laughter and turned away. "Sorry, they look fine, really."

He only answered her by grunting some more, finally getting the jeans over his hips and then with an intake of breath, buttoning them. They felt a little better once he had them buttoned, though still tight. He quickly transferred the remaining shells for the shotgun and a few other miscellaneous items to the pockets of his new pants.

Mary was just searching through a rack of clothing, finding some jeans and a new shirt when Henry's flashlight went out.

"Shit!" He muttered in the darkness.

"What happened?"

"The damn flashlight went out."

She could hear him smacking the light against his palm trying to jar it back on, but it wasn't working. Now only the faintest amount of light penetrated into the store and where they were standing there was almost total darkness.

"Forget it," Henry exclaimed, "it's gone. Maybe the batteries, I guess. Just grab what you found and let's go. You can put it on outside while I stand watch."

She was doing just that when she started to hear that scratching sound again. It was like a thousand toothpicks had been dropped on the floor and were then being dragged about.

"Henry, I hear something and I know it's not my imagination," she told him, a touch of fear in her voice.

"Yeah, I hear it, too. But for the life of me, I have no idea what it is. Come on, let's go, I don't want to find out, either."

He took a step to leave and his boot came down on something crunchy. Whatever it was, it yielded to his weight, but as he moved his other foot, it too, came down on another one, the sound similar to stepping on eggshells.

"What the?" He said, moving his foot in the darkness. He could see nothing and was beginning to get a little creeped out about the situation.

"Mary, there's something on the floor, be careful where you step," he said cautiously, while he continued working his way to the front of the store. With each step he took there was more crunching. It was like he was stepping on seashells; hundreds of them, but the blackness prevented him from seeing what they were.

Mary picked up her clothing and tucked them under her arm and then started for the front, as well. Crunch, crunch, crunch, sounded under her feet and she was starting to feel sick. It was only the not knowing that prevented her from freaking out.

It was when Henry was halfway through the store and the clouds lifted in the sky that the illumination changed. The moonlight shot down and bounced off the dusty mirrors in the store, reflecting the light enough so that Henry was able to see better, though only slightly.

He took the opportunity to look down at the floor and his voice locked in his throat. The floor was a writhing mass of small-shelled black shapes and they were almost entirely covering his legs. He started brushing them off and received a few bites for his trouble.

"Son-of-a-bitch, the little bastards are carnivorous," he screamed. "Mary, get off the floor, now, there's cockroaches everywhere and they like people!"

"Oh my God!" Mary screamed as she jumped off the floor and onto the nearby counter. It was then the sounds of the mother cat and the kittens came to her ears. They were crying in pain, their hissing, screech-like cries filling the room.

In the wan moonlight, through the hanging clothing, Mary could only watch as the insects devoured the cats like land-based piranhas. In seconds, the cats were nothing but hair and bones, the cockroaches burrowing into the flesh to feed on the organs within.

She raised her rifle, wanting to start shooting, but realized the futility of the situation.

"Henry, up here, hurry, they're everywhere!"

"No shit, what do you think I'm trying to do?" He said as he jumped over a wide pile of the little black objects. He pushed a rack of clothing to the floor, and for a moment, the clothing covered the roaches. Like an island in a tempest sea he jumped for it, feeling the crunching carcasses under the material. It was like he was on a living floor, the creatures undulating like water.

Two more jumps and he had reached the counter next to Mary, climbing on top like he was reaching the top of a cliff. Breathing hard and wiping off the rest of the roaches, he let out a yelp when one of the creatures tried to crawl up his leg on the inside of his pants. Slapping the lump hard, he wiggled his limb until the dead bug fell out. He was just glad he had been able to put his pants on before they had popped up. He could see now they were coming out of every crack in the walls and floor, like black water flowing in reverse.

"What are we going to do?" Mary asked, kicking off some of the persistent creatures that were even now scurrying up the counter to try and reach them.

Henry was doing the same and he frantically looked around the room for some way to escape without being devoured like the cats.

"I don't know yet, just let me think," he screamed as he kicked and slapped the little monsters away. He thought maybe they could wait it out until daylight, but that was hours away and the aggressiveness of the roaches was intense.

They'd never make it.

Then he remembered something he had in his pants pocket, something he had only picked up an hour ago that would likely be their salvation.

"I have an idea, just keep them off us for a few more minutes and we'll be out of here," he yelled as he quickly found what he needed and got to work.

The roaches were in for a little surprise and in a few seconds it would all be over.

He hoped.

Chapter 27

"Uggg! They're everywhere!" Mary screamed, wiping another dozen roaches off the counter and her boots. The creatures were never-ending, pouring out of the crevasses and cracks, some slivers in the floor so small only the tiniest roaches would fit.

The mother cat and her babies were gone, devoured until there was nothing left, but still the roaches continued feeding, now consuming the hair and leaving tiny indentations in the bone as they tried to get at the tender marrow within.

Stomping her boots on the counter like a tap dancer, Mary continually crushed dozens under her heels, only to have another dozen replace each one she'd succeeded in killing. They were everywhere. The floor was now a seething cauldron of black and wiggling insects, all wanting nothing more than to feed on the two companions.

Next to her, in the darkness, she could hear Henry doing something, but she was helpless to see him. In her desperation, she began firing her Winchester into the floor, chewing large holes into the floorboards and killing hundreds from the blast, but like a pool of water, the blast holes were quickly filled up again, the black shells of the insects crawling over one another as they moved about. In fact, she was causing more problems for her and Henry. With the floorboards ripped open by the rounds, the roaches now enjoyed even larger holes to enter the store by.

They were so completely trapped it was actually hard to believe it was truly happening. In less than five minutes, the store had gone from being devoid of life to being one giant aquarium of carnivorous insects. Carrion beetles moved about with dung beetles and large cockroaches that couldn't be native to California filled any open spaces on the floor. Though she was constantly battling the little creatures, she had to wonder where they could all have come from. Could there have been some kind of research lab nearby that had set them free when the place had crumbled, and now without human intervention the insects were free to reproduce with impunity?

She was pulled from her thoughts when Henry slapped her on the shoulder. "Okay, I'm ready, hold tight and we'll see if it'll work."

"And what if it doesn't?" She asked, slapping half-a-dozen beetles from her shirt; the creatures falling back into the pool of death only to crawl back to the counter and try again.

"Then we're dead," he stated coldly and then she could see his face as he tried to light the cigarette lighter in his hand. The spark would flicker, but the flint didn't seem to want to cooperate.

"Shit, I think it's empty," he muttered as he kept trying.

"What? Why the hell would you carry around an empty lighter? You mean to tell me we're gonna die because you forgot to get one that's full?"

"It's not mine, I found it in the car, dammit, now shut up and let me think!" He screamed at her. He felt something crawling under his shirt and he slapped at the bump, a roach falling out to land on the counter. Shaking the lighter furiously, he tried again, and this time the lighter worked! A small blue flame sputtered to life and Henry wasted no time. Just before trying to light the cigarette lighter, he had used a piece of wooden molding from the counter and had picked up the closest piece of clothing near to him, wrapping the material around the tip of wood. He was in luck, finding a cotton blend shirt that should burn easily once he had set the homemade torch to burning. He had cracked open one of the shotgun shells and sprinkled the cotton material with the gunpowder. Then, holding the lighter under the makeshift torch, he silently prayed it would work.

The flame licked at the material, and a second later, the torch woofed with a small blaze of blue and orange, the gunpowder feeding the flames. Henry wasted no time, but instead leaned over as far as he could and knocked over the closest rack of clothing he could reach. Holding the torch to one of the housecoats, a lime-green affair just made for old ladies, he set it alight. The clothing caught easily and a second later the rack was burning nicely. Flames licked at other nearby racks of clothing and soon the flames had jumped to the next aisle. Though the smoke was becoming caustic, all they could do was try to hold their breath and wait, the floor still filled with roaches; not that it helped that they were standing on the counter, their heads far too close to the ceiling to receive clear air.

"All right, just give it a little more time and if we don't pass out from the smoke, we can try to make a run for it!" He yelled, his face resembling something out of nightmares as the flames flickered and cast shadows across his visage. The cockroaches shied away from the flames, some rolling over and curling up to die under the intense heat. Though the floor was still covered, there were small, clear pockets appearing where the insects were shying away from the heat, not wanting to get too close to the slowly growing inferno. Clothing on the floors, knocked over and discarded were beginning to smolder, the fire retardant material only adding to the smoke, though not bursting into flames themselves.

Henry still had the torch and he waved it at his feet and Mary's, trying to keep the roaches off them as they waited for the right moment to run.

Ten minutes past and the ceiling was invisible, nothing but smoke filling the store. Both Mary and Henry had their faces in their shirts, trying to use them as filters. The coughing was uncontrollable and Henry had taken to only breathing from his nose, the chemicals in the clothing burning his nostrils, but keeping him from coughing. Mucus dripped down his face like a five-year-old with a bad cold, but he ignored it, waiting for the right moment to move.

He found it seconds later when a rack, blazing, fell over, the roaches scattering.

"There's our chance, Mary, run for it, now!" He screamed, but instead his voice sounded hoarse and dry from coughing. But she heard him, and though she hated to leave her small island of safety, she obeyed, dropping down to the floor, her heels crunching under the piles of small carcasses.

Henry followed and scooped her up in his arms, holding her upright as he ran and jumped over the small pools of roaches. His arms were singed by the nearby fires, but he ignored it. The closer he was to the small blazes, the safer he was from the encroaching insects.

Behind them, the store was becoming a small inferno, the rest of the large room catching fire. Was it Henry's imagination or could he actually hear the high pitched screams as the insects roasted alive, similar to the sound a lobster makes when its dropped into boiling hot water. He didn't know for sure, but he tried to imagine the little bastards were suffering.

Finally reaching the front of the store, he lunged through the shattered window, falling to the sidewalk, Mary next to him. His shotgun was digging into his side and he rolled over to reduce the pain. No sooner did he roll over and look up did he see the rotten, decayed face of a dead man looking down on him with an almost idle curiosity.

Henry lay there, coughing, staring up at the creature. His shotgun was still under him and he didn't know if he would have time to reach his Glock or panga before the creature leaned down and attacked. One bite, one scratch would be all it would take to send him on the last train west.

Controlling the coughing, Henry smiled up at the dead man. "Hey, buddy, can we talk about this?" He asked as his hand crept down his thigh to draw his Glock. The zombie snarled, its dead eyes flaring wide, looking even more evil in the flickering light of the fire.

Then it bent over and lunged at him, just as his hand wrapped around the butt of his sidearm. He was too late!

Just before the ghoul could sink its teeth into him, it was knocked back and away like the Hand of God had slapped it. Looking up and over, Mary was in a kneeling position, her Winchester cradled in her arms as she ejected the spent shell, and proceeded to reload the weapon from the shells in her pockets.

"Thanks, I thought I was a goner for sure," he told her.

She grinned. "No problem, just repaying the favor. So, do you think you can trust me again?"

Henry sat up, checking himself for wounds and finding none. Only his ribs ached, not totally healed yet from the fall from the cruise ship. It already felt like it had happened weeks ago, but was in fact, only days.

"Yeah, I guess so, thanks again," he said, standing up. Looking around, he could see shadows on the fringes of the road. The dead man had friends who were even now moving in to investigate.

"Best we get moving, I think we're about done here. How say you?" He asked her.

Finished with the last shell, she cocked the weapon and nodded. "Fine with me, lets go."

Henry checked his shotgun, adding a few new rounds to replace the spent ones he'd used and then they started moving. The shadows were closer now, and as he moved away from the tiny strip-mall, he looked back and could clearly see the dead faces illuminated in the blaze of the store as they passed by the fire. There were ten or so, all in different states of decay. Only one saw him and Henry turned and shot it in the face, the round striking its neck instead. The ghoul spun on its heels and then stopped. Its head was still attached, its spine and a few pieces of gristle holding it in place, though the head lolled at a ridiculous angle. Henry ignored it then. If it was still interested in him then it wasn't showing it.

"Come on, let's double time it. The sooner we're on the road and out of here, the better."

"Lead the way," she said, following.

"Oh, and Mary..." Henry said, leaving the sentence hanging.

"Yeah, what is it?" She asked.

"The next time you want to go shopping for clothes, leave me out of it, okay?"

She chuckled slightly and nodded. "Sure, Henry, no problem."

They walked in silence for a while, only concentrating on moving quickly and studying their surroundings for potential threats. When Mary felt they were safe, she asked: "So where to?"

"The beach. We need to start from where we were found the other day and work our search out from there. Once we get there, we go find Jimmy and Cindy."

"What about the Reverend. He did screw us over..." She left the rest hanging. Henry thought about it for a second or so. She was right, of course. The so called man-of-God had set them both up to be his patsy. He should pay for that. Plus, it wasn't like Henry to leave an enemy behind, but it was more important to find Jimmy and Cindy, if they were still alive, that is. Either way he had to try. The Reverend wouldn't be going anywhere and once they were away from California it would be unlikely they would ever see the man again.

And good riddance.

"Forget him. We'd have to get back inside the town, and once we did, we'd be outgunned. It's not worth it. Plus, he'll probably think we died when we don't return. Let him think that. Once we're away from here, we'll never see him again; let's just concentrate on finding our friends."

She nodded, agreeing, though she had to admit she wouldn't have minded paying the bastard back for hypnotizing her. Oh well, perhaps in another life she'd get her revenge.

With both jogging at a casual gait, they moved up the road, soon lost in the shadows of the night as the store burned in the darkness behind them like a lone candle.

* * *

The sun was just rising over the clouds when they approached the half mile mark to the main gate of Sunset Bay. They had no choice but to pass by the town as it was the only viable route back to the beach.

Henry and Mary slowed as they approached, noticing an unusual amount of activity around the main gate. From their vantage point they had a clear view of the gate, but could not be spotted by the guards from their position and so were able to watch patiently as events unfolded.

Ducking into the shrubbery lining the highway, both he and Mary watched silently while men ran about moving barricades and shooting any wandering ghouls still moving about the gate.

"What's going on?" Mary asked next to him, squinting hard so she could make out the small figures as they moved about like ants on an ant hill. She was hot and tired, the long night-walk weighing down on her heavily. She was looking forward to finding a place to rest, but now it seemed there was something important happening.

"I don't know, but I wouldn't mind finding out," Henry said as he watched the last of the barricades being dragged away from the gate.

He was about to move his position, wanting to get closer to the area in question, when he heard the distinctive sound of multiple large truck engines. The road seemed to vibrate with their intensity and a moment later, he saw the front end of a large, black eighteen wheeler exiting the town.

But before the semi exited, though, there was a lead car, carrying two in the front seat and three in the back. The car moved forward a few car lengths and then slid back to the side of the road, then moved forward again like a satellite orbiting its larger master, always staying close to the larger vehicle. Then the first semi appeared, rolling through the gate like a demon out of the depths of hell.

"What could they be doing with those?" Mary asked.

Henry shook his head, not knowing, but getting an itch just behind his ear as he remembered seeing those same trucks parked by the lighted warehouse with all the activity the other night.

"I don't know, but I saw those rigs the other night. They were near a warehouse and there was a lot of activity going on. Wherever they're going, I think we should tag along," he said, ducking low when the first car drove by their position, followed by the first semi. One more eighteen wheeler followed, rumbling past their hiding place, a spume of dirt and dust following in the convoy's wake.

"Okay, fine, but how the hell are we going to get into the convoy? If we're spotted, we'll likely be shot," Mary stated while she watched the vehicles roar past, the noise so loud she was tempted to cover her ears.

Henry's head perked up at what he saw next. Coming out of the gate after the second semi was a trail car, a jacked up El Camino with a bright blue paintjob. There was only one man in the driver's seat and another in the rear bed, the passenger's head swiveling around for signs of danger. But the man was looking for rogue zombies, not particularly worried about human enemies and Henry was planning on using that to his advantage.

Just as the second semi rolled past, Henry grabbed Mary by the arm and pushed her into the road. “Fall down and act like you’re hurt. When they stop to check, I’ll take out the driver, you get the guy in the bed,” he hissed at her as she felt herself shoved forward.

If she was going to argue, she wasn’t given the opportunity, finding herself tossed out onto the road like a bag of garbage. She hit hard, scraping her arm and crying out in pain.

Looking up, she saw nothing but the front grille of the El Camino bearing down on her, and for a moment she wondered if the driver was just going to drive over her, killing her as he did so. But the driver slowed, swerving the car and pumping the brakes. The second semi had rounded a bend further up the road and was out of sight, the trail car now all alone. It was the perfect ambush, provided the men didn’t have itchy trigger fingers.

Mary lay in the road with her Winchester under her. From a casual glance, she looked unarmed. The driver’s door opened and the man in the rear bed jumped down, thinking Mary had fallen from the convoy in front of them.

“Hey there, Missy, you okay?” The driver asked while walking over to her. He hadn’t taken three steps toward Mary when Henry shot the man from the edge of the tree line, striking him high in the right shoulder. The guard twisted from the impact of the round, falling backwards as his left arm instinctively came up to touch where the pain was.

He never got the chance to actually know what had happened to him. When the man reached up and touched his wound, his eyes already glazed in shock and surprise, Henry stepped out onto the road and sent another round directly at the man’s face. One moment the man had a face, with eyes and a nose and a mouth. The next his face was nothing but a grizzly mass of red and burnt meat. His body balanced for almost thirty seconds, the legs not realizing the brain wasn’t there to direct them and then the body just crumpled to the ground like the man was too tired to stand anymore and just wanted to take a nap.

At the same time the driver was losing his face, Mary had rolled to her knees and fired twice into the other man, the impact of the rounds tearing his chest to something resembling ground hamburger. The man flew backward, landing hard onto the hot pavement, but he was already dead, his arms lying motionless at his side.

For a heartbeat there was no sound but the cry of a crow in a nearby tree. Mary stood still, not moving, while Henry strolled over to the two bodies to make sure the men were dead, stripping the dead men of their side arms. They were still in sight of the wall and it could be any second that someone discovered them and sent out reinforcements.

Then without preamble, he waved to Mary to get in the car.

"Come on, the guards at the gate will have heard the shots. We'll have company in a minute if we don't go."

Mary stood up, her face a mask of anger. "What the hell was that? You tossed me into the road like an old shoe. What if he ran me over?" She yelled, waving her arms in the air for emphasis.

Henry tossed the side arms into the El Camino and then climbed into the driver's seat. The car was still running and he placed it in drive, slowly rolling up to Mary's position.

When he reached her position, he stopped, grinning up at her angry face. She was so mad he could almost picture storm clouds over her head and bolts of lightning shooting from her eyes like a cartoon character.

"Look, I'm sorry. I didn't have much time to think and it felt like the right thing to do at the moment. In hindsight, you're probably right; he could have just as easily run you down or shot you in the road and gone around you. If it'll make you feel better, I'm sorry."

"You're sorry?" She stood there with her mouth hanging open.

"Yeah, I'm sorry, now are you going to get in the car or are you gonna walk?"

She was about to tell him she'd rather walk, and that he should go to straight to hell, when the sound of another car could be heard coming up the road, followed by gunshots. A second later, only inches from her feet, the dirt exploded, spraying debris in all directions. Mary dropped down behind the car, ducking instinctively.

That decided it for her. Stomping her feet in frustration, she ran around the front of the car and climbed inside. Once inside the relative safety of the car, she crossed her arms and pouted, looking like a little girl with the exception of the Winchester rifle between her legs.

Henry floored the gas pedal, the car shooting forward, the enemy vehicle in pursuit and slowly gaining on him.

"There, now that wasn't so bad, was it?" Henry asked her with a wide grin on his lips and the wind blowing his ash-gray hair around his face. He was almost flying down the road, he was going so fast, attempting to outrun his pursuers and also trying to reach the convoy somewhere on the road in front of him. He didn't know what was going on with that convoy, but he knew wherever those semis were going would be interesting.

What he didn't know was just how interesting.

But first things first. Before he could deal with the convoy, he had to figure out how to ditch his tail or he and Mary would be in hot water all over again real soon.

Chapter 28

"That car is still following us, they're gonna try something soon. We need to deal with them before they do," Mary said, turning around in her seat. The semis were about a quarter mile in front of them and Henry had made sure to keep his distance, not wanting any of the drivers or passengers to see him and know he was an impostor, the actual driver lying dead in the road.

Mary had sent a few rounds back at the trailing car, making it keep its distance, but every few minutes the driver would speed up, slowly gaining his courage back.

"Yeah, I know. We need to figure out what we're gonna do, though that doesn't end up with us getting killed. They must know we stole this car when they found their friends dead in the street. Sooner or later they're gonna make their move, not just taking a few pot shots at us, and when they do, I want to make ours first."

"What do you have planned?" She asked as she glanced over her shoulder again. At the moment, the trail car was about a thousand feet away, not moving closer, but not dropping back. Whoever was driving was wary of them now, respectful of their firepower, but they could block them in-between the convoy and then Henry and Mary would be vastly outnumbered. And that didn't bode too well for their chances of escaping alive.

Henry shot her a quick look. "I'll let you know it when I do, okay? I'm kinda making it up as I go."

She nodded. "Okay, but I suggest you speed it up or they might take the decision out of your hands."

Henry flashed a grimace her way, but that was all, concentrating on not losing the rear semi. If he was correct, then the car they had taken would have been the trail car, making sure there were no problems in the rear of the convoy. So far no one had tried to contact them and that was fine with Henry. The longer they were anonymous, the better. Which was why he had to figure out a way to dispose of the other car both quickly and quietly. If Mary started shooting once they were closer to the rigs, then the men in the semis would be alerted to trouble, so that was out. No, he needed to come up with something that would be silent. The only question was what?

The road they were on hugged a cliff on the right side, the left nothing but a steep incline of trees and boulders. There was a sharp turn in the road just ahead, and just as Henry began banking around it, an idea came to him like a flash of light.

Without telling Mary what he was doing, he slammed on the brakes, the car fishtailing dangerously close to the guardrail, and then before she could ask what he was doing, he slammed the car in reverse and started driving backward, gaining speed as he slowly accelerated.

Just as he reached the bend in the road, the other car came around the turn, and was greeted by Henry coming straight towards them. In his rearview mirror, Henry could see the eyes of the driver, two more men tucked next to him in the front seat. He saw the driver panic, and desperately try to avoid Henry, but instead ended up shooting through the guardrail and over the side of the cliff.

Henry slammed on the brakes and jumped out of the car, running to the broken guardrail. The car was still in mid-air, but just as he looked downward, finding it in the wide open expanse, the car plunged into a small stream at the bottom of the ravine, collapsing in on itself like it was made of aluminum foil. Though flattening, and rolling a few times, the car stayed silent, no eruption of a fireball to be seen. He breathed a sigh of relief. If the car had exploded, then it might have been possible the semi's drivers could have seen or heard it, but the way events had played out, the initial crash was already lost in the cavernous ravine like it had never happened.

Mary ran up to him and looked down at the wreckage.

"Thanks for the heads up," she said, looking down into the ravine and admiring his handiwork.

He shrugged. “Sorry again. The idea came to me so quick there wasn’t time to discuss it. It worked didn’t it?”

“Yeah, guess so, but it would still be nice to be let in on what the hell is going on once in a while.”

He rubbed her shoulder affectionately. “Honey, when there’s time, I promise we can set up a committee, now come on; let’s get a move on before we lose those rigs.”

They both ran back to the idling car and climbed in, Henry shooting forward with a screech of tires. Zigzagging through the curves, it wasn’t long before the rear of the last semi came into view. Slowing down, Henry followed at a discreet distance once again, this time being able to relax a little more without worry of being followed.

Now all there was to do was drive and see where the convoy led them.

Unfortunately, things weren’t going as planned, and an hour later, the engine started to make weird noises that Henry couldn’t identify.

“What’s wrong?” Mary asked from his side.

“I don’t know, but if I had to guess, I’d say it’s the timing chain or something serious like that. I’m gonna pull over and check.”

Turning the wheel to the right, Henry brought the car to a halt, looking forlornly through the front windshield as the rear of the second semi disappeared around the next bend.

“Shit, we’re gonna lose them now,” he snapped; stepping out of the car and slamming the door shut. Opening the hood, he stared at it like it would talk to him and tell him what was wrong with it. The engine was click, clacking like it had thrown a cylinder, making quite a racket. Then as if the engine had sensed it was being watched, it sputtered and died.

“Shit!” Henry yelled out over the ravine. “Mary, scoot over and try to start it again, will ya?”

She did as asked and a moment later the starter was clicking continuously. Henry waited for almost a minute until smoke appeared; the starter overheating.

“Enough, enough, stop please, it’s not working.”

A second later, Henry heard the car door slam and then Mary was next to him.

"So, what now?" She asked quietly, not wanting to agitate him anymore than he already was.

With a sigh, Henry closed the hood. "Now, my dear, we walk. Again. All we can do is hope the location of the rigs isn't to far from here."

"I'll get our stuff and weapons," she said and then went to work, quickly gathering anything of value.

Accepting his shotgun from her with a nod, they started walking up the lonely highway, the sun slowly rising in the sky.

"You know, it seems that all we do sometimes is walk," he said in a dreamlike voice.

"Yeah, I know, but so far only our feet haven't failed on us," Mary said, trying to sound positive.

Henry didn't answer and the two walked in silence for the next fifteen minutes, both of them concentrating on putting one foot in front of the other.

"It's beautiful out here," Mary finally said, breaking their silence as she gazed out at the mountains and trees.

"Yeah, it is. Kind of reminds me of back home," Henry said in a melancholy tone.

Mary was silent for almost a minute and then said: "Henry, do you think we'll ever go back home, you know, back to Pineridge and your house?"

"I don't really know. I'd be lying to you if I said I hadn't thought about it. But what's really there? This past year my home's been wherever the four of us have laid our heads. That hasn't changed."

She smiled at him, pleased with the compliment.

"Henry?" She asked yet again.

"Hmm?"

"Do you think Jimmy and Cindy are really alive? Or is it just wishful thinking."

He stopped walking and turned to her, wiping his forehead of sweat.

"Mary. Jimmy once said that until you see the body, then the person isn't dead. Remember? I've told you that before, too. Well I'm sticking to it. Until I see their bodies, I'm going to keep looking and hope for the best, no matter how long it takes. But don't get me wrong, I'm a realist. It's always possible they're dead, I just won't entertain that idea just yet."

She repositioned the Winchester and grinned. "Fair enough, I'm with you, you should know that. Besides, life's not the same if I don't have that little twit to tease," she said, referring to Jimmy.

He chuckled at that and they started walking again. "I'm sure he feels the same way about you. You know, if they are still alive, I wonder what they're doing right now."

Mary shrugged. "Knowing Jimmy, he's probably stuffing his face while Cindy does all the work."

Henry chuckled. "Yeah, probably. If there's a way for Jimmy to goof off, then I'm sure he's found it already. Shit, he's probably living it up at some small town he found, patiently waiting for us to find him and Cindy.

With their spirits a little higher, thinking about their two missing friends as safe and sound somewhere, they continued trudging up the empty two-lane road.

The road in front of them would continue on for a few more miles and then meander back to the ocean, where the coastal town of Stardust Cove waited, ignorant of its coming fate.

Chapter 29

Jimmy moved across the high cement wall of the town, his eyes trying to see everything at once as he patrolled his area. Despite the decadence of the town, both he and Cindy were fitting in quite well. Cindy was still sleeping at the moment, not being due for work in the bar until noon. Jimmy had drawn a shift on the wall and Bert had told him it was non-negotiable.

The night before, after making passionate love, Jimmy and Cindy had discussed their roles in the town and what their next move should be. They had agreed on remaining for another two days, making sure they were both well rested, then they would take their slowly growing stockpile of food they had both been accumulating and would find a way to sneak out of the town and begin their search for Henry and Mary.

But first he had to finish his shift on the wall, then he would meet up with Cindy at the bar for a quick meal. Then he would leave her to finish her own shift. She had fit in quite well at the Dollar Bar and Betsy had already become a good friend. Cindy had told him in bed the previous night that Betsy reminded her of the mother she'd lost years ago.

Though it would be sad to leave her new friend, Cindy told him she'd be ready and that any ties she made while they were in the town could be cut easily.

After that, they had made love for the second time until both had passed out, exhausted.

Jimmy smiled now, thinking back to last night. How soft her skin had felt and how she had been like a living ball of energy as they rolled around in the sheets together like a single being.

For the thousandth time since he'd met her, he thought how much he loved her and thanked whatever God had saw fit to send her to him.

Jimmy had been on watch for almost two hours, the sun just having risen in the sky, signaling the start of another beautiful Californian day, when the first view of two eighteen wheelers came into view. With the jersey barricades in front of the gate, the truck drivers had no choice but to stop.

Another guard on watch with Jimmy this morning moved closer to him so they could talk better. The man's name was Tyrell and he was a large black man with a deep voice, heavy accent, and an imposing stare. Despite this, Jimmy and he had become fast friends, enjoying each others company while burning the hours on watch until they were relieved.

"Hey, any idea what that's about?" Jimmy asked the large man.

"No, brudda, I's got no idea, but Paco already's called Bert and he's on 'is way," Tyrell said while, fingering his rifle nervously.

Tyrell was referring to the man at the other end of the wall. Paco was a small Mexican man who wore a faded Dodgers T-shirt and matching baseball cap. His English was atrocious, but he was a nice enough guy. Jimmy had taken an immediate liking to him despite the language barrier. Now the three of them raised their weapons and prepared for what would come next as the semis idled softly down below, the rumble vibrating straight up to their feet through the cement of the wall.

At the sound of vehicles behind him, Jimmy turned to see Bert arriving with ten other men. They all looked tired, like they had been pulled from their beds, but all had weapons in hand and grim looks of determination on their faces. The open-bed pickup trucks pulled into the lot with a spry of dust, all the men jumping to the ground and running to the wall. Bert climbed up the ladder and nodded to Jimmy and Tyrell while the other men scrambled up the wall to cover all possible angles of fire.

"What you boys got?" Bert asked. "Paco said something about a truck, but I can't understand what the hell he's saying. The man's voice is worse than a drive-thru window employee at a McDonalds. The only thing he didn't say to me is if I want fries with that?" He finished as he approached the other men.

Jimmy ignored the man's joke and pointed to the two semis and the one car next to it. At the moment, nothing was happening, the tinted windows in the trucks defying any chance at perceiving who was driving, though Bert tried with a set of binoculars.

A few zombies were gathering around the front grille of the trucks, attracted to the noise, but at the moment the area was almost totally devoid of any undead presence. The night before, the men on watch had taken a flamethrower to the crowd of ghouls, burning them to nothing but ash and bone. The rest had run away, their primitive brains had enough intelligence to know to stay by the walls would be death; this time a permanent one.

But as the sun rose that morning, they started to trickle back, wanting the live food they knew existed inside the tall, stone walls.

"Has anyone made contact yet?" Bert asked while scanning the trucks for movement.

"No, brudda, nothin's happened," Tyrell said.

Then the door to the car opened and a man climbed out.

"Wait, the car! Someone's getting out!" Jimmy yelled, pointing with the barrel of his shotgun. Up on the wall the weapon was almost useless, but if anything tried to actually climb the wall, or stayed to long at its façade, then his weapon would be deadly.

Ralph climbed out of the car and walked over to the front of the vehicle. He had a bullhorn in his hand and as the men on the wall watched, he raised it to his mouth and spoke.

"Hello, Stardust Cove! Reverend Carlson sends his best and a token of his wanting to mend our ways between our two people!" He turned and gestured to the two semis. "Inside these trucks are food and supplies. We found a warehouse on the other side of San Diego and stripped it clean. There was so much that we decided to share it with all of you, too. We want to be friends, no more fighting. We need to stick together if we're gonna survive this shit we've all found ourselves in!"

Ralph walked back to the car and leaned on the hood. "So? What do you say? Come out and inspect the cargo if you don't believe me." Then Ralph turned and shot a walking corpse that had stumbled too close to him, blowing its head clean off its shoulders.

Jimmy turned to Bert. "Could what he's saying be true?"

"Maybe, I guess...shit. I don't know what to think," Bert said, stymied.

"You best be gettin' Mr. Merle up here, Boss," Tyrell said as he watched the trucks. Ralph and a few other men were taking pot-shots at any roving ghouls, keeping the area clear, but more were arriving every second, attracted to the activity.

"Best make up your minds quick!" Ralph yelled and shot another ghoul in the face. "It's getting crowded out here!"

Bert rubbed his face, trying to decide what to do.

"Tyrell's got a point, Bert. Merle should know what's happening. Let him decide what we should do next," Jimmy told him.

"Yeah, I know, it's just...there's been so much bad blood between our towns and now this..." Sighing, he picked up the two-way radio on his belt and called Merle. It took a few seconds for a reply and when the fat man's voice came over the speaker, the distinctive sound of a woman giggling in the background could be heard.

"What the fuck do you want? I'm busy doing Mayor's work," Merle snapped into the radio.

Bert sighed again and then quickly filled him in on what had happened and asked what he wanted them to do. Merle waited almost a full ten seconds before returning his answer.

"Well, get that shit inside the walls, we need it. If Carlson is stupid enough to want to make friends, then who're we to stop him."

"But what if it's some kind of trap?" Bert said into the radio. "Maybe I should inspect the situation some more before we let them into the town."

"Trap? Why the hell would they do that? Shit, Bert, stop thinkin' so goddamn much and get that shit inside the walls." Merle said and then the sounds of giggling could be heard again before the man took his finger off the call button on his radio. "Look, I already said I'm busy, so just get it done. Or do I need to find a new security chief."

With a slight dropping of his shoulders, Bert shook his head no, despite the fact he was talking on a radio. "No, sir, you don't. I'll get it done," Bert said and then snapped the radio back to his belt.

"Well, boys, there you have it. The man wants us to bring those trucks inside. But before we do I still want to check them out."

"But Boss, Merle said..." Tyrell started to say until Bert cut him off with a snarl and a glare.

"I know what he said, goddammit, but I'm in charge here and I say we inspect the cargo, now get down there! I want you to go with me, too, Tyrell. You too, Jimmy. Paco, you stay here with the others and at any sign of foul play, you shoot those fuckers."

"Si, Senor," Paco said and stepped away so the others could descend.

Once on the ground, with Bert in the lead, the three men stepped through the small opening connected to the gate and walked out into the open area in front of the walls. The jersey barriers were off to his left and Jimmy wondered just how exactly the trucks would be brought inside the town. But then Bert had said something about a tanker full of gas and he had to assume the same egress for the tanker would be used for the semis...wherever that was.

The men covered the distance in only a few minutes and were greeted by Ralph when they reached the first truck. While they moved through the area, pot-shots were taken frequently at any nearby ghouls.

"I'm Ralph, the Reverend's head of security. So, I guess you guys want to inspect the product, make sure there aren't a dozen commandoes inside waiting to jump out and shoot ya?"

"Something like that," Bert said as he sized up the other man.

"Well, come on then, let's go see."

They walked to the rear of the trucks, with numerous gunshots sounding around them as the men in the crew kept the zombies at bay.

"Best do this quick, if it's all the same ta you. There's more of 'em coming every minute," Ralph said. Was there a touch of nervousness to his voice? Jimmy wondered.

Upon reaching the rear cargo doors, another man was ready, holding the latch, and threw up the door.

Bert whistled softly as he stared at the boxes of supplies. Toilet paper, clothing, dried food and bottles of juice and crackers. It was a goldmine and it was being given to them free, out of friendship!

"See, I told ya. Nothing fishy's goin' on here. Just one town helpin' out another," Ralph said with a wide smile.

Jimmy frowned and reached up and grabbed a box of crackers from the back of the trailer. Opening it, he pulled out one of the colorful interior boxes and grunted when he saw the vacuum sealed bag inside.

"It's real," he said.

"Of course it's real, what else would it be?" Ralph said with a little indignation in his voice.

Bert had also reached up and pulled down a carton of apple juice. Ripping off the cover, he saw six plastic bottles, all still sealed from the factory.

"Son-of-a-bitch, this is really on the level. You guys are just giving this stuff to us?" Bert asked.

Ralph nodded yet again. "That's right. We want to mend the broken fences and shit that's grown between our two towns. This is the Reverend's way of starting that process. Besides, if you fellas saw all the shit we got, then believe me, this is nothing."

"All right then, let's get this stuff inside where it's safe," Bert said, reaching for his radio. "Paco, open the side door, we're comin' in."

"Si, Senior, I do it now," Paco answered back, his voice garbled. Jimmy realized the man had his mouth too close to the speaker when he talked and so his voice came out garbled. He made a note to himself to tell the man later, that is if he could make him understand what he needed to do.

With more sporadic gunfire floating across the road, Jimmy watched as a massive piece of the stone wall was removed from the right side of the jersey barriers. As the wall was raised into the air, Jimmy could see a mid-size crane behind it. The crane was lifting the section of wall out of its slot like a giant Lego set. With the slab now removed, there was more than enough room for the trailers to drive through easily.

"Well, I'll be damned, so that's how you do it," Jimmy said while he watched the crane pivoting on its axis with the stone slab hanging like a giant pendulum.

"Yup, we had an engineer help design it. Pretty clever, huh?" Bert said; proud of the construction like it was his own design.

"So what's the story, should we just drive inside or what?" Ralph asked.

"Yeah, tell the driver's to turn left once they get inside. From there we'll inspect everything better and offload it. But be warned, the men on the wall will still be watching with loaded weapons," Bert said with a hint of a warning.

Ralph grinned like a Cheshire cat. "Wouldn't want it any other way."

He climbed into his car and Jimmy could see him talking into a two-way radio while the driver swung the vehicle around and headed for the gate. Seconds later the trucks began to rumble more, the drivers revving the engines in preparation for moving.

Jimmy, Tyrell and Bert jogged back through the small side door, Tyrell taking a few zombies out as they ran. It was true, it was growing worse outside the walls and the sooner they were all back inside the better. The other men on watch were all busy, now; keeping the zombies from entering the large hole in the wall.

The semis rolled into the opening, and once the last one was past the wall, the crane began lowering the section again. A few ambitious zombies scurried inside while the hole was closing, but they were quickly dispatched by the guards on the walls.

Bert helped direct the semis to the parking area, and within a few minutes the semis engines were turned off, a deafening silence descending over everything after listening to the rumble of the diesels for so long.

Ralph was already out of his car again and walking over to Bert and the others.

"So what's next?" He asked cheerfully. Too cheerfully if Jimmy had an opinion.

"Next, we offload everything and get you and your men set up for the night." Bert told Ralph while the drivers of the semis climbed out of the cabs, the passengers doing the same.

Jimmy noticed one of the drivers appeared to be looking for something under the passenger seat and he walked over and cleared his throat so the man knew he was standing behind there.

"Lose something?" Jimmy asked, casually.

The driver turned around and stopped what he was doing. “Huh? What? Oh, no, guess not. Thought I dropped my cigarette lighter, that’s all.”

“Okay, then, if you’re all set then let’s get with the others,” Jimmy said, this time with an edge to his voice.

The driver nodded, and climbed down from the cab. Jimmy flashed the driver a smile as the man passed him. Jimmy glanced into the cab for a moment, but on the ground there wasn’t much to see unless he wanted to climb up the side of the semi. Deciding everything was fine, he followed the man back to the others.

When everyone had disembarked from their vehicles there were a total of six men, including a shy fellow who wore an old Yankees baseball cap over his eyes. With all the commotion going on in the area, no one noticed him.

“Look, Ralph, about your weapons...” Bert said almost hesitantly.

“What about them? Jesus, man, there’s only six of us. What the hell are we gonna do, take over the town single-handedly?”

The rest of Ralph’s men chuckled at that and Bert had to admit the rival security chief had a point. It wasn’t like they could do much harm, and besides, they would always be under guard while they were inside the walls of the town.

“Fair enough, you made your point. You can keep your weapons, but be warned. One wrong move and...”

Ralph raised his hand to silence the larger man. “Yeah, yeah, I know, you’ll blast us. Shit, I’d do the same if you were under my watch, now if it’s all the same to you, I’m starving. What do you say we let the workers handle the offloading and you show us where we can get a drink and some grub?”

Bert turned to Jimmy and Tyrell. “Jimmy, you and Tyrell get two other men and escort these fellas to the Dollar Bar for some food. When we’re done with unloading the supplies I’ll send someone to get you.”

“Sure, Bert, no problem,” Jimmy said, glad for the chance to see Cindy. She would be getting to work in an hour and he would be able to talk with her and fill her in on what had transpired.

Gesturing politely with his shotgun, Jimmy pointed the way to downtown. "Well, come on then, get goin'. It's that way," Jimmy told Ralph.

Ralph nodded. "You got it, pal, tell you what, when we get to the bar, I'll buy you a beer, how 'bout that?"

Jimmy only smiled, his eyes not matching his lips. "Sure, whatever."

The group headed off, leaving Bert and the rest of the men to offload the food and supplies, but the last man in line hesitated for a moment, watching the activity at the rear of the trailers as the men began offloading boxes of goods. His eyes peeked out from under his baseball cap and a smile crossed his lips, then he moved away, following the others on their way into the town proper.

Chapter 30

Jimmy led his guests, or prisoners, he really wasn't quite sure which one the men were, and the rest of the guards into downtown. They were more than halfway to the Dollar Bar when the prisoners made a break to get away. That was the moment he made up his mind that they definitely weren't guests of the town.

Jimmy was in the lead, with Tyrell walking to the right of the six men. The other two guards, Jimmy wasn't actually sure of their names, but he thought of them as Moe and Curly from their resemblance to the Three Stooges. One had short black hair in a bowl haircut, and the other's head was round with a scraped scalp, only peach fuzz growing in from the last shave of his dome-shaped head

The escape came at the most inopportune time, or perhaps the perfect time, depending on your point of view, meaning whether it was Jimmy's or Ralph's.

Just as the group of ten had reached the middle of town, the debauchery in full swing around them, a fight had broken out near another bar. The brawl had taken place in the street, and from the looks of it, the two men were fighting over one of the local prostitutes.

With the men punching and kicking each other, trying to gain the upper hand, the fight rolled into the middle of the prisoners.

When Moe and Curly took their eyes off the prisoners to try and break up the fight, that was the precise moment when Ralph brought up his elbow and slammed it into Jimmy's jaw.

Jimmy fell backward, hitting the ground hard, seeing stars from the strength of the blow. While he lay on the ground staring up at the sky, in his dazed mind hoping no one would step on him, a firefight erupted over his head.

After knocking Jimmy to the ground, Ralph brought around his sidearm and shot Tyrell in the chest from no more than ten feet away. The black man was thrown to the dirt, his chest spitting blood like a geyser and he opened and closed his mouth like a landed fish, not understanding how he had ended up on the ground dying.

Meanwhile, two other prisoners tackled Moe and Curly, clubbing them in the head and shoulders until they were unconscious. But it didn't end there. Once the prisoners had stripped the two unconscious men of their weapons, Ralph crossed the few feet separating the downed men from him, and in cold blood, shot both men in the face, ending their lives in an instant.

With Ralph discharging his weapon, the crowd around him went into turmoil, men and women running to and fro, trying to escape from whatever carnage had befallen them. In the commotion, Ralph looked for Jimmy, wanting to finish him off before he could get to his feet.

But though Ralph tried to cross the distance to Jimmy, the crowd around him slowed his progress. Jimmy, unaware of the danger about to strike him was even now climbing to his feet, his vision still fuzzy.

Ralph spotted him and raised his handgun, prepared to send Jimmy to hell when a bystander ran by Jimmy just as a round was headed for his chest. The bystander went down in a scream of gurgling blood and Jimmy realized he was being shot at. Ducking down to the ground, his mind now sharp with adrenalin, he duck-walked over to a cart and stayed low, only peeking out when he thought it was safe.

What he saw was Ralph rallying his men as they punched, kicked and sometimes shot some of the crowd as they made their way back the way they had come.

When the six ex-prisoners had started moving away far enough that Jimmy thought it was safe, he started to follow them, making sure to duck behind something each time Ralph would check his back trail. He followed them all the way to the far wall and then he watched as one of the men shrugged off the light coat he'd been wearing to see he had a light weight climbing rope wrapped around his torso. Unraveling it, he then connected a hook from another man who had hidden it on his person, and then after a few swings in a circle, he tossed it up until it caught on the top of the wall. Once he tested it, he began climbing until all six men were on the top part of the wall.

A guard on watch spotted them and sent a short burst at the six men. One of the enemies was caught in the chest and he was knocked off the wall, lost from sight as he tumbled into the bushes that surround the perimeter of the barricade. Then the five remaining men returned fire. Jimmy noticed the man with the baseball cap didn't seem to actually be firing, though the man had his handgun in his hand.

The guard went down in a hail of bullets, lost over the side like a man going into the sea from a sinking ship. Then the five remaining men began running back toward the gate, shooting guards when they became available.

Jimmy cursed under his breath. The damn perimeter guards were being taken completely unaware, and in a matter of minutes, the five prisoners will have reached the sentries at the gate and disposed of them, as well. With the high ground, and the towers at the gate, it would be hard to get at them, but Jimmy had a feeling there was something more at work here. After all, why go to the trouble of getting inside the town only to fight their way out again once they were accepted into the fold?

No, there was something seriously wrong here and Jimmy took off at a run back through the streets to find Bert. The only chance was to warn him and rally the other men before whatever was going down happened.

As Jimmy ran through the streets, he detoured by his quarters, hoping Cindy was still there. He was in luck and she was just about to head over to the bar, already clean and showered with new clothes on. She saw him running toward her and she immediately sensed something was wrong. When he reached her and she saw the bruise on his jaw, she let out a gasp of surprise.

"Oh my God, your face! What happened to you? Are you all right?"

"Never mind that now," he panted, waving her questions away. "We need to get ready to leave now. There's some shit going down soon and I have no idea what it is, but I bet it's gonna be bad and I want you with me when it does."

"But what about Betsy and the bar? My shift starts soon..."

"Screw that shit, Cindy, it's time to go. I know you're getting used to it here, but we need to leave, now come on," he pulled her out of the doorway and into the street. "And we need to find you a gun so you can defend yourself."

She let herself be pulled along, dragged like a little girl by her daddy. She yelled questions at him, not pleased with being in the dark about what was happening.

"Where are we going?" She demanded.

"To the gate. Bert needs to know what's happening and that the prisoners are on the wall."

"Prisoners? What prisoners? Who's on the wall?"

"It doesn't matter right now. Just keep up with me, you're slowing me down."

She was about to protest some more when a loud bullhorn sounded. It reminded Jimmy of an air raid siren, the high-pitched screech filling the air over the town.

"What the hell is that?" Cindy yelled, trying to be heard over the siren.

Jimmy only shrugged, but he knew a siren was never the harbinger of good news.

They raced through the streets and he noticed more people filing out of buildings, some with weapons and firearms. One burly man with a sawed-off shotgun ran by and slowed when he saw Jimmy, recognizing him as one of Bert's men.

"Is it true? Are they really inside the walls or is this another damn drill?" The man asked.

"What, a drill? What's going on, do you know what's going on?" Jimmy asked, his voice barely discernable over the siren.

"You mean you don't know? Shit, that's great when Bert's own men don't know what the hells happening."

"Dammit, man, just tell me what the fuckin' siren means!" Jimmy ordered him.

With a rolling of his eyes, the burly man looked over his shoulder towards the direction of the main gate and then looked back at Jimmy.

"That siren means the dead ones are inside the walls; that's what. If that siren sounds, then we're all in for a world of shit, now if you'll excuse me, I need to get to my post. If that sirens real, then everyone in this damn town who's able to is gonna have to fight or we're all dead." Then he took off at a ground-eating run, leaving Jimmy and Cindy behind.

While they stood in the street, hesitating for a moment, unsure of what they should do, people were moving by them hastily, bumping and pushing past them like a crowd at a rock concert.

"Damn it, Jimmy, what are we gonna do?" Cindy asked hesitantly.

"We do what we have to do to stay alive, that's what. Come on, let's get to the gate and see what's happening. If there's a chance to slip away, we'll take it. Otherwise we fight with the town."

She nodded, accepting his suggestions, and the two fought their way through the crowds. While the flow of most of the people went the other way, like salmon working their way upstream, they fought against the tide until they were on the outskirts of the town, the street in front of them leading to the large parking lot and the large gate with its jersey barriers on the outside. The first thing Jimmy saw were the two eighteen wheelers still sitting in the parking lot, but they looked far different from the last time he'd seen them. The walls of the trailers had fallen down, like the seams had let go and had just fallen outward, leaving only the floor of the trailers exposed. The second was the giant horde of undead that was even now walking toward the town. Jimmy looked over their heads at the trailers and the few ghouls still climbing down or just falling off the bed to the ground.

"Oh my God, the trailers were full of deaders and now they're in the town. We are so fucked it's not even funny," Jimmy said in awe while staring in shock at the approaching undead army.

Cindy was awestruck at the sight before her; the amount of bodies was enormous. There had to be over a thousand zombies shuffling their way towards the town. Jimmy looked up at the top of the wall to see a few guards taking pot-shots at the horde of dead men and women, but even as he watched, three of the prisoners came around the curve on the top of the wall and started shooting. The sentries were mowed down, some falling into the mass of bodies where they were ripped to shreds as they screamed for mercy. The prisoners now controlled the wall, and as Jimmy watched, one of them reached the main gate and began opening it, allowing more roamers inside the town's limits. As for the two missing prisoners, Jimmy had no idea where they had disappeared to.

Jimmy started backing away, knowing to stay where they were would be a death sentence.

"Come on, back the way we came, we need to warn the town before it's too late!"

"But what about the deaders? How to we get out of here in one piece?" Cindy asked while running at his side.

"There's a rear gate at the opposite end of town. We need to get everyone over there. We can get out that way. Once everyone's safe, we can regroup and then try to take out the deaders one by one from the walls. But right now, just run!"

So they ran like the demons of hell were at their backs, with the siren sounding overhead, and the town falling deeper into chaos.

Chapter 31

Henry and Mary had been walking for hours. Their feet hurt and they were hungry and thirsty. The only thing keeping them going was that they knew they were moving in the right direction.

A little more than a mile behind them, they had found the road sign for Stardust Cove, and soon after, the mountains had given way to upper-class homes lining the road, first only a few stragglers, their massive front yards a scene in decadence, and then an entire community of contemporized structures, each with two and three-car garages.

“That’s got to be where those rigs were going. It has to be,” Henry had told her.

“Lead, on Macbeth,” she’d said, too tired to say anything else. The only thing making their trek easier was that they were almost to the shore again. The ocean was less than a mile away and the smell of the salt water invigorated them. Concentrating on walking, they slowly moved up the road, admiring the setback homes that bordered the street.

“What do you say, should we check one for water and supplies?” Henry asked.

She nodded. “Sure, either way it’ll be good to rest a while. After all, those trucks aren’t going anywhere.”

Picking a house at random, they moved up the stone steps until they reached the front door. Even from a mile away, the salt air had ravaged the door and the front of the two-story home, the paint chipping from a year of neglect. Henry shot Mary a brief look, making sure she was ready, and then they stepped inside the gloomy house.

Sniffing deeply, all Henry could detect was the smell of a musty house. One thing about the dead is that they were easy to smell. All that rotting meat was an easy detector if they were near. If the house had unwelcome guests inside, then Henry or Mary would be able to know far before either was caught off guard. As it was, only the smell of neglect came to them and they both walked into the main hall with weapons at ease.

A rat scurried by Mary's foot and she kicked at it. "Shoo, get out of here, you little bastard. Ugh, I hate them almost as much as cockroaches."

"Not me, cockroaches are the top of my list now, then ants, then rats," Henry said while his eyes scanned the hall in front of them. The house was a simple two-story home with a stairway to the right that led up to the second floor. On the wall to the right was a hand knitted picture that read: God Bless This House.

On the main floor there were multiple openings, each one leading off in a different direction. All the doors were presently open.

"Come on, the kitchen should be this way," he said as he began to move deeper into the house. She followed, not really wanting to explore, but knowing they had no choice. If there were food and supplies inside the house, they wouldn't find them unless they searched for them.

"Close those doors as we go by them. That way we don't have to worry about anything popping up and biting our asses off," he told her.

"Okay," she said, closing each one as they made their way through the house.

At the end of the hallway was the kitchen, and after a quick sweep to make sure it was clear, Henry set his shotgun down on the dusty table. "Looks all clear, now lets see if there's anything left. You stand watch and I'll work."

"Okay, it's about time the man did all the work while the woman stood around and relaxed."

He smiled at her joke and then got to work.

The kitchen was full of tiny mouse droppings, the countertop looking like someone had sprinkled peppercorn everywhere. As for the tiny rodents, they were nowhere to be seen. But that bode well for the two companions. If mice were active here, then that could only mean there was food to find.

The cupboards were full of spider webs, the dried husks of long dead bugs littering the bottoms. He searched from top to bottom, becoming discouraged until he began looking on the bottom cabinets below the sink and microwave, closer to the mouse droppings. Reaching into the gloom, he found an old bottle of grape juice and a can of French string-beans, both unharmed by the tiny teeth and claws of the rodents, though the paper on the can of string-beans had the definite signs of being worried at.

Pulling them out of the cabinet and holding them up like a school boy proud of what he'd found, he set them on the table.

"Look at these. Someone got lazy and didn't reach all the way into the back."

Mary leaned closer, inspecting the grape juice. "Good for us. If they were more thorough, we'd be going thirsty right now."

Henry nodded. "Yeah, that is if the grape juice hasn't turned. In the mood for wine?"

She winced, hoping as he turned the cap that the juice was still drinkable. Henry opened the cap and sniffed. Satisfied with what his nose told him, he cautiously took a sip. Smacking his lips, his eyes lit up and he drank half the bottle in only a few gulps, then handed the rest to Mary. He had a big purple mustache on his upper lip; the image reminding Mary of a small child drinking his milk too fast.

"It's good, drink up. I saved you some," Henry said, wiping his mouth with his shirt.

"Yeah, I can see that," she said, smiling, and then downing a quarter of the bottle herself in a few quick gulps before she took a break. Before she could stop it, she let out a belch that rattled the few remaining glass windows.

"Oh, excuse me," she said, slightly embarrassed.

"It's okay, Mary, you're among friends here," Henry told her and then got to work opening the can of beans. Using his panga to slice into the cover of the green beans, he had it open in moments. "Can I drink the bean water or do you want some of it?"

"No, go 'head and drink up, but I want some of the beans," she told him, shaking her head.

"Cool, you know, a lot of the vitamins end up in the water, so even before the world took a nose dive I used to do this. Emily would always pour the water into a glass for me before supper."

Mary nodded, taking another sip of grape juice. Mentioning Emily made them both think of what was instead of what is, and for a moment both ate in silence.

But this time Henry wasn't going to let his mood become spoiled and he drank the bean water, relishing the taste on his lips. It was like eating the beans without chewing. Once he was finished, he grabbed a few with his hand and shoved them in his mouth, then handed her the can.

"Be careful you don't cut yourself on the lid," he told her.

She nodded and ate greedily. The beans tasted like heaven and she marveled at how, when you were hungry, anything tasted good...except rat that is. She'd known people that dined on the rodents as a regular part of their diet, but she swore she'd be on death's door before she would ever consider eating the filthy little animals. She left a little in the can for Henry and then handed it back with Henry finishing off the rest in one bite.

With both feeling refreshed, they were about to head out when the sound of a loud horn filled the house and the surrounding countryside.

"What the hells that?" Henry asked, moving to the front of the house and its dirty windows.

"Sounds like an air raid, like during WW2 at the London Blitz," she said.

Both ran outside to try and see where the noise was coming from, but with all the homes and the wide open street, plus the tall trees, it was nearly impossible.

"Where's it coming from?" Mary asked, looking around for the source.

"No way of knowing from here. But I'll tell you this. If there's an air raid horn sounding somewhere then it can't be good news. Come on," he said as he ran down the front walk, taking the steps two at a time. At the bottom of the stairs was a two-car garage and he kicked in the door, shotgun leveled just in case there was trouble. But the garage was devoid of life, only spiders and their webs inside to keep Mary and him company.

"Look, a car, maybe it still runs" he said hopefully, and moved across the garage to the side of a 2007 Buick Skylark, peeking in the dusty windows at its interior like he wanted to buy it from the long dead owner. It had black leather seats and chrome rims. Whoever had purchased the car had gone all out, buying everything in the package that was offered. The only problem was, as Henry found out when he opened the driver's side door, was that the battery was long dead. Out of shear dumb luck, the owner had left the small reading lamp on, the battery draining down to the point it was utterly useless.

Popping the hood, he had hoped maybe he could somehow jump the car's battery, but when he got a look inside the engine compartment he was greeted to a gutted engine. The battery and other important parts were long gone, stripped by some scavenger.

"Shit," he said, slamming the hood closed. We could have used this to get to that siren...and traveled in style for a change."

"What about those?" Mary said, pointing to a set of mountain bikes hanging from the ceiling by a couple of hooks. There was one for a man and one for a woman, with colors painted accordingly on the sleek frames.

Henry only grunted, his heart set on the car, but he ran over to the bikes and pulled them off their mounts. Pressing on the frame of the man's bike, he frowned. "Tires are flat, probably for a while now."

Mary walked around the garage, the siren muffled inside the stone enclosure. She slowed at a small workbench and then held something long and skinny over her head like she was holding the Olympic torch.

"Hey, look what I found. This should still work."

Holding out his hands, Henry said: "Here, toss it to me and we'll see."

She did what he asked and a moment later Henry was unscrewing one of the small black caps on the front tire, pumping it up with smooth even strokes. Mary had found a bicycle pump, along with a few other handy items like a patch kit and a backpack for riding.

"Looks like the people who lived here liked to ride," she said while examining the garage.

Henry had finished with the front tire and was now working on the back one.

"That's' good for us. We should make good time at least; better than walking, anyway."

When he finished with his bicycle, he started filling hers. In minutes he was done, and after packing a few items that might come in handy in the garage such as the patch kit and a small tool set, they exited the garage and began to ride.

Once outside again, the shrill siren was back to full force, shattering the day with its persistent call. Feeling the urgency of the call despite themselves, both began pedaling faster than normal riding speed; eating up the miles as they rode down the two lane highway.

An hour later they slowed when they saw a massive wall of stone in front of them. The siren was much louder now and had been growing in pitch the closer they came to the town. A few ghouls wandered the road around them, but it was a simple task to steer around them, the bikes whizzing by before the ghouls knew Henry and Mary were within their midst. Henry even began having a little fun, kicking a few in the ass as he drove by them. It reminded him of Jimmy, the childish prank something his young friend would have done the second he had the idea in his brain.

"This is definitely the place," Henry yelled to Mary as he stared at the wall and open gate. For the moment they were alone on the road, the zombies far behind them.

"Look," she said, pointing to the large group of zombies that were filing through the large opening in the wall, more coming out of the woods every minute.

Henry looked to his right and saw ten more ghouls coming their way.

"Shit, I think we need to leave here," he said. "Or we're gonna get caught in a trap. Maybe this isn't the best place to be on bicycles."

He pointed to the new crowd of converging dead and both began turning their bikes around, deciding to go back the way they came. But the road behind them was blocked, more than twenty ghouls now shambling up the road, as they slowly swarmed out of the woods and surrounding countryside.

The siren was a dinner bell to every undead creature in the area.

"Great, what do we do now? I don't have enough ammo to take out all of those and I know we can't move fast enough to fight our way through them, especially not on these bikes," Mary said as she watched the horde slowly draw closer.

"Dammit, I know that," Henry said, fingering the trigger of the shotgun. He was also low on ammo for the shotgun, and he only had two more clips for his Glock. After that they'd be down to using clubs and sticks...plus his panga.

Making a quick decision, he swung his bicycle around and pointed it at the opening in the wall. "Come on, our only chance is to get inside that wall and find someplace to hold up!"

"But what about all the roamers?"

"They're pointing toward the town. We can just fly past them, like out on the road; now let's go before it won't matter anymore!"

He punctuated his statement by shooting a dead fireman in the face, the body falling backward to crash to the ground. The yellow fireman's hat rolled off its head to spin on the ground like a top. But Henry and Mary didn't see this as they were already pedaling as fast as they could into the opening in the wall. Zooming past rotting cadavers, the stench hitting them both in the face, they flew by each one, the reflexes of the dead not up to the task of catching the quick moving bicycles.

Once inside the wall, Henry saw the large eighteen wheelers, the sides of the trailers peeled back like giant cardboard boxes. As he flew by them, he noticed the backs of the trailers had food boxes and a false wall, the boxes now ripped open and crushed under the hundreds of feet.

Weaving in and out of the maze of dead bodies, Henry felt the hackles on his back go up as groping arms came ever closer. Mary let out a yelp when a rotting hand wrapped around her shirt, but the forward momentum had her breaking free in an instant. Looking down, she cringed when she saw the severed hand still wrapped around her arm, and she quickly pried it off, riding deeper into the chaos surrounding her and Henry.

They had made it through the mass of walking corpses and now Henry realized they were still in trouble. Townspeople ran about, screaming and firing at the approaching undead horde. Bullets whined past his head and he realized if he and Mary didn't find cover soon, they would wind up being shot by the bullets filling the air like angry hornets.

Checking over his shoulder, relieved to see Mary still with him, he cut to the right and headed up an alleyway between a grocery store and what looked like a brothel, the scantly clad women now running around in fear. Mary was on his tail and ten seconds later, Henry hit the brakes and slowed the bike, breathing heavily from his exertion.

Mary stopped next to him and both took a much needed breather. At the opposite end of the alley, the cacophony of towns-people continued, fighting for their lives as the hundreds of ghouls flooded into the street, searching for tender flesh to eat.

"What now?" Mary asked, breathing in short gasps.

Henry shook his head, the sweat dripping down his face to fall on his hands. "I have no idea. I've been pretty much making it up as I go along." A dead hooker stumbled into the alley, and when she saw the two companions, she quickly began shuffling towards them. Henry pulled his Glock, waited patiently for the brain-dead creature to stumble closer. As he watched the woman move closer to him, he couldn't help but admire her figure. Once upon a time she had been beautiful, with tight abs and long legs. But none of that mattered now, and when she was close enough, he shot her between the eyes. The zombie dropped like a load of bricks and Henry holstered his weapon.

"There's more where she came from, best we find a place to hold up. Let's go this way," he said and started pedaling again after checking both ways at the opposite end of the alleyway.

The area was clear, the zombies not yet saturating the entire town. Taking the back road behind Main Street, they began pedaling smoothly and with purpose.

Where they would end up next was unknown, but if there was one thing Henry knew, it was that he and Mary would make it out of the predicament he had foolishly gotten them into.

But until that time happened, they would continue pedaling and keep moving.

Chapter 32

One hour ago.

Bert was managing the off-loading of the supplies from the semis when he called a halt.

"Hey, did any of you guys hear that?" He asked the other men. They were busy carrying the boxes of food and supplies across the lot and placing them in the rear beds of pick-up trucks, which would then be used to transport the supplies into the town.

"Hear what?" One of the guards asked. He was a wiry fellow with a thin nose and face that made him look like a weasel.

"That pounding. There, I just heard it again," Bert said.

With the engines of the semis turned off the lot was much quieter, the vibrations of the idling motors finally gone.

Then one of the other men's eyes perked up. "Hey, you're right, I did hear something. Maybe there's animals in the back or something. That'd be cool, real meat for a change. Think it's cow or sheep?"

"Probably dog," another man said as he reached up and grabbed another box. But the box appeared to be stuck. "Hey, what gives?" He mumbled to himself, pulling harder.

The box seemed to be jammed into its nook, but there didn't appear to be any reason for this odd occurrence. Calling Bert over, he pointed to the uncooperative receptacle.

"The damn box won't come out, it's stuck," he told Bert.

"Get out of the way, you pussy, and let a man do it," Bert snapped as he reached up and began pulling. At first the box was immobile, but soon he felt a slight tension, and then with a straining of his arms and back, he slowly pulled the box away from its rectangular brothers. When the box was a foot from the others, the weasel faced guard looked behind it and his face scrunched up in curiosity.

"Hey, there's some kind of wiring behind it," he said.

Bert's face lost all color as he realized it must be a trigger for a bomb. All the maker of the bomb had to do was wait for an unknowing worker to remove it and...boom; bye, bye workers. He closed his eyes, expecting a loud explosion and a bright flash before he saw his creator, but nothing happened.

Opening his eyes, he looked at the other men who were all staring at him like he was mad.

"Huh, guess it's a dud," he said, relief filling is voice. But then the wire went slack and the sound of tiny levers could be heard. One after another, latches undid inside the trailer until there was only silence once more.

All the men stood perfectly still, not understanding what was happening. Then, like someone had pushed the trailer walls from the inside, all four sides fell off the trailer to crash to the ground in a loud noise, the sheet metal collapsing and crumpling as it struck the pavement. Nothing but the frame, roof and the floor of the trailer remained now. But its what became exposed when the trailer's walls collapsed outward that had every guard and worker yelling in fright and panic.

Looking around like newborns, were hundreds upon hundreds of zombies, all stacked together like cattle. They were so close together that if they could still breathe, some would have suffocated in the confined space, but unfortunately, that wasn't a problem.

One second there was nothing but silence in the lot as the guards stared up at an army of the undead now inside the walls of the town. Then the first zombies on the edge of the trailer, pushed from behind by their brethren, fell off the trailer to land on the ground.

Snarling like wild animals, they attacked the closest guards, ripping into their necks and flesh, whatever was exposed, and feeding like it was their last meal.

Then there was bedlam, the men totally losing what civility they had left, most of them beginning to run away, only wanting to escape their impending death while others pulled their weapons and began shooting into the torrid mass of rotting bodies. But there were hundreds on the trailer, stuffed in there like cordwood, and now they were all flowing off the bed and crashing to the ground like a massive wave of water. The tide was enormous and the guards were quickly swept under its flowing mass, ripped to pieces or killed; then reanimating to join the enemy they had been fighting only moments before.

"Sound the alarm; let the town know what's happening, dammit!" Bert screamed, firing his weapon repeatedly as he fought for his life.

Then his jaw dropped when the other trailer, the one barely unloaded, popped its walls and then they, too, crashed to the ground, exposing more of the same dead-eyed ghouls. Watching this happen, he could now see that the supplies only went in about four feet, the false wall keeping the zombies inside. It had all been a trap, a Trojan horse fabricated by the Reverend to finally destroy his town.

Bert reached for his two-way radio, wanting to warn Merle what was happening, but the radio was knocked from his hand as a frantic woman ran by him, bumping into him in her panic; the radio falling to the street to clatter and bounce under the dozens of feet near him. Shooting round after round, Bert slowly tried to escape what he knew was coming, and when he tripped over a fallen guard laying on the ground, falling to the pavement himself, he knew that was it. Looking up at the undead faces hovering over him, he shook his head back and forth.

"No way, man, you're not getting me!" Then he made the sign of the cross and placed his weapon under his chin. Closing his eyes, he felt the first dead hands grab him just as he squeezed the trigger.

Then he knew no more.

His body still warm, the ghouls ripped him apart, hands pulling intestines out and eating them like raw sausage. Bert was torn to bits, gobbets of his body going in all directions until there was nothing left but a bloody smear on the pavement.

Those with his arms and legs and parts of his torso, sat down and began feasting, fighting others who wanted a taste. While around them, the rest of the undead army moved into the town, following the smell of live flesh and moving after the escaping guards and workers.

Then the alarm began to sound, a high-pitched screech that filled the air and foretold of the doom to come for all that remained alive within the walls of Stardust Cove.

More than half of the army moved away from the parking lot, the others staying to feast on their prizes. All the guards were either dead or had somehow joined the ranks of undead, though not too many. The zombies were hungry and for once weren't leaving much to revive.

The sun was just reaching its peak in the sky, the shadows on the ground from the approaching dead men and women almost nonexistent as they tumbled, crawled and shambled their way onto Main Street.

* * *

Jimmy was running at the head of a large group of townspeople, herding them toward the rear gate like a shepherd would his sheep. It had taken almost half an hour to get most of the people to follow him. Leaderless, they ran about like chickens with their heads cut off and it had taken a punch to the face to calm some of them down.

Now he led his flock through the streets of death. Zombies were everywhere and Jimmy had arranged all the guards he could find into lines on either sides of the large crowd. There were almost two hundred men, women and children behind him, the guards shooting anything that came too close to the group. But still there were holes in the lines and many times a ghoul would lunge from some unseen hiding place and sink its teeth into some innocent person.

But they were making progress and a large sigh of relief went up when the far gate came into view at the end of the street. Similar to the front gate, the rear gate was slightly smaller, a large winch-like system built to open the wall enough to let in automobiles and horses.

But as they grew closer, Jimmy realized their only chance of escape was shattered when he saw the winch's delicate mechanisms had been destroyed. He was no demolitions expert, but it looked like someone had set off a grenade in the middle of the machinery, shattering it into a hundred pieces, most of them lying on the ground by the gate.

Cindy cursed when she saw the destruction and turned to Jimmy, her eyes still full of hope.

"What do we do now?" She asked, desperately.

Jimmy shook his head, looking at the other faces in the crowd.

"I have no idea. This was our best hope. Now the only way out is to fight our way through the dead and I don't have much hope that we'll all make it out alive. Most of the people behind us are just civilians. They don't know how to fight."

Jimmy kicked a rock in the road out of his way as he walked up to the gate, inspecting the damage.

"Dammit, one of those bastards did this, they had too. One of the Reverend's men. That bastard, if I ever see him face to face, so help me!"

While Jimmy ranted at the sealed gate, he didn't see the man in the baseball cap on the top of the wall. He had been hiding behind a small sack of sand that the sentries used for defense and now, he slowly leaned over and aimed his weapon at Jimmy.

Before anyone could shout a warning, the man shot his handgun and Cindy watched as Jimmy's head snapped back and his body fell to the ground like a deflated balloon.

"No! Jimmy!" She screamed. Other men saw what had happened and a barrage of gunfire erupted from the crowd. The man in the baseball cap dove behind the sandbags and then began crawling away from the gate, making his way across the wall until he was lost from sight. The wall would wrap around the town and a mile from the rear gate, the front gate would be waiting, though the shooter could drop off the wall at anytime and disappear into the surrounding countryside.

Cindy ran forward with tears in her eyes. Jimmy wasn't moving, and by the way he had thrown back his head, it could only mean he had been shot in the head.

Fearing the worst, she ran toward her lover, though she already knew what she'd find.

* * *

Henry and Mary were at the rear of the same crowd as Jimmy and Cindy as they battled their way through the streets of Stardust Cove. They had found the crowd quite by accident and had joined it after more than half had passed them by. Though they had no idea where they were going, it seemed prudent to stay with other people for as long as they could. They didn't know the town or its layout and could just as easily get lost and wander right back into the mass of undead. Better to stay with the large group and hope for the best.

Someone was leading the crowd at the front, but from where they were neither Henry nor Mary could see who it was.

Both figured it was one of the security guards or someone else in power in the town and had faith that they were being led to an escape route away from the hordes of undead swarming through the city.

While they moved up and down the streets, both Mary and Henry did their part to keep the zombies at bay, shooting any that threatened the group. The other guards had already welcomed them with smiles and nods, grateful for the help, though not recognizing either of them as part of the town.

When the high stone wall came into view, Henry was easily able to see it over the heads of the people in front of him and he smiled at Mary.

"It looks like we're home free. There's another gate over there and the crowd's headed right for it. See? I knew it was a good idea to join these people."

Mary only nodded; her attention busy on shooting a ghoul who came out of a doorway and attempted to attack an old woman near her. She blasted the ghoul in the chest, knocking it back into the doorway it had erupted from. Then she was past the doorway and would have to leave the zombie to someone following behind her if it was still active.

But then the procession stopped and a murmur went through the crowd that the gate's mechanism was destroyed and that they were trapped. Not wanting to just wait idly by while someone else made the decisions, Henry climbed on top of an old vendor's cart to see what was happening in the front of the crowd.

His eyes went wide when he saw, of all people, Jimmy, walking out ahead of the front of the line toward the rear gate and inspecting the winch. Henry watched him cursing at what he found. As for Henry, his jaw was hanging open and he yelled out to Jimmy. But he was so far away his friend couldn't hear him.

"Mary, you won't believe this, but Jimmy is at the front of the line!"

"What? No way, he's here, alive? What about Cindy? Can you see her, too?" She asked frantically, trying to remain upright in the heaving, shifting crowd.

He shook his head, trying to peer into all the strange faces, most seen from the back, but he couldn't see her. Her blonde hair should have stood out like a beacon, but so far she was nowhere to be found.

Then a shot rang out and Henry saw Jimmy fall to the ground at the foot of the wall. Returning fire lanced out from the street as most of the men and women with weapons tried to take down the sniper on the wall, but he was too quick and disappeared around the bend, a roof of one of the nearby buildings blocking his escaping form from view.

"What's happening? Why's everyone shooting?" Mary asked Henry. From where she was she could see nothing and had to rely on Henry's commentary to know what was happening.

Then Henry saw a woman leave the crowd and run towards Jimmy, and with her blonde hair flying behind her in the wind, he knew it was Cindy.

"I found her, Cindy, she's there. But It looks like Jimmy's been shot. He went down and he's not moving."

"What? Oh my God, Henry, we have to get up there and help him," she screamed, tugging his leg.

Henry agreed. Before he dropped back down onto the street, he could tell that no one was in charge up front. The crowd was lost unless someone stepped up and took over.

Pushing his way to the front, he and Mary pushed and shoved while behind them the staccato of gunfire continued, the guards trying to keep the zombies at bay. But there were hundreds of them and only a finite amount of ammunition among the defenders. Once that was gone, it would become a hand to hand battle and then all would be lost.

Reaching the front of the line, Henry breathed in a mouth of air. It was almost claustrophobic in the large crowd, the smells of sweat and bodies permeating everything and seeming to hang over the group like a dark cloud.

Running across the open area, he and Mary could see that Cindy had already reached Jimmy. She was cradling his head in her arms, Jimmy's blood staining her clothing, and her shoulders were shuddering. She was crying.

Henry shot Mary a concerned look and she returned it.

It was too much to contemplate that they had actually found their lost friends again only to arrive seconds too late to save one of them from death.

When Henry reached Jimmy and Cindy, he gazed down on the still body of his young friend and the woman cradling him lovingly, but he already knew what he would find, though it broke his heart to look.

Chapter 33

Cindy looked away from Jimmy's face, her vision blurry from the tears filling her eyes to see Henry and Mary standing over her. At first she blinked, tears running down her cheeks like tiny raindrops as she stared in disbelief at the two people hovering over her with concern on their faces. She couldn't believe what was standing in front of her, how was this possible?

Perhaps it was some bad dream she was experiencing thanks to the shock of watching Jimmy gunned down in cold blood. But then Mary leaned over and squeezed her shoulder and Cindy knew they were real.

"Oh my God, Mary, Henry, we've been so worried about you two guys. You're alive," she said while hugging Jimmy to her breast like a mother would a child. "I can't believe it's really you."

"We could say the same about you two, as well. Is he..." Henry couldn't say it, but instead leaned down and felt for a pulse on his prone friend's throat.

"I don't know, I haven't checked yet," she said quietly, "but when he was shot, the way he went down..." She trailed off; hugging his body to her and then Henry leaned back on his haunches and looked up at Mary.

"Is he alive?" She asked him hesitantly.

He nodded. "Yeah, seems to be." Henry reached out and gently touched the bloody wound that was seared across the top of Jimmy's forehead, just where his hairline began. The wound was shallow, though a small bit of bone peeked through the slice in his scalp.

"Would you believe the bullet only grazed his head? I always told Jimmy he had a hard head, but I had no idea it could deflect bullets."

"You mean...?" Cindy asked while looking down on Jimmy's still face.

"Yup, he should be okay. He'll probably have a hell of a headache when he wakes up, though, and we'll have to get that wound looked at so it doesn't get infected, and it's possible he might have a concussion, but yeah, he'll live to see another day."

"Oh, thank God," Cindy said as she cradled Jimmy harder. She squeezed him so tight she slowly brought him around, back into the world of grim reality. He groaned a few times and then raised his hand to his head, gingerly touching his wound.

"Oh, my head. What happened?" He asked, blinking up into Cindy's face and then looking over at Mary and Henry. He blinked again, not believing his eyes.

"Henry? Mary? Holy shit, is that really you?"

Henry chuckled, and Mary knelt down next to him, cupping his hand in hers. "Yeah, Jimmy, it's really us. We found you, isn't that great?" Mary said smiling, with a few tears filling the corner of her right eye. She quickly wiped them away so Jimmy wouldn't see them. She knew once he was better, he'd never let her forget it.

"Oh, it's great, all right. We found each other only to die a few minutes later by a thousand deaders. It's wonderful," Henry grumbled sarcastically.

Mary shot him a disapproving look, but Henry ignored her.

"No, he's right, Mary. The gate's damaged, it won't open. We're trapped," Jimmy said in a low voice. He was trying to sit up, now, despite Cindy's admonishments.

Henry nodded at his statement. "Yeah, I saw. We're not getting out this way unless you have a tank lying around," he said as he stared at the crowd of panicking townspeople. They were yelling at one another, helpless and scared, milling about with nowhere to go. The guards were still shooting at the rear, holding off the zombie horde, but soon there would be far more than the men could hold off and each gunshot was one less bullet to use later.

With Cindy and Mary's help, Jimmy managed to stand up, though still lightheaded. Looking up at the top of the wall, he frowned.

"Bastard shot me like I was a damn deader. Good thing that sniper wasn't a good shot. You know, you just might have an idea there, Henry...about the tank that is. I'm glad you're here. I was getting an idea as I walked up to the gate before I was knocked unconscious. Maybe together we could work it out. If you're up for it, that is."

Henry smiled at him, glad to see his old friend still alive and ready to fight. "Looks like that bullet knocked some sense into you. Okay, shoot, what's the idea?"

Jimmy nodded and the four began moving slowly back into the crowd, wanting to get some of the guards in on what Jimmy had planned, while Jimmy filled Henry in on his brainstorm.

* * *

Reverend Carlson climbed down off the wall near the front gate and waited for Ralph to pull up in the car the security chief had retrieved from the parking lot inside the town. There were rope ladders hanging unguarded near the gate, once used for the sentries to climb up and down for their turn on watch. Almost all the ghouls that had been milling about outside the walls and inside the semis had flooded into the town, en masse; only a few stragglers hanging around the lot to feed on their recent kills. It had been child's play for Ralph to slip in and get the car and drive it out of the gate once he had returned from escaping Jimmy and the other guards.

When the car pulled up, Reverend Carlson finally took off his baseball cap and tossed it through the open window and onto the dirty front seat. He took one last look around, fully satisfied with the results of his plan, then climbed inside the car, slamming the door with a solid, thunk.

"All right, then, let's get out of here. Our work is done here," he said, glancing at Ralph approvingly.

"Did you close the gap in the wall and destroy the controls to the crane?" Reverend Carlson asked.

Ralph nodded brusquely. "Sure did, Reverend. I shot the controls to scrap metal. They're trapped inside the town like chickens in a hen house with the fox hiding in the shadows."

"Good, excellent work, he replied. "What about the C-4? Did your man have time to set it up?"

Ralph shook his head no. "No, 'fraid not. Nelson was stopped by one of Bert's men before he could complete his mission. He said it had rolled under the seat or something."

"That's too bad. The added explosions would have sealed the deal, made sure no one escaped God's wrath," Reverend Carlson said with a slight twinge of sadness. "If I had known that the C-4 wasn't going to be used, I would have brought the flamethrowers and had the men wait out in the surrounding countryside until I needed them. But I didn't believe they'd be necessary if we used the C-4. See, Ralph, even I can be vain and not plan for every occurrence."

Ralph didn't answer, knowing enough not to take the bait. If it was one thing the Reverend disliked, it was when others found fault in him. No, just because he said he had screwed up, didn't mean he wanted someone to agree with him. Instead, Ralph felt it would be safer to change the subject.

"What about the semis? Are we just gonna leave them back there?" Ralph asked the Reverend.

"No, Ralph, once the dust has settled, they'll still be there. Then we can retrieve our property in a timely manner. But at least now that we're not going to blow the place to Hell there just might be more we can salvage later. In the end, things might work out even better than I had planned. Besides, the dead ones will be more than enough to complete the job."

Reverend Carlson looked into the backseat to see only two men sitting there, both men knowing not to speak unless spoken to.

"Where's Nelson and Rogers?"

"Didn't make it," Ralph said blandly as he spun the car in a circle and headed back down the coastal road that would bring them back to Sunset Bay.

"Pity, they were both good men. Oh well, they're in Heaven now, doing God's work by his side."

Ralph looked askance at his leader, but said nothing, keeping any thoughts he had to himself. The Reverend was right, though. The operation had gone off without a hitch. The town was in turmoil and once the populace had been wiped out by the rampaging ghouls, he would come back with a clean-up crew and destroy any of the zombie horde still remaining. Then he and his men would pick the town clean, thereby building his own town's coffers and at the same time eliminating the threat that was Stardust Cove.

And to top it off, the search party with Wilson was long overdue. Wilson had always been a pain in Ralph's ass; the man always trying to take his job. If he was dead, then that was one more of the opposition gone, leaving Ralph in total power next to the Reverend.

As for Watson and the girl, they must be dead by now, too. Or if they weren't, they should be at least twenty miles from here and still going, probably glad to still be alive. Either way, they were one less problem for the security chief to deal with.

Swerving around a small group of roamers in the road, Ralph leveled the car out and continued onward. He glanced to his side to see the Reverend sitting next to him with a wide, angelic smile on his lips, his eyes on the road ahead. The man was very pleased with himself, and if he was pleased, then that meant Ralph's life would go infinitely smoother for the time being.

Yes, sir, things couldn't have gone more smoothly than if he had tried.

* * *

A short time later, Henry and Mary were on the roof of the closest building from the rear gate and moving at a good clip from roof to roof. The downtown area of the town was designed in an old fashioned layout, with no buildings being taller than two stories. The alleyways were no more than ten feet across at any given time, and all had mostly flat roofs, a few having ornate dormers with wooden carvings and moldings.

Like sprinters in a marathon, they ran from roof to roof, jumping the wide gaps and rolling in the gravel to come up running again and again. By doing this, they were far above the zombie horde infesting the town and safe from further attack.

Every few minutes, they would slow down and get their bearings, making sure they were headed in the right direction. But while on top of the buildings, the landmarks in the town were useless, plus the town had slowly been catching fire, black and grey smoke filling the sky, causing them to have to slow their pace and move more carefully or risk falling through a melted hole in one of the roofs.

Screams of panic and for help carried on the wind to their ears, but they ignored them. They had only one task to accomplish and that was more important than any one person.

Jimmy's idea had been rather simple when the younger man had laid his idea out to Henry. The semis were large, heavy vehicles, and with enough speed, should be able to at least put a dent in the large stone walls. And if that failed, the crashed front cab should make a suitable ladder for the townspeople to use to climb up and over the walls and out to safety.

But first he had to reach the opposite end of the town and the best way, and safest, was to use the rooftops. Mary had volunteered to go with him and Henry hadn't refused her help. He would need at least one more pair of eyes to watch his back while he attempted to start one of the rigs. Jimmy had informed both Mary and him that the keys should still be in the ignitions, left their by the men who had driven the semis inside the walls of the town, but as no one had been back there to check, for all Jimmy knew the semis were gone, the attackers using them to escape after they had broken free of Jimmy and the now dead guards that had been the prisoner's escorts.

With the sun high in the sky, beating down on their backs, the two runners reached the last rooftop at the edge of the town. Across the open road, the semis still sat, their dusty finishes still reflecting the bright sunshine as they waited patiently in the parking lot.

"There they are, just as Jimmy said they'd be," Henry said while scanning the area for possible threats. There had to be at least three dozen ghouls scattered about the road and parking lot, separating them from Henry and Mary.

"If we move quickly, we should be able to outrun them, God knows speed isn't their strong point," Mary said with ragged gasps of air. She leaned over, hands on her knees and tried to catch her breath. She hadn't run so far and jumped so many hurdles in a long time, and though she was in excellent physical shape, without proper food and water, her exertions were beginning to take their toll on her. Neither Henry nor Mary had eaten in almost twenty-four hours except for the juice and the can of beans they'd found earlier in the day.

"Yeah, looks that way," Henry said. He began looking for a way down off the roof and it came to him that the drainpipes seemed fairly strong. Though the building had a fire escape, the alleyway where it dropped into was filled with the undead, making it all but useless.

"I found our way down," he said, moving to the edge of the roof. He reached his leg over the side and kicked the pipe gently, seeing how stable it was. It moved slightly, but seemed to hold.

"I'll go down first. I figure if I just hold on enough to not fly off the wall, then gravity will do the rest."

Mary moved next to him and pushed him away from the edge. "No way, if anyone is going first, then it's me. If it doesn't hold you, then what happens to me? I'm lighter than you. I stand a better chance of making it down to the street without breaking a leg."

Henry wanted to argue with her, but her reasoning made sense. He was almost twice the weight of her. She should have a much easier time then him shimmying down the pipe.

"All right, then fine, get going and watch your back once you're down there. If I'm holding on to the pipe, then I can't help you if you get into trouble."

"Okay, watch me go," she grinned and climbed over the side, making sure the Winchester was secured with its strap over her shoulder.

Like a monkey in a tree, she climbed down, the pipe groaning under her weight, but not breaking. Dropping to the ground a minute later, when she was five feet off the street, she landed like a cat, swinging her Winchester around and watching the road for any signs of unwanted company. At the moment, she hadn't been spotted and she waved to Henry to follow.

Behind her in the alley, cardboard boxes and trashcans filled the urban, narrow canyon, the debris leaving many places for both imaginary and real monsters to hide. The wind blew away from her, any scents in the alley also blowing in the same direction.

Anything could sneak up on her before she knew it was there.

Such as the lone rotting corpse who even now was crawling out from its shelter, slowly creeping up on Mary from behind. It had been around for quite some time, the salt air turning the skin a dark brown, as if it had been cured right on the creature's withered frame. Its skull was almost devoid of skin, its eyes sunk deep in their sockets, giving the dead man a caveman like quality. His clothing was nothing but rags, dozens of layers of filth and blood matting the material until the original color was lost in the ages.

It clacked its teeth together, seeing Mary at the far end of the alley. Though black and brown, the teeth were still strong, more than capable of doing considerable damage to the soft flesh of a human being.

With Henry clanking and grunting as he slid down the pipe, the footsteps of the zombie went unheard behind her, and it was only when it was less than three feet away, that Mary sensed something behind her and spun around, rifle already aimed at the potential target.

Though she was inured to the walking corpses that now inhabited the United States of America, this ghoul was particularly grotesque. As it stumbled forward, claw-like hands out-thrust in front of it, wanting nothing but to grab her and pull her down, she hesitated for a crucial second, the sight of the monstrosity disturbing some primal fear that all humans had deep inside themselves.

Sensing weakness, the ghoul lunged for her, but just before it would have touched her, a large shadow dropped in front of her, blocking the deader from view.

Henry let go of the drainpipe and landed hard on his boots, bending his knees to absorb the impact. Still, his legs screamed with pain. He had let go ten feet up, but after seeing Mary in danger, had risked the longer fall.

Halfway down, he had pulled his panga from its oiled sheath, and upon landing on the hard ground was already swinging it with all his might.

He was off-balance, though, the blade cutting into the zombie's midriff instead of the side of the head or neck, which had been his initial target. The honed steel blade sliced through the entire skeleton like it was nothing but old parchment, the powerful blow driving the blade so hard the brittle bones barely slowed the swing.

The panga rebounded off the adjacent buildings brick wall with a metallic clang, and Henry watched as the top half of the ghoul slid from its body like wet leaves out of a plastic bag.

With a meaty thump, the upper half landed hard, internal organs trailing out of its cavity, resembling something found in the waste can of a butcher shop.

The bifurcated body was still active though; the upper torso already crawling towards them, leaving a red trail of guts behind it like it was an artist's paintbrush painting the alley red and black.

For the moment though, they were safe, and he ignored the crawling creature.

"You all right?" He asked her, staring into her eyes when she realized what had just occurred.

"Yeah, I'm fine, thanks. I hesitated, don't know why, exactly. If you hadn't been there I..."

"Forget it," he said with a wave of his hand. "It's done, now lets get moving. You need to focus on what's coming. We need to move fast and hard, don't stop for anything. If one of us goes down, then leave 'em. If we don't get out of here soon, then all of us are gonna die, anyway. Those rigs are our best way to do that... maybe our only way."

"Okay, let's go," she nodded, her face setting with a grim resolve.

Henry looked out on the open road that led to the parking lot and the main gate for the town. There was almost a half mile to cover, zombies sporadically spread out everywhere. But once they started moving, all dead eyes would be on them. Studying the area intently, his forehead creased slightly when an idea came to him.

They needed something to distract the ghouls so they would have an easier time crossing the flat, open plain.

And he thought he just might have an idea.

He turned to Mary, staring into her eyes. "I need you to do something for me. This time I'm telling you about it before it happens, not like before when I pushed you into the road so we could get at that patrol car. You game?"

Her eyes flicked to the road and the stumbling, wandering forms scattered about and nodded. "Yeah, I'll do it, but so help me, if I'm the lamb for the slaughter, I'll kill you myself."

Before he could answer her, he had to look down. The severed ghoul had almost reached their legs again. Turning, Henry kicked the slimy head like a place kicker, the entire torso flipping back from the blow to land on its back in the alley four feet away. As if nothing had happened, much like a turtle would do, the zombie rolled back to its chest and began crawling back toward the two companions.

Turning back to Mary, never missing a beat, Henry gave her his widest smile, at the same time placing both hands on her shoulders.

"Hey, it's me. Would I ever do that to you?"

Frowning, she nodded and replied: "Yeah, you would."

He pursed his lips at her answer, but said nothing, ignoring her jibe. Then he began filling her in on what she needed to do. While he talked, Mary's frown grew longer until it threatened to drop off her face and land on her boots.

While behind them, the severed ghoul kept crawling towards them, like the proverbial rubber tree ant that wouldn't give up.

Chapter 34

"I can't believe I'm doing this," Mary mumbled to herself as she ran out from the alley and into the street.

She made it more than a hundred feet before the first ghoul noticed her and swung its rigid body in her direction.

But though the first; the undead man was not to be the last. While Mary ran, she waved her arms in the air and began yelling at the top of her lungs, making quite a spectacle of herself. All eyes turned as one to watch her, every zombie within earshot now moving in the same direction: toward Mary.

Not waiting to be caught, she ran around the rotting, stumbling, corpses, doing circles and weaving in and out of grasping hands like a figure skater, sans the ice. She was playing the most dangerous game of tag ever, for if she lost, she wouldn't be it, but would end up being ripped apart by rotting, filthy hands and teeth.

"Okay, Henry, anytime you're ready would be nice!" She yelled across the road, dancing like a ballerina to escape grasping hands.

Henry didn't reply and for a brief moment, she wondered if he was coming. What if he had been attacked and overwhelmed in the alley while she was busy playing the bait in a dangerous game of death? Then he would be dead and she would have attracted every single deader in a quarter mile radius, all wanting to have her for lunch.

And it would have all been for nothing.

Then, just as she risked a glance back to the alley, she saw a figure dart out of the shadows and run towards the two semis. She saw Henry kick a ghoul in the chest, sending the thing falling back to the road where its head slammed so hard on the asphalt its brains began seeping out of the large hole in the rear of its skull.

She knew Henry couldn't use his firearms or risk attracting the attention of every zombie in the area...that was supposed to be her job.

Then she had to look away from him, and concentrate on staying out of reach of wanting hands. One ghoul came a little too close for her liking, and she raised her Winchester, sending a blast at point-blank into its chest. Though it was a pointless gesture, the shot not putting the body down for good, it did give her the precious moment she needed to dance away from it, only to run into the next group coming towards her.

Luckily for her, she had no compunctions about using her rifle, in fact, the more noise she made the better the spectacle she portrayed.

In ones, twos, and fours, they came, slowly tightening the noose around her until there would be nowhere to run. They were everywhere, the stench unbelievable. With the sun high in the sky, baking the rotting meat like an oven, the sweet smell of decay filled the area. Though hardened to most odors and sights of death, even she could feel her stomach jumping inside her, like a cage full of mice in revulsion.

And the flies. The flies were everywhere. Buzzing around anxiously and getting into her eyes and hair.

With the heat of California an ever present entity, she found the zombies of this state particularly grotesque, thanks to the humidity and always high temperatures.

A hand grabbed her shirt and she had to pull as hard as she could to escape being drawn into the clutches of yet another ghoul. This one happened to be an old man, at least eighty when he was alive. An emergency medical bracelet adorned his wrist and she could see the distinctive scar from a triple bypass on his chest, thanks to his torn shirt. The ripped out throat told how he had died, one of thousands who had probably joined him on that fateful day.

At times like this, she almost wished things were like they had been six months ago, when the rain clouds in the sky were deadly, but the zombies on the ground weren't contagious. Back then, if a ghoul attacked a live person, nothing happened but a standard infection from an open wound, and if said person died, they stayed dead. But in the past few months, with the cold temperatures of the winter up north, or just because the bacteria had run through its life-cycle, the rain became safe again. Optimistic, the survivors had crawled out of hiding, believing they would now take the world back from the dead, but Mother Nature had a little surprise in store for mankind. The virus had mutated inside every ghoul walking the earth, each one now a contagion in its own right. To be bitten by a ghoul would cause infection and then death, followed by a return from the grave to walk the earth as one of the undead.

Knowing all this didn't make Mary feel much better. All she knew was that she was gambling with her life, and if Henry failed in his mission, then she was about to lose her last hand in the card game of life.

As she darted in and around hands and teeth, she tried to spot Henry. Wherever he was, she couldn't see him anymore, and she felt her heart begin beating faster from something more than just physical exertion.

Despite herself, she began wondering if she was actually spending her last minutes on earth running for her life with no one to help her. Shooting another zombie in the face, half the head disappearing in an instant, she kept running, knowing she was growing low on ammo and time.

* * *

Henry sprinted across the open road towards the two semis, arms pumping and legs propelling him forward as if his life depended on it; and if not his, than Mary's was certainly in jeopardy.

He knew he needed to move fast, Mary's life was depending on him. As he ran across the two-lane highway and into the parking lot, dodging any ghouls that tried to grasp him, he cast fleeting looks over his shoulder to check on Mary's progress. She was running around like an idiot, screaming and waving her arms over her head. At the moment, there had to be at least thirty zombies approaching her with more on the way. So far she was doing fine, but soon her luck would run out and there would be nowhere else to go.

Upon reaching the front of the first semi, Henry grabbed the chrome bar that was mounted to the driver's door and swung himself up onto the running board. But when he pulled open the door, he hadn't noticed the door had already been ajar, and he quickly learned the cab was far from empty.

A desiccated head, with one missing eye and half a nose, darted out at him like a cobra, trying to bite his arm while he pulled himself up. Henry leaned back, surprised, but kept his cool. As the ghoul tried to pull itself out of the cab, Henry reached up to the top of the door and pulled his body up, doing a chin-up. When his boots were even with the snapping mouth, he stuck the tip of his right boot into the fetid mouth and then stepped down with all his might. Like a tree branch snapping, the jaw of the zombie popped off, only a few pieces of skin from its chin keeping the severed jaw from just falling to the dusty ground. The broken visage and dead eyes looked up into Henry's face with a forlorn look, and the warrior looked down on it and sighed, almost looking sad himself.

"Sorry, about this, buddy, this is gonna hurt you way more than it's gonna hurt me," he said ruefully, while bringing his entire boot up and stomping down on the miserable creature's neck. The spine cracked, skin stretched to breaking, and the head rolled back into the cab and ended up on the floorboards, the blow severing the brain from the rest of its rotting body. Though the mouth and remaining eye still moved, the body was inert. Henry reached out with his left hand and grabbed the corpse's filthy shirt collar, pulling it out of the cab and dumping it onto the parking lot like it was a bag of trash.

With the cab clear, he climbed into the driver's seat, kicking the head off the floor where it had landed, sending it out into the parking lot to bounce, and then roll, away on the ground. He slammed the door shut just as five more ghouls came at him. With their hands and fists pounding on the door below him, he searched for the keys to the truck. His eyes lit up a half-second later when he saw they were still in the ignition.

Makes sense, he thought, as he turned the engine over. From what Jimmy had told him about the town and their tight security, it wasn't like someone could just steal the rig. And even if someone did try, and was fortunate enough to succeed in starting the rig; without permission by the sentries at the gate to depart the town, the massive gate would simply stay closed, trapping the thief.

The engine turned over on the first try, the exhaust behind the cab belching black smoke into the air. Though he was not an expert at driving a large tractor-trailer, Henry had dabbled at it in his twenties; at one time having a CDL license and driving for a local trucking company in and around his home state in the Midwest. But when he had met his wife, Emily, he had given up the long hours and insecure future and had gone into software engineering. Years later he had let the license lapse, not wanting to pay the extra fee for renewing something he didn't believe he would ever use again.

Flooring the gas pedal, the engine roared with power, and all his skills came flooding back to him like he had never stopped driving. Releasing the air brake, he stepped on the clutch and then double shifted into first gear. The truck rocked for a moment while he got the feel of the clutch and its gears; each one as sensitive as a woman's feelings in its own right. Shuddering, the semi rolled forward, crushing five bodies under its massive tires as it slowly gained momentum. On the trailer behind the cab, the trailer's walls were lying on the ground at an odd angle like a peeled onion, only their connection to the bottom portion of the trailer keeping them attached. With the semi beginning to move, the walls began tearing off, falling to the ground to be left in the dust, now only the frame of the trailer still intact.

Shifting into second, Henry grinned.

"Just like riding a bike," he said to himself, pulling on the air horn and letting Mary know he was in the rig and on his way to save her. But when he looked across the parking lot, easier now that he was sitting high in the semi's driver's seat, he looked over the heads of a large group of zombies that were slowly surrounding her. He saw her forced into a corner against the front wall of the town, desperately fighting her unrelenting attackers with her hands and feet. She had nowhere to run and was even now shooting the last of her ammunition into the bodies of the charging horde. Henry stepped on the gas, the truck surging forward, praying he would get there in time to save her from a grizzly death as butterflies filled his stomach in his concern for her fate.

The engine surged with power, and the semi shot forward like a bullet, its front grille dripping blood and gore from the countless impacts with rotting bodies.

He had to reach her in time, because if he didn't, then whatever else came next would all be for nothing and far to difficult to contemplate.

Chapter 35

"I'm out!" Jimmy yelled, letting his shotgun drop from his hands to swing on its strap. Reaching around his back, he pulled a Browning Hi-Power 9mm and began shooting at the approaching army of walking corpses. Bert had equipped him with the new handgun; a replacement for the .38 Jimmy had once carried. The .38 had been damaged by the salt in the ocean. At the moment, the weapon was in the armory, disassembled and waiting for replacements parts.

"Get those children behind us, we need to keep them safe for as long as possible," Jimmy yelled at three women who were sheltering the children with nothing but their arms and a defiant gaze at the undead.

The entire street was filled with a seething mass of rotting bodies, each one desperately trying to reach the townspeople.

Crude barricades had been erected in the street and on both sidewalks, totally blocking the street, everyone just trying to keep the ghouls at bay for as long as it took for Henry to return.

It had been an ongoing battle, and Jimmy had slowly given ground until his back was at the rear wall of the town. The defunct rear gate was right behind him, as if it was mocking him with its presence. A few men were trying to fix the mechanism, but the gears had been shattered to the point it would take weeks to find new parts to fix it.

A few of the younger men and women had used ropes, climbing up the wall only to be trapped on top when they realized the undead were waiting for them to drop down into their midst. But there were far too many women, children and the aged to have them all attempt to climb the wall. And there was no time. If

Jimmy had guessed correctly, he and the others had ten, maybe fifteen minutes left, before their ammo was entirely exhausted.

Jimmy fell back from the front line to assess how things were going and to redistribute manpower. Cindy saw him and ran up to him, Betsy at her side. The owner of the Dollar Bar was a tough woman, hard as nails, and had been instrumental in rallying the townspeople to fight their undead attackers. Also, she alone had been a large help in getting the others to listen to Jimmy, who was still a stranger to the town, and helping to set up the barricades. But the zombies were relentless; one after another they climbed over the wreckage only to be taken down with a blade or a gunshot to the head.

Two men forced their way through the frightened townspeople and stopped when they were in front of Jimmy.

"Ben, Pete, you're still alive," Jimmy said as he shook each man's hand.

"So far we are, but I don't know what's gonna happen in a little while, man," Pete said while he scanned all the terrified faces surrounding him.

"Merle's dead," Ben said flatly as he emptied the expended shells from his revolver and began loading the bullets one at a time. "We just came from there and he's dead. But he's not just dead, dead; he's been totally ripped to pieces; him and one of his whores from the brothel. Don't know which one, though, there wasn't enough left to identify."

"How'd you guys get here from way over there?" Betsy asked the men.

Ben pointed to a side alley. "We hugged the buildings and came up that way. But don't think of trying it 'cause those dead bastards are already filling it up. Shit, nearly ran out of ammo just getting here. The words out that all the survivors are here with you, Jimmy."

"Yeah, about that. Exactly how the hell did you pull that off?" Pete asked, curious. "Shit, you're running things and you've only been here for a few days. I've been here forever, I should be in charge."

Before Jimmy could say anything, Betsy spoke up. "Will you two knuckleheads shut the fuck up? Jimmy knows his shit, and if things go as planned, he and his friends are gonna get us out of this with our skins intact, so shut up and get on that firing line before I shoot you myself!"

Both Ben and Pete's faces went blank, as if they had been yelled at by their mother for getting mud on the freshly scrubbed floor. Without saying anything in return, both men turned and left, moving to the front of the line where they immediately got to work fending off the undead masses.

"Thanks, Betsy, appreciate it," Jimmy told her.

"No problem, hon'. The way I see it, you're the best chance of getting us out of here, so I'm on your side. Now what's next?"

Jimmy glanced to Cindy and she nodded, supporting whatever he said. "I hate to say it, but I'm all out of ideas. If Henry doesn't get here soon, all the people capable of climbing the ropes are gonna have to make a run for it and leave the others behind."

"But we can't. They'll be slaughtered. It's inhuman," Cindy said next to him.

Jimmy nodded, agreeing with her. "Don't you think I know that? But what other options do we have? If he doesn't get here soon we're all going to die, so we may as well try to save as many as we can."

"But where do we go?" Betsy asked. "You heard what some of the men said who climbed up there already. The wall is surrounded by dead ones. Without a vehicle, we'll just be killed outside the walls instead of in here."

"I don't know what to say," Jimmy said sadly, out of ideas.

"Then the town is doomed," Betsy said, her face filled with hopelessness.

"Hey, you guys, we need help over here!" A grumpy faced man yelled from the side of the defending line. Jimmy looked up and saw the man calling out for help. Both he and three other men were punching, kicking, and shooting almost a dozen ghouls as the relentless monsters broke through a part of the barricade that had only been partially defended.

"Come on, it's time to get back to work," Jimmy said, snapping his shotgun closed after loading it with the last of his ammo. "We've got to hold on for as long as we can. Give Henry time to get back here. 'Cause if we don't, then a lot more people are gonna die today."

Without answering Jimmy, the two women only nodded, and then with Jimmy at their side, they all charged into the fray once again to try and hold the line for just a few more minutes.

* * *

Mary shot her last round from the Winchester and then spun the weapon around like a bat and swung upward at the closest ghoul, a dead man in a stained, pinstriped three-piece suit. The butt of the rifle struck the dead man under the chin, breaking his jaw and shattering teeth; the bloody teeth falling to the ground like dice.

Without slowing her movements, she spun around in a circle, the rifle's butt now cracking another across the face, a teenage girl of no more than seventeen. Mary was like a dervish, dancing and swinging, always trying to avoid the grasping hands that tried to pull her down.

Her back came up against the high, stone wall and she knew she was done running. She could see nothing but rotting corpses, with so many bodies surrounding her, blocking her vision and the stench was enough to make her gag and want to pass out. She made herself breathe through her mouth to try and deaden the odor, but it did little to stop the smell from suffusing her olfactory senses and her very consciousness.

She swung the rifle yet again, the butt lodging into the torso of a rotten corpse that should never be able to walk. Like quicksand, the rifle became stuck, the splintered ribcage catching the strap on the end of the butt and preventing her from removing it. Deciding it was useless, she let go, now down to only hands and feet.

Breathing heavily from exertion, she measured her life in seconds, and just as she thought it was over, the horde so close she could almost taste their decay in her mouth, a loud air horn shrilled through the air and broke through the moans and groans of the dead.

The front grille of the semi drove into the crowd of zombies, knocking them over like ten pins, fragile decomposing bodies exploding like water balloons, and a dark-brown ichor rained down in front of the semi like black rain. When the rig reached Mary, Henry slammed on the brakes, the airbrakes hissing in protest.

Leaning over the seat, Henry pushed open the passenger-side door and yelled down to Mary.

"Get in; they won't stay down for long!" He yelled to her.

She stared up at the open door; Henry perched too high up for her to see him clearly. While she battled for her life, lost in the fray, the beleaguered woman had actually forgotten about him, too caught up in the moment and her impending doom.

"Come on, Mary, snap out of it!" Henry yelled to her, revving the engine in anticipation.

Realizing she was wasting her second chance at life, she climbed up into the cab and closed the door. Henry smiled at her, relief filling his eyes.

"It's good to see you in one piece," he told her happily.

She was still too shocked at not being killed. But it was slowly sinking in.

"Oh my God, you saved me."

"Sure did," Henry said, putting the truck in gear and swinging it around to head back into town.

Then she slapped him on the shoulder, hitting him with both hands.

"Hey, quit it, what gives?" Henry asked, befuddled at what was happening to him.

"What gives? I was about to be killed, that's what. You sure took your sweet time!" She yelled at him, her face red with exertion and anger.

"I'm sorry, Mary, really. But I had a few deaders of my own to deal with. I got here as fast as I could. But I made it, you're safe. Hell, you know I would never let anything happen to you."

She crossed her arms and made a: You've got to be kidding me, face.

"If that's so true, then how come it seems for the last few days I'm the bait in every damn trap you set?"

Henry opened his mouth to speak, but stopped when he saw her eyes. He quickly realized that no matter what he said, she wasn't going to believe him. And perhaps she was right. Maybe he had grown careless in the past few days. Any good plan took careful consideration and thought, weighing the odds of failure over victory. But lately it seemed that every damn plan had been made up on the spot. But he wasn't going to tell her any of this. Instead, he just shrugged and put on his best smile.

"I'm sorry, honey, you know I'd die if anything happened to you."

"Huh, good choice of words," she quipped back, but her temper was quieting down and Henry reached out with his right hand and rubbed her shoulder, his left hand still on the wheel.

"I'm glad you made it, I never had any doubt you wouldn't or I would never have had you do it. You should know that, that's all. Plus, it was the only way to get to the rigs so we can save Jimmy, Cindy and the town."

Sighing, Mary turned to look at him. Outside in the road, the semi was crushing and rolling over ghouls like they were made of paper. In the large insulated cab, the bodies barely made a sound.

Thinking of Jimmy and Cindy had her weakening a little more. "I know that Henry, it's just we deal with enough everyday without actively throwing ourselves into danger."

"Yeah, don't I know it, but this is how the world is now. Either adapt or die, right?"

She nodded and then sat up higher in her seat.

"Okay, Henry, let's go get Jimmy and Cindy and get the hell out of this crazy place."

With a smile and a nod, Henry floored the pedal, the semi surging forward, barreling through the streets like a charging bull.

"I hear that, Jimmy and Cindy, next stop. Okay, Mary, buckle up and hold on tight because this ride's gonna get rough."

She did as she was told, holding the hand rail above the door to prevent from being thrown across the cab. Henry swerved in and around the streets, crashing into cars and vendors carts like they were made of cloth. Bodies were everywhere, littering the town like stray confetti from a parade. With so many dead and dying in the street, it was hard to tell who was an attacker and who was a victim. Not that it mattered. Once a person died and came back, they were the enemy. No questions asked or given.

Swinging the semi wide around a tight intersection, the left corner of the bumper caught the building on the corner, ripping out its wall like it was paper-mache. The truck shuddered from the impact, but continued onward. Mary felt something hit the back of her feet and she reached down and pulled up a small block of clay with what looked like a pen sticking out of it. The pen had a small wire leading out of its top that looped around and back into the clay. She held it up so Henry could see what she'd found.

"What's this?" She asked, calmly. "I found it on the floor under the seat."

He turned his head to see what she was talking about and his face went white, his eyes opening so wide they looked like they were about to pop out of their sockets, when he saw what she was holding. Swallowing hard, he stared at the large block of C-4 in her hands. But he regained control of himself and tried to stay calm.

Casually, trying his best not to let his voice crack, he said to her: "Hey, Mary, would you do me a favor and pull that stick there out of the block?"

"Why, what for?" She asked, not understanding.

"Just do it for me, will you, honey, please? Just pull it out. It's no big deal, really." Then he had to look away and watch where he was driving, nicking a corner of another building as he swerved through the intersection.

Shrugging, thinking Henry was being silly, she pulled the detonator from the block and then looked back at him.

"Okay, what now?"

"Now place the stick in the glove box there and then close the door."

She did as instructed, and a second later was finished, though she was now more curious than before.

"Okay, done. Now will you tell me what this is and what's the big deal?"

Henry let out a massive sigh now that they were safe.

"That block in your hands is C-4. Now, I'm no expert, but I bet that amount of plastic explosive would be enough to kill us and level a good chunk of the town, to boot."

Her face went white and she froze, staring at the block of clay in her hands. Her breath came in gasps and she began to perspire.

Henry hadn't seen any of this, concentrating on driving again. Every time he ran over a body, the steering would fight him for a moment. He had to constantly adjust the steering or risk crashing into one of the buildings lining the street.

When he sent a quick gaze at her, he saw her appearance and let out a small laugh.

"Whoa, Mary, relax. It's safe now. That little stick you took out of it was the detonator. With out that, the block is about as dangerous as Playdoh."

"Really? You're sure?" She asked; her face ashen.

"Yup, so don't worry, we're fine."

She slowed her breathing, wiping her forehead with her sleeve.

"Jesus Christ, Henry, you could have said something earlier."

"Oh, yeah? And what would have happened? No, you were better off not knowing until it was safe."

She gave that some thought, and in the end realized he was right. Glancing out the front windshield, she frowned slightly.

"You sure you know where you're going?" She asked him as he turned down yet another side street.

"Me? I thought you knew the way back!" He said in surprise.

Her jaw dropped and she turned to glare at him. "No way, you don't mean..."

"Relax, Mar', I know the way. It should just be around the next corner." Then he swung the wheel and slowed the truck as he made the last turn, leveling the semi out and heading forward again.

With the long trailer still attached to the cab behind him, some of the turns had been tough, the small streets never meant to handle the long rig. And if he needed to prove his point, all someone had to do was walk his back trail to see all the devastation he'd wrought. The corners of the buildings had been ripped apart from when he had made the delicate turns at far too high a speed. He wasn't concerned though. The town was all but lost; now the only thing to do was try and save as many lives as possible and start over somewhere else.

Henry let out a bark of laughter filled with pride and pointed ahead of the rig at the crowd of people in front of them. True to his word, he had reached their destination.

In front of them, no more than a quarter mile down the long road, was the battling townspeople and their massive crowd of undead attackers, though from where they were, neither Henry nor Mary could make out distinctive faces.

At first all Henry saw was a shifting sea of heads, the undead horde struggling to climb over the barricade of old carts, barrels and pallets. For just a second he thought that there were no more survivors, but then he heard the distinctive sound of gunshots over the semi's engine.

Setting his jaw and preparing himself for whatever would come next, he floored the gas pedal and shifted into a higher gear, shooting forward like a rocket. Unprepared for the increase in speed, Mary actually banged her head on the rear wall of the cab.

"What're you doing? You're going too fast!" She screamed, holding on for dear life as the truck barreled down the small road amidst the storefronts and brothels.

"I'm making an entrance, now hold on, it's gonna get bumpy!"

Then he leaned on the semi's horn--the loud proclamation sounding like a cavalry charge to battle--and shot like an arrow towards the middle of the mass of the undead horde, increasing his speed with every second he drew closer to the target.

Chapter 36

Things weren't going so good for Jimmy, Cindy, and the townspeople who were trapped with their backs against the inoperable gate at the rear wall.

Now, even if the people that were capable of climbing the wall, taking their chances with the undead on the other side, wanted to try climbing up the few ropes hanging down from the top of the wall, there would be no time.

The army of the undead had continued pushing at the living humans, and slowly, the humans had begun to fall back until there was nowhere else to go. Their numbers were dwindling, and worst of all, every time a townsperson fell under the assault of the dead attackers, they would rise again and then attack the living, thereby the dead continually added to their numbers while the living defenders were slowly becoming depleted.

Thirty-eight children, the entire towns compliment, sat curled up in tight balls against the side of the broken gate, crying and calling out for their parents. But their parents were too busy to console them at the moment, all of them fighting desperately with every ounce of their remaining strength, prepared to give up their lives to save their children. Ammunition was almost out, most of the men and women now down to using clubs and their weapons as bludgeons.

Jimmy shot three ghouls in the face, one after the other until his Browning cycled dry. When the next dead face appeared, he threw the Browning at it as hard as he could, the weapon only bouncing off the ghoul's nose to land in the street, where it was quickly buried in the gore and blood that now coated the pavement.

He reached down to his hip and pulled the small six-inch hunting knife he'd had there, waving the small blade in front of him menacingly.

"Well, that's it, I'm out of ammo. If anyone has any ideas, I'm all ears!" Jimmy cried out desperately to anyone within hearing.

No one answered; all too busy fighting for their lives.

It was hopeless. Even now, almost every man and woman knew they were only forestalling the inevitable and a few morose parents were seriously considering killing their children themselves to save them from a fate worse than death.

Though it would be the hardest chore any parent could ever do in a lifetime, it would be a mercy that the undead ghouls would never show to the hapless youngsters.

When some of the parents, their faces grim with sadness and exhaustion, moved toward the crying children, Jimmy jumped in front of them, blocking them.

"No, wait, don't do it. Henry will be here, he has to be!" Jimmy yelled, trying desperately to stall the harried parents.

"But what if he doesn't arrive? What if he never made it to the front gate? Then our children will suffer when those bastards rip them to shreds," one father said while waving his arms in the air.

"Jonah's right, if we wait any longer it'll be too late. It's over and we lost, end of story," another woman called out, others taking up her cry, despite the horror of what it would mean.

It was an absolutely despicable situation. These parents were arguing about not waiting to kill their children. But they knew it would be best. A bullet or blade to the head would be infinitely better than what the ghouls would do if they reached the children.

"Please, just wait a little longer. He'll be here!" Cindy said, begging for them to wait.

"It's no use, hon'," Betsy told her. "It's not like they want to do it, hell, they'd sacrifice themselves in a minute if it would save their kids, but it's over. We lost. We're all dead."

"They're breaking through! They're breaking through the line!" Ben's voice yelled, piercing the cacophony of screams and yells.

Jimmy and Cindy placed themselves between the children and their parents. As if things weren't bad enough, they now had to fight off the townspeople.

"You're not getting these children without a fight. My friend will be here. I know he will. We just need to give him some more time," Jimmy pleaded.

"You heard Ben. We're out of time, the lines broken. We've only got minutes if that. Now stand aside or we'll take you out, too," A dark faced man said with an angry voice, despite the fact he had tears running down his face from his guilt at what was to come. He was arguing with a stranger about slaughtering his own children. Deep down, he thought he'd be going to hell, mercy killing or not.

Jimmy looked to Cindy. "You don't have to stay with me. You can try to get away," he told her.

She shook her head, her blonde tresses flowing around her face. Even sweaty, dirty and covered in blood, he thought she was beautiful.

"No way, lover. If you stay here, then so do I."

He nodded, his jaw set tight. "All right then. We hold them off for as long as it takes, not that it'll matter much once the deaders get us."

"We'll do what we can. Henry and Mary will be here, you're right. You have to be."

The two lovers stood side by side, the children cowering behind them. They didn't entirely understand what was happening to them, but in some strange turn of events, the two people in front of them appeared to be protecting them from their own parents. With tears in their eyes, they huddled closer together, while the screams of the dead and dying filled the air. With each tick of the clock, the massive crowd of zombies moved closer to the huddling children, Jimmy, Cindy, and the remaining townspeople.

Jimmy turned to Cindy, shoving a parent away who was trying to get past him.

"You know, I never thought we'd end up dying like this," he called to her.

She smiled back, "Me neither, but as long as we're together, I guess it's okay. I couldn't take dying and leaving you alive to keep dating after I was gone."

He laughed out loud. "Fat chance. You've ruined me for all other women. You're it for me, baby."

"As it should be," she laughed back.

The parents began pushing at them, with the zombies clawing at their backs. If they were going to die, then the parents wanted to send their children to Heaven before they were killed.

Jimmy knew in seconds both he and Cindy would be pulled away, and perhaps killed, by either the parents or the zombies only a few yards away, but then his ears picked up a loud blast from an air horn, cutting through the din of the fighting and dying people.

"Did you hear that? That's a horn. It's Henry, it's got to be! Wait, don't touch the children. Turn around, fight the dead bastards. Help is here!" Jimmy called out; trying to rally the townspeople to him. "We're gonna be okay, fight, damn you, fight!"

With the mass of people fighting and punching and being pushed this way and that, for a brief moment no one heard the horn. But then it sounded again, and faces began turning around, facing the barricaded street. A few shouts sounded that a truck was on the way, but it was hard to hear anything clearly with the battle still in full swing. More than half of the townspeople who had taken refuge behind the barricade had been killed or turned into the undead. Those numbers continued to shrink with every passing minute, but if they could only hold on for a few more minutes, they would be saved.

But a few more minutes was something none of them had.

The horn sounded yet again and many of the undead turned to see what the noise was. Their small minds went to whatever was loudest or flashiest, and the siren was a call to dinner, despite all the humans in front of them. As the ghouls turned to see what this new attraction was, Jimmy began regrouping the men and women still able to fight.

"Come on, people, get it together, it's not over yet! We still have a chance. Fight, damn you all to Hell!" He yelled, and kicked a deader in the face so hard he shattered its jaw. As it rolled backward, away from him, he followed it and brought his heel down hard, crushing its skull beneath his boot. The corpse had been one of the originals, more than a year's worth of decay making its bones brittle.

Then Jimmy saw the semi heading towards him over the heads of the battle and he realized it wasn't slowing. In fact, if he was correct, it was speeding up.

"Oh, shit, he's gonna ram the crowd!" Jimmy screamed. "Fall back, fall back! Get out of the road! Now! Move or you're gonna get flattened!" He yelled, slapping men and women on the back. Pushing them and sometimes kicking some in the ass to get them to move. And all the while he and the rest had to battle with the undead, who still wanted their flesh for lunch.

"Cindy, get those children away from the gate, now!" He ordered her. She heard him, and with Betsy helping, got to work, herding the children like a shepherd herding her sheep.

Ben and Pete popped up and Jimmy quickly informed them of what was about to happen.

"Oh, shit, man, your friend is fucking crazy!" Ben yelled, and then turned and saw the semi barreling down on them, his eyes going wide in fright.

The horn sounded once more, trying to warn everyone in the street of the semi's arrival, and then it was too late, the rig hitting the barricade at speeds of fifty mph or more and plowing straight through with almost no reduction in speed. Wreckage flew in all directions, like it had been shot from a cannon.

Jimmy reached out and grabbed the sleeve of a middle-aged woman who wasn't moving fast enough, pushing her onto the sidewalk, and then he dived to the side of the street himself; his world turning upside down as he tumbled and rolled and was pelted with debris. There was a massive crashing sound that rent the air in twain, and entire bodies and body parts were thrown into the air like a giant blender had lost its cover, spewing its insides across the area and painting the buildings red.

The ground shook and it felt like an earthquake had begun, the land shifting under the townspeople's feet like a living thing.

Striking the ground hard, Jimmy rolled with the explosion until he whacked his head on something hard and a sharp pain was added to the one he already had received from the gunshot wound. Just before darkness fell over him, he heard a voice, but it seemed like it was coming from far away; it was Cindy's voice calling out to him, her voice filled with panic.

Then he heard no more.

* * *

Henry held his breath just before he struck the first clot of undead bodies gathering in the street. They were massed so close together, their anatomy seemed like one giant, blob-like creature with hundreds of hands, arms and heads.

Then the front windshield became covered in blood as the front grille of the truck plowed into the undulating mass of meat. Like a child's foot stomping in a puddle, the semi parted the crowd, sending bodies flying off in all directions.

Then the semi hit the barricade head on and the truck roared with sounds of destruction as wreckage shot off in all directions like a massive grenade had exploded.

Ghouls that were struck head on, either bounced off the massive semi or simply exploded, like an overfilled water balloon. It appeared to be raining blood and limbs as Henry downshifted and floored the pedal yet again. The engine surged in pitch, heads and torsos becoming caught up in the front tire-wells where they were chewed up until there was nothing left but a putrid mass of gristle.

Both Henry and Mary could feel the slight decrease in speed and he hit the breaks, trying to slow the truck, not wanting to hit the surviving townspeople huddling near the rear wall. The massive undead crowd actually began rocking the semi with their large numbers, making Henry and Mary feel like they were back on the cruise ship in the storm tossed ocean.

Henry slammed his boot on the brakes and quickly put the truck in reverse.

"What are you doing?" Mary screamed while blackened, claw-like hands beat on her window.

"Just watch," Henry said flatly. Using his blood-tinted side mirrors, he began backing the semi up.

The instant the truck backed out of the undead crowd, the hole that had been made filled up like it had never been there. Henry backed a good two hundred feet and then, when he thought he had enough room, he slammed the pedal with his foot and the semi surged forward yet again, a battering ram of massive proportions.

Once again, the front grille became enmeshed into the crowd, knocking bodies away as if they were defunct chattel. Blood spilled onto the streets and ran in the gutters, a hellish rainstorm of epic proportions. When he had reached the barricade once more, he stopped and then slammed the truck into reverse yet again.

Backing up, the long, flat-bed, trailer behind the cab plowed into any ghouls foolish enough to get in the way. The bed of the trailer was head height and countless bodies were decapitated from the impact, the severed bodies crushed by the massive wheels of the semi.

Henry did this again and again until the street looked like the floor of an unclean butcher shop. Every time he drove through the scarlet sludge, the tires would sink six-inches deep into the vermilion muck, the suction pulling the red gruel out to spread it across the area like a sprinkler watering the grass.

When he was finally finished, more than three quarters of the zombie horde was either destroyed or lying on the road, twitching.

With less numbers to battle, the townspeople sent up a cheer and quickly formed a front line once again, rebuilding another barricade behind the semi with whatever could be found. As they moved about, their feet slid into the carnage, like they were walking in icy slush, but no one cared. They now had a second chance to make it through alive, and they'd be dammed if they'd throw it away.

With the semi on the inside of the barrier, safe for the moment, Henry dropped down from the cab and looked at the destruction he'd wrought.

But he was far from finished.

Jimmy ran over to him, happy to see him still in one piece. He had a large bruise on his forehead to match the wound received from the glancing shot to the head. He was still slightly dazed from his tumble when the semi had plowed into the barricade, but adrenalin was keeping him alert and standing on his feet. He was about to fill Henry in on what was going on, but before he could say anything, Henry pointed to the open trailer.

"There's no time for talk. Get those kids onto the bed of the trailer and as many others that you can spare. We're getting out of this goddamn place, right now."

Jimmy only nodded; words in short supply at the moment.

With Mary helping, all the children, plus the old and wounded were helped onto the trailer, the steel frame now being used for handholds.

While Jimmy and the others did this, Henry climbed back up into the cab and retrieved the C-4 and detonator Mary had found.

With the C-4 in hand, he now had an easy way to break them free of the town's massive stone wall. With absolute chaos around him, he slid the detonator back into the block of plastic explosive and then ran over to the defunct rear gate. Placing the C-4 into one of the large cracks near the base of the gate, he made sure it was good and stuck, and with a quick look over his shoulder to see where everyone was, he set the timer.

Running back to the semi, he yelled and waved his hands in the air to get everyone's attention.

"Okay, it's time to go! Get everybody else onto the trailer!" He called to Cindy who was in the process of helping a wounded guard up. Outstretched hands waited for him, pulling the man onto the bed with the others already there.

Henry climbed into the cab and sounded the air horn, leaning out the window so people could hear him.

"Get on the damn truck if you want to live!" He yelled at the top of his voice, cutting through some of the bedlam. Jimmy heard him, and with Mary and Cindy at his side, they all quickly climbed inside, the four of them squeezing into the cab, Cindy having to sit on Jimmy's lap so they'd all fit.

"Fall back, fall back! Get onto the truck!" Ben screamed, slapping men on the shoulder as they made a hasty retreat from the now shattered barricade. Though they had tried valiantly to hold the line, once Henry had demolished it, there was just nothing left to use; everything now crushed and splintered and dripping with blood.

The men and women fell back to the trailer, with hands reaching down to pull them onto the bed with the other refugees. The rear trailer was now packed with people, all that was left of the destroyed town.

Slamming the transmission into reverse, Henry began backing up, doing his best not to jolt the vehicle too badly and knock some of his passengers off.

Jimmy shifted in his seat next to Henry, turning his head to look through the rear window so he could check on the rest of the exhausted survivors.

"What's the plan? Even if we have this truck, the damn gates are all sealed and that cement wall is a foot thick."

Henry grinned, knowing something Jimmy didn't. With the semi slowly backing away from the wall and down the street, the zombies filled the gap, still hundreds left to finish the work of their crushed brethren.

With the semi constantly moving, the zombies couldn't get a handhold to pull themselves up to attack the survivors and the people on the trailer were able to easily kick and punch any who tried to climb on.

"Three, two, one..." Henry counted down, staring at his wristwatch.

"What are you...?" Jimmy asked him and then he got his answer.

The semi had moved more than half a block down the street, but the massive stone wall was still clearly visible. In a blinding flash of stone and debris, the gate and a large portion of the wall exploded outward and upward, sending large pieces of stone into the air to fall back to earth, crushing and pummeling the undead horde that had been massing on the outside of the wall.

Jimmy blinked in surprised awe at the sight in front of him. In the rear bed, all went silent as they watched the massive explosion.

At first there was a catastrophic sound as the wall fell in on itself, but then as the dust settled, there was silence, only the ticking engine of the semi and the undead moans of the dead around them.

"All right, then, that should do it. You ready to leave this place?" Henry asked.

Jimmy's jaw was hanging open as he watched the decimation of what had been his deathtrap only seconds before and was now nothing but rubble.

"How the hell did you do that?" He asked in surprised shock.

"Mary found some C-4 in the truck. Guess one of the truck drivers left it for some reason. Though I can't imagine why." He shrugged off the subject as irrelevant. "I don't know; maybe they were supposed to blow up the trucks or something but then something happened with the plan. Doesn't really matter, though, does it. What does matter is we're free."

"Yeah, guess you're right," Jimmy replied.

"Well then go, will you, please? The sooner the better," Cindy said as she stared out the window.

With the semi in first gear, Henry began rolling forward, slowly picking up momentum.

Many more ghouls had been destroyed in the explosion, but with the wall collapsed, the ones that had been outside the range of the explosion now swarmed in. Henry shifted into second gear, and as gently as he could, barreled his way through the thrumming crowd of moaning creatures.

The front grille plowed through the bodies, the sickening sound of crunching and squished bodies rising over the sound of the engine.

With the dust settling around them, the truck forced its way through the horde of dead and out into the fresh air of the day. Henry never slowed, only shifting into third gear and driving down the open road, the survivors still holding on for dear life on the open rear trailer.

One more ghoul was still holding on, a tenacious, wiry fellow with only one leg. He was holding onto the rear bumper, his remaining leg dragging and bouncing on the asphalt while the truck moved down the road. Betsy was near the back of the trailer and she looked down when someone else screamed at seeing the ghoul. With her shotgun in hand, she moved to the spot and then leaned over the edge of the bed, bringing the butt of her weapon down onto the ghoul's head. She had to hit it three more times, and the powerful blows sent vibrations up her arms and into her shoulders, but eventually the ghoul let go, rolling over and over in the road until it finally stopped.

A cheer went up in the crowd of refugees, parents hugging their children, thankful to be alive.

Henry drove for almost three miles until finally pulling over onto the side of the road. The road went into the distance in both directions and there was nothing but an open plain on one side and what appeared to be an overgrown orange farm on the other. It was a good place to rest and set up camp. With guards posted it would be easy to keep an eye out for any unwanted guests and everyone was exhausted, needing to rest. Plus, there were still plenty of fruit on the trees for food.

Henry turned off the motor and climbed down to the ground, where he was abruptly almost knocked over by Cindy who had run around the front of the cab to get to him. Now that she knew they were all safe, Mary was free to show her happiness. Inside the cab, she'd held her tongue, not wanting to celebrate before they were truly safe and not wanting to distract Henry from driving. The semi was pretty beat up and the steering fought Henry every mile they drove away from the beleaguered town.

"Whoa, there girl, easy, you'll break something," he joked.

"I can't believe we did it, Henry. I really thought that time was it," she screamed into his ear, laughing.

She was covered in blood spray, her blue eyes peeking out at him. She was smiling so hard her face looked like it might crack, and when Mary ran up to them, as well, she nearly knocked them both over.

Then Cindy and Mary hugged, jumping up and down like school girls.

Jimmy moved next to Henry and slapped his friend on the back. "Well, old man, I don't know how you did it, but goddammit if you didn't. You saved all these people." Jimmy shook Henry's hand. "Not to mention my ass, too. Congratulations and thank you."

Laughing, Henry waved the compliment away. "Hey, it was your idea. The C-4 was just a little extra add-on."

"What would you have done if you hadn't found the explosives?" Jimmy asked.

Henry shrugged. "Don't know. Maybe ram the gate. But I'm glad I didn't have to try that particular plan out."

"Amen," Jimmy said and then looked up when Ben and Pete walked over. Both men were also covered in blood, as was almost every one of the refugees.

Ben held out his hand, as did Pete, and Henry quickly went through with introductions. Then Pete was called by someone off on the crowd, and with a wave of thanks to Henry, he ran over to see who needed him.

Ben gestured with his head across the plain and said: "There's a stream just over that small hill and we're gonna go in groups of ten to get cleaned up. But the question is; what happens after that? We can't stay here forever. We need more food than just oranges to live on, and without more weapons, we won't last long."

Henry barely gave it a thought, but instead tossed the man the keys to the semi.

"Here, take these. Maybe when you're ready, you can find someplace down the road. The tanks almost half-full, so you should get at least a hundred miles or so." He shrugged. "I don't really know, exactly. I'm not that good with how far one of these babies can go."

Ben's eyes lit up and he shook Henry's hand again. "Wow, thanks, thanks a lot. We won't forget this. You're welcome to come with us if you want. All of you. We've been talking, and as far as we're all concerned, you guys are one of us now."

"Thanks, Ben, that's real generous, but we're going the other way. But I wish you good luck, we all do," Henry said, looking at Jimmy, Cindy and Mary for confirmation.

They all nodded in return that they agreed with his assumptions.

Ben smiled, not really understanding why the companions wouldn't stay with him and the other survivors, but respecting their decision.

"All right, then, good luck and thank you again...from what's left of the entire town." Then he walked away, jingling the keys in his hand happily.

Jimmy turned to Henry with a curious look on his face. "What's next for us around here? I don't know about you, but I want to put this place as far behind me as I can. And you just made that a little more difficult now that you gave away our ride."

Cindy nodded in agreement, as did Mary.

"Yeah, especially after what Carlson did to me," Mary said. "I want to never see this place again, no matter how sunny and beautiful the rest of it is. But how are we going to leave here safely with no vehicle?"

Henry listened to their concerns, nodding when appropriate. “Listen, guys, I totally agree with everything you’ve said, but almost everything we’ve been through since we’ve arrived here is because of one man. And if there’s any justice in the world, then that man needs to pay for what he’s done, so there’s one more small chore that we need to do before we can wipe the dust of this place off our backs.”

He gathered them closer and Henry laid out what would be done next, the others sometimes protesting and other times offering ideas of their own.

When he was finished laying out his plans, he stopped and turned back to the refugees who were already setting up a makeshift camp with fires and water from the nearby stream. A few had begun picking oranges, carrying them in discarded buckets found scattered across the field under the trees.

“You know what? Maybe these people don’t need to leave their homes so soon. I think I have a way for all of us to get what we need.”

“What do you mean? They can’t stay in their town, it’s been overrun,” Mary said while watching the townspeople resting and just giving thanks for being alive. Children were smiling and laughing, their parents hugging them and keeping them close. After coming so close to the worst fear any parent could have, they were all so thankful it felt like their hearts would explode from gratitude.

Henry nodded, agreeing with her as he also studied the refugees.

“Yes, Mary, I know that.” Then he pointed to Mary and Cindy. “Look, you two go get Ben, Pete and anyone else who seems to be somewhat in charge around here. We have a lot to talk about with them,” he told them both.

Mary and Cindy did as requested, moving off to talk to the refugees and gathering people together who would want to listen.

“So you think you’re plan will work?” Jimmy asked, idly.

Henry watched both women move off into the settling camp, then he turned to look Jimmy straight in the face.

"Yeah, I think it will, but listen, we've got time to work out the details. When we leave, I want no mistakes. So once we've rested up, we're gonna stage a small revolution."

Jimmy smiled, wanly, not fully understanding what Henry was intending. But he knew he was itching for some payback and would go along with him regardless.

Henry had decided they would stay with the refugees for a day or so, resting up and relaxing. For Jimmy and Cindy it would also be a chance to say goodbye to new friends. Cindy especially had become close friends with Betsy.

Also, while they recuperated, it was good to be around a large number of people; the more eyes to watch out for trouble the better. Sentries had already been posted and a schedule had been fabricated. Fallback plans had been made so that if there were any serious problems, such as more ghouls arriving than they could handle, then everyone would retreat back onto the trailer and then they would simply drive away to someplace safer.

It was a good system, and with fruit and water at their disposal, it would be as good a place as any for the companions to rest and enjoy the reunion of finding one another again.

After they'd rested, though, the companions had one final task to complete, and then they, too, could move on to clearer pastures.

Chapter 37

Reverend Carlson leaned back in his chair and stared at the wall of his office. City Hall was silent now, the hour well past midnight. But he liked it quiet. This was when he did his best thinking and scheming. A small cd player was off to his right, playing an old Willie Nelson tune. He closed his eyes and listened to the song, reveling in his power.

A soft rustling sound came from outside his office window and he turned around in his chair to glance outside. A shadow moved by the window, and when he leaned forward to get a better look, he saw it was only one his men making his rounds. Though a man of God, the Reverend wasn't exactly a trusting man. There many men, and some women, who would love to take his power and rule the town in his place. And now, with Stardust Cove destroyed, his town stood alone in the area, a glimmering jewel that he alone controlled.

A few survivors had arrived in the past three days and some had been welcomed, after they had been indoctrinated into the town's affairs, so to speak. Thanks to the new arrivals, he now had a growing slave labor force that could do almost anything. He had already begun plans for fabricating a massive stone wall of his own, similar to the one that had surrounded Stardust Cove.

In a year's time, maybe less, his town would be impregnable.

He had sent a scouting party out to inspect the ruins of Stardust Cove and the party had yet to return. He wasn't worried though, with almost all the zombies in the area now hovering around the extinct town, it made it much easier to move about the areas outside his own fences.

Tomorrow, more missions would be sent out to explore the military base and the surrounding cities.

He leaned further back in his chair, threatening to topple over, only the brackets under the chair preventing him from doing just that.

Another shadow moved across the door of his office and he stopped moving, staring at the door intently. At first he thought it was probably Nelson, or maybe it was Ralph, come to see if he was needed anymore tonight before turning in.

But when no one knocked, he began to grow nervous.

Sitting upright in his chair, he reached for his handgun sitting within reach on his desk. The M-11 felt good in his grip, giving him a false sense of courage.

"Nelson, is that you?" He called out, trying not to let the worry he was feeling seep into his voice. He knew he was being silly. No one would dare try to attack him, not with all his men on guard. There was Nelson outside his door in the hallway and Jeffers was walking the area around City Hall. All he had to do was press the button under his desk and a red light would light up in the hallway, alerting the guard he was in trouble.

When no one answered, he knew something was wrong.

Pushing away from his desk, he stood up and walked over to the door, but not before grabbing the two-way radio from the shelf against the wall. He could call Ralph now, but if it was all a mistake, then he would look foolish in front of his second-in-command and that wouldn't do. Walking to the door, he paused, then opened it slowly and peered through the crack to see a pair of legs lying prone on the floor and the hall bathed in darkness. Someone had done something to the lights.

"Nelson, you all right?" He whispered. He waited patiently for more than a minute, but when no one answered, he opened the door a little more, now stepping out into the dim hall. He had drawn his gun and was prepared to shoot anything that was out of the ordinary.

Silence greeted him and he moved to Nelson's prone body, kneeling down and feeling the guard's throat for a pulse. There was a slight pulse, and on closer inspection, he could see a large, red bruise on the man's forehead.

Reverend Carlson stood back up, gun waving in his hand as he called out to the empty hallway. "Who's there? Come out you bastard. Face me if you think you have the stones!"

At first there was no answer, but then footsteps could be heard coming up the side stairs that led to the basement and ground floor.

With his gun aimed at the stairwell opening, Reverend Carlson waited, ready to squeeze the trigger the second the person showed themselves.

He was so focused on the stairwell; he didn't hear someone coming up behind him. Suddenly he felt a hard blow to the back of his neck and he crumpled to the floor.

He lay supine on the floor, on the brink of unconsciousness, while shadows moved around him, his vision blurry from the blow to his head.

"Go ahead, kill me and get it over with," he grunted up at the shadowy form above him.

"Oh, I wouldn't worry about that, Reverend. Don't worry, I give you my word, I won't kill you. We have a few things to discuss first," a voice said from the dark. The voice sounded familiar, but he couldn't place it.

"So we got him, what do we do with him now?" A man's voice, someone young, but one he'd never heard before.

"I say we just kill him and be done with it, thanks to him a lot of people are dead and homeless. Shit, just killing him is too quick for the bastard," another said. A woman's voice, also one he'd never heard before.

"Just get him up, I know exactly what we'll do with him," said another voice. A man's voice, the same voice that had first spoken to him, probably the one who had struck him from behind, but in his daze he still couldn't put his finger on it.

"Hey, I think he's still with us," the unfamiliar woman's voice said again.

"I got it," said the young man's voice, and then he felt another blow to his head, and heard no more.

* * *

Reverend Carlson slowly came back to consciousness with a splitting headache. At first he didn't know where he was, but slowly, his vision cleared and he realized he was in a cage on the stage he used for rallies. The cage wall at his back had a large canvas covering it. He thought he heard sounds coming from the other side of the canvas, but then a voice talking to him caught his attention.

"Ah, look who's up. Have a good nap?" A man's voice said. The Reverend looked up into the face of Henry Watson and his jaw dropped.

"You, but you're dead. You died at the base," Reverend Carlson said, his mouth dry and scratchy. God he could use a drink of water.

"Nope, afraid not. Not that Wilson didn't try, mind you. And that thing you did with Mary, well, I gotta tell ya, that was pretty damn clever. Hypnotizing her, that was brilliant. But it didn't work out and now I'm back. Miss me?"

Reverend Carlson shifted inside the cage, he was sitting down, his back against the canvas wall and he slowly pulled himself to his feet.

"Let me out of here, you bastard, or so help me, I'll hang you by your balls and cut your throat!"

"Tsk, tsk, Reverend. Are those what a man of God would say? Doesn't sound that holy to me," Henry joked back.

"What do you want with me? We can make a deal, Watson. Just tell me what you want. I can get you almost anything. You want a car, weapons, food? Just name it."

Henry seemed to think about the offer for a moment. "Well now, that's a nice offer, Reverend, but I've already got a car. Oh, and the scouting party you sent out to investigate Stardust Cove won't be returning anytime soon. As for weapons, well, those men had some great stuff as well as a good supply of ammo. And as for food, we're doing okay in that category, too. Seems your scouting party had a few days worth of rations with them. All in all, they were a real Godsend. I thought me and my friends were gonna have to walk all the way back here."

"There must be something you want, anything!" Reverend Carlson screamed.

"Well, there is one thing you could do for me, actually," Henry said with a tone that said he might be succumbing to temptation.

"What, name it and it's yours, just set me free."

Henry's face went from laconical to menacing. His eyes creased into slits and his jaw set tight.

"Well, Reverend, after all the shit you've done to me, my friends, and the town of Stardust Cove, you can die real slow for me."

"You're gonna kill me? But that's not justice."

"Justice? Justice is overrated, buddy. Now there's only vengeance, and to tell you the truth, it's better than nothing."

"But I can make amends, invite the survivors to come and live here with me and my people," he pleaded.

"Oh, really. Do you mean like the refugees you've already brought in these past few days to be used as a slave labor force? Well, I'm sorry to disappoint you, but I found them and set them free. In fact, they're probably at the guard's barracks right now taking care of the opposition."

Gunshots and shouts of alarm floated over the town, adding proof to Henry's words.

"Sorry, Reverend, but your little mad plan is over. In fact, I think the survivors of Stardust Cove are going to enjoy living here with the rest of your people."

"What? That will never happen. My people won't stand for it," he spit back, anger in his eyes.

Henry shrugged. "Perhaps, but I think once all your stormtroopers are dead, they'll come around to it. I met some of the people who live here when I was here and they're just like the people from Stardust Cove. The only difference is you and the lies you filled their heads with. When you're gone, they'll get along fine."

"Fuck you, Watson! You won't kill me. You're not a murderer. We both know that, so let me out of here and I can stand trial. My people will defend me, I know it."

Henry nodded at that. "You know, that just might happen if you were to get free, and I can't let that happen. As for a trial, well, those days are gone, just one more casualty of the apocalypse, I guess."

The Reverend crossed his arms. He was feeling safer now, sensing Henry wasn't going to kill him. Both of Henry's hands were away from his weapons.

No, the man wasn't going to shoot him.

"Well, so long, Reverend, see you in the funny pages," Henry said as he walked off the stage.

"Watson, come back here, you fuck. Don't you walk away from me. I'll find you, you bastard, so help me, and when I do, I'll rip your heart out! You'll burn in Hell!"

Henry stopped at the bottom of the stairs and walked around the stage until he was looking up at the Reverend in his cage.

"Hell, Reverend, maybe you're right. Since things went to shit last year I've had to do a lot of pretty bad things to survive. And if killing is a sin, then I know I'm going to hell. But I tell you what. You can do me a favor, all right?"

He picked up a rope that had been draped across the stage. The end connected to the canvas and Henry now yanked it as hard as he could. Up on the stage, in the Reverend's cage, the canvas was pulled out of the way to reveal the opposite side of the cage. On the other side was a slavering ghoul, rotting face, bowels hanging from its open stomach wound and scarlet mouth, just drooling in anticipation of what was to come.

Where there was once only a small hole for an arm to fit through was now a five foot wide opening. A few wires had been connected to the canvas, enough to keep the idle ghoul from pushing through, but now that the opening was exposed, it snarled and groaned like a wild animal.

The Reverend screamed in fright and seemed to try to squeeze into the opposite corner of the cage, but the ghoul ignored his futile attempts to escape. Pushing through the hole, leaving large chunks of rotten flesh on the sharp points, the ghoul forced itself into the Reverend's side of the cage and began ripping him to shreds. Blood sprayed through the mesh of the cage, splattering across the stage, and the entire time Henry watched quietly.

His face showed no emotion while he watched the Reverend being eaten alive.

Dropping the rope to the ground, he leaned forward while the Reverend screamed into the night for mercy. Though he knew the man couldn't hear him, Henry finished his sentence from before he pulled the rope.

"Do me a favor, Reverend. When you get to hell, tell the devil I'm coming, but it won't be for a long, long time."

"No! You bastard, someone help me! Ahhhh!" The Reverend screamed as he tried in vain to keep the zombie off of him. His screams rising in pitch at each tear of his flesh. "But you said you wouldn't kill me, Watson. You said you wouldn't kill me!

Henry's face was devoid of emotion.

"I lied," he said coldly.

Then he turned and began to walk away, while the Reverend screamed for the mercy he refused to give to others.

"Yell all you want, Reverend, the Lord Himself can't hear you," Henry said over his shoulder, keeping his back to the shrieking man. He had seen more men than he would care to count torn apart by ghouls and he had no need to see another. Walking away from the podium, he was soon lost in the shadows, his rigid form disappearing into the night.

As he walked back to the opening he and the others had cut in the fence that surrounded the town, the Reverend's shrill screams followed him like the wind blowing through a cavern.

When he finally reached the fence, Mary, Cindy and Jimmy were waiting.

On the small field behind them sat the small Volkswagen they had accommodated the day before from the search party the Reverend had sent to inspect his handiwork. As for the guards, their bodies were lying in a ditch along the road somewhere, cooling in the night air. Henry had actually given the men a chance, offering them the choice of being tied up with the refugees instead of death, but like they were living in the Wild West, they had refused, drawing their weapons and firing. But Cindy and Mary had been in the tree line, waiting, and had mowed the men down like wheat.

"You all right? I heard the screaming and the gunshots and was starting to get worried," Jimmy said, lowering his weapon when he saw it was Henry.

Once Henry had gotten the Reverend inside the cage, he had sent the others back to the opening in the fence, wanting to do the rest on his own, not wanting to stain the souls of his friends anymore than he needed to.

While waiting, Jimmy had been nervous, not enjoying his position out in the open. They were exposed outside the fence and anything could be lurking in the dark. So far it had been quiet, thanks to the fact that almost every ghoul in the area had already been rounded up by the Reverend for his macabre purposes.

“Yeah, I’m fine Jimmy. Everything okay out here?” Henry asked as he crawled through the hole and then quickly began securing the cut wire fencing so no curious zombies could find the hole and sneak into the town.

“Everything’s copasetic. How ‘bout the Reverend? Is he...?” Jimmy asked.

Henry finished closing the hole and stood up. “He won’t be bothering anyone ever again.”

Jimmy nodded. “That’s good, I guess. He was an evil bastard.”

Henry and Jimmy walked back to the car, and he climbed in, taking the driver’s seat. It had always been something unspoken with the four companions. Henry usually drove. It had been that way since the first time they had met and he had saved them with his wife’s Dodge Caravan.

Mary and Cindy had been a few yards away, watching the area for signs of trouble and now they returned to the car and climbed into the back seat just as Henry started the car. With a crunching of rocks and gravel, the car moved away from the fence, and Mary leaned over the front seat and kissed him on the right cheek.

“What was that for?” Henry asked, the headlights cutting through the night as he drove onto the main road and headed away from the two towns of Stardust Cove and Sunset Bay.

“That was for doing what had to be done, and for keeping the blood off the rest of our hands,” Mary said softly.

He reached up and squeezed her hand, smiling in the darkness of the car.

“Anytime, honey, anytime,” he said, his voice cracking slightly. She didn’t notice, though, so she leaned back in her seat and began talking to Cindy about where they might go next.

"You okay, there, old man?" Jimmy asked from the passenger seat.

Henry cleared his throat. "Yeah, I'm fine, now stay sharp. I want to be far away from here by sunrise and anything could be out here on the road," he snapped at him, sounding gruffer then he meant to.

Jimmy only nodded and did as he was told, gazing out the windshield, his eyes trying to peer into the darkness past the headlights.

Henry let out a deep breath and slowly breathed in again. He was thankful for the darkness that surrounded them inside the car. Because in the darkness, none of his friends could see the one tear that slid down his left cheek; the wind from the open windows quickly drying it so that, perhaps, it had never been there in the first place.

With a night bird calling from the surrounding treetops, searching for its mate, the Volkswagen drove under the trees, the bird fluttering for a moment, disturbed by the vehicle's passing.

Soon the taillights were nothing but dim spots in the night, and then, they too, disappeared, leaving the road quiet once more with the exception of the night bird's symphony, a sweet melody that was lost on the wind.

Minutes later, after the car had completely disappeared, a lone figure stepped out of the tree line onto the deserted road. It heard the bird's song and looked up into the branches of the tree, its dead eyes searching for the source of the sound. It gazed up in vain for almost five minutes until its dim intelligence forgot what it had been looking for.

Then, taking one step forward, it started walking down the highway after the Volkswagen.

There had been meat in the car and it was hungry. And though the car was probably miles away and still going, it didn't matter to the feeble brain of the ghoul, and so, with never-ending persistence and tenacity, it took another stumbling step forward, and then another one after that, until its shambling form disappeared down the lonely road and was lost in the darkness.

THE NEXT EXCITING CHAPTER IN THE DEADWATER SERIES!

DEAD UNION

By Anthony Giangregorio

BRAVE NEW WORLD

More than a year has passed since the world died not with a bang, but with a moan.
Where sprawling cities once stood, now only the dead inhabit the hollow walls of a shattered civilization; a mockery of lives once led.
But there are still survivors in this barren world, all slowly struggling to take back what was stripped from their birthright; the promise of a world free of the undead.
Fortified towns have shunned the outside world, becoming massive fortresses in their own right. These refugees of a world torn asunder are once again trying to carve out a new piece of the earth, or hold onto what little they already possess.

HOSTAGES

Henry Watson and his warrior survivalists are conscripted by a mad colonel, one of the last military leaders still functioning in the decimated United States. The colonel has settled in Fort Knox, and from there plans to rule the world with his slave army of lost souls and the last remaining soldiers of a defunct army.
But first he must take back America and mold it in his own image; and he will crush all who oppose him, including the new recruits of Henry and crew.
The battle lines are drawn with the fate of America at stake, and this time, the outcome may be unsure.

In a world where the dead walk, even the grave isn't safe.

DEADFREEZE

By Anthony Giangregorio

THIS IS WHAT HELL WOULD BE LIKE IF IT FROZE OVER.

When an experimental serum for hypothermia goes horribly wrong, a small research station in the middle of Antarctica becomes overrun with an army of the frozen dead.

Now a small group of survivors must battle the arctic weather and a horde of frozen zombies as they make their way across the frozen plains of Antarctica to a neighboring research station.

What they don't realize is that they are being hunted by an entity whose sole reason for existing is vengeance; and it will find them wherever they run.

DEADFALL

By Anthony Giangregorio

It's Halloween in the small suburban town of Wakefield, Mass. While parents take their children trick or treating and others throw costume parties, a swarm of meteorites enter the earth's atmosphere and crash to earth.
Inside are small parasitic worms, no larger than maggots.
The worms quickly infect the corpses at a local cemetery and so begins the rise of the undead.
The walking dead soon get the upper hand, with no one believing the truth.
That the dead now walk.
Will a small group of survivors live through the zombie apocalypse?
Or will they, too, succumb to the Deadfall.

DARK PLACES

By Anthony Giangregorio

A cave-in inside the Boston subway unleashes something tha should have stayed buried forever.

Three boys sneak out to a haunted junkyard after dark and fin more than they gambled on.

In a world where everyone over twelve has died from a mysteriou illness, one young boy tries to carry on.

A mysterious man in black tries his hand at a game of chance at local carnival, to interesting results.

God, Allah, and Buddha play a friendly game of poker with the fat of the Earth resting in the balance.

Ever have one of those days where everything that can go wrong does? Well, so did Byron, and no one should have a day like this!

Thad had an imaginary friend named Charlie when he was a child. Charlie would make him do bad things. Now Thad is all grown up and guess who's coming for a visit?

These and other short stories, all filled with frozen moments of dread and wonder, will keep you captivated long into the night.

Just be sure to watch out when you turn off the light!

THE MONSTER UNDER THE BED

By Anthony Giangregorio

Rupert was just one of many monsters that inhabit the human vorld, scaring children before bed. Only Rupert wanted to play vith the children he was forced to scare.

Vhen Rupert meets Timmy, an instant friendship is born. Running away from his abusive step-father, Timmy leaves home, mbarking on a journey that leads him to New York City.

)n his way, Timmy will realize that the true monsters are other dults who are just waiting to take advantage of a small boy, all lone in the big city.

Can Rupert save him?

)r will Timmy just become another statistic.

SOULEATER

By Anthony Giangregorio

Twenty years ago, Jason Lawson witnessed the brutal death of nis father by something only seen in nightmares, something so norrible he'd blocked it from his mind.

Now twenty years later the creature is back, this time for his son. Jason won't let that happen.

He'll travel to the demon's world, struggling every second to rescue nis son from its clutches.

But what he doesn't know is that the portal will only be open for a inite time and if he doesn't return with his son before it closes, hen he'll be trapped in the demon's dimension forever.

ROAD KILL: A ZOMBIE TALE

By Anthony Giangregorio

ORDER UP!

In the summer of 2008, a rogue comet entered earth's orbit for 72 hours. During this time, a strange amber glow suffused the sky.

But something else happened; something in the comet's tail had an adverse affect on dead tissue and the result was the reanimation of every dead animal carcass on the planet.

A handful of survivors hole up in a diner in the backwoods of New Hampshire while the undead creatures of the night hunt for human prey.

There's a new blue plate special at DJ's Diner and Truck Stop, and it's you!

THE DARK

By Anthony Giangregorio

DARKNESS FALLS

The darkness came without warning.

First New York, then the rest of United States, and then the world became enveloped in a perpetual night without end.

With no sunlight, eventually the planet will wither and die, bringing on a new Ice Age. But that isn't problem for the human race, for humanity will be dead long before that happens.

There is something in the dark, creatures only seen in nightmares, and they are on the prowl.

Evolution has changed and man is no longer the dominant species.
When we are children, we are told not to fear the dark, that what we believe to exist in the shadows is false.

Unfortunately, that is no longer true.

DEAD RECKONING: DAWNING OF THE DEAD
By Anthony Giangregorio

THE DEAD HAVE RISEN!

In the dead city of Pittsburgh, two small enclaves struggle to survive, eking out an existence of hand to mouth.

But instead of working together, both groups battle for the last remaining fuel and supplies of a city filled with the living dead.

Six months after the initial outbreak, a lone helicopter arrives bearing two more survivors and a newborn baby. One enclave welcomes them, while the other schemes to steal their helicopter and escape the decaying city.

With no police, fire, or social services existing, the two will battle for dominance in the steel city of the walking dead.

But when the dust settles, the question is: will the remaining humans be the winners, or the losers?

When the dead walk, the line between Heaven and Hell is so twisted and bent there is no line at all.

RISE OF THE DEAD
By Anthony Giangregorio

DEATH IS ONLY THE BEGINNING

In less than forty-eight hours, more than half the globe was infected.

In another forty-eight, the rest would be enveloped.

The reason?

A science experiment gone horribly wrong which enabled the dead to walk, their flesh rotting on their bones even as they seek human prey.

Jeremy was an ordinary nineteen year old slacker. He partied too much and had done poorly in high school. After a night of drinking and drugs, he awoke to find the world a very different place from the one he'd left the night before.

The dead were walking and feeding on the living, and as Jeremy stepped out into a world gone mad, the dead spotting him alone and unarmed in the middle of the street, he had to wonder if he would live long enough to see his twentieth birthday.

Book One of the *Undead World Trilogy*

BLOOD OF THE DEAD

A Shoot 'Em Up Zombie Novel by A.P. Fuchs

"*Blood of the Dead* . . . is the stuff of nightmares . . . with some unnerving and frightening action scenes that will have you on the edge of your seat."

- Rick Hautala
author of *The Wildman*

Joe Bailey prowls the Haven's streets, taking them back from the undead, each kill one step closer to reclaiming a life once stolen from him.

As the dead push into the Haven, he and a couple others are forced into the one place where folks fear to tread: the heart of the city, a place overrun with flesh-eating zombies.

Welcome to the end of all things.

Ask for it at your local bookstore.
Also available from your favorite on-line retailer.

ISBN-10 1-897217-80-3 / ISBN-13 978-1-897217-80-1

www.undeadworldtrilogy.com